Praise for *Ar*

"Soehnlein delivers a sprawling portrait of our darkest days, capturing all the anger and heartbreak and heroic love that forged who we are today. If you want to know how it felt, read this."

—Armistead Maupin

"Just when a moment in history is about to be forgotten, an author comes along to capture its passions and struggles and hope. Soehnlein has performed that magic for readers here. *Army of Lovers* will become essential reading for years to come. Read it now; be moved, enraptured, emboldened, and reminded of what it was like to be young at a turning point in history."

—Andrew Sean Greer, Pulitzer Prize-winning author of *Less Is Lost*

"Army of Lovers comes at a crucial time, when the most devastating years of the AIDS era are sometimes remembered only for their despair and not for the love through action that brought so many changes. An evocative and beautiful book that reminds us of the deepest power of witness—it can sometimes take years for its clarity to shine through, but it can also help us find our lost once again through the precious telling of their stories."

—Manuel Muñoz, author of *The Consequences*

"In this vivid novel set in 1980s New York, the stakes could not be higher. While facing down monoliths like the FDA and the Catholic Church, Paul must navigate the ordinary desires, anxieties, and heartbreaks of youth. Drawn from the author's lived experiences and rich with yearning and tenderness, *Army of Lovers* is a must-read for anyone searching for agency in an indifferent world. The story of ACT UP remains strikingly relevant today, and K.M. Soehnlein is just the writer to tell it."

—Alia Volz, Author of *Home Baked: My Mom, Marijuana, and the Stoning of San Francisco*

"*Army of Lovers* is astonishing, devastating, a small time machine made of words, a survivor's novel, a queer coming-of-age story—collective by necessity and also deeply particular—one perfect tear-stained facet of the kaleidoscopic scene that was ACT UP/Queer Nation in early '90s New York. I was there, I knew these people, and I wanted it never to end"

—Andrea Lawlor, author of *Paul Takes the Form of a Mortal Girl*

Army of Lovers

a novel

K.M. SOEHNLEIN

AMBLE
PRESS

2022

Print ISBN: 978-1-61294-247-6

Amble Press First Edition: October 2022

Printed in the United States of America on acid-free paper.

Cover designer: Kevin Clarke
Cover photo: Eurivaldo Bezerra
Book designer: TreeHouse Studio

Amble Press
PO Box 3671
Ann Arbor MI 48106-3671

www.amblepresspublishing.com

This novel is a work of fiction. All characters and events
described by the author are fictitious. No resemblance
to real persons, dead or alive, is intended.

Excerpt from *To the Lighthouse*, the Virginia Woolf novel that
is quoted in this novel is in the public domain.

"My first well Day – since many ill –," the Emily Dickinson poem
referenced in this novel is in the public domain.

This book is written in memory of
Bradley Ball,
Lee Schy,
and
Maura Soehnlein

and dedicated to all those who acted up.

Sad and free
Sad and free
—Black Box, "Everybody Everybody"

An army of lovers shall not fail.
—Rita Mae Brown, "Sappho's Reply"

Part 1

Harmony Moore Has to Die

Our voices roar. We lie on our backs on the floor of the state senate building, twenty-seven of us, arms linked. Our chants reverberate: *No More Business as Usual! What Do We Want? Money for AIDS! When Do We Want It? Now!* I gaze up to the lights in the vaulted ceiling of this modern, concrete building—they call this style brutalism, and yes, it's the brutal world we're shouting at, hard and square and indifferent. The brutal indifference of our government led us here, to block the glass doors of the legislative chamber, demanding to be heard.

But as our chants fade, it's clear that we're not actually *blocking* anything, because the powerbrokers aren't here. Maybe they cancelled their session knowing we were coming. Maybe it was poor timing on our part, though timing was what ACT UP did best. Knowing where to strike and when. Knowing how to make an impact.

Those of us who have organized this "die-in" confer: Do we move somewhere else? Find a more meaningful target? Our media people say no, stay, this is where the media is.

I see Derek heading toward me, leading a reporter and a cameraman. Derek is my boyfriend. His dark, thinning hair is combed neatly, his shirt is buttoned up and tucked smooth. He's part of our media committee. He carries a walkie-talkie and a clipboard thick with paper.

The reporter crouches, leans toward Amanda, at my side, and asks what the protest is about. She shakes her long, honey-colored locks out of her face. Her brows narrow, her caramel eyes shine. "Women with AIDS die twice as fast as men," she says, "but the New York state AIDS budget doesn't include any funding for programs specifically targeting women. Healthcare is a right."

The reporter, a pink-skinned guy with a helmet of gelled hair, shifts his microphone to me. He asks how long we're going to lie here blocking these doors. I say, "People are dying while the state government takes the day off." He waits for more. "I'm staying here until Governor Mario Cuomo shows up and tells me what he's gonna do for people with AIDS." As the cameraman steps back to get a long shot, Derek nods at me, at Amanda. We've done our part. We've learned the chants, we've delivered the sound bites. We've gone through civil disobedience training. We know why we're here. This is an *action*.

Also true: When demands are not being met, monotony sets in. The reporters get their footage and leave. They'll file their stories while we stay on the floor, waiting for the police to disperse us.

Our angry chants get tedious, even to our own ears, and we become silly. *Act Up, Fight Back, Fight AIDS* becomes *Act Up, Fight Back, Fry Eggs*.

How Many More Have to Die? becomes *Harmony Moore Has to Die!* There's an ongoing, shifting narrative of this Harmony Moore—who she is and how her death might solve our problems. Eliot, lying near me, says, "Albany is her second favorite city in the state of New York."

The head cop finally calls out the official directive. "This is your last warning. If you don't leave, you'll be charged with resisting arrest."

No one moves. The top brass huddle together, muttering, while the rest of the cops stiffen and stare hard at us. They've put on latex gloves. Someone in our group starts up, *Your Gloves Don't Match Your Shoes, You'll See It On the News*, and others pick up the chant, taunting, mocking, until this too runs its course. What do the police think of us? (Did I wonder it then or am I wondering it now, all these years later?) AIDS activism is a new thing in 1988, but here in Albany, is this just one more routine protest at the state capital, though campier than usual? Or are they disgusted by us: diseased faggots, loudmouthed lesbians, interlopers?

They stream through the crowd and one by one pull us to our feet. I feel an officer's grip on my upper arm. As I stand, he yanks my hands behind my back. He binds my wrists with hard, thin plastic, a zip tie. This is a surprise. Cuffs aren't the norm. Usually they just guide us onto a bus. But these are state police.

It's night outside, dark but for streetlights, and cold. My friend Dale is on the sidewalk, bandana wrapped around his long hair, camera hanging from a strap around his neck. He darts out in front of me and shouts, "Say AIDS!" Despite the cuffs and the uniformed officer at my back, pressuring the pace, I smile. Dale's flash erupts and blinds me. The cop orders me to keep moving.

Albany wasn't our most significant action—that would be our protest at the FDA, when we forced the federal government to shift how AIDS drugs were approved. It wasn't the most controversial—that would be St. Patrick's, when the media decided we'd gone too far by demonstrating inside a Catholic cathedral. I wonder how many people even remember our arrests at the state capital.

I remember.

That night, I got to know Eliot.

In that cell, I met Zack.

They're gone now, Zack and Eliot. So is Dale, whose camera captured me being hauled away.

Later, when Dale gives me a print of this photo, I'll note that I look incongruously happy. The Paul in the photo, smiling into the flash, doesn't yet know he's going to spend a night in jail. My light blue eyes have a giddiness to them. The lock of blond hair curled across my forehead strikes me as boyish, which is not so strange, since I'd been a boy just a handful of years earlier. It's an image of in-between: I'm still wearing the fraying peacoat I'd worn every winter since college; I haven't yet bought the leather jacket that will be my uniform. I haven't yet shaved my head. I'm not quite *queer*.

In New York City, where ACT UP has been doing civil disobedience for many months now, the usual drill is that we're put in big holding cells and processed as a group. That's safer for us, because not everyone gets treated the same by the police. This is true now and it was true then. Floyd told me he wasn't going to Albany to get arrested because he didn't know what the upstate fuzz would do with him: 6'2", scarecrow skinny, and politically astute, he's a Black man uninterested in keeping quiet. As it became clear we were being put in jail cells, I thought of Floyd, probably back in New York at The Bar on East 4th Street and Second Avenue, smoking a cigarette between his pencil-thin fingers. Floyd's gone now, too.

The twenty-seven of us who have been arrested are paired off and told to wait in front of cells that line one side of a long corridor. Once we're locked in, we can hear but not see each other. Are there other arrestees in here, too? Or is this cellblock set aside for out-of-town protestors?

Eliot and I stare out through the bars at the cinderblock wall. The whole place has a sickly aspect.

"Is the wall yellow, or is that the lighting?" I ask.

"It's the color of jaundiced flesh," Eliot says. "I've seen hepatitis. I know."

"I've never been in a jail like this," I say.

"I've never been arrested at all," he says.

"You haven't?"

"No. Someone's got to stay free to keep track of the rest of you."

Eliot is ACT UP's administrator. Don't call him "secretary." He's been very clear about that. At the group's packed, noisy weekly meetings, he sits behind a table at the front of the room, taking the minutes in longhand. I've seen those notes, his tight penmanship slanting to the left like a criminal's. And now he *is* a criminal, in jail for the first time for dying-in. At meetings he speaks only when a contentious moment calls for someone to cite Robert's Rules of Order (which is always referred to as Roberta's Rules of Order). Who was Robert anyway? I should have asked Eliot.

Eliot has a dark, trimmed beard; thick, dark eyebrows; and black eyes, all of it stark against his sun-starved skin. He is striking in an obvious way when you see him from across the room, like a dangerous-looking character actor, one who never gets cast as the lead because his features are just a little off. But he is striking in a different way up close, holding tension around his eyes and pressing his plum-red lips tightly together. In meetings he seems distantly cool, but here I see suppressed emotion; I see a man who has learned to be self-protective so that no one can call him weak.

"I'm having my French Resistance moment," Eliot says. "And you? Did you always dream you'd wind up a political dissident?"

"The short answer," I say, "is that Larry Kramer yelled at me at a gay and lesbian student conference. Not just at me. At a whole room of us. He was the keynote speaker: *This half of the room, stand up. You'll all be dead in five years. This half of the room, what are you going to do about it?* He was so Old Testament."

"I've heard that spiel. It's effective, I suppose, though I wasn't impressionable enough to be swayed by Uncle Larry."

"I knew who he was," I say, feeling the need to explain. "I'd seen *The Normal Heart*. It affected me. I was with Amanda—you know, we went to college together, and we drove down from upstate New York for this conference. And Derek was there, too. That's how we met—while Larry was telling us we had to fight or die."

"You kids," Eliot says.

4

Activism has taken over my life. Multiple meetings every week, poster-making, civil disobedience training, outreach. I've turned down a temp job to go to this demonstration. I've dropped old friends who don't share my urgency about AIDS. I want to be seen as a grown man, someone to be taken seriously, someone who can lead. But I guess, to Eliot, I give off—what? Idealistic youth?

"So how did you wind up doing this, if you're so jaded?" I ask him.

"I went looking for other HIV-positive men who had the same analysis of the crisis as I did. We were having these conversations in the community before Larry Kramer took the microphone and claimed it was all his idea." Eliot lowers himself onto the bench in our cell. He crosses his legs, and in an accent that I think is meant to be Scottish says, "Give me a boy at an impressionable age and he is mine for life!"

This, I will come to learn, is very Eliot: the grand statement that opens up questions, followed by the pop-cultural toss-off—like this one, from *The Prime of Miss Jean Brodie*—that shuts things down.

A guard brings another guy to our cell, another one of us I guess, though I don't recognize him. His face is half in shadow under the brim of a New York Yankees cap. "Get in," the guard commands, voice tense.

He steps in and the iron lock clangs behind him. "Hi boys. About to get cozy in here."

"I should have reserved a suite," Eliot says.

"Three's company," I say. "I'm Paul."

The new guy holds out his hand, pushes back his cap. His eyes, which are somewhere between brown and green, lock on mine. "I'm Zack."

I like the sound of that, the buzz and clip. I like the way he lets his leg fall against my leg as we both take a seat on the floor. Zack leans back against the wall and releases a long breath. I wonder if he's tired, or maybe freaked out about being in jail. Probably both.

"Did you come up on the buses with us?" I ask. Our group had gathered that morning in the West Village, in a haze of cigarette smoke and take-out coffee and damp early spring air. From there we rode chartered buses up the New York Thruway. I have no idea how we'll get back; the buses have already returned.

Zack says he got a ride from a friend, that it was a last minute decision, that this is his first ACT UP anything. He talks about the big rally that kicked off the day's protest, how he'd heard the writer Vito Russo's speech, how his words had inspired. "He kept talking about AIDS as a war but we're the only ones who are fighting it. *They don't care because it isn't happening to them.*"

Eliot says, "He was magnificent."

"After we heard him," Zack continues, "me and some guys went all around the city, lying down on the sidewalk, making chalk outlines around each other. Then we'd write, *AIDS is happening to you too,* and stuff like that. Then the cops caught us." He lowers his voice. "They were pretty fucking scary."

I steal a sideways glance at him. Light brown skin. Thick eyelashes. Glossy hair curling out from under his cap. He looks biracial, or multiracial, white European mixed into something else. I notice paint splattered on his work boots, in many colors. Artist? Housepainter? Both?

I was already telling myself stories about Zack. I still am.

There we are: Eliot, cross-legged on the bench. Zack sitting close to me. I feel alert but exhausted. Eliot says he believes they can keep us for eighteen hours, maybe longer. Then the guards show up with food. Wet tuna salad on white bread too soft to support the gloppy weight, half-pint cartons of milk that bring back school-cafeteria memories. From down the hall, street-tough activists groan and gasp at the meal.

A voice calls out, "Steven, did you order the tuna, too?" There's no answer. "Steven?" Again: "Steven?"

In the pause that follows, I wonder: in our world of guys named Michael and David and John, is there really no Steven here?

"Steven?"

A new voice: "Steven, answer her!"

Eliot stands up, wraps his pale, tapered fingers around the iron bars of the cell and calls out, "Fine. *I'll* be Steven, and yes, I ordered the tuna!"

"No—," this is Amanda, from somewhere down the hall, "I want to be Steven."

"Steven," yells someone else, "I'm sharing my cell with Steven."

"I'm rooming with Steven, too. He drank all my milk."

There are more calls for Steven, from Steven, to Steven, about Steven. The *S*'s blossom into sibilance, the *E*'s elongate enormously— *SSSSSSTEEEEEVENN*—as giggles spread from cell to cell and laughter erupts out of all proportion. We are officially stir crazy.

I look at Zack, whose serious face has softened for the first time. This makes him seem younger, and I feel my story about him shifting: he's had a hard time of things, was toughened up at an early age, but there's still sweetness underneath it all, if you just give him a chance. Marlon Brando in the '50s, Paul Newman in the '60s.

Eventually silence descends, until someone very quietly tries, "Steven?" and is met by voices shouting, "Shut the fuck up."

"Sssssssorrrrry."

Zack lays himself against the wall, closes his eyes and shifts his body away from me. I don't take it personally. Comfort is elusive here. It hits me again: we're in *jail*. I wanted to get arrested. I didn't think about my freedom. But this is real.

Eliot catches my eye. "How about we trade shoulder rubs, Steven?"

So here's what I learn about Eliot. He came to New York to be a singer, but gave that up and now has a job at a TV network, in the RCA building. He works in a cubicle outside the office of his boss, a woman who invites him in to smoke cigarettes and gossip and who looks the other way while he does massive amounts of photocopying for ACT UP. He lives in Hell's Kitchen. I picture this apartment: photos in silver frames on a piano, matching furniture bought in a department store, a cat purring along hardwood floors. But the image is erased as Eliot describes a studio that is "all hell, no kitchen." He tells of battles with his landlord over the rat-infested, garbage-strewn alley ten floors below his window. He swears he can hear the scampering of their tiny claws against the aluminum garbage cans. We share some things in common: kind, well-intentioned mothers who cried when we came out, crushes on boys who ostracized us in high school, one serious sexual relationship with a girl, briefly. But unlike me, Eliot has fended for himself since age sixteen, when he tried to kill himself, then decided it was better to just leave home and survive on his own.

He says he changed his last name to sever his family's claim on him. He chose Vance, from Vivian Vance, Ethel on *I Love Lucy*.

He says, "I'm happy to be the sidekick."

He says, "Maybe that's a Canadian thing."

He left behind an older lover in Calgary, a lawyer he met when he was seventeen and lived with until he moved to New York. "We never officially

7

broke up," he says.

He tells me how they went together to get AIDS tests. Ralph, who fucked all through the '70s, came back negative, and Eliot who'd only fucked a few times in the days before anyone knew to use condoms, found out he had it. "He won't break up with me because I'm positive," Eliot says, "and I won't break up with him because he's forty-five and doesn't think he'll ever find another boyfriend. It's a tragic romance."

"Romance is having someone to spoon with at night," I say, then wonder once more if I sound young and impressionable.

Throughout all of this, Zack is listening. I catch his eyes peeking open, watching us beneath those lush lashes.

Eliot lays himself out on the narrow bench, announcing, "Mama gets the best bed," though I've just learned that he's twenty-eight, only six years older than me. He hands me his leather jacket to use as a pillow. I take a place on the floor next to Zack, who right away curls around me, his breath on my neck. Just like that I'm hard.

It might have been midnight, it might have been two. I shut my eyes, blocking out the yellowy light, the imprisoning bars, the jaundiced wall. I worry that I'll be awake all night in this alien environment.

But I fall asleep quickly, wrapped in Zack's arms, atop Eliot's leather jacket.

I haven't told you much about Derek yet, which seems unfair, because Derek came first. He'd been my boyfriend since before I finished college, the first guy I ever told "I love you." We lived together on the Lower East Side; we'd made all our New York friends together, as a couple. Our names blended together for people: *PaulNDerek*.

There he is, the next morning, in the back of the courthouse with other ACT UP folks, watching the legal proceedings unfold. I'm relieved to see his smile, which telegraphs his own relief at seeing me. When I wave to him, I'm reprimanded by the bailiff, who tells me to keep my eyes forward, on the judge, who is in a foul mood. He lectures our lawyers, Howard and Jocelyn, both in their thirties and looking disheveled, as if they slept in yesterday's jeans and t-shirts, too. "Our lawyers" is misleading, because they're activists like us who happen to be lawyers, the same way some of us happen to be graphic designers who create images for protests, or happen to be doctors who bring their medical expertise to the issues committee. This Albany judge is angry about our *disruptive behavior*, our *hubristic expectation* that we can get away with *criminal irresponsibility*, the *heavy burden* we've placed on the taxpayers by *overloading the system*. Jocelyn counters with a firm defense of nonviolent civil disobedience, remarking on the clarity of our message, the urgency of the issues we are addressing, the limited amount of actual disruption caused. Howard remarks that our overnight incarceration was unnecessary punishment and seeks an ACD for the twenty-seven of us in the group—"Adjournment Contemplating Dismissal"—which would erase the arrest from our records if we don't get arrested for the next six months. This strikes me as reasonable on paper but unlikely to work since getting arrested is what we do. The judge accepts the ACD, though not without making it clear he doesn't have to; by rights he could put us through the system but he wants things to *return to normal*—which sounds so offensive to our ears as we suffer through this horrifying epidemic—but which means we can go home.

Outside the courthouse, I hug Derek, who right away asks, "Did you eat?" and then says, "God, I sound just like Marilyn"—his mother, forever foisting food on those around her while picking at her own meals like a bird.

"They fed us the basic food groups," I say, "flour, salt, fat and dairy."

"Was it awful in there?" he asks.

"Could have been much worse."

Derek stayed overnight with a local activist, who put a bunch of the New Yorkers up on couches, on the floor, wherever there was room. "I got to sleep next to Miguel. Such a hunk," he says, pointing across the milling crowd to a big brown guy, muscley and animated—then he switches gears to tell me about all the work he and a few others did to get us out of jail and arrange transportation back to the city. There are shuttle vans and cars awaiting. I feel grateful to be taken care of like this but not yet ready to be ripped from my affinity group.

I see Zack staring in our direction. He catches my eye, and I wave him over. In the light of day I see that he's taller than I realized, over six feet, with a long, lean torso and a firm ass that looks great in his jeans. "You got a ride?" I ask him.

"Yeah," he says, then tousles my hair. "Thanks for spooning, Kiddo. That was nice." He offers Derek his name, shakes his hand, and then scurries off.

Derek raises his eyebrows at me. "I'll tell you about him later," I say, which is how it works for us—we disclose everything, including, especially, our crushes.

One more good-bye that day: Eliot's. He pulls me into a hug, clamping his arms so tightly around me it almost hurts. This, I'd learn, was also very Eliot, the unexpectedly tight hug, as if it would be the last you ever shared.

But of course it wasn't. We were both back at the ACT UP general meeting the following Monday night, Eliot taking minutes and me reporting to the floor about the arrest of our affinity group, now calling itself the "Steven Twenty-Seven." While a group of us stand together at the front of the room, I say, "I'm still waiting to hear from Mario Cuomo, and when I do, I'm going to ask him: why are you putting people in jail when the state legislature is letting us die?"

A chant starts up—*Arrest the Real Criminals, Arrest the Real Criminals*—like a high-speed train approaching, then gone in an exhilarating whoosh. I look around for Zack, but he isn't there.

As the meeting adjourns, Eliot pulls me aside. "Come to my birthday party," he says, adding almost as an afterthought, "Would you bring a cake?"

I've never made a birthday cake before. It's possible I'd never *bought* one. But of course I said yes to Eliot Vance.

The night of the party, Derek and I were mad at each other—I remember that now, though I can't remember why. We'd been dating for a year, and living together for most of that time, and we seemed to have entered into a stage where we could bicker over anything. I was probably annoyed that he was running late, which was a constant with him. He'd probably had enough of me suffering over the birthday cake, which I wanted to make from scratch, then changed my mind, running all over the city at the last minute to find one special enough for Eliot. "Just grab something at the corner market," Derek said, which made sense, though I wound up buying an elaborately decorated layer cake from a bakery in Little Italy. I think it cost me thirty dollars when I was earning ten an hour as an office temp.

We meet Amanda at the subway entrance. From down the block I see her petite, firmly upright frame, her wavy hair cascading over the shoulders of her black jacket, her black leggings and red cowboy boots. I see that she's also holding a box with a birthday cake in it. "That's hilarious," she says, looking from mine to hers, a store-bought cake like Derek had wanted me to get. "Eliot asked you, too?"

I nod, feeling a stab of embarrassment: Eliot hadn't trusted me to deliver.

In Hell's Kitchen, a dingy neighborhood of narrow streets behind the theater district, we find Eliot's building, tall for the block. We take an elevator to the eighth floor, then walk down a narrow corridor lined with so many doors it's clear that this is a building of subdivided units. We step into Eliot's high-ceilinged studio, which is organized around a well-worn sofa that is also Eliot's bed. Bookshelves line three of the walls. When I look closely I see that the books are two lengths deep, one stretch of books pressed to the back, the other lined up in front of them. Philosophy, religion, theory, literature, pop culture: more than you could read in a very long lifetime.

"The cakes go over there," Eliot calls out, already tipsy, bubbling with glee. He sweeps his arm to a long table—a door stretched across filing cabinets—where I see, all in a row, a dozen different cakes. There must be one from every guest at the party. I burst out laughing at the sight of them.

A bar has been set up, bottles of booze already being drained. A guy I've never met before, shorter than Eliot, probably Jewish, with scholarly glasses and a barrel chest, is pouring cocktails. Eliot throws an arm around him, proclaiming, "This is Lenny, we've known each other two weeks, and we're in love." Lenny rattles the cocktail shaker, as if deflecting this extravagant announcement, but his eyes fix so much admiration on Eliot that I know there is something real going on here. Eliot waves his drink toward Amanda, Derek and me. "These are the new kids, the hope of the future!"

"Here's to hope," Lenny toasts, his voice a marvelous mix of optimism and irony.

I drink quickly, trying to make the jitters subside. Jitters, because I *was* still the new kid, and for all the gritty glory attached to these memories, I remember as well what it was like to feel awkward at a party, planning an exit not long after entering. I'd had little practice in high school or college, never having been claimed by a social world before. Yet here I was, among the select few invited by the ever-surprising Eliot to come bearing cake.

I watch Derek cross the room toward a sexy Latino in a tight t-shirt whom I recognize as the guy he'd snuggled with in Albany, Miguel. His voice booms, and there's something inviting about his speaking style, the eye contact he makes. I step closer and he asks, "Martin Luther King or Malcolm X?"

"MLK," I say. "Nonviolence."

"I told you," Derek says.

Miguel shakes his head. "Turning the other cheek doesn't work when you're dying of AIDS."

"Score one for Miguel," Derek says.

"That's a great line," I say, "but I'd rather be part of a great political movement."

"That's a false construction," Miguel says.

"Your drink is empty," Derek says to Miguel.

"I'm not done with you," he says to me, his eyes twinkling.

I know where this will lead: late in the evening, Derek will ask me if we should take home this sexy, hunky, fired-up guy, and I'll say yes, which is what our sex life is all about these days, as exciting and expected as that.

"I'm taking requests," Lenny announces, standing over Eliot's turntable and browsing his records.

"But only from me!" Eliot calls out.

It's an hour later, and Eliot has requested "Stairway to Heaven," pulling us all into a vortex of nostalgia for the acid rock past. When the song ends, Eliot yells "Encore!" and I watch Lenny drop the needle back down. The plaintive guitar melody starts up again, greeted with groans and laughter. Some of us sing along, and some play drunken air guitar, and somewhere in the middle of this, Eliot disappears into the bathroom. Amanda is lighting birthday candles. The room grows bright with the glow reflecting off all those squares of white frosting.

Deep into the third playing of "Stairway," Eliot reemerges in a platinum wig that has seen better days and a black, beaded cocktail dress. He forges a crooked path between the furniture and his cheering loved ones, one gloved hand pressed coquettishly over his beard, and the other, which we all take turns kissing, extended like a courtesan's. "Charmed, charmed," he repeats, in a soft, posh accent.

He makes his way to the apartment's only window, which faces the alley. Amanda brings him the biggest of the cakes—the one I bought. In a blur of flame, drowning out Led Zeppelin, we sing "Happy Birthday."

"Before I make a wish," Eliot says, fluffing his cheap wig, "allow me to introduce myself. My name"—dramatic pause—"is Harmony Moore."

"Harmony Moore has to die!" several of us shout enthusiastically.

But the laughter slides into an uncomfortable hush as Eliot lingers, candle flames flickering in his dark, messily mascaraed eyes. "Yes, it is true, I have to die."

Then he turns away from the cake and throws open the window.

I feel a clench deep inside, a primal tightness below my navel: the fear that he is about to finish what he'd told me he attempted at age sixteen.

"I have to die," Harmony repeats. Pause. "But not tonight."

I exhale, relieved. I'm not the only one.

"Tonight, I am making a request to the gods. I have asked for a reprieve so that I may enjoy my birthday. And they have agreed. In return, there must be a sacrifice."

"I sacrificed my eardrums to 'Stairway to Heaven,'" someone calls out.

"I'll sacrifice my virginity," calls someone else.

Harmony Moore bends down to blow out the candles that haven't already melted into waxy puddles on the buttercream, then takes the cake in her hands, exclaiming, "A sacrifice!"—and tosses it out the window.

If there were twenty of us in the room at that point then there were twenty different reactions: laughter, shock, shrieking one-liners. Harmony calls for another cake, extinguishes its candles in a gust of breath, and sends it out the window, too. "Cake," she commands. "Let me throw cake!"

A chant swells up from the party: *Throw Cake, Throw Cake, Throw Cake.*

As the platters are passed, fire-brigade style, from the table to the window, I understand just how far this will go: Harmony Moore will toss them all, not leaving even one for us to eat. After the first few, she stops making wishes and just throws them out, lit candles and all, cast from her hands into the city night, spinning like flying saucers doomed to crash-land among the rats.

The exhilaration swells, and it is like that frightening and glorious moment at a demonstration when the front line, arms entwined, chests and chins thrust forth, casts aside police barriers and steps as one brazen mass into a busy street or onto government property—wherever we've been told we cannot go.

When it is over, when "Stairway to Heaven" is finally replaced by something less mournful, I lean out the window and look down.

I feel the softness of tears in my eyes. Harmony Moore's sacrifice has painted the shadowy alley in a pattern of bright bursts of color, like the interconnected streaks on a painter's palette. I imagine that our bodies might look like this, during one of our die-ins, if you could watch from a great height, like a god.

I was wrong about one thing that night: Derek and I do not bring home sexy Miguel. Instead, they leave together, and I stay behind. This wasn't our usual arrangement—we weren't hooking up one-on-one with other guys at that point—but I'm not done with the party. "Go have fun," I tell Derek, imagining that this is a sign of how mature our relationship has grown, rather than how distant.

I linger at Eliot's with the last of the guests, each of us kissing him at length, another birthday wish that no one can refuse. I throw myself into it. Our tongues slosh around just a little too long, then we break apart laughing, and it's someone else's turn.

Amanda steers me to the door, leaving Eliot in Lenny's arms. We debate cab or subway. It's late. We flag a cab. She says, "That was fabulous and a little manic, don't you think?"

"I can't believe I spent so much money on a cake that no one got to eat."

"But you'll remember it forever." Which has turned out to be true.

In the cab, whizzing downtown, she and I sit close, fingers braided together. And then at the same time we face each other and start making out, which is also fabulous and a little bit manic, one more unexpected kiss in a night no one wanted to end.

In my apartment, I lie on my back, on top of our bed. Derek and I hauled this beast up two flights of stairs not long ago. I'm looking up at the ceiling, webbed with cracks, which seems to spiral away and lower itself down onto me at the same time. I'm drunk but I'm also aware, sharply aware, of my solitude. I've lived in this Lower East Side apartment for half a year, but I've never spent a night here by myself. I haven't spent more than ten minutes by myself since New York and ACT UP took hold of me. I've forgotten how it feels to be alone.

Note to Self #1: Why did you join ACT UP?

Because there was a photo in the Village Voice of gay men in ACT UP getting arrested by the police.

Because the text beneath that photo said these protesters, some of whom had AIDS, were angry about the high cost of AIDS drugs. They were angry at the pharmaceutical companies. And Wall Street. And Ronald Reagan.

Because I read the Village Voice every week cover to cover in my upstate college town.

Because at college, I took a class called Political Theory and Gay Politics, taught by the only out gay professor on campus.

Because in that class I learned the Theory of the Single Ally: A voice crying out in protest is nothing without an ally. But once a single ally is found, change has already begun.

Because I came out to my best friend Amanda, who then came out to me.

Because Amanda and I talked all the time about politics—abortion, apartheid, No Nukes, the invasion of Grenada, how Reagan and Thatcher were evil twins intent on destroying every cultural gain of the '60s and '70s, how society treated gay men and lesbians like second class citizens, how our generation had to change that.

Because we traveled to New York City for a lesbian and gay student conference where I met Derek, and after that we became boyfriends. Because Larry Kramer was the keynote speaker at that conference.

Because it was 1985 and we finally knew about HIV, and HIV always led to AIDS, and because gay men were the ones—not the only ones but the first ones—identified as "AIDS carriers," AIDS was my problem.

Because when Larry Kramer yelled at us and said we would die of AIDS if we didn't do something about it, the thing he said to do was join ACT UP.

Never Be Silent Again

And so, our first ACT UP meeting.

Derek, Amanda and I find our way to the Gay and Lesbian Community Center, an old school building in the middle of a West Village block. Its brick façade might be disintegrating into red dust; inside, dull fluorescent light falls onto peeling wall paint and discolored floor tiles. Voices buzz from a room just beyond the reception area. I immediately sense that this is a vital site but hurting, like the community it serves.

The table near the door welcomes us with flyers: info about safe sex, pamphlets from other AIDS groups, contact sheets with names and numbers with 212 area codes. I take a contact sheet, fold it in fourths, and slide it into my back pocket, already staking a claim. The flyer with ACT UP's logo—lean white font on slim black rectangle—is covered with defining language: *outraged, mismanagement, direct action, AIDS.*

Chairs are being pulled from a supply closet, clanging open noisily amid the low roar of conversation.

"Take a chair and have a seat," a tall man tells us. Southern accent, drapey pants, twinkle in his eye. The three of us grab chairs, open them up, join a half-formed row, halfway back. The tall Southern guy walks to the front of the room and joins the people up there who are in charge. They confer, they gesture, they laugh. Then he faces us and declares, "This is ACT UP, the AIDS Coalition to Unleash Power. Hello darlin's, I'm Nicholas."

My mother would have dubbed Nicholas a long drink of water: skinny torso, string bean arms, prominent Adam's apple jutting from a pale, elongated neck. I deem him "granola"—drawstring pants from South America, sandy hair hitting his shoulders.

Christopher, next to him, is the opposite: a powerfully built body under a black t-shirt with the words "Silence=Death" beneath an upward-pointing pink triangle. This seems to be the group's official t-shirt, for sale on the front table, $10. Christopher's blond hair is military short on the sides but fuller on top, gelled into waves. His eyes are like a tiger's: flecked and golden, almost spooky.

Big Christopher offers a tiny wave. "How many of you are here for the first time?"

Amanda's hand goes up. I raise mine and nudge Derek to do the same. Around the room, others identify themselves. I clock: a Black man in his thirties; two butch white women; three guys near my age, white, white and brown; a white older guy who looks like he came from work; a much older guy in a fanciful fedora; two guys with the same haircut, younger, black and brown; a skinny guy wearing hoop earrings and a shiny blouse. And us, three white recent college grads with no jobs.

ACT UP has recently staged a protest outside the White House where sixty-five people were arrested. I'd seen this in *The New York Times:* pictures of demonstrators carried away by cops wearing rubber gloves (the heavy yellow ones my mother wears when she washes dishes), and posters with Ronald Reagan's face looking demonic in Day-Glo colors above the word "AIDSGATE." The report on this protest comes from Mike, who says ACT UP has demanded a statement from the Capitol police acknowledging that you can't get AIDS from skin-to-skin contact. "The gloves were unnecessary, and they send a dangerous message to the public."

Mike has AIDS. I know this because I can see a lesion on his neck, and another on his upper arm, blotches like grape jelly on his olive-hued skin. Otherwise he doesn't look sick: he has a dancer's body, strong across the shoulders and solid at the core. He has wide, flirty eyes that I want to just gaze into, thick walnut-colored hair, and a Roman nose.

They're all so different from each other: Mike the charismatic rebel. Nicholas with his theatrical, Southern hippie vibe. Tiger-eyed Christopher, the intense gym queen. The next guy up is different again: Floyd, a lean, dark-skinned African-American with expressive hands and authoritative diction. He is dressed all in black, down to his shiny boots. His hair is shorn to the scalp and runs down into perfectly trimmed sideburns. What they all seem to share is the same riveting energy, some sense of purpose that I want, too. I look to my left: Amanda is leaning forward in her seat. Then to my right, where Derek has his arms and legs tightly crossed. He might be less sure about all this.

Floyd is speaking with the cadence of a preacher: "We've got a chance to make a powerful impact on our people, on our city, on our community. I'm talking about the Lesbian and Gay Pride Parade. We are going to march down Fifth Avenue in force and show them who we are and what we have to say. We've got the permit. We've got the vehicle. There *will* be a float. Now, brothers and sisters, we need to decide together: what will we do with this opportunity?"

"Ten minutes for discussion," says Christopher.

Derek looks at his watch. He is going to time this.

A man stands up and suggests a massive coffin, to be carried by pallbearers, marked on its sides with the number dead from AIDS. Floyd asks if a coffin is the right image to mobilize action. He calls on another man, who says he wants to see a *pile* of coffins on a float, "one for every AIDS death."

"That's thirty thousand coffins," Floyd notes.

"We're going to need a bigger vehicle," Nicholas drawls. Some people laugh. It's good to know laughter is OK. Discussion continues:

We should be stressing people living with AIDS, not dying from it.

I'm imagining an AIDS garden: cut flowers for the dead, potted plants for the living.

We need to burn Mayor Koch in effigy—he's done nothing!

We've gotta build on the Washington protest. Reagan just said the word AIDS for the first time, six years into this epidemic.

Reagan believes the only innocent victims of the virus are babies born with it and the rest of us should be rounded up and quarantined.

The Reagan comments strike a nerve. From around the room, people hiss. This delights Amanda.

Christopher says, "I'm facilitating, so I'm not supposed to make any suggestions—but what if we build a concentration camp, a right-wing vision of HIV quarantine? A group of people with AIDS behind a barbed wire fence, with uniformed guards marching alongside wearing yellow rubber gloves. And then Ronald Reagan leading the way like some evil mastermind."

Floyd nods. "We'll forgive you for stepping outside of your role, Christopher, since that is clearly an *inspired* idea."

Next to me, Amanda raises her hand. Floyd points toward her. "The sister with the long hair has the floor."

"I'd like to see a diverse group of people in the camp, not just white gay men."

"Right on," Floyd says. "Are you volunteering?"

18

"Yes," she says. "But I want to be a guard."

The room whoops. Amanda is beaming. I grab her hand and squeeze.

"That's ten minutes," says the guy taking notes at the table up front.

"The lovely Eliot, ladies and gentlemen," Nicholas says. I look at Eliot for the first time: the pale face, the trimmed beard, the air of watchful judgment. Eliot gives a royal wave and lets his gaze drift out across the room. In my memory, he takes note of me, too, though I've probably manufactured that detail because of how important he later became. Our night of sharing a jail cell is still many months away.

Derek nods and taps his watch, clearly impressed. "Ten minutes exactly."

"I'd like to make a motion that we agree on a federal focus," Floyd says, "and on the idea of people *living* with AIDS, to be worked out in committee."

Christopher says, "Do we have a second?"

Voices shout, "Second!"

"All those in favor?" Hands go up everywhere. The three of us raise ours, too, already feeling included.

"Opposed?" A smaller number of hands—the coffin people, the Koch people.

"The motion has passed," Nicholas says, pushing a long lock of hair behind his ear. "Well done, darlin's."

All three of us sign up for Gay Pride duty, and Amanda and I sign up for the outreach committee, too. Derek looks over the committee list and writes his name under Media. "Why not?" he says. "Gotta do something with my useless communications degree."

We step out into the balmy, late-May night and say our good-byes to Amanda, who is staying uptown in a studio apartment that her father rents but never uses. It seems absurd that Derek and I must return to our families in the suburbs—New Jersey for me, Long Island for him—but it's only been a month since I graduated, and we haven't figured out our plan. We walk to the subway holding hands, something we never do, and which I'd possibly never seen anyone do back in those days when public affection between men on the streets of New York was as rare as a bar without cigarette smoke.

In college I would take walks by myself to some far corner of campus, carrying a notebook, writing drafts of screenplays inspired by confessional poetry and coming of age novels, full of feelings I could barely put words to. I had a vibrant, inquisitive mind—I see that now—but I'd led a sheltered life, so that hard truths, when they hit, overwhelmed me. I was a person capable of great love, a young man absolutely boiling with sexual desire, but always with the lid on, rattling from the steam. I had no outlet. I felt that no one could know my true self or they'd shun me, mock me, even destroy me. I'd been picked on by boys all my life—made the butt of jokes, insulted, physically intimidated. These boys had glimpsed my queer spirit—a questioning mind, keen emotions, eager eyes—and they knew how to squash it. Girls were my true friends. I spoke in their rhythms, I played their games and listened to their music. I had a soft mouth that I would apply lipstick to in the mirror while wrapping a bath towel into a turban. But I was not protected like girls were, which made me a target. I learned to tamp down feelings except in my notebook or in stories I composed in private and showed to no one—stories populated by boys who were bolder than me—or as prayers to Jesus, who I believed cared and listened, like a gentle older brother who could wrap me in his arms and make it all okay.

And then, when those lonely solo walks had become unbearable and praying had ceased to work and I'd learned to drown explosive feelings in boozy binges with my fellow film students, Derek appeared. Whenever I look back and wonder, why Derek, why was he the one?, I land on this: he smiled. We were strangers in the same room at a student conference, and I was staring at him, and he caught my stare, and he welcomed it. Had he been blank-faced or scowling or even intensely cruising, I would have shied away, but his smile invited me in. It said, *let's start something*. That was all I needed. My strong, gentle, older-brother-savior had arrived.

He was physically smaller than me, but his body looked sturdier. He was sinew and lean muscle, with dark fur on his chest, cheeks shadowed in stubble, sprouts of hair on his knuckles. Today we'd call him an "otter" but we didn't have that term yet. Did we even have "bear"? I don't think so, not in New York in the '80s. I didn't learn those subdivided categories until I moved to California, at the end of all this. Everything is different now, including how we talk about ourselves.

Later, as his lover, I got used to his complaints about his appearance: going bald too soon, chin too weak, eyes too squinty in photos. But from the start I liked his approachable face. Too hot intimidated me. Hot guys were good for faraway crushes. I'd nurtured dozens of them all through high school and college, silently man-crazed and furtive, aware of male bodies as they slid into and out of desk chairs, shirts rising up from the waist, sweaters pulled overhead in stuffy auditoriums, exposed flesh, treasure trails, the elastic bands of underwear, the bulges below, the mesmerizing outline of an ass in snug jeans. I had acted on my desires before Derek, but so what? I barely remember those first few quickies: a drunken blow job at a party, a 3 a.m. hand job in a dorm lounge, a jock waving me into a library bathroom stall and telling me to put my cock in his ass, just like that, like it was nothing, like there wasn't the risk of disease. I mostly remember feeling unskilled and uncomfortable, ready to flee as soon as one of us had an orgasm.

But Derek—I notice him at Columbia, at the student conference where Larry Kramer delivered his fiery call to action and helped put this whole story in motion. Derek is a boy who draws people toward him. No sooner has he entered a room than he's waving someone over, or a friend is calling his name, which is how I learn it even before we speak.

Amanda and I are at a presentation about safe sex when Derek takes a seat down the row from us, talking animatedly to the next guy over. I nudge Amanda and mouth the word *him*. She follows my eyes and says, "Introduce yourself," but I've never before said hello out of the blue to a stranger who's captured my interest.

"Everyone has the virus," says the gay doctor giving the presentation. "That's the assumption you should make. When you fuck, use condoms, which should be latex. The lube should be water-based not oil-based. No Vaseline. Avoid exchanges of bodily fluids. Oral sex is safer if you don't take cum in your mouth." I am terrified of all this risk but also thrilled to hear this handsome man talking frankly about what guys could do together in the middle of this epidemic.

When it's time to ask questions, Derek raises his hand. "What about getting cum on your skin? If you don't have any cuts, is that safe? What about dried cum?" The doctor is answering, "When you're talking about semen, *on* you is better than *in* you." Instantly, my mind fills with an image of Derek naked with cum (mine) drying on skin (his). This is the moment when he catches my stare, the moment he smiles, the moment I smile back and decide it won't be so hard to introduce myself after all.

We spend the rest of the day going to conference events together. I bring him back to my hotel room, where I am sharing a bed with Amanda, who has gone downtown to a bar called the Cubby Hole with a group of women she met today. She calls the hotel late to say she's not coming back that night. So Derek stays over, and together we try out the latex condoms and water-based lube handed out earlier by the older gay guys determined to keep us younger gay guys safe.

The next day I drive back to school. I call Derek from a payphone at a rest stop and tell him I miss him. That night he calls me at my off-campus apartment and says he's cleared the weekend, he's coming to visit. And that's how it begins: he drives four hours upstate in his two-door Datsun. Next, I take a bus to the city to meet up at the apartment of one of his friends, where we can spend the night on a pullout couch or a futon on someone's floor. When we're apart, we write each other letters. We talk on the phone nearly every day. And just like that my real life erupts out of solitude. I put as little effort as I can into my finals. I half-ass the short film I'm directing for my senior project. My grades take a last-minute dive, but I hardly notice and don't care. I have love in my life.

For the first couple weeks after college, I do little but sit in the backyard on a patio chair with my shirt off, slathered in sunblock, reading novels and creating pornographic fantasies of studly delivery men. I mail resumes to video production houses in Manhattan and wait for someone to offer me work. Derek and I see each other when we can, but many hours are spent without him in New Jersey, where I mow the lawn, help my father clear junk out of the garage, shop and cook with my mother, drive my sisters to their jobs at the mall.

My mother is a petite Irish woman with blue eyes and freckles who never raises her voice. My boyish face, pale skin and tendency toward insecurity come from her. My father has a killer smile and strong opinions, even at times a temper—I've inherited a bit of that, too—but he's mellowed as I, and my two younger sisters, Lisa and Michelle, get older. Lisa attends a local college and dates a guy who stands awkwardly at the door while my father chats him up before their dates ("the third degree," Lisa calls it). She and her girlfriends—who sport big hair and talk in loud voices—are always dressing up and going out to parties. Michelle, in contrast, is shy, with just a single best friend who comes over almost every day when their high school classes let out. They close themselves behind her bedroom door, play records, and giggle in voices rarely raised above a whisper.

The announcement of my sexuality the previous year left my mother crying, my father angry, Lisa embarrassed about what her friends would think, Michelle silent and fleeing from the tension. "Don't you know what's out there?" my father demanded of me. The likelihood of getting sick, he reasoned, should make me think twice about coming out.

22

My mother told me she knew I was gay from an early age. I was an excitable little boy who often raided her makeup bag. But now she fears I am resigning myself to a life of loneliness.

"I have Derek," I tell her.

"For now," she replies sadly.

He comes over for visits. They are kind to him, but refer to him as my friend, never my boyfriend, much less my lover, which is the word I like. Among my family, I live in the realm of what is not discussed.

The weekend after that first ACT UP meeting, Derek is staying over for the night. We are supposed to sleep in separate rooms—my parents' rule—but after they go to bed, I make my way stealthily to the family room in the basement, with its TV and pile of board games, to join him on the pullout sofa. We wake to the ringing of the telephone and then my father shouting for me to pick up. Shaking off sleep, I stumble to the extension. "Hang up, Dad."

"Are you upstairs?" he asks.

"I'm downstairs. Hang up."

He clicks off. Then a male voice asks me, "Is this Paul or Derek?"

"Paul. Who's this?"

"Christopher from ACT UP."

Christopher of the tiger eyes and rock-hard pecs. "Really?"

"Yes, really. You volunteered for the Pride contingent." He sounds bemused, exasperated. Behind me Derek stirs. I mouth: *ACT UP.* His eyes go wide.

"The parade is tomorrow and we don't have anyone for the booth on Christopher Street."

"OK. We can do that. Me—Paul—and Derek."

"It means you're *not marching*," he says, making sure I don't miss this point. "Everyone's marching, and no one wants to work the booth, but we need the booth manned—I mean *staffed*—all morning."

"We'll do it, yes." I gesture to Derek for pen and paper.

"You will? Oh, that's great." He gives me the where and when, his voice softening with relief.

I slide back under the sheets and tell Derek, "I think we just made Christopher's day."

"I'd like to make Christopher's day," he says, flashing me a dirty smile.

I roll onto him, my hands on his chest, my fingers stroking his soft black fur. We are kissing when my father's voice calls down, "Your mother and I would like to speak to you. Upstairs."

There is a lecture coming: you-know-the-rules-about-sleeping-in-this-house. But I am ready for a fight. The stasis of summer is over.

We drive into the city on Sunday morning and make our way to Christopher Street—*Christopher's Street*, we now call it (and we'll call it that forever). The June sun is already blazing. Sidewalks are filling up with parade-watchers claiming spots. Anticipation hums in the air like a live wire, strong as the smells from the food booths: roasted chestnuts, baked pretzels, meat-on-a-stick.

The ACT UP booth is made of plywood and two-by-fours, painted black, looking sturdy but not quite ready. Standing behind it is a guy with a cool, rockabilly haircut and a bulky camcorder on his shoulder, aimed at the crowd. Catching sight of us, he lowers his lens. He has big features: large, round, dark eyes, a wide nose, a big smile that reveals a gap between two Chiclet teeth. "I'm Raymond," he says. "Everyone else went uptown for the start of the parade."

"Are you going or staying?"

"I'm with a video collective assembling footage as a tool for community organizing and resistance." It just rolls off his tongue. Then he laughs. "It's agitprop. That's what I'm about."

I want to ask him more—I'm excited to talk to someone my age about filmmaking—but he's already packing his camcorder away and hoisting a bag over his shoulder. "All yours," he says, leaving the booth and slipping into the crowd.

Derek and I look at each other. "I guess we're in charge," I say.

"So, we just sell t-shirts?"

"First—a makeover."

We stretch "Silence=Death" and "AIDSGATE" shirts over the nail heads protruding from the plywood and arrange the merch in display piles. We trade the shirts we put on that morning for these ACT UP images, and it's like a comic book hero's transformation. I suddenly have all this power. In the middle of the street, I shout, "ACT UP, fight back, fight AIDS," as if it's the most natural thing in the world. Derek calls out, "Get the hottest t-shirts at the parade." Right away, people are heading toward us. They've heard of

ACT UP, or they're curious who we are. "How do I join?" someone asks.

"I don't think you really *join*," I say. "I think you just participate."

"Come to the Monday night meeting," Derek says. "That's what we did."

We hear the parade before we see it—the roar of the Dykes on Bikes, the swelling cheers from the crowd. The hum I'd felt in the air is now a vibration moving through me. Next march the AIDS groups, the biggest being GMHC, the Gay Men's Health Crisis, so many men in different stages of illness, some walking tall and waving to the crowd, some frail and grim and supported by others. This doesn't seem like the same population I saw at the ACT UP meeting, which was younger, more visibly healthy, angrier.

Then I hear them—an upswell of noise, a shift in energy—and see them, a mass of marchers behind a black banner, wide as the street, proclaiming We'll Never Be Silent Again, a mass of voices chanting the words over and over: *We'll Never Be Silent Again. We'll Never Be Silent Again.*

Next comes the flatbed truck. Perched on the cab like a vulture is a guy in a gray suit and a Reagan mask, laughing maniacally, arms raised in triumph—the ghoulish overlord of the concentration camp. On the four corners of the flatbed are watchtowers anchoring a barbed-wire fence. Men and women of different ages and skin tones stare out like prisoners. Guards in military camo, dark glasses and yellow rubber gloves flank the camp in formation. There's Amanda! It's easy to spot her among all the tall men. I wave but she's focused—staring straight ahead, emotionless in her role.

The next wide banner says Treatment, Not Testing and behind this marches the group, huge in number, far greater than I'd seen at the meeting. Where have they all come from? Have they joined along the route? Derek and I take up the new chant: *No! More! Business-as-usual! No! More! Business-as-usual!* It's all so much grander than I imagined.

It's not just a float in a parade. It's a battle cry.

Later, familiar faces begin popping up back at the booth. There's tiger-eyed Christopher, long-haired Nicholas, bearded Eliot, fashionable Floyd. Christopher goes right for our cash envelope, counting the pile of bills we collected.

"After you guys marched by, we couldn't sell them fast enough," I say.

"If you want to capture someone's attention," Eliot says, "send Dachau down Fifth Avenue." He's wearing a suit—*he* was our Reagan. I hadn't realized that. It's hard to connect his animated performance during the parade to his silent secretarial presence at the meeting.

Mike shows up next. I try not to stare at his lesions, but I want to know, see, understand. Mike walks directly to Christopher, who wraps his beefy arms around him. They kiss, and I realize they're a couple. Of course—the two hot guys. I wonder, is Christopher infected, like Mike? I was still new enough to form questions like that, thinking of these men as "infected," afflicted, other. Different from me.

Eliot catches me watching them and mutters jaggedly, "Ah, young love," though he looks younger than either of them, and I'm younger still, an interloper sizing everyone up.

Christopher announces, "Paul and Derek from New Jersey sold a shitload of t-shirts."

"I'm actually from Long Island," Derek says.

"If you insist, darlin'," Nicholas drawls, and everyone laughs.

Then there's someone else entering the booth. "Make room for Uncle Larry," Mike bellows.

And there he is, Larry Kramer. I recognize him right away: the small, dark intense eyes behind wire-rimmed glasses, the mouth in a frown, the Oxford shirt buttoned high. He looks small and ordinary, not like the fearsome prophet at the podium, the self-proclaimed Cassandra who raised his voice to the sky. I introduce myself, saying, "You're the reason I'm here. You made me stand up at a college conference, and then you told me I was going to die."

"Well, I've got to get people's attention," he stammers, perhaps abashed at meeting one of the young men he's terrified with his recruitment speech. "It's getting worse all the time. They're trying to pass a bill in Congress preventing people who test HIV-positive from entering through customs! ACT UP needs to fight this *now*."

"Definitely," I mutter, deer caught in headlights, knowing nothing about this particular bill.

He holds up a t-shirt. "So how do we do this?"

"Um, you just sell them for $10," I say.

"Tell people they're the hottest shirts at the parade," Derek says.

Larry looks dubious.

"It works," Derek says. "Hottest t-shirt at the parade," he shouts for the hundredth time.

Larry joins him, but he calls out, "Clothe yourself in your anger!" and soon he's making a sale, too.

"That's just rich," Eliot says, watching Larry with a smirk. Seeing my confusion, Eliot explains that three weeks ago, "Uncle Larry" delivered a dramatic farewell on the floor of ACT UP, furious about the group's direction.

"Furious about what?" I ask.

Nicholas offers me a cigarette, balancing his own at the corner of his mouth. I'm not much of a smoker, but I take one and puff lightly. "He claimed," Nicholas says through clenched teeth, "that we were wasting time getting approval for the money to pay for these very shirts." He scrunches his brow and tightens his gaze as he and Eliot imitate Larry's accusations in unison: "*You sissies! People are dying and you're arguing about t-shirts?*" And then they both break into giggles.

Christopher walks over, still clutching the cash. "You guys have done well," he tells me. "You're free to go."

But we don't have anywhere else to be.

Note to Self #2: Why are you telling this story now?

For years I tried, but it hurt too much, in too many ways: The hurt of grief and loss, which is bottomless, and the hurt of betrayal, which shuts one down. There's the hurt that feels like failure, which is really just deep-rooted shame; and there's the excess that follows success, which can go rancid, and that hurts, too.

Now there's this man at his laptop making sense—or lacking that, making stories—from memory, this refurbished "Paul," asking questions of himself, older now than those older friends who died.

Why now? Perhaps because there's a new wave rolling in: the young who want to rename the world and make it new again, discovering those of us who've been waiting on the shore, something precious in our arms to be preserved.

Survivors? Sure. Elders? If you insist. There's the need to unburden oneself of what's been borne. To testify. To witness.

Call it hope, which is stronger than hurt.

Part 2

Direct Action

The target is the federal courthouse in downtown Manhattan. We're protesting the ban on HIV-positive people entering the U.S., the one Larry spoke to me about.

The afternoon is muggy and hot, the sun high in the June sky. Taking a cue from guys like Christopher and Floyd, I have dressed all in black. By the time I meet Amanda in the West Village, at a diner, I'm sweating. Amanda is in black, too, her hair tied back with a very femme pink bow. Though we're both recent college graduates, she's been living at her father's place in the city and already looks like a New Yorker: dark sunglasses, fashionable backpack, street-ready, thick-soled boots. I buy us iced coffees, and she gives me one of her Marlboros. On the subway downtown, we complain about the humidity, about being broke, about trying to find work in film production.

Emerging above ground, we immediately spot the "SILENCE=DEATH" and "AIDSGATE" signs. The throng is already edging into the plaza, dozens of black t-shirts flooding the streets like an oil slick. I find Derek with a clipboard in his hand. As a member of the media committee, he's gotten here early to help wrangle the press. "Looking *official*," I marvel.

"I'm just doing what they tell me," he says. "Once we get the news crews positioned, the arrests are going to start."

Ahead of him, Nicholas bellows, "Derek from New Jersey! Come with me."

Derek laughs. "From *Long Island*." He hurries to catch up with Nicholas.

Amanda pulls me into the thick of the crowd. Chanting slogans in public takes some getting used to—we're all trained from an early age to keep our voices down. But we rehearsed together at the Center the night before, so when someone shouts, "We'll never be silent again," Amanda and I join in and repeat the words over and over in rhythm with everyone else.

Moments later, Nicholas's distinctive Southern voice is booming through the bullhorn: "Make room, ladies and gentlemen, here they come." A line of activists begins to snake past us. I step aside, feeling my heart speed up.

There's Raymond, the guy with the rockabilly hair from Pride. Today he's not carrying his camcorder. Today he's going to be arrested. I keep my eyes on him as he takes his place on the courthouse steps among the protesters, who are a vision of the twentieth-century New York melting pot: Jewish, Italian, Irish, Puerto Rican, Greek, Black. I want to be up there among them, participating, not observing, I want to be that kind of man, although "man" is hardly how I think of myself. And yet there is Raymond, no older than me, looking fearless.

Among this group I see Mike, with his handsome face, thick hair and fit body. Mike with his lesions. He carries a sign:

LIVING WITH AIDS 2 YEARS AND 3 MONTHS, NO THANKS TO YOU PRESIDENT REAGAN.

Unlike most of ACT UP's polished, uniform graphics, this sign is handmade: white posterboard covered in red and black magic-marker letters. The numbers peel off so they can keep on rising. The target's name is removable, too, changed for the occasions. At City Hall, it will be "Mayor Koch." In Albany, a year from now, "Governor Cuomo."

I nudge Amanda. "He's incredible, isn't he?"

"I hear he used to dance on Broadway, but no one will hire him now."

It's absurd to think that those few KS lesions mark him as having a deathly illness, because Mike is so full of life, so strong and vigorous it seems like his fist, pumping the air, could shatter the sky.

"I want to be with them," I say to Amanda.

"Should we?" Then she answers her own question, "Yes, before we change our minds." She pulls me onto the plaza and up the steps. We sit among the others. I squeeze her hand tighter. She takes the hand of the guy on the other side.

Two other boys from the crowd—carried along on this furious wave—sit down next to me. They're dressed alike: buzzed heads and t-shirts with band logos. My age, maybe a little older. One of them intertwines his fingers in mine and says, "I've never done this before."

"Me neither."

"I have to pee," he says. The other guy gives him a kiss on the cheek.

I probably have to pee, too, but mostly it feels like I've left my body, gazing down at the mass from which we've just emerged: other ACT UP folks, media people with cameras, random onlookers, and many, many police, all wearing rubber gloves. Where is Derek? I hope he can see me, because I'm about to get arrested, and I realize I have no idea what happens next.

I pick up the chant—*"Ronald Reagan you can't hide, we charge you with genocide"*—feeling it move through me and soar like an anthem. We raise our interlocked hands, a gesture at once triumphant and heavy with grief.

The police converge on the steps, dropping their hands on the demonstrators. This triggers an eruption from the crowd—*"Shame, shame, shame, shame!"* I watch, heart thumping, as one by one Mike and Raymond and the other men and women are led away by police. My stomach clenches, my breath becomes shallow. The police reach Amanda, lifting her to her feet, and then a cop is grabbing my arm, yanking me up and away from the buzz-cut boy at my side, forcing me down the steps. I get thrown off balance and stumble. He tightens his grip and shouts, "Move it."

"Take it easy," I bark.

In the crowd, an older woman with long, frizzy gray hair calls to me, "Don't resist." I catch her eye and nod and attempt to keep pace with the cop, who after all is doing exactly what we need: making arrests in front of the cameras.

Up ahead is the police bus. I see Mike, already inside, lowering a window and thrusting himself out, waving his homemade sign. I watch as press photographers circle around and snap pictures: angry face, angry sign, angry demonstrator under arrest. And then I step onto the bus, too.

We are kept together in a big holding cell. Everyone jokes and converses and makes introductions. People are curious about me and Amanda and Timmy and Keith—the two buzz-cut boys—all of us first-time arrestees. From across the cell, Christopher, his intense tiger-eyes fixed on me, calls out, "Paul from New Jersey, have you and your friends gone through CD training yet?" I feel my face go red. CD is civil disobedience; getting arrested is something you're supposed to practice with the group. "It's not always this easy," Christopher says. "Be prepared next time." I feel chastened but also included: there will, without a doubt, be a next time.

Hours later, the last light of day fading, the evening bearably warm, we are released "under our own recognizance." Lawyers have arranged this, and no one seems too worried about our pending trial date. ACT UP has only been around for four months, but in my eyes, people like Mike and Christopher and Raymond are already seasoned veterans.

"I can't believe you just went ahead and did that. I looked up and there you were." This is Derek, outside the precinct, waiting for me, a little tense.

"We got swept up in it," I say. "Sorry to worry you."

"We upped the numbers—thirty-two of us! That's good for media," Amanda says.

"I know, I'm on the media committee. I've been working all afternoon."

"OK, Mr. Big," Amanda says.

I give Derek a kiss. He manages one of his disarming smiles.

Timmy pushes himself into the conversation. "Aw, so cute."

I introduce Derek. Keith is skinnier, with finer bones and a lightly freckled face. Timmy is broad-chested and blue-eyed. With their matching buzzed heads and rock t-shirts, I've assumed they're boyfriends, though I wonder now. I'm learning not to make assumptions about relationships, the same way I've gleaned that you don't ask anyone what his HIV status is. You wait for people to tell you the important things, in their own words.

The five of us walk uptown, talking over each other, excitedly recounting the day. We eat Chinese food, we buy beer and drink out of paper bags, and we end up at the Pyramid Club on Avenue A, a dark, narrow space with a stage in the back where a drag show is starting up, emceed by a queen named *Tabboo!* "The exclamation point is included," she tells the crowd. The only drag I've seen is on stage, *La Cage aux Folles*, but this scene has nothing to do with sequined gowns or feather boas. It's pure punk: makeup that calls attention to itself, dollar-bin dresses, torn fishnet stockings. "It's all trash, no glamour," I say to Timmy.

"The trash *is* the glamour," he says, in an accent that's pure Brooklyn, with a hint of a soft *s*, a little *ith*.

At the end of the night, Derek drunkenly throws one arm across Timmy's shoulders and the other across Keith's and says, "Fellas, it's time to take us home."

Keith says, "Oh, you're one of *those* couples," and he and Timmy laugh.

I'm embarrassed for a moment, though Derek is not discouraged. "You're not going to send us back to the suburbs, are you?"

Amanda takes this as her cue. "I'm going uptown. You boys have fun."

"I'll go with you," Keith says.

"I don't need an escort."

"I do," he says with a giggle, and loops his arm through hers. We kiss them good-bye.

Timmy says, "Looks like you're all mine."

"Is this OK with Keith?" I ask.

"We're not boyfriends. He's my sister. We're practically the same person."

A cab pulls up and Derek gets in, then Timmy, then me. Timmy has already given an address and is making out with Derek when the cab driver turns to face us through the partition. "Well if it isn't the boys from New Jersey."

It's Nicholas, behind the wheel! His hair is pulled back into a knot.

"What are you doing here? We just saw you at the demo!"

"That was hours ago. A lady's gotta earn a living."

"You're the facilitator," Timmy exclaims. "You're famous!"

"That's a new one." Nicholas laughs deeply as he pulls away from the curb, adding, "Please secure your own oxygen mask before assisting your child."

"I'm not their child," Timmy says, "I'm their sandwich meat."

"Would you lovelies like to smoke a joint?" Nicholas asks.

"I'm too drunk," Derek says, though I reach for it eagerly.

The high hits me right away, and the moment blooms into something magical. The thrilling surprise of Nicholas being our cab driver is not just because, as a leader in ACT UP, he is "famous," but because in recognizing us he reflects something special back our way, too. I notice that he's left the meter off. Free ride! The whole day—the protest, the arrest, our new friends, the drag show, this chance encounter—feels not quite like real life, but instead like the story my life is turning into.

Never again did I hail a cab that had Nicholas at the wheel, but that night taught me that such a thing was always possible. New York City was becoming much more intimate, knowable, full of offerings. You just had to be there to receive them.

The next afternoon, I am back in New Jersey. The front porch with its peeling wicker furniture, the gauzy curtains in the windows, the refrigerator door littered with coupons, Catholic mass cards, and school portraits of our cousins' children: it's all so familiar, but now so alien, as if I have time-traveled back to an era before plague and chaos. I am missing Derek, Amanda, Timmy and Keith—all of my new friends. I join my family at the dinner table, not knowing quite what to say.

The *Bergen Record,* our local newspaper, is sitting on the kitchen table. I flip to the Metro section and there it is, a short article about yesterday's demonstration. I've read the *Record* my whole life. My first job was delivering this paper door to door. Now, indirectly, I'm in it, one of the "thirty-two protestors arrested." There's a photo of Mike, holding his sign out of the window of the police bus.

We have just taken our seats, as we do every evening at six, and are about to eat pork chops and egg noodles and a salad made of iceberg lettuce. My mother peers over my shoulder and reads the headline aloud: "AIDS Victims Act Up." She emits a small sound of pity and sympathy.

"His name is Mike Savas," I say.

"Who? In the picture?"

"Yeah. I was there, at that protest."

"You were?" She looks across the dinner table at my father, who looks at my sister Lisa, who looks at Michelle, a wordless question pinballing between them.

"Did you get arrested with the AIDS victims?" my mother asks.

"We don't say *victims,* Mom."

My father says, "Could you think about the tone you take with your mother?"

"We say People With AIDS."

"Who's we?" Lisa asks.

"Those protesters?" my mother asks.

"It's a group called ACT UP. And I'm not trying to take a tone," I say. "I just don't want you to sound ignorant."

Michelle, who is still in high school, takes the paper from me and starts reading the article. "They want money from the government for research."

Without quite planning it, I'm suddenly telling them about the hideous legislation being pushed through Congress, about the forces creating stigma rather than solutions, the insidious rhetoric about how AIDS hasn't yet hit the "general public." Even as I speak I'm surprised at how articulate I sound, at how much I've absorbed already about the politics of AIDS. I look at Michelle and ask her if she knows what civil disobedience is, warming up to admitting that I was among those arrested, but then I catch Dad and Lisa suppressing what looks to me like laughter. Nervous laughter, maybe, but still. "Is this funny to you?" I ask.

"She just spilled her drink," he says, pointing to a splash of iced tea on her shirt.

"I spazzed out," she says. "He was laughing at *me*, it wasn't about you."

I push back my chair and stand up. "Forget it."

"Where do you think you're going?" my father asks. It's never been OK to leave the table in the middle of a meal.

"How would you like it if it was *me* with those marks on my skin?" I ask.

"It's *not* you, thank God," my mother says.

"It could be," I say. "Think about it." They stare at me, silent and anxious, and I leave the room, my pulse pounding. What does it mean to confront them with my new knowledge but not be able to capture their attention? Yesterday I was chanting about genocide on federal property; today I am arguing across a plate of egg noodles in New Jersey.

I call Derek from the upstairs phone. "It's time," I say, "to get a place of our own."

A knock on my bedroom door. I grunt unhelpfully, and my mother lets herself in. "Are you going to talk to me?" she asks.

"I talk. No one listens."

"Come on. I'm trying to understand." Her pale blue eyes have a worried intensity. "Tell me, how is your health?"

"I haven't been tested, if that's what you're wondering," I say. "But I have no reason to think I'm HIV-positive."

"Maybe you should take that test, so you know for sure."

"What good would it do?"

"It's always better to know." In her voice I hear the terror she must surely feel, thinking of her son getting sick. "There are treatments, right?"

"There's *one*. A drug called AZT. It's expensive, and people say it makes them sicker."

"What about these experimental drugs, the ones you're trying to get for the people with AIDS?"

As she speaks, she rubs her hands together. For years my mother suffered from eczema—"bad skin" we always called it—and though the problem has long since cleared, at anxious moments her hands repeat the old motions, as if she were still rubbing herself with ointment, trying to heal.

"Mom, I'm being safe, you don't have to worry."

"Worrying about you is what I do." She is a stereotypical Irish mother, on alert for calamity at every turn. When I'm at the wheel, with her in the passenger seat, she rides with her hand on the dashboard, bracing for a crash.

I don't want to get an HIV test, but she repeats, "You'd be better off knowing," so I tell her I'll think about it. When she hugs me, I melt a little. I'm not too old to need my mother.

I can't sleep. I think of everything I saw the day before. The group of us assembled on the federal courthouse steps, our arms raised, the police leading us away, the frizzy-haired woman telling me, "Don't resist." I think of sex with Timmy, the first guy Derek and I have brought home together. I think of the condom on Timmy's cock as he fucked me.

I think mostly of Mike Savas and his sign, about what it means to live with the disease marked on your body, feared and fearless. Those lesions seem to me like medals bestowed upon a warrior who has excelled in combat. I imagine one for every sexual conquest, one for every orgasm. My mind fills with this vision—Mike as a centurion. I peel off his armor, lay him down on my bed, straddle him, let him penetrate me. I want him to open me up. I want him to fuck his power into me. I put our bodies through every position I can imagine. There's no condom in this fantasy, because I want him to make me into a man like him, not *infected* but powerful: a man unafraid of the stares of passersby or the grip of the police, a man brave enough to call out government crimes on his handmade sign.

My orgasm is explosive and noisy. As I catch my breath, I feel sure that everyone in the house has heard me, not only *heard* but somehow witnessed the visions I've conjured. My parents will look at each other and shake their heads and say, "See? He wanted it. He said he was fighting it, but he wanted it."

Strong Language

Summer 1987. It's so long ago now, hardly real at all, the stuff of nostalgic TV shows and Internet memes. Every day was different, and every day was full. My résumé, and my film school degree, had started to yield work on commercial production shoots. I'd get up early and take a bus or a train to the location, which could be anywhere in the city. I'd run around, a gofer, getting yelled at by the people in charge, feeling low. When I had no work, I'd sign up at another temp agency, relying on my fast typing speed to make money doing office work in high-rise buildings. I'd eventually rendezvous with Derek, sometimes at an apartment we had found through the classifieds in the *Voice*. We'd jockey for position among other potential renters to catch a landlord's attention. We were looking for our love nest, though mostly we saw roach traps, small scuzzy places that seemed overpriced to me, as downtown rents were on the rise. From there we'd rush to whatever ACT UP committee or planning meeting we'd signed up for, and after that we'd go out for beers, finally crashing with anyone offering a couch or bed or floor for the night.

I slept poorly in strange apartments but I loved seeing how these New Yorkers lived: their scrappy furniture, the art they hung on their walls, and most of all their books. I said yes to any book that anyone pushed on me— critical theory, queer novels, monographs about artists I didn't know back then but who are essential now—and I'd stuff these into my backpack with my extra t-shirts and the toiletries of my youth: Colgate, Mennen Speed Stick, Paul Mitchell Mousse.

I spent a lot of time with Amanda. She was full of contradictions: extroverted except when she withdrew into quiet thought, sensitive even when at her toughest. She was a natural activist who would stand for hours on a street corner in Harlem or the Lower East Side, handing out ACT UP leaflets to strangers, but had also confessed to me that she was afraid of the dark and slept with a light on. She never wore a bra or shaved her armpits but also splurged on golden highlights for her hair, which she tied back with a girly pink headband. I had handed her résumé to my film production contacts, though her lack of experience, and the men's-club sexism of the industry, meant that she rarely got hired. I admitted to her my lifelong ambition to be a writer, and so she took me along to a night of lesbians reading poems, the first poetry reading I'd ever been to and the first room in which, as a young white man, I found myself a minority.

In the summer of 1987, there is so much to learn, and lessons are doled out to me all the time. On this particular weekend, a group of us are at Dojo's, the best place for cheap food in the East Village, gathered around a table and editing text for the ACT UP business card. We are the outreach committee, a handful of young guys like me, plus Amanda, Floyd and Raymond, his camcorder in a bag at his feet. At the head of the table is Rochelle, the woman who'd warned me not to resist the police during my arrest. She's a brilliant professor with decades of activism in the feminist and queer movements, whose wild hair, crooked teeth and Moroccan sandals made her less intimidating than she might otherwise have been; she's like a slightly eccentric, favorite aunt. Together we dissect every phrase of the text.

"What about this line?" I read: "By 1991, more people will die from AIDS each year than were lost in the entire Vietnam War."

"More *Americans,*" Rochelle corrects. "That number doesn't include Vietnamese deaths."

Someone wants to use the word "genocide," but Raymond isn't sure. "The government's failure on AIDS has absolutely been deliberate, but genocide? I'm uncomfortable with Holocaust metaphors."

"We're already reclaiming the Nazis' pink triangle on our t-shirts," Amanda says. "We had a concentration camp float. Why not use strong language?"

"The point is to get people involved," I add.

"Which people?" Floyd asks suddenly. He's been sitting at the foot of the table, smoking and not saying much. I've caught his eye a few times and seen something impatient there, something I haven't understood. "To which *people* do most of you imagine that you're speaking? Are you trying to reach people of color like me, especially those poor folks disproportionately affected by AIDS? Perhaps the junkies just outside this restaurant on St.

Mark's, sharing their needles? Is your meticulously crafted business card for them?"

He has commanded everyone's attention, and not only at our table. The restaurant seems to have hushed.

"No, I think most of you imagine that you're speaking to other well-intended liberal lily-white people like yourselves, folks who just need a good slogan to be persuaded to join your comfortable committee. But you'll never get the words right because as Brother Baldwin said, *you don't know where it's at*. You don't know the truth, not about them—about yourselves. You don't know how to look inside and see your own fear and the responsibility you bear for the state of the world today. I for one am not going to sit around and educate you any further." With that he stands up, scraping his chair on the floor. He puts a hand on Rochelle's shoulder and says at half-volume, "Sister, none of that was for you. I know you've lived the struggle. But please, can you hurry these children along?" And with that he sails out of the restaurant. I am breathless, instantly overheated, defensive and confused. It was my comment that triggered him.

I look at Raymond, who is shaking his head. "I identify as mixed race, and I am committed to building a coalition, but maybe I haven't been speaking from that subjectivity clearly enough."

Amanda lights a cigarette. "It's not helpful to walk out. I don't think a woman can afford to walk out of a room like that."

Rochelle says, "What Floyd's saying is true: we're not going to speak to all communities with this. It's a business card, it's meant to reach people who will respond to a tool like this, which is people of a certain class. That doesn't mean we don't continue with our process, it just means we expand our agenda."

The conversation goes on haltingly at first, as we absorb Floyd's words, and then with some regained enthusiasm, but for me, it is unbearable. Who am I to haggle over words when I can't see the big picture, don't understand my own relative position in our coalition? I've never thought of myself as lily-white; I'm Irish and German, the son and grandson of immigrants, a kid who's worked jobs since middle school, is paying off student loans, is basically broke all the time. But I see too that I am someone who has been able to gain certain skills, who can expect a résumé to be answered when mailed, who can *choose* to get arrested and not feel endangered. Today we have a word for this, *privilege*, an analysis still being invented and articulated at tables like that one, for people like me who had so much to learn.

• • •

Afterwards, Raymond asks Amanda and me to walk with him to Tompkins Square Park, where he'll be videotaping a couple of community organizers, "recovering IV drug users passing out information about clean works." I know nothing about IV drug use, and I've never been to Tompkins Square; I've never walked east of Avenue A into Alphabet City, the grittiest, crackiest part of downtown. But I say yes. After what just happened, of course I do.

The sidewalks are covered in dark splotches: chewing gum, spit out and flattened into shapes that look like lesions. The sky is a heavy gray. There's a newly visible desperation to the people we pass, or so it seems. On St. Mark's Place, beneath soot and rust, buildings of limestone and brick with ornate scrollwork under each cornice and iron bars over every window suggest a lost era to which we are still somehow connected. But am "I" part of "we"? Or am I an interloper? At the corner of First Ave., Raymond stops and insists that I try Stromboli's pizza, best in the city, he says. We've just eaten rice and vegetables, but we gobble down slices. Across the street is Theatre 80, where old movies are screened. Out front, grooved into the sidewalk, are handprints and autographs of bygone Hollywood stars. I see Bette Davis' name etched in concrete. "Bette Davis?" I marvel. "Here?"

"Used to be a premiere movie theater," Raymond says, "and before that a Yiddish stage." He conjures up an era when the surrounding tenements were filled with the Eastern European Jews who built these blocks into a nightlife district.

"When you said you identify as mixed," Amanda asks Raymond, "what exactly did you mean?"

"My mother is Panamanian, my father is a Sephardic Jew. People read me as white. By some definitions of 'Hispanic,' I am, but I grew up mostly in Ohio, where I was the darkest kid in school and everyone called me a spic."

"How long have you lived in New York?" I ask.

"Four years. Right out of high school." He's living now in a storefront on 13th Street, just off A, with an older artist named Pierre, who painted their street-facing windows black. "It's like living behind a wall of mud," Raymond says.

"Plus you can hear everything on the sidewalk, right?" Amanda asks. "That's what I hate. There's always some man yelling at some woman."

It all sounds heart-thumpingly seductive to me: Avenue A, the noise of the streets, an artist named Pierre. "I'd settle for anywhere that's not my parents' house," I say.

Raymond looks at me, surprised. "I assumed you lived in the city."

"Yes!" I say, with a fist pump, which makes them both smile.

"I need to get out of my situation," he says. "Pierre and I aren't lovers anymore, and he's been dealing coke and speed, which is too much temptation."

"I hate drugs," Amanda says. "They destroy poor people."

"I love drugs," Raymond says. "I mean, they love me."

"I did coke with some of Derek's friends once," I say.

"Once? Maybe you do seem a little suburban," Raymond jokes.

Amanda says that she's looking for a place, too. Her nomadic father has announced he's reclaiming his tiny rent-controlled studio uptown, where she's been staying since graduation. "We should all get a place together," she says gleefully.

"We could convert a commercial space for cheap," Raymond says.

"I'm in!" Our communal future blooms: the furniture we'll drag in from the street, the video-editing station where we'll assemble Raymond's agitprop footage, the painted floor on which our ACT UP friends will sprawl, making posters for the next demonstration. I can see it all: the graffiti-tagged freight elevator, the potluck dinners, a giant window I stare out of while banging away at my typewriter.

As we reach Tompkins Square and pass through its wrought iron gateway, I feel newly energized by the grimy city; these smart, open-hearted new friends; even the pizza, a crisp, tangy, genuine New York *slice*. We pass punks with studded collars and wire-sharp Mohawks, and the homeless who are camped on the park's inner green in a labyrinthine village built from shopping carts and tarps. A musty human stench intermingles with incense, patchouli, a waft of food frying in oil, marijuana rolled into thick blunts and smoked by dim-eyed men in zippered jackets. I see the three of us, in our black boots and cuffed jeans, our Silence=Death buttons pinned to our Silence=Death t-shirts, playing our necessary part in this cityscape. There's hope for me still, I think.

Raymond leads us to a table where a guy with dreads and a woman with hoop earrings and a head wrap are demonstrating how to sterilize works with bleach, passing out pamphlets about needle exchange. The discrepancy between gay men contracting HIV sexually and drug users contracting the virus from shared needles is one that ACT UP has only just begun to address. As Raymond rolls tape, interviewing them about their mission, another man steps up to the table, identifies himself as a recovering addict, and announces, "The only path is strictly clean-and-sober."

"There's more to this than just-say-no," the woman in the wrap answers.

"Let's talk it through, brother," says the dreadlocked guy.

Debate ensues—abstinence versus harm reduction—and voices are raised, but in the end the stranger leaves wishing "Blessings" upon the couple. Raymond is about to turn off his camera when I blurt out a question: "What language does someone like me need to use to communicate to the people you work with?"

The woman leans her head to the side. "You learn what to say when you listen. You been listening?"

I nod.

"Well, that's a start."

When I meet up with Derek that night, I gush to him about this idea of living in a converted workspace with Raymond and Amanda. "What about our love nest?" he asks.

"But this could be that and so much more. We'd have our own area but we'd also be with other people."

"Where is this coming from? Our own 'area'?"

"I'm just thinking out loud."

"We have a plan," he says. "Let's keep to it."

I try to find the words to express to him that feeling of arriving, of discovery, of being absorbed into the park, into the city. Of taking Floyd's exasperation and trying to turn it into something beyond my own sense of guilt. But Derek simply says, "I've been to Tompkins Square. It's dirty and kind of scary, isn't it?" I want him to see the person I might become, who might shed his old skin and earn a place in this vibrant and risky world. I want to, but I don't yet have the language.

We find an apartment on East Houston, at the corner of Norfolk, two floors above a "monument store" full of mortuary marble and uncarved grave markers. Our landlord runs this store, and we sign our lease atop a granite tombstone. A morbid start, but we shake it off because upstairs, our place is full of light, with a big bedroom, two closets, and a spacious main room comprising a kitchen, eating area and living room. We'll pay $500 each a month for rent, which is a lot. We'll spend $400 more putting bars on the fire escape windows. Derek's mother, Marilyn, is getting rid of her kitchen cabinets, so we claim them. Nicholas, with his history of do-it-yourself communal living, takes charge of installing them for us. We amass furniture, a combination of secondhand stuff and cheap, sleek pieces from Conran's. We get our first CD player, though our music is all on vinyl or cassette. We buy a coffee maker. Coffee hurts my stomach but I am determined to drink it, the same way I've willed myself into smoking cigarettes and liking red wine. We shop for groceries and stock our fridge—then we watch produce rot and milk go sour, because we're too busy to cook.

Out the windows, it's always noisy. A man and a woman endlessly shout obscenities back and forth from a few doors down Norfolk. I ask Derek, "If they fight so much, why don't they just break up?"

"I don't think she's his girlfriend," he says, and I realize what I've been hearing: not one woman but a series of them, with the same man, who turns out to be a pimp, and probably a heroin dealer, too. In the mornings, the super, Nelson, who is always drunk by noon, sweeps syringes off our stoop.

One day I step out of the building and quickly realize the two guys I'm walking behind are carrying Uzis. I spin around and walk briskly in the opposite direction.

I am quickly in debt and a little scared of where I live. But I have a Manhattan address. A fire escape. A subway stop one block away. A new bed I share every night with my lover. Our names on a lease. A home.

I'm back in New Jersey, in a mall, at a store called Fashion Fabrics with my mother, picking out material for curtains. This is her idea. She's sewn curtains for every window in her house, and insists on doing the same for me and Derek. At first I protested: no, don't bother, I'll figure it out, but I could tell this hurt her feelings. It was Nicholas who said, "Darlin', refusing your mother's help is like pushing her love away." His own mother died when he was young, and he holds a particularly sentimental point of view on the subject of appreciating your mother, if you've got one to appreciate. Things between Mom and me have been strained since my eruption at the dinner table. So I call her back and say yes. Today, I show up with our window measurements written down.

It's a humid summer day so the air-conditioned mall is crowded, though Fashion Fabrics is an oasis of calm amid the harried mothers corralling their children and the raucous high-schoolers who've commandeered the food court. Here, tungsten lighting warmly bathes bolt after bolt of fabrics for clothing, fabrics for upholstery, fabrics for drapes.

"How about this?" I say, pulling up a corner of charcoal gray.

"That's too thick, it won't let light through."

"I thought that's what curtains were for."

"Depends what you need."

I'd only thought about decoration, not function. "I guess for the living room, we should let some light in, but block it out in the bedroom."

"Oh, so you're *both* late sleepers," she teases. I take that as a good sign.

I am rifling through blacks and grays, but she keeps suggesting patterns and plaids. "Nothing busy, Mom. Think urban."

"Black is so depressing." I catch her glance at my clothes—black jeans, black t-shirt.

"Our couch is gray and the chairs are black—that's our style."

"If your blacks are even a little bit off, it'll look tacky."

"Ah, good point. Derek will kill me if it's tacky."

"What about stripes?" I frown. She keeps looking.

In the end we go with a deep violet for the bedroom, and a bluish-gray that she says will liven up the living room though I worry it's too militaristic. When I approach the register with my credit card she says, "Put your money away."

A week later, she and my father drive into the city. When I buzz them in, he yells, "Come down to the street, we pulled in front of a hydrant." Sure enough, their little Plymouth Champ idles at the curb, flashing its hazards. In my mother's outstretched arms are the curtains, folded like laundry. The blue I see on top is brighter than the one I picked out. In a rush she says, "It's not what we bought but I had another idea and thought I'd give it a whirl and you can see for yourself."

"Take a look," my father says, pulling the top piece off the stack, letting it unfurl. She's alternated the blues in thick vertical stripes, with black piping between them. It's striking, and expertly sewn.

"You like?" she asks.

"I love it. Come up and help me hang them."

"We haven't parked the car."

"That shouldn't be a problem."

"I don't need any broken windows," my father says.

"It's the middle of the day—"

"Barb and Phil had their window smashed right around the corner from St. Patrick's Cathedral," my mother says. "In broad daylight!"

Barb is my mother's chatty best friend, a wonderful gossip with absolutely no city-smarts. "She probably left something on the seat," I say.

"Just a little carry-on bag that had an extra layer in case she got cold, and a couple of cans of diet soda and snacks for the ride home."

"The ride home to New Jersey?"

"People get hungry."

Dad shakes his head. "You can't leave anything in the car. Even a little temptation, they're all over you. Everyone knows that."

"So," I say slowly, "let's clear out your car, and then why don't you both come up and see the apartment?"

"Another time," Dad says. When I look to Mom, she averts her eyes.

"OK," I say, confused. Why drive all the way here and turn away at the front door? But as I watch them drive off, I know why. They're not yet ready to step into our love nest.

Now that we live in Manhattan we go out all the time. One night in the West Village we run into Floyd. "I'm reading *Giovanni's Room*," I tell him.

"Are you now," he says, looking me over, and I try not to be intimidated.

"You mentioned Baldwin at the outreach committee, and I'd never read him."

"But you picked the only one of his books with no Black characters."

"Yeah, I noticed that."

"They wouldn't let him publish a book that was gay *and* Black, not at first," he says. "Try *The Fire Next Time*. That's the truth you need."

Derek asks, "Do you want to get a drink?"

"You buying?"

"First round."

"That's a start."

Floyd steers us to the Ninth Circle, a bar we've never been to before. Inside it's sad and a little seedy. Floyd sits on a barstool, legs crossed, smoking a Kool and sipping a grasshopper. "This has been my drink since I first came to New York. Oh, I used to have fun here," he says. "In the '70s, this was *the* place."

"Did you come here after Stonewall?" I ask.

"Child, I was *at* Stonewall." He's smiling now. "The Stonewall wasn't much for fancy cocktails. You went there to dance. To this day, when I hear Aretha Franklin's 'Think,' I go right back to that summer when we fought the police. All of us dancing with our hands in the air, singing 'Freedom!'"

"People claim that Judy Garland's death set off the riot," I say.

He shrugs. "Judy was beloved, but I'm not sure she deserves credit for our rebellion. The harassment was constant, especially for us Black brothers and sisters. You'd sit on a stoop with your friends, enjoying a summer night, and the po-lice would tell you to move along, threaten to arrest you for loitering. But we didn't move along, we just put more asses on more stoops! You had to be on the streets if you wanted to claim the streets. They couldn't arrest everybody."

As we exit the bar, he sits down on the stoop and gestures to us to do the same. "Come on, children, feel it with me. *Lounge*."

We sit, and then lounge, spreading ourselves out like we own the steps. He says, "Back then you'd have your one pair of jeans."

"Just one?"

"That's right, your second skin. You'd buy them shrink to fit. Put 'em on, step into the shower and soak. You'd let them dry onto your body, and you'd wear them 'til they were falling off. Today you all want new, new, new. But back then you walked around with your history showing."

"Ooh, girl, I can see your history," I joke.

"That's right. Read it and weep."

He takes us on a tour, pointing out bars that were open twenty years earlier, and places where bars used to be, and places where cruising happened that were now either desolate or gentrified. He points to the Oscar Wilde Bookshop. "Before we had a community center, you could go here and ask questions. What's the best happy hour, where's the protest march beginning, what's the number for the VD clinic?" Walking us down Christopher Street, he says, "A year after Stonewall we marked it with what we called Christopher Street Liberation Day. That became Gay Freedom Day. Then someone decided to rename it 'Pride.' As far as I'm concerned, that was the beginning of the end."

"The end of what?" Derek asks. "We were blown away by what we saw at the Gay Pride Parade."

"Once you're celebrating pride, instead of freedom, you're just saying 'look at me.' But freedom—"

"Just another word for nothing left to lose?" I finish.

"Yes, child, that's right. The white woman who sang that song was half a dyke herself. She knew the score."

As we travel toward the West Side Highway, Derek lets Floyd in on our joke, that we call this "Christopher's Street." Floyd frowns. "Oh, Christopher. That big boy, I worry about him," he says. "Too bottled up. Let it out! Let it all out!" At the highway he shows us the former site of the leather bar where the movie *Cruising* was shot; the community protested the production, citing exploitation. "Frankly, at first I thought it was a lot of fuss about a movie. But it was a fuss that had to be made, you know? This was our neighborhood, our drinking establishments, our fucking, and they were turning it into another tale of a homicidal queen."

"I've never seen it," I say.

"It's a fascinating study about the heterosexual male's longing for cock up the ass, and how he'll kill rather than admit that's what he wants. Which is the story of the human race, if you ask me. But no one ever asks."

"Movies are important," I insist.

"Is that so?"

"It was documentaries like *The Times of Harvey Milk* that taught me about our history."

"The White Nights. That was something, in San Francisco, when they rioted against the verdict. I wish I'd been there. Angry queers—a beautiful thing. Which is why I like you ACT UP boys."

Derek says, "We should burn something. Cop cars. Office buildings."

I stare at him in surprise. "You've never even gotten a traffic ticket."

"Start a little smaller," Floyd says, giving Derek's hair a ruffle. "Break a window. See if you can get away with that." Derek hates anyone messing his hair, but he almost purrs under Floyd's touch.

At our next Monday meeting, Mike announces that a doctor who was with ACT UP since its first demonstration, on Wall Street back in March, has died. (March seems forever ago. I remember myself on campus, taking my gay politics seminar, reading about ACT UP in the *Village Voice*—preparing, without quite knowing it, for the life I'm now living.) I'm not sure if I knew this doctor, who Mike says was Christopher's roommate, who'd set up Mike and Christopher on their first date. Christopher is standing in the back, not speaking, tightly coiled, his tiger-eyes haunted. Mike finishes, and the agenda continues, no moment of silence, just on to our next action: a weeklong picket of Sloan Kettering Hospital, where a federally funded AIDS drug trial is underway. The issues committee reports that half of those enrolled will be given a placebo. ACT UP's position is that all participants should be given actual medicine.

Our picket lasts from morning rush hour until evening. We hold up signs, chant, pass out the business cards the outreach committee wrote, and talk to the media. I arrange my work schedule so that I can do three different shifts. During the first one, I find myself picketing alongside Mike, his sign now reading:

LIVING WITH AIDS 2 YEARS AND 5 MONTHS, NO THANKS TO YOU SLOAN KETTERING.

"You're famous in New Jersey," I tell him.

"What I've always aspired to," he says.

"No, really, there was a photo of you in the *Bergen Record*." I tell him about that argumentative dinner with my family.

"I force my family to keep up," he says. "My brother's really come around."

I point to his sign. "Can I ask, what date do you mark that time from?"

"My first HIV test. Who knows how long I had the virus before that."

I've never thought about that, the virus circulating among bodies before anyone knew it was there. Gay liberation must have seemed like an unstoppable path of progress toward a perpetually bright horizon. And then the ground opened up and swallowed half the tribe. I feel newly robbed of an entire generation of gay men older than me. I don't quite know how to say this to Mike, so instead I ask, "I heard you were a Broadway dancer. What was that like?"

"Oh, baby, I could tell you stories."

"Tell, tell," I say eagerly, as our picket circles the sidewalk again. Mike starts talking: that time he auditioned for *A Chorus Line* and realized he'd slept with the choreographer *and* half the dancers in the room; the time he was in a show with Lauren Bacall, who made a pass at a straight costar then made this guy's life miserable when he turned her down; the night on Fire Island when the boy he was fucking had to rush back to his sugar daddy, and the next day at brunch when Mike spotted the boy sipping mimosas with Leonard Bernstein.

"The mythical Fire Island," I say, with wonder in my voice.

"I still have a share," he says. "Want to come see?"

Adventurers Camp for Boys

What I knew about Fire Island, I knew from novels. I'd pored over the lyrical *Dancer from the Dance*, with its sexy, inscrutable hero, Malone, who everyone wants to fuck and who gets fucked by everybody, but in a blank way that just didn't make sense to me. (Were there really people lucky enough to have that much sex but incapable of enjoying it?) There was the unwieldy *Faggots*, written by Larry Kramer himself, with its neurotic, nebbishy narrator, bitter because every New York gay guy in the '70s was having sex without shame except him. Both books climaxed on Fire Island, with big parties where all the characters converged, like in a Victorian novel but with overdoses and fisting.

Derek and I take the subway to Penn Station, where we catch a train out to the sleepy former farming village of Sayville, and from there catch a taxi to the ferry that goes across the bay to the Pines. The difficulty getting here seems to be the point. You had to *want* it. I've heard guys my age downplay Fire Island, like Raymond, who says, "It's an elitist scene, all about real estate," though he's never been. I don't know what a "share" like Mike's actually costs, but I'm pretty sure my temp salary won't get me one. The island's inaccessibility marks it as another ghetto, but one far enough off the map to ensure safety that couldn't be guaranteed closer to home. Far enough away to have fun without looking over your shoulder.

The sky is still light when our ferry pulls up. There, waving to us from a bar overlooking the dock are Mike and Christopher, both shirtless and gleaming; Floyd, wearing dark sunglasses and a scarf around his neck, like a French movie star; and Nicholas, who has gotten a very short haircut that has washed the granola right off of him. The fifth guy is Roger, a boyish stockbroker I recognize from meetings. They gather like my family at

Kennedy Airport when my grandmother visits from Ireland. Margaritas magically appear, festooned with umbrellas and tiny, plastic, curly-tailed monkeys. Everyone talks at once, volleying the inside jokes they've already developed during their stay. Around us men sit quietly sipping cocktails, eyeing us, the loud young crowd.

I am hungry to take it all in: the boats bobbing lazily behind us, the total absence of cars, the men pulling wagons full of groceries along faded boardwalk planks. At the next table, a bronzed, bare-chested man uses a disposable plastic razor to shave his shoulders. "Mary," Mike whistles, "that is not up to code."

"If he starts shaving his balls," Floyd says, "I'm leaving."

"If he starts shaving his balls," Roger says, "I'm asking for his number."

Derek and I get tipsy fast—empty stomachs plus tequila plus excitement—so Mike and Christopher offer to carry our bags, the better for us to navigate the narrow boardwalk in the dusk. It would be easy to take a drunken tumble into the sandy scrub where, we're told, killer deer carrying ticks full of Lyme disease lurk, ready to ruin everyone's health all over again.

"It's Labor Day weekend. Where's the crowd?" I ask. Mike tells stories of what it was like here ten years ago, at its peak, and I think of all the articles I've read in the *Voice* and the *Native* about how AIDS hit the Pines like a force-five hurricane. There's no revelry from the dimly lit vacation homes along our path. It's like being in a stadium after a huge concert has ended; the place still hums with energy, but too bad for you, the show's over, everyone's gone away.

Mike's rental is two stories high and planked in wood, with sliding glass doors. A flagpole on the roof flies a white flag with black lettering, readable in the firm bay breeze: ADVENTURERS CAMP FOR BOYS.

"Mike went to that camp," Christopher says. "When he was thirteen."

"That was its honest-to-God name," Mike says. "A little voice in my head whispered, 'One day you'll need this flag.' So I stole it."

"Did you already know it was ironic back then?" I ask.

"Girl, that's how I knew I was gay. I had a superpower the other thirteen-year-olds didn't: irony."

Mike presents us with white t-shirts that have the same logo as the flag. The other guys have them, too, and that night we all put them on, like a costumed gang from *The Warriors*, and descend on one of the Pines' two dance clubs.

The colored lights are blinking and the music is blaring—Pet Shop

Boys, Erasure, Jody Watley singing *"Hasta la vista, baby"* —but we have half the dance floor to ourselves. I keep trying to hold onto the thrill of being included among this group of fun-loving men, but there's absolutely an element of *trying:* trying to be the life of the party, trying to ignore the pall.

When I articulate this to Christopher, he says, "Honey, why do you think Mike invited you and Derek? You're the hope of the future. Now, dance!"

I throw my hands up and swivel my hips and twirl in place under the lights, single-handedly prepared to make up for an entire generation of disappeared dancers.

Back at the house, we squeeze into the hot tub. Christopher and Mike can't keep their hands off each other. Nicholas and Floyd seem to be pairing up. Roger, who is really cute and really flirty, has been labeled the weekend's *sandwich meat,* up for grabs by one of the couples. These guys have an ease with each other that blows my mind. I've never been in a hot tub with six men—never actually been *naked* with six men, never played on a team that showered together, never joined a gym or sat in a steam room. Before this year, the only group of male friends I'd claimed was in high school, the cluster of "brains" I sat with in the cafeteria, who rehearsed a never-ending performance of playing gay: lisping speech, flapping wrists, calling each other "thweetie." At Adventurers Camp for Boys, everyone talks that way too, calling each other "girl" and "Mary," using "she" as the default pronoun, but of course it's different: not a teenage steam valve but an adult badge of freedom.

Here in the bubbling water, I am aware that I haven't entirely shed that adolescent self. I feel like a boy, with not enough muscle or body hair, and balls that don't swing in a manly sac like Mike's or Floyd's. In the bathroom, I spy razors and shaving cream, electric hair clippers, toner to splash on freshly shaved skin, tiny scissors for attacking nostril hair and trimming wild eyebrows. These items reignite in me an old, secret desire for an older brother, who could teach me to shave, taming his facial hair with a razor gliding across foamy skin as he leaned nearly naked toward the bathroom mirror, faucet hissing at his crotch, wiping the mirror clean, meeting my gaze with understanding eyes. I only shave once a week, and even that's a stretch. Fuzz grows under my nose, and a little patch near each ear might soon, I hope, bloom into sideburns, like on the activist boys I admire and am becoming more like, one baby step at a time.

Everyone splits into their separate rooms. Derek and I make eyes at Roger, but his attention is firmly on Mike and Christopher, and we watch all three disappear behind a closed door. "Well that's that," I say to Derek, who replies, "They're probably all positive, so—" He doesn't finish. Doesn't have to.

That night, while Derek and I have sex, I close my eyes and attempt to revisit the fantasy of Mike fucking me unprotected, but I can't locate it. I've repressed it out of guilt or fear, or maybe from a sense of responsibility—my hope-of-the-future understanding of what it means to commit to survival. It's confusing to want to be like Mike and also to have organized my life around not getting the virus that defines him for me—the thing that makes him angry and strong, that makes him a warrior. It is my good fortune to have been invited to share this weekend, but I'm aware that it derives from his *mis*fortune. Without AIDS, there'd be no weekend at Adventurers Camp for Boys. Maybe that's why Mike wanted us here: so that he could be known to us, not just as icon but as friend—not just the activist in the evening paper, but a big sister gossiping or an older brother passing on cultural instruction—all of us together soaking up this dream, under a flag he stole just for us.

ACT UP meetings are flirty, cruisey, full of eye contact and kisses, hugs hello and stronger hugs good-bye. The guy next to you might throw his arm over your shoulder in the middle of a discussion. At demonstrations, you'll grab hands with boys or girls, not only to block traffic but for the feeling of togetherness. We kiss each other on the lips, kisses that sometimes linger, sometimes deepen, sometimes last. You want—I wanted—to kiss everyone.

But mostly, I want sex. I'm almost twenty-two. I feel too old to be this inexperienced.

Until Derek, I'd only been with a couple of guys in college. Our night with Timmy had been our—my—first threeway, something we'd talked about but never made happen before. It was drunken and fast, with tangled limbs and lots of giggling, trying to make three bodies work together for pleasure. Now, with our own apartment, we invite Timmy over to play. It's a revelation how different he is from Derek: the size and shape of his cock, the way he kisses, the fact that he openly asks us what we're "into." "Let's just do what feels good," I say. I haven't broken down sex into likes and dislikes. Anything that starts with a guy and ends with an orgasm is what I'm into. But Timmy knows what he wants: to kneel in front of us and suck our cocks 'til we cum all over his furry chest.

It's a weekend evening, and some combination of twilight and streetlight pours into the living room through our blue curtains, throwing an underwater glow onto Timmy's buzzed head, casting us into the deep sea. I meet Derek's wide eyes, witnessing his wonder at being worshipped like this, and I know I must appear the same to him. We're feeling identical pleasure, shared reward. I dive in for a hungry, sloppy kiss with Derek, and as my eyes close I flash on a memory of driving a car along a rural back road in upstate New York on a lonely and desperate night during college when I impulsively turned off the headlights and plunged myself into the pitch black without stopping—I drove blind in the dark, heart racing, gripping the steering wheel, not slowing down, knowing I might crash, even die, nearly manic with the accumulating risk—and then I hit a bump and swerved and got scared, turned on the lights, righted the car, slowed down a little, then a little more, and at last pulled over. I sat panting in the idling car, smell of petroleum and scorched rubber in my nose, wiping away angry tears, angry at myself, at the world, at my family and God, with no notion that life was going to improve. That was just eight months ago, right before I'd met Derek, before I could even imagine there was a life like this waiting for me. I open my eyes and, there he is, Derek, and there's Timmy, the radiant blue light wrapped around us. This is my life, my luxurious life, this is our home, this is me and Derek getting better together.

After, the three of us shower, plucking rubber-cement flecks of cum from Timmy's hair, soapy hands roaming across each other, happy happy happy. We walk up Avenue A to Odessa Restaurant and stuff ourselves on pierogi and blintzes. On this night, everything feels uncomplicated.

Later, I ask Derek if he'd do it again. "With Timmy? Duh, why wouldn't we?"

"I mean, with other guys."

"Is that what you want? You want to get slutty?" He says this in a jokey, leering voice that doesn't hide the truth under the question.

"I want us to cultivate a whole slutty brotherhood."

"Just a big gay sex orgy with a revolving door."

"Fucking all the time—"

"Safely, of course—"

"Of course—"

So that's what happens: we bring back to our apartment a string of boys from ACT UP.

Raymond is next, surprising us both with how eager he is to bottom. He brings out in Derek a top energy I didn't know he had: Raymond's ankles in

55

his hands, their pelvic bones banging as Derek slams his wrapped cock inside of him, their eyes locked. It's hot to watch, but I'm slightly outside of it, not feeling the sensations. Raymond is someone I want to impress, he's worldly and experienced and smart, he makes videos and has rock-star hair. (I want hair like that; I've been growing mine out but I can't make it stand up like his, my hair is too fine.) But maybe I don't want to fuck him, or can't fuck him, the way he needs to be fucked. Maybe a triangle in bed is not always equilateral.

There is Gilberto, who I met through the outreach committee, though he quickly grew restless there and formed a new one, the Majority Actions committee, a linguistic reversal of the usual language of "minorities." Gilberto was born and raised in the Bronx, and has street smarts that peel away in bed, turning him surprisingly gentle, planting kisses all over us. And there is Mick, who is Italian, and Kyle, who is Chinese, and Mikey, who is pale and freckled and has a British accent, and Martin, who is Black and from Georgia, and William who is Black and from Brooklyn, and two different Jewish Davids, and John who is blond and John's friend whose name is also John.

We repeat with Timmy, who wants to fuck me like he did that first time but surprises us both when the screwing starts. Derek sits back and watches Timmy order me around, making me beg to get fucked, using a mean voice and calling me names: "You like that dick, fag?" I like it, I do. He fucks hard, pulls out, peels off the condom and shoots all over me, and then right away he's back to his cheery self, with his soft speech pattern, saying, "Guesth I pushed that a little far."

Derek says, "It got kind of intense."

"I'd beat up any straight guy who called you fag," Timmy says.

"I was into it," I say quietly, though I don't have the words to say why.

Later, I tell Derek that I wanted Timmy not to pull out, to cum inside the condom, I wanted to be fucked until I flew out of my body. What I'm talking about isn't purely physical. I want sex without worry, without fear of death. I want transcendent sex like I've read about in novels and watched on scratchy VHS copies of '70s porn. I want gay sex like it used to be.

"Don't you think that's the reason we're even alive?" Derek challenges. "Because we didn't start earlier, because we were taught the rules, and we keep to them?"

"I know that."

"It's a matter of math," he says: the year of birth or sexual awakening, coupled with the year the virus appeared, in relation to the year safe sex as a common practice began. Guys like us, at this stage of the epidemic, are healthy by circumstance, by luck. You're not supposed to tempt fate.

But I couldn't help it, I wanted more: more partners, more intensity, deeper feeling, more knowledge.

Note to Self #3: The mechanics of sex in the middle of the AIDS crisis.

You kissed a lot. Everyone agreed kissing wouldn't give you AIDS. Even so, positive guys talked about negative guys being afraid to kiss them.

You sucked cock, because most people agreed cocksucking didn't transmit HIV. But you heard about people who seroconverted after oral sex. So you didn't let anyone cum in your mouth. Or if you planned to let them, or if you were worried about HIV in precum, which some people said you should be, then you made sure you didn't have cuts in your mouth, and you didn't floss or even brush your teeth before sex, which was weird, because what if you'd just eaten dinner, and also gross because everyone smoked.

You wondered if it was true that the only cases of oral HIV transmission were because the guy in question had just had extensive dental work. You heard that story repeated, and you tried to figure out what kind of guy went on a cocksucking, cum-swallowing binge after extensive dental work.

You fucked with latex condoms and water-based lube. You didn't cum inside.

You could get condoms free at gay bars. One of the AIDS health groups started packaging two condoms with only a single mini-lube in a little baggie. Were you supposed to squeeze out exactly half and save the rest for the next fuck?

You tried to buy lube in the East Village but it was hard to do. The gay-owned shops were in the West Village, and the Duane Reade only had KY, which was unappealingly sticky and medicinal. It would be years before lube was everywhere.

You bought lube with nonoxynol-nine in it. People said it killed HIV. But it was nasty and left your butthole irritated. One time I used it and afterwards was bleeding down there, which was exactly the thing you didn't want to happen, so what the fuck was up with this nonoxynol-nine anyway? People called it "detergent."

You wondered if anyone really knew anything for sure, even though it was 1987 and there'd been six years to figure shit out.

If you and your partner were both HIV-negative, was it okay to fuck without a condom? It should have been, because negative guys couldn't transmit what they didn't have, but all the literature said ALWAYS use condoms for anal. You might be infected and not yet know it, or your partner might be. Because even if you'd just been tested you could have been infected in the last six months which wouldn't show up on a test. I suppose you could have NO SEX for six months and then get tested, and your partner could do the same, and then, maybe, you'd be sure. BUT YOU COULD NEVER BE SURE. That was the message.

Like, one night Derek and I were rolling around in bed, just the two of us, getting into it, and I have his cock lubed up and he's playing with my hole and I just throw my leg over him and sit on him, and he says wait, get a condom, and I say, I think it's okay, just for a little while, and he

says OK and fucks me from below while I ride
him, willing myself to shut out all the thoughts
about what is okay and what isn't and just letting
myself enjoy the sensation of my lover fucking
me unprotected, but not for long, because even
though this can't be risky since we are both HIV-
negative it feels like the BIGGEST RISK because
what if we aren't really negative, that's why there
are rules and we are breaking them.

Because sometimes you break the rules because
you have a body that makes its own logic.

We read everything we can about AIDS—in the *Times*, whose spotty coverage
we critically dissect; in the *Voice*, where you could count on political analysis
but not medical information; in the *Native*, once an essential community
newspaper but now a voice of conspiracy, editorializing doubt about HIV
as the cause of AIDS. We are always sifting fact from speculation, resisting
the pull toward paranoia. I retrace the steps of every sexual encounter, no
matter how essentially risk-free it was, worrying through the details. Little
nicks on my fingers bloom into gaping wounds, passageways for disease. A
canker sore in my mouth throbs like a laceration, its sting a signal of doom. I
grope under my jaw for swollen glands, the first sign of infection. Adulthood
is a world of anxiety, where every choice is a burden. I have inherited my
mother's propensity for worry. Now I have something to worry about.

We get our first HIV tests at CHP, the Community Health Project, on
the second floor of the Center, just upstairs from where ACT UP meets.
A volunteer nurse pokes my arm with a needle. I watch my blood fill the
syringe. I'm told to come back in two weeks for the results. Yes, back then
we waited. The idea of it today seems unbearable, when no one waits for
anything, certainly not HIV test results.

After the clinic we go to The Bar, a dive at the corner of Second Avenue
and Fourth Street that our friends have started to claim as a hangout. We
are on our first beer when Nicholas walks in. He's just woken up, late in the
day, having driven his cab all night. I tell him we just got tested. "You did?"
he asks. I'm surprised he sounds so surprised, because he was the person who

had first mentioned CHP to us; he was volunteering there, a sort of trial run for nursing school, which he's contemplating. He's tired of being a cabbie.

"As soon as we left the clinic, all I could think about was fucking," I say.

Derek says, "Calling Dr. Freud."

"That doesn't surprise me," Nicholas says. "Fallibility. Mortality—"

"Also general horniness," I say.

Nicholas lights a cigarette and talks with the butt dangling from his lips. "So, darlin', mind if I ask why?"

"Why what?"

"Why get tested?"

I voice the usual things—*it's better to know than not know, there might be treatments, it's your responsibility.* Then Derek interjects, "He promised his mother."

"I told her I'd *think* about it."

Nicholas laughs, almost cruelly. "You can lie to your mother, if that's the only reason."

"So you think getting tested is a bad idea?"

"The tests aren't perfect. The results take a long time and they don't necessarily cover the previous six months, when the virus can lie dormant. And if your insurance company finds out, you're fucked. Plus—call me paranoid—but I'm not convinced our government won't compile lists of the infected. I mean, I lived through Nixon, and Reagan makes that crook look liberal."

I sigh. "I've done oral and rimming with a dozen guys. I've been fucked by people who don't know their status."

"But you haven't fucked, or more to the point *been fucked* by anyone without a condom?"

"We don't even fuck each other without them," I say.

"Well," Derek says, "that one time—"

"You didn't cum," I say.

"But precum is—"

"Ladies, ladies," Nicholas interrupts, waving his cigarette to shush us. "Look, it's probably more important for you to test for hepatitis, if your tongue's been up an asshole."

"Exciting!" Derek says. "Another test!"

"You two are wound up," Nicholas says, quickly fixing this with another round of beer, plus shots of tequila that make me light-headed. I bum a cigarette, which causes Derek to shoot me a disapproving look.

A week of poor sleep and bad dreams follows. Waiting for results makes me irritable with Derek, frustrated with all his little neuroses, things that would usually roll right off, like the fact that he sleeps in his underwear instead of naked like I do, or the way he frets constantly about his thinning hair. I hear him arguing on the phone with his mother, Marilyn, and instead of listening supportively when he's off the call, I tell him he should stop speaking to her, since all she ever does is upset him. "You're not helping," he says, and he's right, which only underscores how helpless I feel.

Two weeks later, at the clinic, I sit with a doctor, a middle-aged gay man with pink skin and tired eyes. The fact that he's a doctor and not a nurse alarms me. "Here are your results," he says, handing me a computer printout. My gaze skids across the white paper, but the black marks blur together. He puts his finger on a box in the corner. I read the word NEGATIVE.

"Good news, right?" He takes back the paper. "Questions?"

"Wait," I say. "Let me see that again." There's my name, and there's the word *negative*. It's real. It's right there in print. I'm okay for now.

Derek's results are negative, too. We mark this with a kiss, though we don't go to The Bar to celebrate. Our walk home is oddly quiet. A storm heading in our direction has taken a sudden swerve out to sea, but we're still bracing for the impact, still expecting it.

Part 3

The Place Where We Live

I learn to go limp.

In the weeks leading up to demonstrations—or the days, if that's all we have—we educate ourselves and prepare for arrest. There are older guys in our ranks, like Floyd, who've been around since Stonewall, and women like Rochelle, the professor, with years of feminist activism, who give us history and context. And skills, too. Tonight we're being trained as marshals—people whose task it is to steer a protest away from trouble, whether that means a pothole in the street or a cop hungry to make arrests, deliberately provoking the crowd. The training is run by Bryn, a lesbian whose voice is deeper than any man's in the room, and Will, a mop-haired straight guy who introduces himself this way: "Everyone thinks I'm gay, but I'm actually a leftist Quaker raised by Jewish Communists," to which Bryn replies, "That's the gayest thing I've ever heard." They give us lessons in nonviolence, some of them terrifying: If cops on horseback charge at the demonstration, sit down in the street—*sit down?*—because the horses will stop. And: If you see a cop harassing a protester, demand his badge number. And: When you're about to get arrested, go limp.

During a break, I spot Timmy, who I haven't seen much of in the past few weeks. "Where you been hiding?" I ask. He stands next to a guy with mutton chop sideburns and a bandana over shoulder-length brown hair, who points a camera at me with the words, "Say AIDS!"

"For real?"

"Your mouth makes a good shape when you say AIDS."

"OK. AIDS!" He snaps a picture.

"This is Dale," Timmy says.

"I'm his new *boyfriend*," Dale says, while Timmy rolls his eyes, as if the label is up for debate. "Timmy convinced me to join the revolution."

"I told him he could take pictures of cute boys," Timmy says.

"Speaking of which, there's another one." Dale lets out a honking laugh like Pee-Wee Herman's—a replica of a laugh—and then cuts across the room, camera up to his face.

"He's interesting," I say.

"He's a goof, which is what I need these days." His expression shifts, and he says, "You heard about Keith?"

I shake my head. "What? I haven't seen him since we all went to the Pyramid together."

"He died two weeks ago."

"Really?" I say, stunned.

Timmy's eyes are clear, blue and penetrating, and when he locks them on me, I know that if I say another stupid thing like "really?" he'll eviscerate me.

"I'm so sorry," I say.

"It was PCP that got him."

I know what that means: *pneumocystis carinii pneumonia*.

"He had trouble breathing and next thing you know we're in the emergency room."

All I know of Keith comes from the long, fun day last June that began with our spontaneous arrest on the courthouse steps and ended with him laughing at me and Derek for our drunken proposition. I remember him walking off into the night with Amanda, while Derek and Timmy and I piled into Nicholas's cab. Now Timmy fills in Keith's life for me: how they met in an art class at a state university up the Hudson, then moved to the city and squatted on the Lower East Side until they were booted out; how Keith went from spray-painting on the walls of abandoned buildings to starting a tiny gallery in the back of a bar; and how just six months ago he'd been hired to teach a design class at Pratt. "Everything was looking up for him," Timmy says, "but since he didn't have a full-time job, he never had health insurance." PCP smothered his lungs before he'd even been tested for HIV, and he had lain in a city hospital bed half-ignored by doctors until Timmy ran through the halls screaming for medical help. "I totally went *Terms of Endearment* on them," he says.

Bryn and Will call us back to order. They play the commanding officer to those of us sitting on the community center's linoleum floor, telling us we're trespassing and need to move. We don't move. Then, "If you do not leave, you will be arrested." We don't leave. Then Bryn and Will put their hands on us, and we go limp, our arms crossed over our chests, our legs together, bodies like pine planks. If you don't go limp, if you struggle in any way, it's considered resisting arrest, and once you resist, cops have a green light to beat you up. Don't get beaten up. Go limp. The cops will drag you by your shoulders, or, if you're lucky, lift and carry you to the paddy wagon like a corpse. We practice this together. We make it fun.

But for me, the pressure in the room has changed. The demonstration we're training for, in Albany, now has a human face, the buzzed head and freckled skin of a boy I shared my first arrest with and flirted with at a drag show, who between that moment and this one suffered and died, uninsured, drowned by poisoned fluid in his lungs. We are protesting the statewide issues related to AIDS, but its threat has never felt more local. Who among those surrounding me today will be gone, like Keith, before our next protest?

Albany is where I started this story—my night in jail with Eliot, meeting Zack for the first time, The Steven 27. *(Ssssteeeeven!)* I have one more memory to add to those. It's the van ride home, and I'm seated next to Derek, with Amanda in front of us. Next to her is Jocelyn, one of the two lawyers who negotiated our release. Jocelyn was impressive, even intimidating, in front of the judge—butch, serious, armed with her ethical rhetoric—but now I suspect something is wrong even before she turns and announces, "You guys, I'm freaking out."

"Do you need anything?" Amanda asks. "Water? Medication? A back rub?"

She shakes her head. "All my friends are dying."

There's a pause, and then Derek says, "It's so fucked up."

"No, I mean *all* my friends—my closest friends—are dying." She tells us she was at the hospital three times that week, visiting three different people, one sicker than the next. Two were gay men and one a bisexual woman, all in their forties, a circle of older siblings who adopted her when she was new to New York: they'd brought her out dancing, taught her how to do shots, helped her write her application to NYU Law School and schooled her in attracting the right lovers and repelling the creeps. "What am I supposed to do?" she asks.

"You're doing this," I say, waving my arm wide. "This protest."

"And all the time you give to ACT UP," Derek adds.

"But how is this going to save Michael's life, or Peter's, or Donna's?"

"It won't," Amanda says. "But maybe you'll save ours."

Jocelyn laughs and cries at the same time, and then buries her head against Amanda, who strokes her and whispers as Derek and I watch, struck dumb. Out the window a pastoral landscape breezes by, gleaming, verdant, indifferent. I wish I had more to offer Jocelyn. Everyone I know is *not* dying—Keith is the first I could call a friend—but so many are positive. Eliot. Mike. Others who speak up and self-identify at meetings. We are two decades younger than Jocelyn's decimated circle, but unless our activism works, her state of desperation will soon be the place where we live, too.

1988. Early spring. Winter still hanging on. Amanda is moving in with Raymond, a third floor railroad on Tenth near B, facing Tompkins Square. The lease belongs to one of Raymond's many exes. How any twenty-two-year-old has had this many lovers is a mystery to me. Raymond's my age but it seems like he's squeezed in extra years.

On moving day I help Amanda carry her stuff up the narrow, dimly lit stairs: two suitcases, a crate of pots and pans, a typewriter and nineteen boxes of books. The apartment opens onto a kitchen with a bathtub running along its left-hand wall. Beyond the tub is a sink with a splotchy mirror above it. Beyond that, a phone-booth-sized space houses the toilet. The rest of the kitchen has a gas stove, a noisy fridge, a wobbly table with mismatched chairs and a wall of exposed shelving, mostly empty until we unload Amanda's cookware. Adjoining the kitchen, across a waist-high half-wall, is a windowless area, more a passageway than a room, with a futon on the floor. This is where Amanda will sleep.

Past this, through a doorway without a door, Raymond emerges, in jeans and a sleeveless t-shirt, barefoot. He's cut his hair—the rockabilly locks have been shorn nearly to the skull. He looks older, tougher, almost intimidating. But his smile widens, and he waves me in to show off his room, the largest in the apartment, with three windows facing the north side of Tompkins Square Park. Through bare tree branches, I see the empty basketball courts, the old-timers in winter coats pulling shopping baskets on wheels, the homeless and their ever-growing encampment, the hardcore kids looking amped up on speed. Raymond's mattress is on the floor, too, surrounded by stacks of books and videotapes and the odd piece of tossed-off clothing.

More clothes, including a dark, wrinkled suit, hang from wire hangers on an industrial garment rack. A desktop made from a slab of wood sits atop stacked milk crates. All of this fills me with excitement: his underwear on the floor, books by Deleuze, Fanon and Didion next to the bed, Raymond's inky blue cursive on the pages of an open notebook. I recall our sex, how ferocious Raymond had been bottoming for Derek, and I wonder if we—or they—will fuck again, here on this mattress in this perfectly disorderly room.

"I got you a housewarming gift," Raymond calls to Amanda, who is already moving some of his books out of the way to make space for hers. He produces an open bottle of Scotch, fills three juice glasses, and we toast: "To changing the world."

"I love it here," I tell them. "Will your ex be back?"

"No, he moved to Seattle. But no one ever gets rid of a cheap apartment."

"Can we get *our* names on the lease?" Amanda asks.

"I hope, one day. For now, the less contact with the landlords, the better."

She ties her long hair back. "I've lived in four different apartments, none of them my own. Did you know that only a tiny percentage of leases in New York are in women's names?"

"Real estate," Raymond says, "is the greatest crime."

"Wait, is that true? About women and leases?" I ask.

"I heard it from Jocelyn, who does housing law," she says. Ever since that tearful ride from Albany, Amanda and Jocelyn have been seeing each other. ("It's not a relationship," she insists. "We're just comfort-fucking.")

Our conversation hopscotches from apartments to housing and homelessness in general to homeless people with AIDS in particular (ACT UP now has a committee specifically devoted to this issue) and then to the larger question of how ACT UP should proceed as it grows. Raymond keeps using the term "coalition building," talking about the need to connect with other affected communities, to continue to build a national movement. Amanda makes the point that it's hard to get lesbians involved since we aren't doing actions specifically around women and AIDS. "Rochelle has started hosting Dyke Dinners at her place in Brooklyn," she tells us. "We're trying to figure out, in the middle of the AIDS crisis, what exactly is a lesbian issue?"

"I haven't had a real focus since the outreach committee dissolved," I say. Outreach was deemed too broad, and other committees—housing, women's, majority actions—have replaced it, each with a better-defined focus and less of a white-guilt problem. "I need to figure out another way to contribute," I say. "Am I just a body getting arrested?"

"You'd be a good facilitator," Amanda offers.

"Me?"

"You're good on the floor," Raymond says. "You don't ramble like a lot of people."

"I didn't know anyone was paying attention," I say. It's true that I've been more vocal over the past few months than I was last year, when it was all so new. "I'll drink to that," I say.

Raymond stops me from refilling his glass. "I still have my nightly push-ups." This makes me laugh, but he's serious. "I'm trying to get to fifty."

"Be as butch as you need, honey," I say.

Amanda sighs. "Gay men and working out. It's all about not looking like you have AIDS, right?"

"Maybe. But also, we're a bunch of peacocks." I glance back toward Raymond, as he drops to the floor, arms flexing with his effort. I reach for Amanda's cigarettes. "So, did you hear about Keith?" I tell her what Timmy told me. She remains strangely silent, her face inscrutable. "Amanda?"

"Goddamnit," she says at last. She pours and downs another shot. "I had sex with him."

"With Keith? It's been, like, forever since you've slept with a guy." She glares at me. "Sorry, let me try that again. Are you okay?"

"It was more emotional than physical, though it *was* physical. He was fun, we got carried away, he wanted to eat my pussy, said he hadn't done that in years."

"Timmy said Keith didn't know his status until he got sick."

"Would you come with me if I got tested?" she asks.

"Of course. But if you were safe you have nothing to worry about."

She exhales. I wait for more, realizing more is not coming. I take her hand. "Do you want to talk about it?"

"Later."

"Say no more. I get it, I totally get it."

I feel unprepared for this, that they were lovers, that their sex was perhaps unsafe sex, that even an established friendship like ours has its secrets, which means, of course, that all of my newer friendships are full of unknowns, too. I am betrayed by my own naiveté. Why am I caught, again, feeling foolish? But I feel resolved, too, determined to open my eyes, to stop acting like a suburban boy with city dreams. I live here now. I must be tougher.

• • •

Derek's mother, Marilyn, once walked in on us in Derek's childhood bed, and after that, she told Derek that I made her "uncomfortable." This was right after graduation. We weren't fucking, just naked and close, but she'd scurried away trembling. Now that we live together, we get the occasional invitations to dinner which, if refused, lead to guilt trips Derek finds crippling. So we take the train to Long Island where she and her husband Fred live in a big, split-level home kept spotless, especially in its all-white living room, which we are forbidden to enter. Marilyn doesn't cook. On holidays a Jamaican woman named Jessa fixes big, delicious meals, but mostly we go out to restaurants, or Fred announces, "Let's get takeout," and within a half hour a Chinese delivery guy arrives laden with grocery bags holding a dozen different containers. At the end of the night, before catching the train back to Manhattan, Derek packs the uneaten food into his bag, and this precipitates a showdown. Marilyn says, "What're you doing?" "What does it look like, Mom?" "Derek we're going to eat those." "No you're not. You're going to let them rot in the fridge until Jessa comes over and throws it away." "It's not yours to take." "Fred, are you going to eat these leftovers?" "Why, you guys need money?" This embarrasses Derek so much that he unloads his bag and leaves the food on the counter saying, "Never mind. We're *fine*. Enjoy the leftover moo-shu." Then, on our way out the door, Marilyn hands *me* the food, saying, "You're right, you need it more than us," and before Derek can protest, I say, "Thank you," and we leave. We graze on the leftovers for days, Derek grumbling with every bite how *manipulative* his mother is.

He has a key to their house, so when they travel, we go out to their place and use their pool. In the summer of '88 we invite a bunch of friends for a party, and in the middle of it, Marilyn phones. I stand near Derek as he talks to her, motioning the rest of us to quiet down: "Just a few people, Marilyn, don't worry, we're not wrecking the house, we'll clean everything up, we won't bother the neighbors," placating and reassuring until at last he explodes at her and hangs up. He turns and announces, "She says she's going to have to drain the pool."

"Good," someone says, "then I won't feel guilty about peeing in it."

"And I won't feel guilty about cumming in it."

"And that turd I left in there won't be a problem."

"Should we start the blood-orgy?"

Derek laughs despite himself.

71

Nicholas, in earshot of the entire call, says, "Derek, honey, call your mama back and ask her where she keeps her coffee filters."

"I'm not calling her back!"

"Then give me the number and I'll ask her."

"You wouldn't."

"Wanna bet?"

"Nicholas, she probably doesn't even know where the coffee filters are. Jessa's the only one who knows anything."

"Give me the number."

I watch all of this with titillated glee.

Nicholas into the phone: "Hi, Marilyn, this is Nicholas. No, ma'am, we haven't met. We're looking for your coffee filters... That's right, we're making coffee... We found the beans and the grinder, but not the filters... Uh-huh. Okay... Yep, there they are. Kind of out of the way, no?... Absolutely, we'll rinse out the pot before we leave. I'll personally do it myself... Very nice to meet you. Fun party, by the way. Bye, darlin'!"

Derek stares, stupefied. "How freaked out did she sound?"

"She sounded just fine. Knew exactly where the filters were: first cabinet on the right, third shelf, next to the wheat germ."

"She has wheat germ?"

I say, "If anything's put back in the wrong place, she'll know it."

"If anything's out of place," Nicholas corrects, "she'll *get off* on it."

"But I'll never hear the end of it," Derek moans.

"Now you're just tempting us."

Indeed as the day goes on, the boys hide things for Marilyn to find when she gets home—like a Speedo, skimpy and shiny, still smelling of chlorine, tucked under the couch in the forbidden, all-white living room.

OK, I know this sounds childish. But I ask you: What was that "draining the pool" about, if not the sharp stick of stigma poking at us? And didn't she once scold Derek and me, with clucks of her tongue and worried, darting eyes as his hand brushed my cheek in a restaurant, for our public affection? Marilyn and Fred were sensible middle-of-the-road moderates who were not our enemies but had not extended themselves as allies, either. My parents were better on this front, but they too were only making small steps forward. We all came from families like this, many of them worse. A family member at an ACT UP meeting was as exotic as a snow leopard. One night, when Gilberto was giving a Majority Actions report, he introduced his grandmother to the room, and we all rose to our feet applauding as if

Judy Garland herself had risen from the grave. Beneath our furious surface, we were starving for allies, for their approval and their presence among our ranks. I felt angry at my mother and father, the way I felt angry at anyone who hadn't personally taken up the cause of AIDS activism. Why were we fighting this alone? Wasn't our struggle our families', too? Today, older than my parents were then, I understand how frightened they must have been to see their son vilified and marked for disease. But in those dark, heady times, the lines seemed clear: we fought—for our lives, for our love, for basic respect—without their help.

Note to Self #4: Remember all the details of the pool party.

Broke into the liquor cabinet, which was locked behind a sliding wood panel.

Sawed a quarter-inch off the end of that panel in order to get it relocked at the end of the day.

Posed for photos for Dale around the pool, on the diving board, on the inflatable rafts, and in every room in the house.

Witnessed this interlude:

Eliot sits in a poolside lounge chair, wearing a wide-brimmed straw hat and dark glasses, covered from neck to ankle in a loose kaftan, reading the autobiography of Shelley Winters.

Nicholas, smoking a cigarette on the deck: "Eliot, you're too young to be a Kaftan Queen."

Eliot, not looking up from his book: "You're only as old as you feel, and today I'm feeling dusty."

Walked in on Derek fucking Raymond on all fours in Derek's childhood bedroom, in front of a mirror that had a Duran Duran decal on it.

Watched for a moment but didn't join.

Found a bottle of just-expired Valium and passed it around.

Raided Marilyn's closet. Applied Marilyn's lipstick.

Watched Mahogany on the VCR while high on Valium wearing Marilyn's clothes.

Got into a late-night drunken argument with Derek.

Made up and slept it off.

Seize Control

Me: "Welcome to ACT UP, the AIDS Coalition to Unleash Power. We are a diverse, nonpartisan group of individuals united in anger to end the AIDS crisis."

Amanda: "If there any members of the New York City police department or any other law enforcement agencies here tonight, you are required by law to announce yourself."

Me, after waiting: "They never do."

Amanda: "But we always assume they're here."

We are the new facilitators at the big Monday night meetings, elected that summer along with Gilberto and Timmy after the original facilitators, Nicholas and Christopher, stepped down. Eliot remains our administrator, our North Star at the table behind us, keeping the minutes in his tight penmanship. Facilitation involves lots of pointing: to people who want to speak, to people who must be cut off because their time has run out, to corners of the room where committees and affinity groups gather at the end of the night. Each week I know more of the people I'm pointing to. Now and then, it's someone famous, brought to the group through some personal connection. Susan Sarandon shows up to lend us her support, the first celebrity willing to attach her name to our actions. Larry Kramer reappears, always managing to stir up the room, usually by attacking it for not keeping to his idea of what the agenda should be. Keith Haring is there one night to present us a t-shirt design we can use for fundraising. He is wildly applauded but he seems embarrassed to be thanked for doing his part.

Our t-shirts are our uniform: SILENCE=DEATH. AIDSGATE. THE GOVERNMENT HAS BLOOD ON ITS HANDS, ONE AIDS DEATH EVERY HALF HOUR, with its huge scarlet handprint. Haring's iconic hand-drawn figures above the words KNOWLEDGE IS POWER. These images transform us, erasing the self that exists outside the room, the person you are all week long, the person you were before becoming an activist. They renounce isolation and celebrate belonging.

One night I call on a gray-haired woman who introduces herself as a chemist who previously worked for a pharmaceutical company. She speaks firmly, if a little awkwardly, about the class of drugs that includes AZT, still the only approved medication for people with AIDS. "I've been looking closely at the federal drug approval process, and I've discovered some important things about clinical trials." She continues in detail, finishing with, "I'll talk to anyone who's interested."

"Where will you be after the meeting?" Amanda asks.

"Oh, um, well, I'll be right here."

We thank her and start to move on, but then someone else jumps to his feet, saying "Wait, wait!" I recognize him: Vito Russo, the writer, one of our most persuasive voices. He says, "What this woman just told us might be the most important thing anyone has said here all night. I'll be talking to her after the meeting, and I encourage anyone who wants to follow up to be here, too." A week later, the small group that gathered announces a new subcommittee, Treatment and Data. Their first move is to use the Freedom of Information Act to collect and compile all available governmental data on AIDS research. A comprehensive report has never been put together before, not by anyone.

We are about to increase our knowledge at an exponential rate.

The folding chairs are being collapsed and stacked, dozens of people are milling about, and I am at the front of the room, attempting to unruffle the feathers of a man upset because his agenda item was given too little discussion.

Behind him, another guy waits his turn—tall, in a shapeless blue button-up shirt and chinos, clothes for an office job. Stepping forward, he asks, "How've you been?" then adds, "Albany?"

It's Zack.

"Hey! Cellmate!"

"Yeah, Zack."

"I remember, of course, hi—"

"Finally made it to a meeting."

"That's great," I say, feeling my face heating up.

He says he's sorry he didn't come sooner, he's been working long hours and isn't "much of a joiner," but he remembers me saying that in ACT UP everyone does what they're able to do. That stuck with him. He's a graphic artist and has an idea for an image, based on the chalk outlines he and his friends did on the sidewalk in Albany. His voice is deep and soft at the same time, his face is a blend of features: light eyes, wide nose, beautiful mouth. Even his dorky work clothes are appealing, the way Clark Kent always strikes me as sexier than Superman. His fingers tap the tabletop between us, punctuating his words nervously. I'm pretty sure I'm the only person he's talked to all night.

"So who should I—?" he is asking.

"Sorry, what?"

"Who should I talk to about designing a poster?"

I point to where Gilberto and the folks on the actions committee are absorbed in planning. Zack looks, then hesitates. I say, "I'll walk you over and introduce you."

At the next Monday meeting, I'm standing near the back when I spot Zack. Instead of his chinos, he wears black Levis pegged over black boots and a white t-shirt emblazoned with one of our agitprop images: a vintage photo of two sailors in a deep kiss, bold letters spelling out READ MY LIPS. These clothes reveal his body: broad shoulders and shallow chest tapering to a lean waist. He wears the NY Yankees baseball cap he had on when we first met. Under it, his hair has been buzzed to a military shortness. I entertain the notion that this is not Zack but Zack's twin brother. He looks incredibly sexy but also *less* sexy than the nine-to-five dork he appeared to be last week.

Then I realize he's with *Raymond*, who's looking very buff from all those push-ups he's been doing. How do they know each other? They stand among a group of fit-looking guys all dressed in their activist-wear, faces stern under their brush cuts until a joke makes one of them break out in a toothy smile. They have the fearsome magnetism of a street gang from the fifties, the Sharks, the Jets, the Wild Bunch. I can feel other people in the room take notice, too. In donning this uniform and standing among them, Zack is announcing he's here to stay.

He catches my stare and lifts his chin, a greeting that makes me blush. Raymond waves, too, smiling his gap-toothed smile. Then Zack drops his arm over Raymond's shoulder, a gesture I feel in my gut.

"There should be a word for it," I whisper to Derek, at my side.

"For what?"

"When a guy I have a crush on hooks up with a guy *you* have a crush on."

Derek scans the group of them and shrugs. "ACT UP is becoming trendy."

Zack had seemed like my special discovery, but the opposite is true. His appeal is obvious to anyone. He's one of those hot guys I swore I'd never fall for.

Amanda and I are facilitating again on the night Christopher makes a proposal for a new national action. At the front of the room, with Mike at his side, he announces that they've met with a national coalition of AIDS groups, including other ACT UPs now forming in cities from Miami to San Francisco. They are proposing a massive action to "seize control of the FDA."

Why the Food and Drug Administration, why not Congress, why not the White House? A lengthy discussion follows, led in part by Treatment and Data, whose research has illuminated how the healthcare system is engineered to keep information from those who require it most: people with AIDS and others in need of life-saving treatments.

Excitement quickly grows. This demonstration is about everything we've been fighting for: speeding up the drug approval process, getting funding for a registry of treatments, circulating information about clinical trials. A few voices complain that this action has been pre-decided in committee, expressing anxiety about behind-the-scenes power. The loudest naysayers are from the ISO, the International Socialist Organization, a group no one knows much about but whose members have been showing up lately, casting seeds of doubt about nearly everything. I've heard grumbling that they are police or FBI plants, deliberately disrupting our solidarity.

A young ISO guy proclaims, "In the spirit of Stonewall, this should be a decision by the people, not the committee elites."

I see Floyd emphatically raise his hand. I call on him, and he bellows, "Don't lecture me about Stonewall. I *am* Stonewall."

Amanda calls on Vito next, who says forcefully, "This is exactly the large-scale mobilization we need to make a national impact." Amanda and I are a good team, friends who can read each other's cues, familiar with the players in the room and which voice would best be heard when.

It's time to vote, but Christopher says, "One last thing." Amanda sends me a questioning look: do I know what's coming? I shake my head. Christopher takes a big breath, and as Mike lays a hand on his back, says, "I came to this meeting directly from my doctor's office. I had HIV test results waiting for me. The test came back positive." Throughout the room, shuffling and chatter cease. "I'm standing up here tonight as a person with HIV whose life depends on the treatments the FDA is keeping from us."

How is a facilitator supposed to segue out of *that*? *Thank you, Christopher*, won't cut it. I look to Amanda, who addresses the room: "Whether we have the virus, or don't have the virus, or don't know our status, we are all in this struggle together."

From the depths of the room, a voice cries out, "ACT UP, fight back, fight AIDS," and everyone instantly picks up the chant: unified voices, thunderously lifting Christopher's confession to a rallying cry.

The action is overwhelmingly approved.

On our walk back to the East Village that night, Amanda, Raymond, Derek and I discuss Christopher's announcement. I say that I thought it was courageous; for all our talk about saving lives, people don't always speak about the virus in personal terms. Amanda counters that she found it manipulative. "The group should be allowed to debate a new action without having personal test results used as an emotional lever," she says.

"That sounds judgmental," Derek says.

"It *is* judgmental. I've made a judgment, okay? And if I knew Christopher better I'd tell him to his face. Maybe I'll write him a letter."

"You can't know what he's going through," Derek says.

"And you do?" she shoots back.

"As a gay man—" he begins.

"Right, I'm just a woman, I can't get AIDS." She throws up her hands and walks past him. Derek gives me a look—*what did I do?*

Raymond calls out, "You're both right. Courageous *and* manipulative. He saw an opening and he went for it."

But Amanda doesn't look back, so I run to catch her. "What's up?"

She lowers her voice. "You know, I never did get tested."

"The offer still stands—I'll go with you."

"I'm terrified," she says. "I'm having the most vanilla sex with Jocelyn, worried that I'm positive and going to give it to her. But the worst part is this weird voice in my head saying, *If you have it, you'll be a more authentic activist.* How self-loathing is that?"

"You're not the only person who's romanticized the virus."

"I'm probably the only woman who has, though."

"You're beating yourself up about your sex life," I say, throwing an arm over her shoulder. She rests her head there for a moment, but she quickly begs off, heading back to 10th Street with Raymond.

That night, I stay up, wired, smoking in the living room. I call Christopher, who sounds surprised to hear from me. I try to speak supportively. *I'm sorry you're positive. How are you feeling? We'll attack this together.* Words like that. He thanks me for calling, but it's late, it's been an intense day, and he needs sleep. After he hangs up, I'm left feeling that I'm still just Paul from New Jersey to him. It's been more than a year, but our friendship hasn't deepened. Maybe I've never gotten past admiring him and Mike; they were out and proud while I was still a teenager, repressed and unaware. And now this test result. Sure, I can claim that we'll attack it together, but he's the one living it, while I stand outside his experience at something like a safe distance.

Amanda and Raymond are throwing a party because *we all need one*, Raymond says. Amanda's test results come in right before; mine too, both of us negative. "More to celebrate," I say to her, and she just tilts her head knowingly because in a world of HIV-positive friends you don't flaunt being negative, and on top of that you never feel like it's real or that it will last.

When Derek and I get to their apartment, Raymond is DJing, switching between a CD player and a cassette boom box, playing guilty pleasure pop like "Never Gonna Give You Up" and "The Way You Make Me Feel." When he manages a transition without a gap between songs, the crowd cheers and he lifts his muscled arms over his head, calling out, "Throw your hands up, queens!" I don't know this side of Raymond. He's changing. I don't see him with his camcorder the way I used to, though I have seen him out at Rock-n-Roll Fag Bar dancing without a shirt, showing off new definition.

The air fills deliciously with perspiration and smoke, the fumes of liquor, the smells of the street wafting through open windows. Liquor flows, beer bottles pile up in the kitchen, voices nearly overpower the music. Boys begin stripping off their shirts, and soon there is wall-to-wall flesh, glistening under strings of lights that crisscross the ceiling.

Zack arrives late, traveling with those boys that Derek dubbed trendy. He gives me a brief kiss on the cheek that stops my breath, then I watch him move to Raymond, who grabs his face and plants a big smacker on his lips. I'm jealous. There's no other word for it. I hate that I'm jealous, but I am. It's not just that Raymond and Zack have something going on. It's that Raymond and Derek had sex, that Raymond and Amanda are roommates. He's everywhere. Even his spotty DJing wins over the crowd.

Late in the sweltering night, a bunch of boys announce they're going across the street to jump into the park's fountain. The rest of us cram in around the front windows, craning our necks. Sure enough, there's Zack, Raymond, and three other guys crossing the street wearing only underwear and combat boots, clutching their shirts and shorts in their hands. Ten minutes later, they return soaking wet. Their shining bodies send a new volt of sexual energy through the crowd. Amanda stands up on a chair at the center and drunkenly announces that if boys can go topless, so can girls. She pulls off her shirt, and the room erupts. I see Jocelyn pressing her lips together. She keeps her shirt on.

Eventually everyone is kissing someone. Derek calls me over to introduce Jean-Paul, "from ACT UP Montreal" (who knew?), and lures me into a sloppy three-way make-out. Jean-Paul is cute but sort of a stabby kisser. I step back and let Derek find their rhythm. I sense someone's eyes on me—and sure enough, there's Zack across the apartment, looking our way. I offer him a little wave, and he blows me a kiss. And then Raymond calls his name.

Seize Control of the FDA is a new kind of action for us, not a centralized march or a rally as much as a bombardment of street theater. Everyone attends the same teach-ins about the issues, everyone is trained in how to talk to the media. No one isn't a spokesperson. Plans for civil disobedience are kept within small, independent "affinity groups," a term we've taken from the civil rights movement. Each group makes its own plans, and on the day of the action we'll swarm the campus of the Food and Drug Administration, a mass of moving targets.

Activists are coming to Rockville, Maryland from all over the country. Our new head of the media committee, Leo, has a background in celebrity publicity, and he's promised coast to coast media coverage, saying, "We're going to make it so easy for reporters that they won't be able *not* to cover us." Derek heads to D.C. with him a few days early to lay the groundwork, but I stay behind because I promised my parents I'd go to a family wedding upstate.

My family drives into the city to pick me up, and this time all four of them come up to see the apartment. My sisters have insisted on it. I've cleaned and straightened up, and it's a sunny afternoon so the space is bright and inviting. Lisa's impressed that we've set up a stocked bar. Michelle lingers in front of my bookshelves looking at titles. I show off Mom's curtains, and I can see she's pleased. Dad's taken with the installed cabinets, looking closely at Nicholas's handiwork. "You've done well," he says, laying an approving hand on my shoulder, which I count as a breakthrough.

My wedding outfit on the other hand—a plaid '60s suit bought in a thrift store on 8th Street—goes unmentioned. I've pinned a button reading SEIZE CONTROL to my lapel, and when relatives at the wedding ask about it, and even when they don't, I tell them about the demonstration I'll be attending the next day. The words AIDS and activism seem to scare people, and I watch eyes glaze over and fear take hold. When I complain to Lisa that no one's willing to engage on the issues with me, she says, "They still think of you as an altar boy who never causes trouble."

I get drunk. Very drunk. "Pace yourself," my mother tells me during the cake-cutting, taking my umpteenth Scotch out of my hand and replacing it with coffee. "I'm not that bad," I insist, gulping the coffee then returning to the open bar for a beer. I wake to a screeching alarm clock, a pointy nail poking rhythmically into my temple.

Carpools to Maryland have been arranged through ACT UP. I'm in a car driven by Nicholas, who finds my murderous hangover hilarious. He sits at the wheel, smoking nonstop and monologuing about the years he spent in a D.C. rowhouse, part of a short-lived vegetarian commune that made money selling weed and acid and charging admission for weekly drag shows—"highly improvised catastrophes," in his words. It was there he met his first lover, Harper. Ten years later they reunited just before Harper got sick. Nicholas stayed with him all the way to his death.

He drops me at the hotel where Derek and Leo have transformed a room into media headquarters, a buzzing, beeping communications zone where faxes go out, calls come in and countless press kits are assembled in glossy black folders. That night, we meet at a Unitarian church that donated its space to us. Bryn and Will are doing last-minute marshal training. I'm among those teaching newcomers how to go limp, how to demand a badge number, what to do if you're put through the system. At the FDA, we'll be spread out over a lot of space, and marshals will have to keep up with whatever unfolds, wherever it happens.

October 11, 1988. The affinity group I'm assigned to marshal is made up of all my friends—Amanda, Raymond, Zack, Timmy, Dale, Rochelle, Nicholas, and half a dozen more—brave and flawed and scared and righteous. Our t-shirts proclaim HEALTHCARE IS A RIGHT. We spread out in the parking lot, lying in front of parked cars, painting outlines around each other. Raymond captures this on videotape, preserving each crime-scene silhouette, which we fill with accusations: MURDERED BY RONALD REAGAN, BY GEORGE H.W. BUSH, BY THE HEAD OF THE FDA, BY SEXISM. DEAD FROM LACK OF AIDS MEDICINE. HOMELESS AND DYING. KILLED BY CORPORATE GREED. We use water-based paint, which is longer-lasting than chalk but can be washed away, so we can't be charged with permanent defacement.

All around us, actions unfold in a symbiotic dance between police and affinity groups, between our army of empowered spokespeople and the national press lapping up stories. Signs and banners wave against a gray cloud cover. I absorb a cacophony of chants. I clock bodies perpetually in motion. Late in the afternoon, timed with the evening news, all eyes lift to the building's marquee, above the main doors, where Roger is fastening an enormous SILENCE=DEATH banner across a row of second-story windows.

Roger is one of the Adventurers Camp posse, a former stockbroker with a knack for sneaking in where others can't, which might have something to do with the years he spent on Wall Street passing as straight. Up above the crowd, a white rag knotted around his head like a samurai, he raises his arms in rebellious triumph. A ladder is pushed up to the marquee, and other demonstrators stream upward to join him. Below, a handful of people are rushing the front doors, two big glass panels framed in metal, locked together with a heavy-linked chain. Demonstrators ebb and flow, push and pull. The doors tremble, buckle, and then, finally, burst. The shattering glass sounds musical, percussive, the climax of a symphony.

Then it gets ugly. Police in riot gear push into the crowd, headed right at our affinity group, which drops cross-legged to the pavement and links arms. I hang back, keeping track of our numbers. Raymond takes the first blow while he's videotaping, caught unaware by a riot shield battering him from the side. His camera goes flying, a cop kicks it away, and another cop spins Raymond around and cuffs him. The police are all over us—they're not local, they're federal—and they don't ask us to disperse, they just yank people apart, twisting arms behind backs, snapping cuffs onto wrists. "They're too tight," Amanda calls out, "you're cutting off my circulation," and as she tries to wriggle free a cop grabs her by the hair and pulls her away. I run to follow, yelling, trying to see his badge but he's covering it with his free hand. *"Step away, sir,"* he commands while I demand a name and number, *"Step away!"* but I get up in his face, "YOU'RE HURTING HER, LET HER GO," and then his arm swings up, crooked like a wing, his elbow connecting *CRUNCH* with my jaw.

The blow stops me cold, sends me backwards, wobbling, breathless, the pain a boomerang in my skull, my vision blurring as I feel myself going down. Someone catches me, steadies me; it's Rochelle, she's whispering, *"come with me, this way,"* guiding me out of the melee, away from the arrests, getting me to sit on the ground and getting others to form a circle around me, a shield from the police, still marauding through the demonstration, snatching people up, a frenzy of arrests, I can't see much of anything, can't make my mouth work, but I hear sirens, I hear shouts, I hear talk of bodies hauled onto police busses, other bodies dropping down in front of those busses, stopping them from driving away, I hear chants rising up, *Let Them Go, Let Them Go, Let Them Go.*

The next Monday, Christopher reports to the floor that two of the drugs we targeted for faster approval—one treating blindness and another that prevents AIDS-related pneumonia—have been quickly approved. The chemist from our treatment committee says we will now apply pressure to the FDA for the *next* step: to make these drugs available for people with full-blown AIDS who don't meet the rigid enrollment standards for clinical trials but stand to benefit from their effects. "Parallel trials" for this population is our new goal. Our agenda, always revisited and refined, is again moving forward.

I understand then what I couldn't as I left the FDA amid shattered glass and mass arrests and the uproarious pain in my jaw: this was a triumph. The policies we've been promoting from the sidelines are no longer being ignored by the establishment. The work we're doing is starting to make a difference.

Insubordination

My jaw isn't broken, as I feared, though it takes X-rays to figure this out, and I wait days before getting them. Derek wants me to see a doctor immediately, but I don't have health insurance—I'm a temp without benefits—so I sit around popping aspirin and applying ice, hoping the pain will just go away. The irony of having been injured while wearing a t-shirt proclaiming healthcare as a right, and then having no access to healthcare beyond the emergency room, is not lost on me. It's to the emergency room I go, accompanied by Amanda, similarly uninsured, who wants someone to look at her neck, which has been aching since that same cop dragged her away. Our wait in the ER is endless because we're a low priority among people bleeding from wounds, convulsing from drug withdrawal, or just shrieking until someone pays attention. My X-ray results reveal a tooth fractured at the root and likely nerve damage. I'm going to need a root canal. *How the fuck am I going to afford that?*

I'm given a referral to the dental clinic at NYU, low-walled cubicles filled with dental chairs, the whirring of drills filling the air. I'm assigned to an anxious intern named Olga, an immigrant from the Soviet Union in a skirt and heels, who tells me gravely, "You are first root canal for me." After every half-step in the procedure, she pauses and says, "Wait please one minute," leaving me alone in the chair, mouth propped open and lined with a dental dam, while she searches for her supervisor, who is apparently in high demand because it takes many, many minutes before he returns with Olga, usually correcting what she's done. My visit stretches, two, three, four hours, and the longer it goes the darker my thoughts become. She's doing it all wrong, she's probably damaging something; as I sit here with my mouth open I'm definitely contracting an infection that will cross over into my brain, and isn't this what they want, isn't this our right-wing government's plan, to give poor people substandard care, letting them—*us*—die off faster? *We die, they do nothing* is not just a chant, it's the truth behind all those horror stories about people with AIDS lying on gurneys in the corridors of hospitals waiting for rooms, ignored.

This is where your mind goes in the middle of a plague.

At last Olga gets to drilling into the root, but again she stops, mutters in Russian, and scurries off in a panic. When the supervising doctor arrives, I pull off my bib. He tells me I can't leave, but if there's one thing I've learned in ACT UP it's that you push for what you need: "Get me someone who knows what they're doing, give me a prescription for something stronger and get me out of here." In short order a more skilled dentist appears and quickly finishes this part of the surgery, leaving the rest for another day. I'm sent home with a bottle of Valium.

For a day or two my speech is slurry, muffled—mouthy me, without a usable mouth. Derek enjoys asking me questions and then saying, "Oops, sorry, never mind," as I garble a reply. He gets me to laugh through the aches. The painkillers make me dopey, which is pleasurable for about a day and then frustrating. I want my mind sharp. There's a lot to deal with, not least of which is ACT UP's attempt to force justice from the federal police: not just for my injury and Amanda's (she still doesn't know what's wrong with her neck) but also the lengthy detention of all the arrestees on the day of the protest, who spent hours in a holding room on the FDA campus without access to legal or medical attention. There's also the matter of Raymond's camcorder, yet to be returned or even acknowledged as confiscated.

Derek takes it upon himself to call my parents, who drive into the city and tell me they'll pay for the rest of the root canal, just get to a dental surgeon, quick.

I joke with Mom and Dad that I had to get beaten by the police before they'd pay a proper visit—more gallows humor, but they roll with it. My father, I can tell, is unnerved by what's happened to me. He has been slow to embrace my newfound civil disobedience. Isn't there another way to accomplish your goals? he wants to know. He was raised by German immigrants, and taught to stay within the lines. You never provoked the police. Broken glass and painted pavement are provocations. But he's alarmed by my stories of what happened at the FDA. Beating up on sick people, pulling young women by the hair? The police, in his view, must play by the rules, too, especially at a demonstration like ours, with a true purpose. The FDA's response proves that much. "There's a method to your madness after all," he says, which I score as another breakthrough between us.

This prompts me to offer an olive branch. "I need to apologize to you both," I say. "I got way too drunk at the wedding, and I hardly remember the ride home. I think I probably embarrassed you, and that wasn't my intention." I've thought of this more than once in these days spent lying around on painkillers, the idea that if I'm going to be engaged in their lives, I need to meet them halfway. I need them on my side.

"We appreciate that," my father says. "I hope you know we want the best for you."

My mother says, "We talk about it a lot, what you're doing. We're listening. We're trying to understand."

My mother pokes around the apartment and dubs us "The Odd Couple." She's noticed Derek's tidy desk, his shirts hanging in the closet according to color, the neat line of his shoes by the bed. My own desk is a clutter of paper scraps bursting out of journals; my clothes are piled in the corner, clean and dirty mixed together. I leave books everywhere, face down, splayed open. "You've always been a little scruffy," she says.

I comment that she looks tired—is it just her usual fretting, magnified by my situation, or is she under the weather? "They've been working me too hard," she says, gossiping about the busybodies in her office at a company that manufactures vitamins.

She's brought me powdered nutritional supplements and a blender—the same one that usually sits on the kitchen counter in New Jersey, gathering dust since my parents moved out of their jogging-and-fitness phase. I wind up living off that blender, liquefying ice cream and peanut butter, plus Mom's supplements, as I recuperate. The whir of the blade brings back memories of high school parties, when I'd make frozen cocktails for friends while my parents were out. Rehabilitation or intoxication: the blender delivers results.

Derek turns out to be a scattershot nurse, hovering when he's home, but not home very often. He has a new, full-time job as a publicist at a nonprofit agency dedicated to combating poverty. He doesn't have any background in this, he just learned how to do publicity in ACT UP. He's still doing ACT UP work at nights, so I don't see him much while I'm home healing.

Get-well cards and flowers from friends arrive—an outpouring that catches me off guard. Best of all is an envelope from Zack, with a drawing inside that he's made for me: my face with a big bruise near the mouth, a speech bubble rising out: *I'd like to make a motion to prosecute the asshole who did this to me.* Next to it is another cartoon face, Zack in a Yankees cap, saying, *Second the motion!* At the bottom, he's written, *Get back in the fight soon, Kiddo.*

I receive a surprise visit from Eliot, whom I haven't seen socially since the night he threw flaming birthday cakes out the window. He's carrying a large box covered in taped-together leaflets from past ACT UP actions. "One of the administrator's duties," he says, "is coming up with creative ways to recycle our outdated flyers."

Inside the box, to my astonishment, is a brand new VCR.

"With love from the Coordinating Committee," he says.

"Really?" The coordinating committee is made up of representatives from all the other ACT UP committees. When people complain about behind-the-scenes power, it's this unit they're talking about. I pull the sleek black apparatus from the cardboard. I've never owned one before.

"I have been instructed to make clear that this was paid for from *personal* contributions. Let the record show, the ACT UP treasury was not touched."

"Generous and ethical," I say. "Now what am I going to watch?"

"Funny you should ask. I've taken the liberty…" His dark eyes twinkle as he passes me a sheet of loose-leaf paper with a handwritten list of titles. At the top of the page it says A QUEEN'S CINEMATIC EDUCATION in Eliot's distinctive administrative penmanship. "Nicholas made some contributions as well. The more psychedelic ones, in case you're keeping track. And my sweetheart Lenny, who you may not know is a bit of a scholar of silent pictures, made sure we included Garbo."

I scan the list. I haven't seen most of these. The next day I'll make it to Kim's Video, on Avenue A, and get myself a membership.

Note to Self #5: What was on the list of A Queen's Cinematic Education?

The 5,000 Fingers of Doctor T
Auntie Mame
Barbarella
Beyond the Valley of the Dolls
The Boys in the Band
Carmen Jones
Cruising

Dark Victory
The Devils
Gentlemen Prefer Blondes
Imitation of Life
Juliet of the Spirits
The King and I
The Lion in Winter
Mademoiselle
Marat/Sade
The Misfits
Nights of Cabiria
Ninotchka
Queen Christina
The Prime of Miss Jean Brodie
Rosemary's Baby
Singing in the Rain
A Streetcar Named Desire
Sunset Boulevard
Sweet Bird of Youth
Tommy
Valley of the Dolls
Wait Until Dark
West Side Story
Who's Afraid of Virginia Woolf?
The Women

"New Yorkers are terrible hosts," Nicholas once said to me. "Our apartments are too small and the plumbing is ancient." But it's been a season of parties, and now there will be one more. Timmy and Dale visit during my recovery week and announce that they're moving in together. They've been dating for less than two months. The shock must be pretty clear on my face.

"He turned me into a lesbian," Timmy says. "Our housewarming is going to be our Lesbian Coming Out Party."

Dale adds, "Except it's the other way around. I rented a commercial loft to live in, and the first time Timmy spent the night he was like, 'This is too big for one person, I should move in with you.' He just wants to get his name on the lease so when I die from AIDS, he can keep it."

"I'm no fool," Timmy says, and they bust out laughing together.

So this is how I learn that Dale, who makes everyone "say AIDS" before he takes their photo, is a person with AIDS himself. Timmy seems so happy and at ease with Dale, though I can't help but be scared for him. After Keith's death, isn't he setting himself up for more pain? I guess he's just thinking, fuck it, why wait? The usual caution doesn't apply when you're living under siege.

The date they pick for their housewarming is the same weekend as my twenty-third birthday. When I mention this, Dale gets really excited. "We'll make it a Lesbian Housewarming and a Twenty-third Birthday Party." I try to protest, but he won't hear it. "Invite all those cute boys you're always kissing."

"Once you get your mouth back," Timmy says, "you gotta make up for lost time."

I've missed the sex we had with Timmy, our first fuckbuddy. Not that there's been a shortage of boys since then, but he was so fun and uninhibited. Later, I express this to Derek, but he says, "Just think of it as, we get to hand our Timmy off to this other great guy. Share the wealth."

Sometimes Derek is so mature it's hard to believe he's just a year older than me. Other times I feel like the grown-up in this relationship, taking care of my neurotic boyfriend and all his mommy-issues.

Derek has recently bought a Macintosh—a first for either of us—and now he spends his after-work hours learning computer programs. He uses a graphics program to make an invitation for Timmy and Dale's party. On one side: a picture of them posing American Gothic-style in front of a U-Haul. On the other: a big "23" and the words "OLDER THAN STONEWALL," with a photo of me as a little boy, wearing short pants and clutching a doll.

On a Friday night, while Derek is at a media committee meeting, I take the invitations to The Bar to hand them out. Boosted by liquid courage, I invite too many people, from my ever-widening circle of activist friends and other folks I'm meeting in the East Village.

The bathroom at The Bar is small and lit with a red bulb. A trough wide enough for two, but often crammed with three, is squeezed between a cold-water sink and a single stall housing a reeking, hissing toilet. I'm at the trough when someone steps next to me, unzips and begins to whistle a jittery tune. I turn my head—it's Zack.

"Hey, Kiddo," he says.

"Hey. What are you whistling?"

"The pee song." He blows a few more notes and piss hits porcelain. I look down at his large hand, holding his soft cock, the arc of his stream catching the light. "It always works," he says

"I'm inviting people to my birthday party."

I pull a flyer out of my back pocket, which he reads as he zips up, muttering "Only twenty-three!" I realize I don't know his age. Is he twenty-five? Is he thirty-five? I can't actually tell. "So what do you want for your birthday?" he asks.

"A cure for AIDS?"

"Everyone wants that. What do *you* want?"

I watch him stuff the invitation in his pocket, and I think about that little square of paper going from my pocket to my fingers, which were holding my dick, to his hand, which was holding his, to his back pocket, and I say, "I want you to come."

"I'll come for you," he says, which actually makes me gasp.

I stay in Zack's vicinity for the rest of the night, as people drift over, taking invitations and offering drinks, which I start to refuse when I realize I'm drunk. The jukebox plays music that seems old to me, Patti Smith and Talking Heads and Bowie, mixed in with new stuff, Neneh Cherry and Guns 'N' Roses, and then out of nowhere, Billie Holiday's "Strange Fruit," which seems to hush the room momentarily before sparking a discussion among the ACT UP boys around me about why our activism hasn't inspired any important music. Someone talks about the folky lesbian stuff that we've all been listening to (Michelle Shocked, Indigo Girls, Phranc), and someone else mentions rap, though we don't know of any out rappers. Who's going to make the music for our revolution?

Finally, it's just me and Zack on the bench, passing a cigarette back and forth, a column of smoke rising up from the shared ember.

He's in his street wear—white t-shirt, black jeans—and I realize I haven't seen him again in the blue broadcloth shirt and chinos. "What are you doing for work?" I ask.

"I'm freelancing now. Consulting."

"Through an agency?"

"Mostly just drumming up my own clients." He pauses, as if considering what to reveal. "I got fired."

"What for?"

"*Insubordination.*"

"I love that word."

"A big word for a bad attitude." I watch his expression go dark, and then he says, "Fuck it. People are dying, right?"

"I think you pretend to have a bad attitude, because it works for you."

He fights back a smile. "How'd you get so wise, Kiddo?" he asks, and combs his tobaccoey fingers through my hair.

I'm not sure I actually like "Kiddo," which he seems to have settled on, or that I'm ready to be tousled and flirted with so intently. I ask, "Where's Raymond?"

"You keeping track?"

"Maybe."

He lifts an arm to drop it across my shoulders, then pauses and sniffs. "Jesus, I worked up a stink."

I lean into him and sniff. "Eau-de-Zack," I say, and then add, "I want it all over me."

"You're trouble, Kiddo."

"I'm actually not. I'm in an open relationship. Unless the problem is you and Raymond?"

"It would be weird the next time I see Derek."

I don't quite get it, but I don't push, either. Only later, replaying our conversation, will I realize that he deflected my question about whatever agreement exists between him and Raymond.

On the street, he puts a kiss on my lips. It lingers long enough to count.

I watch him head to the subway, his gait a streetwise strut. I stay there after he's disappeared from view, my head spinning with alcohol, staring into the void and feeling . . . alone.

Note to Self #6:

Alone? Really? Why are you such an emo drama queen? You're surrounded by people who've been looking out for you, giving you gifts, letting you know you're cared for and loved—

True, true, it was more friendship than I'd ever felt in my life. More community.

But?

But there's this other thing, a primal hollow, filling my physical being the way water soaks a sponge, and it made me feel older than my years. It came from wanting and not getting—desire without fulfillment, which only increases desire. It expands, seemingly limitless.

That sounds like the closet: what can't be fulfilled, the earliest known shame.

Yes. Because it was a hunger not just for one guy—though he was the trigger, stirring up something primal—but for something grander, for dissolution, a loss of self. It was a hunger to be absorbed into another body, when bodies were forbidden. A hunger for infinity, when even the finite seemed impossible.

Once you feel that, can you ever forget?

I haven't forgotten. Are we ever free of what shaped us?

Timmy and Dale's loft is in a nondescript area above 14th Street, which should mean Chelsea, though it's too far east, too close to Fifth Ave. "The Ladies Mile," Dale calls it, using a name from the Gilded Age, when the streets radiating out from the famous Flatiron Building were home to the city's most fashionable boutiques. That seems preposterous in 1988, when the area is festering and dirty, and the park across the street is one you avoid at night. It isn't a place for *ladies.*

Dale and Timmy have done a lot of work to make a home out of what was recently a yarn factory. From raw space they've built out a bedroom, a kitchen and a photo darkroom for Dale. Most of the space remains wide open, with high ceilings and giant windows. Dale's photographs hang unframed on the walls—pictures of our friends, with Dale's handwritten captions beneath. One shows Timmy and Keith making goofy faces above the words WE MISS KEITH. The tone is naïve but captures the heart of the matter: we miss the ones who've died, and we don't fully grasp how it keeps happening.

For the party they've taken the "Older than Stonewall" theme and tricked the place out in late '60s hippie detritus—bolts of paisley fabric and strings of love beads. "Stonewall was the same summer as Woodstock,"

Nicholas reminds us, with a tale of his own teenage love affair at Yasgur's Farm. Mix tapes play Jefferson Airplane, Sly and the Family Stone and Aretha Franklin. A bright red liquid dubbed "Flower Power Punch" is ladled from a stockpot. A TV monitor plays an edited loop of footage from our demos mixed in with old cuts from TV shows that were already in reruns when I was a boy—*Gilligan's Island, My Three Sons, Petticoat Junction.* There's another loop of stills from vintage porn playing in the bedroom, where the lights are low. "You guys didn't have to do all this for me," I say, genuinely awed by the effort.

"We tried to work with the lesbian housewarming idea," Timmy says.

"It was a little too high concept," Dale finishes.

Dale has set up a backdrop for photos, a giant print of the U-Haul truck that they used on their invitation. They've put out a box of drag, which spills wigs, costume jewelry, crazy hats, boas, Elton John sunglasses and weird props like antique fans and damaged dolls. When he wants a cigarette break, Dale hands his camera to Raymond, who hangs a pair of red, waxed lips from the top of the backdrop, like mistletoe, and announces it's now a kissing booth.

Raymond calls me over and tells me to stand under the lips. Then he sets the self-timer, joins me in front of the camera and dives in for a kiss. It's too big, too sloppy, almost a parody of "making out," and it generates catcalls and whistles from the room. When I pull back, with a startled burst of laughter, the first person I see is Zack. I make a jokey face, but he doesn't respond. Then Raymond looks at Zack, too, and Zack holds his gaze, his expression clouding. I shuffle away quickly. Whatever their drama is, I don't need it.

I spy Derek in the bedroom with a group of boys kissing and groping each other, some I recognize, including one I met at The Bar when I was handing out invitations. It's far more innocent than the porn looping above them. There's no door on the bedroom, just a curtain of glass beads that creates a kaleidoscopic spray of light across the half-naked bodies. Happy birthday to me.

From across the loft, I hear an angry voice: Raymond, standing chest to chest with Zack like a couple of rutting stags. Zack shoves him, and then Raymond comes back, pushing harder. Zack regains his balance, lifts his leg into a roundhouse kick and nails Raymond in the hip. Raymond howls—it stops the party. "Get a grip on your fucking testosterone," he yells at Zack. "Stop playing games with me," Zack yells back. Raymond takes another forceful step forward, Zack catches his arm and twists it until Raymond cries out again. It's all happening so fast. Now people rush forward to pull them apart.

I see Zack grab his jacket. A moment later he's out the door. I follow, but when I reach the street, he's halfway up the block. I call his name. He keeps walking. I call again. This time he stops and turns. I can't see his eyes under the brim of his cap, but I think he recognizes me because he surrenders the tension in his upper body. I sprint to him.

He's trembling.

"What happened?" I ask.

"He brings out this side of me I hate. What the fuck am I doing with him?"

"Do you want to talk about it?"

He looks at me with a wounded gaze. "Go back to your party."

"Zack, I'm concerned about you."

"I'm going home." He starts walking again, and I move alongside. His body is tense. When I put my arm on his back, he flinches. I rub small circles there, wanting to calm him. Finally he slows down, stops. Our eyes hold.

I pull him by his hand toward the nearest wall, the side of a building above a staircase descending to a basement door. And then we start kissing, mouths open, wet and connected, hands all over each other.

"Come here," he says, and leads me down the stairs into a dark alcove. The air stinks of piss, but that doesn't stop us. Lips lock, fingers grab at the bottom of our shirts and the top of our jeans, touching flesh, panting. Just as I'm thinking, this is actually finally really happening, he stops and lets out a pained little moan.

"What?" I ask.

He holds my face in his hands. "Don't do this," he says. "I'm too fucked up."

"We both want to, why shouldn't we?" My words rush out while my mind's eye sees Raymond's face, in shock after Zack kicked him.

He says, "It's not tonight—it's my whole life, it's a fucking mess."

I try to protest, but he tells me to go back, not to worry about him, he's sorry for ruining things. I see how confused he looks. I've wanted this, but this is not the way I wanted it.

He kisses me once more, fast, then trots quickly up the stairs, while I fix my clothes. By the time I get to the street he's far down the block.

Back inside, Raymond is still apologizing for the public brawl, and everyone seems to be absolving him, which I suppose means that Zack is considered to blame. This doesn't strike me as entirely fair, nor does it surprise me. Zack is a cool enigma, full of *attitude,* whereas Raymond is a favorite: smart, accessible, fun. I feel responsible for it somehow. I feel certain it was my kiss with Raymond that lit the fuse.

Four a.m., I'm home with Derek, opening gifts: a drinking cup with Farrah Fawcett's face on it, a pillow silk-screened with HAPPINESS IS A WARM FUZZY, a small balsa-wood diorama of a locker room shower—figurines of naked men with boners—under a sign marked "YMCA." From Dale, I get a print of a photo he took of me at a demonstration, holding up a sign reading, THE GOVERNMENT HAS BLOOD ON ITS HANDS. ONE AIDS DEATH EVERY HOUR (soon to be updated to every ten minutes.) I've never before seen a picture of me at a protest. It's the best of all the presents, the one that truly marks me at twenty-three.

The last thing I unwrap is a navy blue NY Yankees baseball cap. Tucked within is a postcard—a picture of Sal Mineo looking longingly at Elvis Presley. On the back: *Happy Birthday to an angry young man. Zack.*

Derek frowns. "How about *from* an angry young man?"

"We're all angry."

"Not like that. He's trouble. You should steer clear."

I haven't mentioned the kiss in the stairwell. I'll fill him in, eventually, I tell myself, once I understand it better. Should I have followed Zack to the street? Did I take advantage of his confusion? What do I want out of this?

Zack makes himself scarce for a while, and the gossip fades. But for me, the incident with Raymond sticks, a reminder that for all the bonding and good feeling among these new friends, ours is still a world prone to overheating, emotional discombobulation, even violence. Being gay doesn't save us from being male. As activists, we harness our aggression; as men together in our everyday lives, we might still succumb to this poison. Zack's struggle with his feelings makes him seem very alive to me, a work in progress, a safe yet to be cracked. I feel linked to him by desire, plain and simple, but also by some sense that I *get* him. There's something buried that wants to come out, something we share.

Derek might be right, maybe I should steer clear of Zack, but I don't want to. I want to put myself in his path.

Part 4

Intensive Care

ACT UP is two years old.

We mark the anniversary in March 1989 with a demonstration dubbed "Target City Hall." Our fact sheets focus on the paltry amount for AIDS in the city budget ("one half of one percent"), the housing shortage ("5,000 people with AIDS live on the street"), the ten-month wait to treat IV drug users with AIDS ("who on average have six months to live"). Mayor Koch has always been high on our list of nemeses. Larry Kramer contends that Koch's closeted homosexuality was at the root of his failure to respond to the epidemic, and once again, right before this demonstration, Koch gives an interview to *Newsday*, in which he makes the claim, "I'm heterosexual." Those words wind up on the newspaper's cover, which one of our sassier affinity groups repurposes into posters. KOCH: I'M HETEROSEXUAL. AND I'M DIANA ROSS... AND I'M JOAN OF ARC... AND I AM MARIE OF ROMANIA.

Target City Hall is the biggest act of civil disobedience on behalf of people with AIDS to date. Three thousand protestors. Two hundred arrests. Waves of affinity groups move into the streets around City Hall, each with its own tactic. I'm marshaling, which is hectic and tense, with so much going on in so many different places. At the end of the day, I'm at the police precinct, calling in to my answering machine, trying to track down everyone who's been arrested.

In the middle of my messages is one from my mother. She leaves a number with a 201 area code, not one I recognize. When I call, she picks up after a few rings, coughing, voice raspy. "Your father brought me to the emergency room last night," she says. "It was hard to breathe."

"Are you in the hospital?"

"An infection in my lungs. Pneumonia, maybe. They don't know yet."

"How do you feel?"

"I'm all right."

"You sound…not so good, Mom." I remember how tired she has seemed, for months now, since I first remarked on it last fall.

"They're running tests," she wheezes. She says they're checking for hepatitis, tuberculosis, HIV.

"HIV? Why?"

"I used to be a nurse. I could have had a needle-stick."

"That was so long ago."

"They're not ruling anything out."

Her symptoms came on suddenly, which argues against HIV—though I know it's not unheard of for someone to be fine on Monday and hospitalized with PCP on Tuesday. A flood of thoughts: everything I know about transmission of the virus, everything I've learned about IV needle users, sensationalized media stories about infected healthcare workers. I can't quite absorb this curveball, my mother as a potential "innocent victim."

She puts Dad on the phone, and he fills me in. She couldn't sleep, her breathing so labored that by morning the emergency room was the only option. "She hasn't been herself for a while," he notes, voice hushed. "It's definitely *something*."

The next day, I sit alone on the bus to New Jersey, reversing the suburb-to-city passage that has framed the transformation of my life. The hospital is only thirty miles from Manhattan, but the ride stretches out, impossibly long. Mile by mile the landscape becomes less urban, which has the effect of making me feel *more* urban, a city boy at last. The congestion around the Lincoln Tunnel gives way to the factory outlets and sports facilities of the Meadowlands, which morph into shopping malls and cineplexes and, gradually, tree-lined towns: front lawns, little girls on bikes, teenage boys loping down the sidewalk bouncing basketballs.

I step off the bus into diesel fumes. Then it pulls away and the air clears. I make my way on foot to the hospital, inhaling childhood memories, dense and quick: A walk to the town center on a weekend afternoon with no goal other than buying candy. Perusing vinyl at the record store, picking out Styx, Fleetwood Mac, Donna Summer, but only daring to glance at the cover of a Village People album called "Live and Sleazy": the cowboy with that lean hard body, the construction worker with the remarkable mound in his pants.

I can't buy it here, the guy working the register is the brother of a girl I go to school with, I'll get it at the mall instead. Eating at the Cantonese restaurant where I took my junior prom date, Erica, drinking beer out of cans in the parking lot, ordering chicken chow mein and—I cringe to remember—cracking jokes about dog meat in the food. I put off kissing Erica until the last possible moment.

A right turn at this intersection would point me toward a strip mall with a movie theater, the one where I saw *Making Love* with three female friends, listening to their chorus of groans when the male characters kissed, agreeing that it was "weird" and "gross" but committing to memory Harry Hamlin's oiled torso as he strained through push-ups then stood approvingly in front of the mirror, nearly naked, gleaming, Olympian.

The past that rises up burns with secret desires, failed masculinity, casual bigotry, the effort of *passing*. The balmy spring air is a blanket of censure, calling up years of masks, years lost to silence within the dominant culture. I understand silence. Until ACT UP, it has always been the way to navigate risk.

Nothing has prepared me for this: my mother in a hospital bed wearing an oxygen mask, her face without makeup, her hair barely brushed, her skin pale, her eyes full of fear. She says they still don't know what's wrong, why her lungs are straining, why she feels pain all over. She pulls the mask off to tell me this, her voice a strained rasp, weaker even than she sounded on the phone. I blink away tears, not wanting her to see.

You can't know what you've been protected from until that protection is taken away, and what I understand now is that my mother has protected me from any hint of her vulnerability. She's always been gentle and kind—a soft person, is how I once described her—but now I grasp this as a form of strength and stability. I've thought myself independent these past couple of years, living with Derek, separate from my need for her; now I know that I've taken her existence for granted, a frame around my sense of self: I have a mother. She loves me. I count on her being there if I need her.

"Can you help me?" she asks, indicating her bedding, which has gotten tangled. I pull back the top sheet to untuck the sheet beneath her. The flimsy hospital gown has bunched up at her waist, and I glimpse her naked body, the rippled flesh of her thighs, the rust-red tangle of her pubic hair, her white stomach and breasts.

"There's no modesty in a hospital," she says, as I pull her gown over her, drape the top sheet, avert my eyes. She seems as vulnerable as a little girl, but I'm the child: gazing upon my mother's body as I have not since my earliest years.

A nurse appears, orders Mom to put the mask on, asks me to leave during a sponge bath. I step into the hallway, where I find my father, returning from a doctor's conference. Everything I've held back erupts: "What the hell is going on here? What are they telling you? Why don't we know anything?"

"They're trying to figure it out," he says. "They're talking about a ventilator. That's so *invasive.*"

His hands are shaking. I give him a hug, hold on tight. Whatever this is, it's only beginning.

I've learned enough in ACT UP to know what has to be done: corralling doctors, monitoring nurses, asking questions, writing down answers. But she's still undiagnosed. We're still waiting for hard news.

Her HIV test comes back negative, but I can't shake the idea that the results are wrong, that in her years of nursing she must have been stuck by an infected hypodermic. False test results are not unheard of. There's so much still unknown about the human immunodeficiency virus. Some doubters in the gay community still call HIV *the virus believed to cause AIDS,* as if the medical establishment has failed to identify the true nature of the epidemic. This seems crazy to me, but I understand why these doubts have traction: the government was absent from the start, the research establishment took its time, the media was slow to report the story. The people who got sick were the wrong people. In the eighth year of the epidemic, the science remains rudimentary.

I call Amanda, asking to meet at Café Mogador in the East Village. The look on her face when she arrives tells me she that she's picked up on my distress, but I hold off spelling out the situation until our Middle Eastern eggs and cappuccinos are served.

"Isn't it so ironic?" I ask her. "The very last person I could imagine with AIDS is in the hospital, and they're wondering if it's HIV?"

"They? I thought you said the test was negative."

"Well, me."

She puts her hand on mine. I've been tapping my fingers on the table nervously. "Your mom is sick, and you're worried. Just try to get the facts."

...

I bring Derek to the hospital, and when the front desk nurse asks if he's family, I say, "He's my significant other," using that strange, borrowed phrase—*significant* how? *other* what?—because in this moment it seems apt: official, descriptive, just vague enough. The nurse's eyes volley between us. I try to see what she's seeing: two guys in their early twenties with short-cropped hair and SILENCE=DEATH buttons pinned to denim jackets. She's probably never before faced a significant other who is significantly of the same sex.

She writes out two visitors badges for us. She points toward a bank of elevators, different from yesterday's, and says, "Your mother has been moved to Intensive Care."

Upstairs, we find my father on a couch, his posture slumped. Our eyes lock.

He says, "It's cancer."

His voice cracks as the dreadful word passes his lips. *Cancer.* It hovers and unravels in my ears: *Canz-er. Cannnnzzzzzzzzzzrrrrr.*

Then he utters a string of medical syllables: "Lymphomatoid granulomatosis."

This, it seems, is our diagnosis.

It's a form of lymphoma. "Non-Hodgkin's lymphoma," he explains, struggling to find his voice again. "'Non' isn't better, in case you're wondering. It's actually worse." A cancer of the lymph system, of white blood cells, revealing itself through nodules in my mother's lungs, filling them with fluid. There was no "infection." There is only this malignancy, multiplying, in her lungs.

They'll start her on chemotherapy—another word that fills me with dread. *Chemo,* I know, is as rough as cancer itself, a destructive regimen of chemicals that hits the body hard, all over, in an attempt to stop bad cells from doing worse. Chemo means weight loss, nausea, hair falling out, teeth going soft. To stop the blight, you scorch the earth. You scorch the earth so the ground might be green again.

We go to her. I can see the fear in her pale blue eyes. The eyes are all I have because her face is covered from the nose down by a milky-white plastic mask holding a respirator's tube in place. She's been muted by the machine that is now breathing for her.

A writing tablet and pen sit on the bedside table. She writes: *It will be OK.*

"I know, Mom. I know. I'm going to talk to my friends and find out what we can do. There might be hospitals in New York…"

She looks at Derek. *You two take care of each other.*

Derek says, "Don't worry about The Odd Couple."

My sisters are there, too, neither of them succeeding at keeping up a brave face. Lisa cries demonstratively; Michelle sniffles and looks at her feet. We all come up with words meant to soothe, the same words always spoken in situations like this—*you'll get through it, it'll be all right in the end, we're going to fight*—words so cliché as to be hollow.

But fighting is all I know how to do.

Amanda puts me in touch with Hillary, a young dyke new to ACT UP, who works at the NYU library. She walks me past the front desk and shows me how to access medical journals usually reserved for grad students and researchers. She helps me look up pulmonary lymphomatoid granulomatosis—PMG—guiding me through indices and bibliographies, locating the limited information available about clinical trials for appropriate drugs. I pass on this information to the doctors in New Jersey.

I visit Rochelle at her Brooklyn apartment. Her long history in the women's health movement has overlapped with breast cancer research, and she owns a collection of videotapes about alternative medicine. We watch them together on her couch, while I scrawl notes. Doctors—outspoken rebels in their fields—argue for curing sickness through prevention, diet, exercise. Aging itself is a sickness, one asserts, spurred on by environmental factors. Cut out meat and double down on nutrient-rich leafy green vegetables. Consider juicing. Yes, I tell myself, when she gets out of the hospital I'll juice leafy green vegetables for her every day. I'll buy the juicer now! Rochelle cautions that none of this should substitute for Western medicine, but should augment it. Yes, we'll do it all: Eastern, Western, clinical trials, meatless diets. Drugs. Herbs. We'll attack from every flank.

Cancer, I learn, is not just a disease but a system, a flow of millions of dollars from government to pharmaceutical companies, from foundations to researchers to hospitals to patients. (Always patients at the bottom.) Cancer is international conferences. Cancer is endless studies. Cancer is careers. The "Cancer Industrial Complex," Rochelle calls it. I wonder: if AIDS becomes treatable, will it be like this? "ACT UP needs to model itself as a healthcare movement," she says. "We have to think beyond *drugs into bodies*. We need a cure. Otherwise this is where we'll wind up. Money flowing in every direction, but no real change."

The big news story that summer is the controversy drummed up around the photographer Robert Mapplethorpe, dead from AIDS that spring. His images—cocks (hard and soft), male couples (some interracial) decked in leather and S&M gear, a bullwhip jammed handle-first into Mapplethorpe's own asshole—were to hang in Washington, D.C., but they've been denounced on the floor of Congress and the gallery has cancelled the show. On the bus to New Jersey, I read out loud to Derek the questions posed by a *NY Times* article: Are these photos art or pornography? Is the gallery, funded in part by the National Endowment for the Arts, guilty of using "taxpayer dollars" to fund "obscenity," as North Carolina Senator Jesse Helms has fulminated? I read a quote from Helms: "*We've got to have some common sense about a disease transmitted by people deliberately engaging in unnatural acts.*"

"How did the thing about tax money," Derek asks, "turn into 'gay men spreading disease'?"

"Defunding the arts is just a front. It gives them a way to demonize us."

"And of course he really hates that it's black and white men together—"

"Fucking racist."

"Fucking homophobe."

In the air-conditioned commuter bus, I shiver, less from the cold than the realization *we* are the immoral men discussed in the newspaper: promiscuous, unnatural, obscene. I scan the coach for anyone who might be looking sideways at us, but no one glances back. Everyone wears blinders. Don't get involved: the suburban mantra.

The hospital's receptionist has gotten used to us, acknowledging me and my *significant other* with a smile as she waves us by.

My mother seems weaker with each visit. I ask the questions my activist training has taught me: names of doctors, names of procedures, whom to call for follow-up, are there other options we should explore? My mind can easily go blank in the face of an answer laden with medical jargon, and I often fail to understand what I'm being told. But I have learned *not* to nod in agreement, to assume there is always another question.

I persuade my father to get the doctors in New Jersey to have a biopsy examined by a specialist in New York. There is an oncologist at Sloan Kettering who had worked on a PMG drug trial. Through an ACT UP connection, forged in the aftermath of our picket line two years earlier, I've gotten this man's contact info.

So on a weekday in early summer, I transport a tiny sample of tissue, a sliver of my mother's sickness prepared and packaged by a doctor in New Jersey, to a specialist at Sloan Kettering, who will examine it through a microscope, run tests and reveal, we hope, a solution. I think about that speck of cancerous tissue smeared on a laboratory slide—how insubstantial it is. I am the messenger, carrying precious cargo, the conduit between one half of existence as I know it—the contained past—and the other half, the uncertain future. The journey that day feels monumental, the gesture enormous. But it is over soon enough. I leave the sample with someone who will deliver it to someone else, who will get it to the big shot oncologist. I've *done* something. But after that, the only thing to do is wait some more.

Affirmations

Derek and I get tested again, not just because we're supposed to—the clinic at the community center now recommends anonymous HIV testing every six months—but because all this recent exposure to hospitals and illness has made us aware of our bodies' vulnerability, all the things that could go wrong. We do a full screening—HIV, but also hepatitis, chlamydia, gonorrhea, syphilis.

Our intake volunteer is a clean-cut white boy wearing a V-neck sweater over a button-down collar. "Aren't you two cute enough to eat," he says as he pumps the blood-pressure balloon.

"We might even be on the menu," Derek replies, not missing a beat.

"Waiter!" the guy says, "Check please!" And he actually winks.

He seems cheesy to me, but then again, I don't mind living in a world where your STD tests come with flirtation instead of shame. Derek exchanges business cards with him on our way out. His name is Michael. There's always another Michael. This one, according to his card, works for a bank as an analyst, whatever that is.

A week later, back at the clinic for our results, Michael isn't there. "I'm going to call him," Derek says.

"Yeah, why not?" I wasn't really interested in Michael, but at that moment I'm sailing on the relief of our test results: all negative. I have antibodies to hep-A, which means I've been exposed without developing symptoms—my immune system is strong. We'll both get the hep-B vaccine, which means one big injection today and then two more over the course of follow-up visits.

"Small fucking world," Derek announces a night later, telling me that Michael showed up at Committee for the City, where Derek works, to volunteer for a benefit.

"What is he, a serial volunteer?"

"He asked about you. Said he hopes he's still on the menu."

Which is how it comes to be that late in the night after the big benefit—held at the Waldorf Astoria and chock full of face-lifted society women who are too rich, too thin, and doted on by semi-closeted gay men who pick out their dresses, do their hair, and usher them past the flashbulbs—Derek and I are walking up the steps to our apartment with Michael between us. He wears an expensive suit and a shirt with cufflinks. We wear secondhand blazers, black jeans and Doc Martens. I've recently buzzed off my hair, nearly to the skull. The supervisor at my temp job told me I looked intimidating, but Michael runs his hand over my bristly scalp saying, "I get hot for downtown boys." I count that as a victory.

He produces a little plastic baggie puffed thick with shiny white powder. I've only tried coke once, hanging out with some of Derek's college friends, mostly actors and musicians, and in truth I'm wary of any drug stronger than pot. Coke and crack are the same thing to me, and I see every day in my neighborhood what a mess crack makes of people. But Michael is nonchalant. He grabs a CD—Grace Jones, *Slave to the Rhythm*—wipes the cover with a monogrammed handkerchief, and then divides up slender lines with his AmEx card. He rolls up a bill and sniffs. Derek mimes the old gag about holding back a sneeze, threatening to blow the blow everywhere. Michael says, "I'd have to spank you if you did."

I do two lines quickly and almost immediately feel consumed by a greed for *everything*. I pull Michael's cock through the fly of his suit pants and start sucking, aroused by the idea of degrading myself to this capitalist with his handkerchiefs and coke and credit cards. "I like this," he moans. "I like you boys. I like what you're doing." In the blaring blaze of the blow being *liked* churns in me like a primal craving, deeply rooted in adolescence, when I was friends with popular kids but never one of them myself, tagged along to parties though never actually invited, heard "fag" whispered behind my back and then heard it everywhere—and suddenly I'm not hard, or maybe I haven't been all along. My mind's eye flies open like a gate in a storm, revealing a vast, flat landscape, above which I hover, peering in every direction, feet unable to touch down.

Michael works on me, but…nothing. "Why so serious?"

"His face gets that way," Derek says. "He thinks too much."

"Maybe it's the coke," Michael says, a hint of the South in that *mybee*.

"I'm flying," I say. "Don't worry about me."

Michael commands Derek, "Fuck my face." I go back to the living room to snort a third and a fourth line off of Grace Jones, and then come back to watch my lover top this handsome white boy. They are spectacular together, pure fireworks, moving through different positions while Michael narrates porn-style: *oh, yeah, give it to me, I need it, harder, oh yeah, fuuuck yeah*. Derek pulls out, peels off the condom and aims, while Michael unloads onto his own hairless belly, then scoops it all up into his mouth. I'm at their side, encouraging them but not physically in it.

We shower together, soaping each other up and jockeying for warmth under the nozzle. I can see by the way that Derek lingers over Michael—who was lithe and muscular in a way that I've never been—that he's smitten. Michael is built like a teenage gymnast, firm in all the right places. His voice has that trace of a Southern lilt slipping in and out. I tease him about it, saying I could imagine him in a tailcoat with a debutante on his arm, making his parents proud.

"If my parents spoke to me," he says. "Which they don't, not since they found out I was positive."

Hearing this isn't a shock anymore, but my mind recalibrates what I know about him—the banking job offset by the volunteer work, the delight he takes in his piggy sexuality, the cum he lapped up greedily, something I don't allow myself, not with strangers. "That sucks," I say.

"Oh, they're praying for me. It's cheaper than giving me an allowance." He says that they supported him through music school—he'd been training to be a classical pianist—but after he came out, they cut him off. "Luckily I have a head for business," he says. "I'll be OK."

We invite Michael to stay over. He asks if he can play us something before bed, and he pulls a cassette tape out of a Walkman in his coat pocket. I'm expecting perhaps his own piano playing, but he says it's a "meditation."

"What kind of meditation?" I ask.

"Louise Hay. She's a healer."

"New Age?"

"She doesn't use that term. She's inspirational. She's able to get people to fight disease through the mind."

"Oh, boy," I say. Derek shoots me a look. I add, more politely, "Probably not my style."

"Give it a listen." Michael presses play and climbs into bed between us. "These affirmations have been so helpful to me."

The sound begins, an airy woodwind-and-piano melody with a

whooshing behind it like the surf. Then a deep, mellifluous female voice enters, expanding like gas to fill the room:

"You are whole. You are complete. You are filled with love. Let the love flow out from your heart. Let it surround you. Accept the love back inside. Feel it enter your arms. Love your arms. Feel it enter your legs. Love your legs. Feel it move toward the center of your body. Feel it enter your glands. Love your glands. Your glands are not swollen. Your glands are perfect. They are filled with love. That love is God. God is not diseased. God is you, and you are love, and love is perfect. Say it out loud: I am perfect."

"I Am Perfect," Michael intones, startling me. "I know it sounds corny, but it's important to *believe*."

"I think," I say, trying to be delicate, "that your glands are swollen because your body is fighting infection, so if you imagine them *not* swollen—"

"But that's so literal."

"*Glands* is a funny word," Derek says lightly. "Don't you think? Glands, glands, glands."

"You're silly," Michael says.

I wonder, what if I brought this tape to my mother's hospital room? She couldn't say "I am perfect," because she can't speak with that tube down her throat. Would she write the words on her pad instead? And is this any different than the prayers to God that my father surely utters, or the wishes I involuntarily cast out to the ether—*Please make her better*—wishes delivered to no named entity but nonetheless beseeching and hopeful? Still, the voice lingers in my ears, Michael's dubious guru insisting that I love myself. Her message is a drug insinuating itself into my system, promising something better. I want to believe that affirmations can outsmart the natural force of the body and its million mechanisms. I want to believe, but I don't.

They fall asleep, but I'm too wired, so I get up and go to the living room, where I blow cigarette smoke out the window and stare at the new apartment tower that's gone up on the other side of Houston Street. Rows of windows flash with light, or shine blackly, or tease with passing silhouettes. I begin assembling biographies—who in that building is also wracked with insomnia, or worried about money, or stuck with bad luck; who is weeping over a broken heart; who is numb from booze or painkillers, in front of a blinking, narcotic TV? Is someone readying for an after-hours club? Is someone cramming for an important meeting? Does someone over there also have a mother with cancer, a friend with AIDS? Streetlight coats my skin with a blueness that seems the exact color of the cocaine high. But "high" is the wrong word. I'm buzzing with alertness, but it's covering desperation: We heard back from that oncologist at Sloan Kettering. He suggested varying the course of chemo—a step, not a breakthrough.

In the past week, I went ahead and bought a juicer. I intend to juice vegetables this weekend, practice for when Mom gets off the respirator and can swallow again. So now, in my coke-fueled insomnia, I leap up, get dressed, and leave the apartment. I walk to the all-night Korean market on Avenue A, fill a bag with cabbage, melon, spinach, parsley and oranges, plus a pack of Marlboros. Back home, I put the produce in the fridge, bag and all, and then go back to the window and smoke cigarettes, those cancer sticks, until dawn.

Martyrs

I wake to a phone ringing in the next room, and I hear Derek answer, his voice bleeding through the walls. I've fallen asleep on the couch. On the coffee table is a full ashtray, butts broken and acrid, and that little baggie of coke, resting where Michael left it, not empty. Suddenly Derek is in front of me, clutching the cordless like a ritualistic talking stick. "That was Nicholas on the phone," he says. "Chris killed himself."

I'm not quite alert yet. "Chris—?"

"Nicholas got a call from Eliot, who heard from Mike, who found him."

"Christopher?" Tiger eyes, tight shirt, *PaulNDerek from New Jersey.*

"I can't believe it," Derek says.

From behind him, Michael appears. "I have some experience with this. I volunteer at the suicide prevention hotline."

"Prevention seems beyond the point," I say. Michael smiles patiently, as if I'm the one who has missed the point. What do I know of suicide? There was a girl in my high school who supposedly left a bitter note, the subject of endless speculation and gossip. There was a guy who jumped off the roof of my college dorm, who everyone said was troubled. But Christopher?

I ask Derek, "How did he—"

"I don't have the grisly details."

Michael crouches to couch-level and puts a hand on my leg. "Suicide is kind of a virus. It's good to keep a watch over those who were close to the deceased, who often feel despair after the shock wears off and might be susceptible to the same idea." He holds my gaze, his face grave.

"I'm not suicidal," I say.

"I didn't necessarily mean you."

I look at Derek and question, "Mike? He doesn't strike me as…"

"Neither did Christopher." Derek looks completely stunned. "I saw him just a couple days ago. We were working on a press release—"

"People are set off by all kinds of things," Michael says. He leans in to peck me on the cheek, and says to keep the coke. Derek walks him to the door. From the couch I watch them whispering, then falling into a lengthy hug, then locking lips, until Michael finally leaves.

We go to Nicholas's place on Second Street, just a couple blocks from us. He's been awake since the call came at dawn and seems sort of liquid and numb when we arrive. He brandishes a coffee pot in one hand and a joint in the other. "Options, darlin's," he says.

His apartment, like Amanda's, has a freestanding bathtub in the kitchen, the first thing you see when you enter. Beyond that, the space opens up railroad style, one tiny room onto another. The walls are hung with the amateur, anonymous paintings he buys from flea markets and the blankets of East Village peddlers—flowers, sailboats, strong women, dandified men— some of them quite detailed and accomplished, others naively charming. We sit on mismatched, broken-in armchairs while he tells us stories.

He met Christopher the night Larry Kramer first spoke at the community center. He met Eliot and Mike and Floyd that night, too. They were among the people who gathered a week later and kicked all of it off— just four months before Derek and I got involved, but in the life of ACT UP, a previous wave, the founders' generation. They were so different from each other—Mike a chorus boy, Eliot an assistant at a TV network, Floyd a stylist, Christopher a bartender, Nicholas a taxi driver—but their shared urgency and outrage was enough for them and a handful of other men and women to build the infrastructure out of nothing.

Nicholas tells us how early on, they went away for a weekend retreat to bang out a plan for running meetings, making decisions, all that procedural stuff we now took for granted. "It was Christopher who insisted on Robert's Rules of Order," Nicholas says. "He'd been studying political organizing. The idea of a coordinating committee was his, and decisions by majority vote. I'm a hippie from Virginia; before ACT UP, I hadn't organized anything bigger than my drug stash. He was Chris when we met, but he felt so reinvented by ACT UP that he asked us to call him Christopher."

"That's how we knew him," I say.

"But we *didn't* know him," Derek says. "We just looked up to him. I was just with him, and the idea that he could have been on the verge of this—"

"To him we were still Paul and Derek from New Jersey."

"And I'm not from New Jersey!" Derek says, his familiar protest now tinged with tragedy instead of irony. *Were* we known to Christopher? He made such an impression on us: the thick blond hair in its militaristic cut, those exotically colored eyes, that body. I'd never seen him wear anything but a tight t-shirt, a thick leather belt holding up snug denim, and black leather boots with laces up the front, like a biker. His street fashion had been adopted by a lot of the younger guys in ACT UP, Zack and Raymond among them. Christopher's look had become the unofficial ACT UP uniform.

And now he's gone.

A memorial service happens a few weeks later in a side room at the community center, thirty or forty of us in attendance, standing up one at a time to tell a story. Eliot leads things off, because it turns out he's known Christopher the longest. I didn't know they went back to before ACT UP. (The cosmic irony of memorial services: learning new things about your friend's life at the very moment you mark its end.)

Eliot is speaking with a strange affect, a kind of dramatic stage whisper, as if he's putting on a performance, not emceeing as much as playing the role of emcee. He tells us he met Christopher at City College in a political science class, both of them making up units to get their undergrad degrees. He says they were "the two big queens in the room, trading references to Emma Goldman and Thelma Ritter." This gets a laugh, but I see something else in Eliot's tense, dark eyes: bewilderment. "We became friends," he says. "It seemed unlikely to me. I'd never been friends with anyone who looked like him. But we had more in common than you'd think. For example we'd both turned tricks, though you can imagine he made a lot more money than I did." More laughs. "He hadn't had any opportunities in life, except the ones you get when you look like that. And that was a burden, too, the kind of attention he attracted. I'd see it at our actions. He was so coiled up with energy, I was terrified he'd be pounced on by policemen who'd mark him as a prize to bag, a trophy kill. Well. He was not a trophy to me. He was someone I loved." No one's laughing now.

I remember how at my first Gay Pride, I saw Eliot look askance at Christopher and Mike's public affection; I understand now how complicated his feelings were. Eliot loved Christopher, differently, I think, than Christopher loved him. Christopher chose someone else as his beloved—Mike, who was a lot like him: the fit bodies, the undeniably handsome faces. Together they were pepper and salt, Mike's Greek swarthiness to Christopher's Adonis gold—the couple everyone envied. But here's Mike now, talking about how hard it was to love Christopher. "He said we had to keep separate apartments, even though I owned mine, which was bigger and had good views, while he lived in a dark studio on a shitty block in Chelsea." Mike tells us about dealing with Christopher's family, who showed up to clear out his belongings, addressing Mike with a Midwestern, "Thanks for everything but we'll take it from here." He tells us how he and Eliot scrambled behind the parents as they cleared a path through the apartment, how they'd rescued Christopher's AIDS research from the garbage bags his parents were stuffing with belongings. The family took the corpse back to Missouri for a Christian funeral, which Mike attended, though he was denied a chance to speak. "There was a lot of talk of the wayward son returning to the Lord," Mike says. "Very few people shook my hand."

Nicholas stands next, gathering his long limbs together before speaking. I expect he'll retell the stories of Christopher's early contributions to ACT UP, but what he says is, "I'm furious with him. If Chris wanted to die, why didn't he strap on a bomb and walk into the Oval Office? Why didn't he walk up to Senator Jesse Helms and shake hands with that bigot and blow them both away?"

Yeah, *why?* If the point of our world was to stay alive, what did it mean that one of us ended his life? I'd always seen Christopher as a warrior—like Mike, like Floyd, like all of our angriest, most vocal activists. How was it possible that even our bravest might not be strong enough to overcome hatred, to say nothing of this incurable virus?

I find myself clenching and unclenching my fists.

On our poster, the one plastered all over the city, the one I've held over my head at demos, Silence=Death sits atop the words Turn your Anger into Action. We all know what to do with our anger toward the government, the medical establishment, the media. But what if you're consumed by anger about your own state of being? How do you protest that?

Eliot announces there's time for a couple more, so I make myself stand. I say, "I just want to share a memory," and talk about being with Christopher on Fire Island, at Mike's, and the moment when Christopher commanded me to throw my hands in the air and dance, saying that Derek and I were the hope for the future. "Did he run out of hope? Did we fail him? Were we supposed to do more?" I ask. Then I have to stop, because my mouth has gone dry.

The room seems very quiet, until Mike answers me: "No."

I look at his grave face and decide to sit. "Look," he says, standing again, "HIV has messed with our lives. I never got another major role, and Christopher gave up his plans to get a degree so he could do activism all the time. But it also revived our lives, because we met, we fell in love, we got to know all of you. The fucking virus and the fucking bigotry it's spawned are what me and Christopher had in common, and we vowed to fight it to the end. And he did, he fought it to the end. Don't let his death tell you otherwise." His voice is so strong, his passion can't be ignored. It sets fire to us all. I feel it like a dare: *never* give up hope, never give up the fight.

We walk out into the street as a group, heading for a restaurant. As we cross an intersection, someone lifts a photo of Christopher in the air and a few others start chanting *How many more have to die,* stopping traffic, but just for a moment. I walk alongside Raymond, whom I've hardly talked with since my birthday, when he and Zack fought. "This is like a political funeral," he says of our impromptu procession, and he mentions Latin America, Oscar Romero in El Salvador, the mothers of the disappeared in Argentina— remarks I'll remember years later, when people start talking about political funerals for real, when we run out of all other options.

But in the moment I wonder: *is* Christopher's suicide political? Everyone spoke of him as if he was beaten down by the homophobic world. Now we're chanting as if he's died of AIDS rather than from a fistful of pills and a plastic bag over his head. When people die in ACT UP, we cast them in a heroic light, which confers nobility, even immortality: they are martyrs in an ongoing battle, speaking truth to power, condemned to die by an indifferent system. But what if death isn't a matter of politics? What if death is just death? What do we do with that?

**Note to Self #7: You went to a lot
of memorial services.**

There was the one in the Quaker Meeting Hall
off Gramercy Park, most of the men in suits and
the women in skirts, a large family in attendance.
People spoke when the spirit moved them. The
whole thing felt refined and well produced. On
the way out, we were all given a mixtape of his
favorite songs.

There was the one in the loft, half the people sitting on the floor, a joint being passed, the whole thing an animated political conversation. The deceased was a defiant chain-smoker and people were invited to light up. The air got so hazy that people started to cough and then leave, and we never quite regrouped. I stayed until the end and woke up with a nicotine hangover.

There was the one in The Bar at three in the afternoon, daylight streaming through the window, showing the dinge we never saw at night. There was no official "program." People got drunk in small groups. At four thirty, the lights were dimmed and the bar opened to the regulars. A group of us stepped outside. We wanted to keep drinking, but not there, like it was just any other night.

There was one in the nightclub in the meatpacking district. A DJ spun while we all stood on the dance floor watching video clips of recent demonstrations, edited for the occasion and projected onto a wall of flaking paint, giving the images a mottled texture, like something found in an archive.

There was one in Tompkins Square Park that turned into a political funeral, the body of my dead friend carried through the East Village streets. I'll get to that one. I will, though I'm dreading it.

Turn Your Anger into Action

Summer in the city. So hot and sticky. Everyone a little turned up, prickly. Derek comes home from work in a terrible mood. The honeymoon at his new job is over. Yes, they're raising money to help lift people out of poverty, but the donors are all society types and the sycophants who suck up to them. He names a famous socialite on their board whose husband is a bigwig Republican Party supporter. "She signed up Al D'Amato as the honorary chair of our next event," Derek says, slapping his forehead, incredulous.

D'Amato, senator from New York, has spent the summer aligning himself with arch-conservative Jesse Helms against the National Endowment for the Arts. They've proposed an amendment that prohibits the NEA from funding "obscene" and "blasphemous" art. I've been starting to cook something for dinner—on a rare night when we're both home—but when I ask him to help me by grabbing a pan out of the cupboard, he fumbles it, causing a big clattering of pots and pans that gets noisier as he tries to shove everything back in place. "Never mind, I'll get it," I say.

Derek shuffles off into the bedroom. The phone rings, and the machine picks up. It's his mother. *Don't talk to her while you're in this mood,* I think, but soon he's circling the apartment with the cordless, complaining about the job, telling Marilyn how he won't work in this environment, with these soulless people. "When I talk to my administrators about AIDS," Derek says, "all they can handle are *innocent* babies born with it. Not the mothers who are infected and need treatment. And gay men, or junkies who shoot up? No, no. Too controversial." She should just let him vent—but of course she has to convince him why he needs to suck it up and hold onto this job—and he should just take her with a grain of salt but instead he accuses her of not supporting him, *never* supporting him, and then it's not about the job but about their dynamic, that lifelong conflict, and soon he's shouting, "Don't call me again," and the phone is flying across the room. I brace for an impact, but it hits the couch, force absorbed with a dull thud.

"Maybe we should go out to dinner," I say.

An hour later we're with Michael, our cocaine-and-affirmations fuckbuddy. I don't know if he called Derek or Derek called him, but now he's joining us for dinner. Since Michael volunteers where Derek works, he makes for a good sounding board. He knows the players. He keeps telling Derek to *visualize change* before he can expect change to happen. "That's true for your boss *and* your mama," Michael says. "Right, Paul?" He pronounces my name "pol," not "pawl," and he keeps trying to include me, though I'm sort of checked out. There's a connection between Michael and Derek that I'm outside of. I even tried to say that to Derek: you go without me, but that just made him feel guilty, since this was our dinner night. "Let's stick together," he says, so I roll with this new plan.

The restaurant on 9th Street falls somewhere between fancy and dive, with a backyard patio draped in twinkling lights and a menu that offers roast chicken and T-bone steak, but the staff is surly, the table wobbles and the "ice water" is tepid. The waitress wordlessly drops three menus on our table and vanishes, refusing eye contact with us as we wait, and wait, and wait to place an order, our hunger exaggerated the longer we're ignored. The place is full, so at first we put up with the slowness, making jokes about how we're *visualizing* the waitress returning to our table, *visualizing* her carrying roast chicken to us, and then, after Derek approaches her directly to ask her to take our order, only to be told to "Return to your seat, I'll get to you," *visualizing* terrible things happening to her. After a while we're just perplexed; it seems like more than just the usual busy-restaurant wait. Even unflappable Michael wonders aloud if maybe, for some reason, we're not wanted here. But why? Are we too loud, too young, too cheap-looking? Too gay?

"Fuck this," Derek says, and pushes back from the table. Michael and I get up and follow. Derek storms from the patio back inside, toward the door to the street. And then I see him pause at the waiter's station, where there's a tray full of salads, each plate piled in greens drizzled with orange dressing. I watch Derek slip his fingers under the edge of the tray and flip up, sending the salads sliding to the floor. A busboy nearby, a young Puerto Rican guy, reacts with a shout, but we're already out the door to the sidewalk. The busboy yells "Stop!", and in that pause, Derek turns back to the restaurant, lifts his leg and kicks.

I watch his boot make contact with the restaurant's plateglass window.

It's true, isn't it, that moments of sudden, jarring action can slow everything down, isolating each image, each sound? And so it is now. I see the glass resist, I see it buckle, I see fractures scurry outward in hairline trails, and then I see it burst, surface shattered, a vacuum of air in its place, the musical chiming of shards cascading into the restaurant and onto the sidewalk. I've only heard that sound once before, at the FDA, when demonstrators stampeded the front door. But that had been epic, monumental, a revolutionary roar. This is different. This is Derek kicking in a plate glass window.

I see: Derek's dawning awareness at what he's done, Michael's wide-eyed disbelief, and then our waitress framed by the empty window, screaming, "I'LL FUCKING KILL YOU."

One of us yells "RUN!" and so we run; I'm in the lead but Michael goes whipping past, roadrunner style. Derek is at my side, I can hear him swearing. I look back and the waitress is shouting, "Stop them!" The busboy clutches the metal hook that lowers the gate that covers the destroyed window.

Michael is at the corner, opening the door to a cab that's miraculously there. Then we're all in the back seat, shouting, "Drive, just drive!"

It turns out New York cabbies will actually do that. The driver hits the gas, swerves into traffic and speeds uptown. Through the rear window the waitress and busboy stand at the corner, helplessly pointing. We tell the guy to take the FDR Drive uptown, to keep driving, we'll figure out where we're going. He doesn't ask for more. If anything, he seems to be enjoying this.

I turn to Derek, trying to form a question.

"I just wanted to hurt the restaurant," he says. "I didn't think it would *break*."

Michael says, "But the salads—" and then gets quiet. After 59th Street he tells the driver to exit the FDR and drop him at Second Avenue. "I'll walk home from here," he says, while we idle at the curb.

Derek says, "Call me?"

Michael says, "You two try and take care, okay?" Then he's gone.

We keep the cabbie driving for a long time, up to Harlem, practically to the Bronx, before we say it's okay, he can head back downtown now, to the West, not the East Village. I watch the meter rise. By the time we're done, it'll cost as much as dinner for two. Meanwhile, I'm still hungry.

"Maybe you should have cooked," Derek says.

...

Later we recount the episode to Nicholas and Amanda, framing it as you'll-never-believe-this to their shocked faces. "That's a lot of testosterone," Amanda says.

"This is not what ACT UP means by turning your anger into action," Nicholas drawls. "You ever think of therapy?"

"With what money?" Derek says. He went to a therapist as a teenager, after his parents' divorce, a process he now calls traumatizing. As for me, therapy is an alien concept. Therapy is for crazy people. Sure, maybe what Derek did was crazy, but he doesn't need a therapist to tell him that.

In the days that follow, I catch myself secretly admiring him for kicking in that window. I want to break things all the time. He actually did it. But when I voice this to him, he blows up. "It was the dumbest shit I've ever done! I could have hurt someone, I could have been arrested. Don't encourage this side of me."

After that, he begins to withdraw. He quits his job, stops going to ACT UP meetings. I come home from work and find him in his underwear, phone pressed to his ear, talking to one of his old friends, his pre-activism friends, the actors and musicians he used to go to clubs with. Some of them are now making names for themselves. He tells me he wants to get back into "the arts," where he originally thought he'd end up, but then one night he goes out with his old crew and comes home in a deeper funk than before. "They're so superficial," he says. "They go out to dinner with their personal assistants but make them eat at a separate table."

One afternoon he appears with a new, above-the-ears haircut, carrying department store shopping bags filled with button-down Oxford shirts and pleated chinos, brown leather belts and loafers. One of those old friends, it turns out, has a contact at an ad agency. "They're looking for creative," Derek says.

"Creative what?"

"That's the department. The people who come up with the ads. Though I think I'd be better at accounts, they're the ones who do all the schmoozing."

"You can sweet-talk anyone," I say encouragingly, but I complain to Amanda, "Can you imagine Derek in the land of the gray suits?"

"We all need better paying jobs," she says, "but come on, be realistic."

"It's like he's giving himself a personality transplant. He's trying to sand off all his sharp edges."

His first agency interview leaves him seething. "They were so fucking condescending. This guy flicking his finger at my resume, saying, 'I'm not *familiar* with the college you attended.'" At a second interview he is offered an unpaid internship to see if he's a good fit. "They actually asked if I was a team player," he says. "I told them, 'Depends what team you play on.' I laughed at this, but apparently no one in the room found it funny. I got one of those pressed-lip smiles, *We'll be in touch*, so, yeah, no. Fuck your internship."

Weeks pass uneasily. Derek reads *The New York Times* in a rage, slapping the paper and complaining about their AIDS coverage. He crumples unpaid bills into wads which he tosses at the garbage. If he misses, they lie on the floor until I get tired of looking at them.

It's time to call in the big guns.

I invite Floyd over. "Put on some pants, Derek," he says upon entering. "And someone fix me a drink." I mix a grasshopper. He lights a cigarette, drops into a chair and lounges. "Now child, tell me why I have not seen you around the Monday night meetings."

"It's obvious I need a break from ACT UP," Derek says. "That whole scene has made me crazy. It makes all of us crazy. Look at Christopher."

"You seem pretty crazy without it," Floyd says, and when Derek tries to speak, Floyd lifts a finger into the air, meant to shush. "Child, do you have any idea how many well-connected queens are in that room? Who already know how hard you work? Who might have a job lead for you?"

"I can't use ACT UP as an employment agency."

"Good Lord, do I have to knock this into you?" Derek looks confused. Floyd says, "You don't run from your people at times of stress. You *lean* on them."

So Derek rewrites his resume, listing ACT UP Media Committee under his experience, and carries copies in a folder to the next meeting. Of course everyone is happy to see him, relieved and wondering where he's been. You don't just disappear in ACT UP without creating worry.

Within a week he has a new job in the public relations department of AmFar, the big AIDS research foundation.

He keeps the button-down shirts, maintains the haircut, but returns the pleated pants and loafers. Now he works late nearly every day, but he comes home energetic, not frustrated. After he banks his first paycheck, he tells me he's made an appointment with a therapist.

Part 5

Fingerprints

I wake from an agitated dream, sticky with sweat, disoriented by the sense that I was supposed to *do* something. But what? I call my father, who has no news from the ICU. I call Derek, already at work and too busy to talk. My sheets are damp—why do I keep waking up in a sweat? I call Dr. Leone, whom Eliot recommended after my jaw injury, and ask if I should be worried about night sweats. They're a sign of a compromised immune system, right?

"Is it very hot in your bedroom? (Yeah, it's stuffy.) How many blankets are on your bed? (A couple.) How much did you have to drink the night before? (Four or five beers at The Bar.) You might want to look at that," he concludes, which is annoying. Five beers is something to look at? When I say that I've just had an HIV test, he says, "Get another one in six months."

I get a surprise call from my sister, Lisa, who is in the city for a job interview at a clothing company. We meet up at a Tribeca bar that I've been to once with Derek. Most of the bars I hang out in are total gay dives, no place for my suburban sister, but this one shines with chrome and marble. We pound a couple of vodka martinis each. She wants my advice about college. She's only weeks away from graduation, but since Mom's diagnosis, she's spent more time in the hospital than on campus. She's thinking about withdrawing before finals, though Dad tells her she has to finish. "Your mother would want that," he's insisted, and I tell her I think he's probably right. Our mother got a nursing certification when she was young, but didn't finish her bachelor's degree until her thirties. When she looks in the rearview mirror, she sees a missed opportunity.

But Lisa's distraught. "I can't concentrate. I'm afraid I'll fail my finals. You can't make them up if you fail, you know?"

"So you'd retake your classes next semester?"

"Yeah, after Mom gets better."

I try to absorb *better*, not sure if Lisa believes this is or is just willing it to be true. "Assuming the chemo works," I say, "and she goes into remission—"

"—then we'll all breathe a little easier."

"No pun intended."

"Ugh. Really?"

"Sorry. Couldn't resist."

She wants to get dinner, but I'm facilitating at ACT UP. "Do you have to go?" she asks.

"You could come."

"I don't think it's for me, but you know I support your cause."

"It's not a *cause*. My friends are dying."

She falls silent. My words sound like a rebuke.

"You should come to a meeting some time," I try, more softly.

"I'd rather just be with Mom, you know?"

Now I feel rebuked. I've been going to the hospital less frequently, sitting at her bedside, searching her eyes above the ventilator's mask for signs of life. On the not-terrible days, the sparks are there. We catch her up on our lives while she writes short phrases on her pad. We grab at what the doctors dangle before us: *vital signs stable, chemo proceeding on course*. There was no *cause* attached to my mother's illness, no committee to join, no target for protest. It had no shape, and I felt so useless. I'm worse than useless, really, because my sister has reached out and I've failed to feel her pain, which is a failure to admit my own: these terrible emotions I'm too scared to voice.

Cardinal O'Connor is quoted in the *Times* referring to "the immorality of condoms." At our next Monday night meeting, Gilberto holds up a fact sheet with statistics: how many New Yorkers are sick, how many are dead, how many women are HIV-positive. In big letters:

**WE DEMAND THE CATHOLIC CHURCH
RETRACT O'CONNOR'S STATEMENTS
AND ADMIT THAT CONDOMS SAVE LIVES.**

That such a retraction is unlikely doesn't matter. The very unlikelihood of the demand gives us purpose. Our response will be a march that night as soon as the meeting ends.

From the floor an objection is raised: the fact sheet doesn't say anything about abortion. And why is there no mention of needle exchange? Gilberto responds that since this is not a full-fledged action, but a zap meant as a quick response, the focus is designed to be narrow. Leo says that the media committee has already tipped off its contacts. It's a slow news night. We'll probably get live coverage. He adds that he'll include reproductive rights and needle exchange in our talking points.

"This one's a no-brainer, people," I say from the front of the room, where I'm facilitating. "What else are you gonna do—go home and watch the rest of us on the news? Come on. Who's joining me?" Hands fly into the air. Facilitators usually stay cool in a room that runs hot, but tonight I'm all adrenaline.

Through the crowd, I see Zack, beaming approval. When the meeting ends, he finds me and says, "Nice hat." I'm wearing the Yankees cap he gave me, its white, stitched NY logo still shiny, where his is worn and dingy.

"I never got to thank you for it. You've been scarce."

"It's the Raymond thing. That was bad."

I nod. "I wanted to ask you—that night, my birthday, you saw me and Raymond kissing, and then—"

"There was a lot going on that night."

"You mean it wasn't all about *me*?" That makes him laugh.

We leave the community center and pour onto Seventh Avenue, an orchestra of car horns blaring behind us. Normally I prefer larger actions, where everything is worked out in advance, and anyone planning to be arrested has been trained. Zaps never have enough marshals or designated legal observers. When things go wrong, they can go very wrong. But tonight I don't care. I'm among those leading one chant, *"Hey hey, ho ho, Cardinal O'Connor's got to go,"* into another, *"They say don't fuck, we say fuck you."* Our voices echo like rolling thunder.

We move onto Christopher's Street, toward the river, the gayest part of downtown, where the archdiocese still maintains an office. It's next to an old stone church that's fronted by a wrought iron fence, about six feet high.

The police show up soon enough, but they hang back at first, taking the temperature. It's that crucial moment when the demonstration can go in any direction: organize into order or splinter into chaos.

Near me, I hear voices starting up a new chant: *"Take the fence, take the fence."* Moving fast enough, a person could be over the fence and onto the steps of the church before the police could do anything about it.

Then I think: not *a person*. Me.

I turn to Zack. "I'm going over," I say. "Come with me." I slide to the front, grip the iron bars and begin to hoist myself up. Hands beneath me, not just Zack's but others', lift me higher, as I claw my way over the top—but my grasp is loose and as I tumble to the other side I feel a sharp, iron tip rip into the palm of my hand—*OW!* A cheer swells up from the street as I land on the steps. Now Zack is coming over the fence, too, and Gilberto, and then another guy whose name I don't know, and then two women—one of them is Hillary, Amanda's friend who helped me at the NYU library, and the second is someone new. The six of us raise our arms triumphantly.

Men in blue start moving in from the periphery. The crowd boos them, a bass vibration intermingling with the cheers and the chants.

Through the iron bars, people hand us fact sheets. We carry them up the steps. "Does anyone have tape?" Gilberto asks. Hillary rummages through her knapsack, produces a box of thumbtacks. We pin a grid of leaflets to the wooden doors of the church. The din behind us gathers into a roar: "*ACT UP FIGHT BACK FIGHT AIDS—*"

And then the cops are also scaling the fence, swift and agile—they must be the most in-shape cops in Manhattan. They've removed their badges. They're not fucking around. One of them pushes me against the papered-over doors, face-first, a white flash of pain erupting from my jaw. He yanks back my arms. I feel the snap of plastic cuffs. My hand is throbbing where the skin is torn. Next to me Zack is cuffed, then Hillary and the other woman. Gilberto is shouting at a cop, then he's suddenly doubled over, wincing, his dark hair flopping into his eyes. He's been clubbed in the ribs with a nightstick. He gasps, on his knees, while the cop cuffs him, too. The crowd cries, "*Shame, Shame, Shame!*"

A voice announces we're under arrest, but there's nowhere to go. We're closed in. On the other side, Leo is leading a news camera and reporter through to the fence. The reporter shouts questions, but the cops block him from us. I turn my head and find Zack, who offers a silent nod.

At last a wizened elder from the church is escorted through the crowd by police. He unlocks the gate. Now the cops push us out, guiding us roughly to a waiting police van. "Where are you taking us?" I ask, but no one answers. From every side, voices demand, "*Show us your badges*" and "*Let them go.*"

Eight of us, cuffed, are thrown into the windowless van: the six who climbed the fence and two more nabbed from the crowd. Gilberto shouts that he's in pain, they bruised his ribs. "*Shame,*" we shout, out of sync with the chanting outside. The van door is slammed, and our voices reverberate in sudden dark. I hear the whoosh of tires as the vehicle creeps away. Will they put us through central booking? That would mean a night in The Tombs, where arrestees from all over the city are held. Will they separate the women, or hold us as a unit? I start to worry that there might be real charges, that the church could make a point of keeping us in the system, which would mean bail. Has ACT UP ever bailed anyone out? Will we be allowed phone calls? I could call Derek, who worked late today and didn't come to the zap. The only person I know who could cough up money is my father, but I won't call him, not now, when he's very likely at the hospital.

Zack sits next to me, his face readably euphoric. "That was incredible," he says. "I wish we could see it on the news."

"Here we are again," I say, thinking of Albany, wanting to reach out and take his hand but the cuffs prevent it.

When the van stops and the doors open up, the first thing I see are the lights of the Brooklyn Bridge above us. We've been taken to a precinct tucked at the edge of the Lower East Side. Police lead Hillary and Shanna to one cell and put us six guys in another, where a couple of very down-and-out men sprawl on the benches. One of them stirs long enough to say, "Shut up, I'm sleeping." We're firing questions at the police, who ignore us and disappear for a long while.

I'm thirsty and I have to pee. My hand is streaked with dried blood, the gash glistening red. Gilberto lifts his shirt and shows us the impact of the nightstick, skin blooming into a wide, discolored bruise.

There's no buoyancy among us, no sibilant sissified joking. The cell feels colder and drearier the longer we're there, and we sit with arms and legs entwined to keep warm. Gilberto repeatedly calls out, "I need medical attention," until one of the men on the bench, dressed in rags and scabbed across his skin, shouts, "You're not the only one, faggot." Gilberto gets in the guy's face, while some of us try to ease him away, until a cop appears like a stock character from an old movie commanding, "Break it up, break it up."

We're marched out at last, joined by the women, and by Jocelyn, in t-shirt and jeans, roused from home late at night for legal help. We're being charged with two counts of trespassing, plus resisting arrest for Gilberto, a cruel irony since he's the battered one. The police want to fingerprint us; if we refuse, we'll be kept in the system. We huddle to discuss. Zack says, "Who cares if they fingerprint us?" and I answer, "They'll send it to the FBI," and Hillary, in an unwavering voice, says, "I assume I already have a file." Gilberto says: "I want to go to the emergency room," which one of the officers picks up on, answering, "If anyone-a-ya refuses, you all stay"—a coercion that Jocelyn protests is illegal but which, sadly, works. I've never been processed before. I watch the ink stain my fingertips as I make a set of marks next to my name.

Our fact sheets were tacked to the church doors only long enough to be cheered and photographed. Was it worth it? It had to be. It was bigger than me, bigger than any one of us or any single action. You throw your little stone, the pond ripples; if you throw enough, you alter the shape of the shoreline.

And yet those ten black smudges on the white page felt personal. How can I explain it? I saw in them the endpoint to my day—the visible outcome of the sticky agitation I felt when I woke, the tension with my sister, the Cardinal's outrageous statement, the chance to take action—all of it leading to this: sunrise, exiting a police precinct with ink on my fingertips. I'd become a person for whom a day could turn out this way, and now it was official. I'd crossed a line. We cross them all the time, these delineations between who we've been and who we're becoming, but only rarely are they as clear as black on white.

In the dawn light, Hillary and Shanna flag a cab to take Gilberto to the emergency room. Jocelyn tells us she'll be in touch about our charges. As a group we share weary good-bye hugs.

And then it's just me and Zack.

A Deep Pit of Love

At first, it's not a decision I make, not a conscious one anyway. Zack says, "I'm hungry," so we walk to a diner that's already open and serving breakfast. I use their payphone to call Derek, who groggily picks up. I tell him I'm out of jail, I'm fine, I'm getting food, I'll see him later. He says he's going into work early so he might not be here when I come home. "Don't wait for me," I say, already feeling guilty for what I'm about to do.

As I return to the table, Zack studies me from beneath the brim of his cap. My body reacts, a chemical rush under my skin that catches my breath in my throat.

He lights a cigarette. "So how's the ball and chain?"

"Ball and chain? That's not very nice."

"Sorry."

"He's working a new job."

"Same here," he says. "I'm freelancing at an agency doing the campaign for a new cigarette brand called Dakota. Supposed to appeal to masculine women."

"So you're designing ads?"

"Yeah, the model is this broad-shouldered, stern-looking chick with skinny hips. But her hair is long and blonde! Can't be too butch." He looks at the cigarette in his hand. "I should quit."

I take it from him and drag, keeping my eyes on him. "Derek's going to work soon. I told him I was fine, not to worry."

"Worry?"

"When I don't come home right away."

He takes my hand and weaves his fingers through mine. "So does that mean you're coming to Brooklyn?"

"Brooklyn?" I exaggerate the horror, though in truth I'd go to the farthest

131

reaches of Staten Island just to be with him now. I lean across the table for a kiss. The brims of our caps bump; he flips mine sideways and we try again. His lips are chapped. My mouth is dry.

I say, "The last time we tried this, it didn't go so great."

He comes around to my side of the booth, pulls me close and locks his open mouth to mine, and from there we just melt together, the world around us fading to insignificance.

"Yeah, that's better," he says.

On the train, he takes my hand and walks me to the door at the end of the car. We step out onto the exposed platform, and he slides the door behind us. "Ever ridden like this before?" I shake my head no. The train picks up speed, the station lights disappear behind us, and the darkness becomes a clunking, thumping, rhythmic rush. He drops an arm over my shoulder, steadying us both as everything shakes, jangly and metallic. At the next station, the train rushes along the express track without stopping—white glare of overhead fluorescents, yellow caution stripe at the edge of the platform, people flickering like phantoms trapped in a bright box. Then—*whoosh*—darkness again. "We're going under the river," he shouts while cool air, ripe as wet dirt, envelops us. I hold onto my cap and watch Zack's face flicker in the intermittent streaking of work-lights deep in the tunnel—his eyes wide and shining, his lips parted, pure joy. The speed of the ride lodges under my skin, joins my body to it. "Let it out!" Zack shouts, and we throw back our heads and howl into the blackness until our throats go raw.

"Are you fuckin' crazy?" some guy barks at us as we reenter the train, laughing and collapsing dizzily into seats for the rest of the ride.

We emerge into a neighborhood half Caribbean Black, half Orthodox Jewish. Zack lives in a building wedged between a bagel shop and a clothing store with a Jamaican flag in the window. The intermingling aromas of garlic and ganja rise through the airshaft as we climb flights of stairs. I follow him into his dark apartment, immediately hit with the smell of oil paint. When he flicks on the lights, a cluttered room comes into view. There's a mattress on the floor, a pile of clothes spilling from shelves, and a long wall papered with pages from magazines, ACT UP flyers, art reproductions (a lot of Rauschenbergs, I think), and postcards of well-known women, most of them Black—Lena Horne, Billie Holiday, some I don't know. I see a photo of Raymond holding his camcorder. *Don't be jealous,* I warn myself. Everywhere, leaning against other surfaces, are small canvases, and near the windows that face the street stands an easel with a half-completed painting. Zack walks over and flips it face down, saying, "That one's not ready."

"You're a painter—I didn't know."

"All kinds of things you don't know," he says, "yet."

He lights a joint and passes it to me. The pot hits me hard, sleep deprived as I am, and I flop onto the mattress. Zack lies down beside me. My heart rate doubles, feeling his heat. He rolls onto his back, pulls me on top of him. I push up his arms and inhale deeply the musk buried there. Eau-de-Zack. We kiss, for a long time. Shirts come off. His lean body has more hair than I expected, tight, kinky curls in a trail up his stomach, fanning out at his chest, patches of it on his shoulders. I put my mouth on one stiff brown nipple, then the other, lapping at his skin. He moans through it all. He compliments my body but I just shake my head. My body is soft, a boy's body, nothing.

When I've imagined this, I had an idea what would happen: I wanted to be overtaken. His taut physique, his laconic attitude, the violence I'd seen with Raymond—my fantasy grew effortlessly from these impressions. But Zack has his own ideas: his mouth on my cock for a long time, then his hand full of lube as he slides a rubber on me, pushing me on my back, straddling me, guiding me in without struggle. He's so warm.

He rides me with his eyes closed, as if by not looking at me he can reveal more of himself. I haven't seen many guys in this state, giving over to getting fucked as if it's an emotional, not just physical, experience. (Derek doesn't writhe like this, on the rare occasions when I've fucked him.) I wonder if Zack will return to his more stoic self when this is over—I'm already worried about when this is over, knowing it'll never happen again, and then wondering if it might, if I could be with Zack, whatever *be with* might mean. Another fantasy: living in this messy apartment with him, waking together and fucking him in the morning before we dress for work. This vision—routine, domestic—bumps aside my earlier fantasy of domination. I'm already rewriting my understanding of him.

He shoots his cum on my belly, then reaches right away for a towel and wipes me up. I pull out, peel off the rubber and get to my knees. He's still shuddering from his orgasm while I finish myself, aiming fat splatters of jizz at him while he urges me on.

Minutes later, lying together naked as if it's the most natural thing, I ask him what went wrong with him and Raymond. "He wouldn't do that for me," he says. "He wouldn't fuck me."

"So you're only a bottom? Isn't the whole top-bottom thing kind of limited?"

"I know what I need."

"You guys broke up over sex?"

"It was more like jealousy—we brought that out in each other. Pushing each other's buttons." He looks me in the eye. "I did see him kiss you at your party. I said I was into you, and he made sure I knew he'd already had you."

"With Derek," I say.

"I don't know how you and Derek do it. Have an open relationship."

"It evolves over time—"

"It's just not romantic, you know?"

I want to say what I've figured out, that romance is sustained through effort and negotiation, but Zack flops back on the mattress and throws his arms wide, proclaiming, "I want to fall into a deep pit of love and live there."

He's never looked this vulnerable. In that moment I think: I'm not done with him. Not at all. I curl into his side.

When I open my eyes, I'm sucking in air, agitated by a dream, disoriented. Midday light blasts through uncurtained windows. There's Zack, up on one elbow, watching me, looking serious.

He says, "I should have told you this last night."

"What?"

"You're negative, right?"

I nod, waiting for him to say, "Me too," but he doesn't. The bad dream I had rushes forth: a fiery apocalypse, a wall of flames speeding toward me. I see a fountain, tall and tiered like the one in Central Park, the one with the angel. I jump in, thinking *I'll hold my breath underwater until the fire passes.*

He gets up and goes to the canvas he turned over the night before. He looks at it, shaking his head. I catch a glimpse: city buildings, some crumbling, one with figures in the windows. His style is illustrative, flat, blocks of color outlined.

Uncertain, I say, "Zack?"

He looks at me and says, "I tested positive six months ago. I had a month of a flu thing and then a month of recovery and then three months of getting healthy and getting my strength back, working out, juicing, eating right. I even stopped smoking for a while."

I feel myself dropping, not into a dark abyss but into a bright glare, the fluorescent glow of a hospital room.

He says, "I should have warned you."

I shake my head. "We were safe."

"I'm talking more an emotional warning."

And I know exactly what he means.

I wish it were last night again, not now, not this.

But I wave him back to the bed. "Come here."

He approaches carefully. "I feel like I tricked you into fucking me."

"Yeah, well," I say, "we've established that you're an insubordinate bottom."

His mouth falls open, and then he laughs. "Yeah, well," he mimics with a comic growl, "fuck me again."

We make out for a while, our hands all over each other, but I stop before it goes too far. "I need to get home," I say. I don't say, *to Derek*. I don't say, *I need to figure out what to do with what you've just told me.*

As I dress, he goes back to the easel, sits in front of it, studies the canvas. I want to ask him about it, but he speaks first, saying, "You'll come over again soon." It isn't a question.

Everything I know about him warns *no*: the intensity of his failed relationship with Raymond, the fact that I lied to Derek to be here, Zack's HIV status, which inevitably means illness. My mind zooms to my mother in her hospital bed. *No.* But I've never wanted anyone so badly, so I say yes.

On the street, West Indian women in colorful head scarves pull grocery carts behind them, stopping mid-block to gossip and laugh with each other. Hasidim park their cars half on the curb, charging out amid rapid-fire conversations. As I walk down the sidewalk in last night's clothes, I wonder what I look like to anyone else. I'm not "Paul from New Jersey" anymore. I'm the guy who's been arrested multiple times, whose mother has cancer, whose friends are infected with a deadly virus; the guy who's coming back here soon to spend more time with this new lover, who's just revealed the worst thing possible. I am the guy the world keeps coming at with more and more shit, the guy who's going to learn how to handle it.

Staying Behind

Note to Self #8: Summer of '89.

I think, maybe, in the history of ACT UP—
not this refracted personal story but the
documented accounting of names, dates,
medical breakthroughs—that the summer of
'89 should be spoken of as a peak, because of
the International AIDS Conference in Montreal.
Amid a gathering of the world's researchers,
clinicians and policy wonks—the very week
democracy protestors were being massacred
in Tiananmen Square—ACT UP took over the
stage at the opening session, demanding, and
getting, a place at the global table for patients
and activists. Going forward, scientists would
increasingly make decisions in accord with the
people affected by the virus. Amanda, Rochelle,
and Hillary were there, insisting that women
with AIDS be enrolled in clinical trials of new
treatments. Gilberto and the Majority Actions
committee were there, calling out racism in
research, pushing for inclusion of people of color.

Derek, Raymond, Nicholas, Mike, Floyd, Roger,
Timmy, and Dale, they were all there, putting
their bodies on the line.

I stayed behind.

...

I stay behind because Mom's situation is too precarious, and I finally have a long-term placement at a magazine publisher: reliable income, much needed. But there's another reason: Zack. He won't be in Montreal, which means we can be together. I haven't told Derek about the day I spent with Zack. I keep thinking I will, but . . . I'm afraid of his reaction? Uncertain what Zack means to me? Yes and yes, and also this: the desire to keep a precious thing to myself.

I'm back in Brooklyn, in that paint-fumed walk-up, where over the course of the night we fuck and nap and get take-out Chinese and fuck again. Later, I'm lying on his mattress, writing in my journal, while Zack snips images out of old magazines and vintage books bought off a street vendor's blanket. This is for a new project, a collage. He says he doesn't know what it'll be, but the seed of it was our recent arrest. "So it's political?" I ask.

"It's more like, the pieces of me breaking apart and then coming back together," he says, which explains the collage, I guess, though I've never actually seen a visual artist at work before.

"Maybe I'll know more tomorrow," he says, "when you're back."

"Tomorrow?"

"Don't tell me you're not free, Kiddo."

"Well, I need to go—I mean, I'm planning to be at—" As my words sputter, I'm aware that I haven't yet said anything about this. "My mom's in the hospital. In New Jersey. She's pretty sick."

He stops. No more ruffling of pages or snipping of scissors. "The hospital."

I tell all—diagnosis, ventilator, Sloan Kettering, waiting. He sits next to me, drawing out things I haven't admitted except in my journal: the battle against hopelessness, the guilt that I'm not doing enough, the utter bewilderment that there's not more to do, while she gets worse.

He says, "You must be so sad," a simple and obvious sentiment but one I haven't yet voiced: *My mother has cancer and that makes me really fucking sad.* "It's okay to let it out," he says, which is all it takes, and then I'm crying the tears I haven't yet shed, while he holds me and rocks me in his arms.

When I'm nearly through, the reservoir drained, I say I'm sorry—feeling selfish for crying over a terminal illness to a guy who's told me he's HIV positive—but he shushes me. "Kiddo, my mom passed when I was thirteen, so I get it. I do."

"Your mom? I had no idea."

"She was sick for a lot of years. Diabetes, kidney disease, other stuff. It was really drawn out, and by the time she died I was sort of ready."

"But thirteen?"

"Yeah, not a good age. Raging hormones and no words for it. I've basically been the same ever since, haha."

"I want to see a picture of you back then," I say. "I bet you were adorable."

He shakes his head. "I was skinny and nerdy. And I had a big head of kinky hair, like hers. After she died, my father cut my hair short, and he always made me keep it that way."

And suddenly I get it, or think I do. "So your mom was Black?"

"She was mixed," he says. "Her father was Black, but he died young, and her mother, my grandmother, came from this WASPy family and they did everything they could to raise her white. And then my dad's side is all Scottish or something and they just never knew what to do with me."

I have so many questions, but he says, "Let's talk about it later," protecting himself, perhaps, or just being supportive of me at this moment.

The next night, after the hospital, the bus ride back from New Jersey, and the long subway trip to Brooklyn, I'm back at his apartment. He's started a new work, a painting of an apartment building with its walls removed. The people inside are made of found images collaged onto the painted surface. The central figure is a fashion model, a Black woman torn in half, her body spilling out objects: light bulbs, cigarettes, pill bottles, seashells, open books, human hands. Zack's personal image bank. When I ask him what it's about, he frowns. "It's hard to explain my work."

"You said something last night about pieces of your identity—"

"Yeah, that." He nods, pauses, and I wait it out until he continues. "After we talked, I started thinking about my mom and how she's still with me. Like, I'm carrying around these memories, but also, I literally came from her body. So I'm carrying that body in me, right?" Another pause. "When you're biracial, and your family passes, you don't really have an identity. There's what people see on the surface versus what's true inside." He shakes his head, out of steam again. "It's better if I say less."

The next night I don't go to the hospital at all, nor the night after that, nor the next one. I stay with Zack, locked away from the world—him working on his art, me inspired by him to spend more time writing, to put down on the page all that's been happening over the last two years, then taking breaks to smoke, fuck or curl together, listening to the neighborhood churning outside. Derek's return is imminent, and on the last night I'm meant to spend with Zack I feel nearly nauseous with the idea of this coming to an end, so paradoxically I start trying to find a reason to get out of seeing him.

Then a reason presents itself: Eliot. I've been leaving reports on his answering machine about my Queen's Cinematic Education—"Dear Harmony: The first half of *The Boys in the Band* filled me with gay pride and the second half filled me with gay shame."

He finally calls me back at my temp job. "Paul from New Jersey! You've left me such lovely messages."

"Which you have not returned, Harmony."

"I've been in the hospital."

"My God, are you okay?"

"To quote our friend Dale, I'm AIDS-OK." An infection, he says, avoiding details. He's out now, resting at home. I tell him I'm coming over after work; my job is not far from his studio in Hell's Kitchen.

He greets me in a fancy silk bathrobe, though the pajama pants beneath are tattered at the hem. "I would have visited you at the hospital," I say.

"Lenny brought me books, and Mike made sure I had the crossword puzzle every day, though after he went to Montreal I had to rely on the kindness of strangers, who are never as kind as one wants."

"You could have called even if you didn't *need* anything," I insist.

"My mind won't hold more than two phone numbers—"

"Eliot—"

"—and when you have a parade of visitors the nurses get bothered. Did I put *One Flew Over the Cuckoo's Nest* on your list? Nurse Ratched, the ur-nurse."

"Are you really okay?"

"Top drawer," he says. "That's a quote from another of your movies."

"*The Women?*"

"*Auntie Mame.*"

"I haven't gotten to that one yet."

"Then you have a lot to look forward to. *Oh, l'amour, l'amour.*"

"How's Lenny?" I ask.

"Lovely," he says. "Lovely Lenny must love me lots, since he's negative and I'm positive. You and Derek better hold onto each other, like Paul Newman and Joanne Woodward, against all odds!" My thoughts go right

139

to Zack. I want to ask Eliot more—how do he and Lenny negotiate their different statuses?—but he hands me a glass of wine and says, "Dr. Leone doesn't want me drinking, but ask any Italian, *vino rosso* is medicine."

We sit on the foldout couch. On the coffee table is a stack of books. "I'm getting rid of these, to make room for more," he says.

"Do you really read them all?"

"I read all the novels and the *important* celebrity bios." He flicks his hand at *Shelley Also Known as Shirley*, the memoir of Shelley Winters. "I think I'll keep that one." He moves it to an end table, next to an alarm clock whose numbers blink the wrong time, as if the power went out and he forgot to reset it.

He's still wearing his hospital bracelet. "Would you like me to cut that off?"

"Yes, but carefully. I'm thinking of having it bronzed." His arm is thin, the wiry dark hair against the ghost-pale skin like underwater grass beneath a stream. He tells me to take a book. I see iconic works like *The Plague, Querelle, Howl and Other Poems*. Inside each one I discover an embossed circular seal: a ring of tiny stars around the words FROM THE LIBRARY OF ELIOT VANCE.

"I still can't believe you named yourself after Vivian Vance."

"She always got the short end of things, the dowdy dresses, the froggy husband. But without her, Lucy's jokes wouldn't have worked. She had *timing*."

He lights a cigarette—menthol—and holds out the pack. "Take. It's one less for me. Dr. Leone says I must quit. Apparently it could kill me."

I light one and puff. It's like breathing Scope.

He says, "The menthol takes the edge off the aerosolized pentamidine."

"Are you on that already?" It only just got FDA approval.

"Dr. Leone made sure."

"My mother hasn't had a cigarette in twenty-five years," I say. "She jogs. She cut out white sugar. She could hardly be healthier. Except for the lymphoma."

"Does it feel real to you?"

"It feels a little more real talking about it."

"Illness makes death easier. Gives us time to prepare. Unlike—" He pauses, clears his throat. His voice turns serious, all the frippery gone. "I was going to say unlike Chris, but suicide is different. The signals were there— comments he made, a sudden sorting out his affairs, paying off debts, that sort of thing. He insisted he owed me forty dollars. I have no idea from what!

So why didn't I see it coming? To this day, I still expect him to walk into the Monday night meeting and complain about the agenda." He points to a slender volume, Virginia Woolf's *To the Lighthouse*. "Poor Virginia had to try several times before she got it right. Chris didn't fuck around."

"I'm so sorry, Eliot, about Christopher. It's really awful."

"Thank you, dear. Sincerely."

When I open the cover of the Woolf, I discover that the text is upside down! The cover's been glued on wrong.

Eliot smiles at my discovery. "I bought it for a nickel in a used bookstore. I recommend reading it on the subway and seeing if anyone stops and stares."

I open to a random page: *Always, Mrs. Ramsay felt, one helped oneself out of solitude reluctantly by laying hold of some little odd or end, some sound, some sight.* "Melancholy," I say.

Eliot nods. "All the best novels are."

I leave with a bag of books. *To The Lighthouse* is in my back pocket, tucked tight like a piece of Eliot I want to keep safe, or at least close. My thoughts are jumbled in the buzz of wine and cigarettes. As I walk through sketchy Times Square, the lights of porn emporiums blink like beacons that have always been there and—so I thought, silly me—always would be.

I decide I don't want to skip out on Zack after all. I call him; he's home.

On the subway to Brooklyn, I open Eliot's book, invert it and begin to read.

The International Lesbian Panty Exchange

There's really only one person I can talk to about Zack, the person who's known me longest. After Amanda gets back from Montreal, we meet at Café Mogador to resume what's become a weekly breakfast date. I tell her everything, wanting her to revel with me in the beat-by-beat romance of it all, but I can't read her response. "There's more to Zack than what Raymond's probably told you," I say. "When I'm with him, I feel like I have all his attention. You know how Derek's always looking in three directions at once?"

"I want you to be careful," she says.

"Because he's positive?"

Her expression changes. I see that she didn't know. "Is he simply positive or does he have full-blown AIDS?"

"I think he's asymptomatic. He didn't mention any opportunistic infections. I didn't ask for his T-cell count." I cross my arms. "It's not the most important thing, his status."

"Of course not," she says, then adds quickly, "but you haven't told Derek?"

I shake my head. "I'm afraid of messing things up."

"Between you and Derek?"

"Between me and Zack."

"So you're falling for a guy whose medical situation you don't understand, and you're keeping it secret from your lover, who you usually tell everything to."

"God, when you put it like that . . ." I reach for her cigarettes, fumble to extract one, spin the lighter's metal wheel under my thumb with no results. She takes the lighter, shakes it and sparks the flame. Our eyes meet as I inhale, an understanding passing between us. "Tell me about *your* love life, please. Save me from myself."

"Two words: dyke drama." She and Jocelyn are done, she reports, after a big, blowout argument. "She said I was too male-identified."

"But she has so many male friends."

"But *I'm* fixated on male approval. Do you remember at my party, when I took my top off? Apparently I was *stripping for the male gaze.*"

"I do remember that. She was *not* into it."

Their breaking point came after a shouting match on a West Village sidewalk between Amanda and one of Jocelyn's friends. This woman declared that gay men were exploiting lesbians by turning them into caretakers and nurses. Amanda had responded passionately—*AIDS was a women's issue, too! Women in the movement were not simply "carrying water" for gay men! ACT UP was taking on the Catholic Church about abortion rights, not just AIDS!* But none of it made a dent. "It was like being back in college and debating separatism."

"Didn't Jocelyn stand up to her friend?"

"Honestly, I think she's burned out from fighting all the time."

"Did you know she showed up at the crack of dawn to bail us out of jail?"

"I heard that," she says. "From Hillary." Now she smiles, and I know her well enough to recognize something in that grin.

"Are you and Hillary—?"

"Yes! We got together in Montreal, but we've been circling each other for a while." It had started on Pride weekend, when ACT UP zapped Manhattan's marriage license bureau, singing "Going to the Chapel" and lining up two-by-two for licenses, which, of course, were refused. Amanda and Hillary were a "couple" for that protest, which led to a movie date, then another to see Karen Finley perform. Before Montreal, they hadn't had sex— "which is a long wait for me," she notes.

Hillary doesn't seem like the take-it-slow type, either. During a recent demonstration against the CDC, she scaled the outside of a building to hang a banner: WOMEN DIE FROM AIDS FASTER. It took many members of the New York City Police and Fire Departments to take down what she'd single-handedly put up.

But—complications! Hillary also has an on-and-off thing with Shanna, who was arrested at the church with us, and Shanna recently went on a date with Rae, who Amanda flirted with at an informational meeting for the NYU film program (to which she's applying) and who, she learned, used to date Jocelyn. "Hello," she says. "It's the International Lesbian Panty Exchange."

We laugh at this, but later, in a letter she writes to me, she admits that the breakup with Jocelyn struck a nerve:

*I have felt lonely being with so many men all
the time. Some nights I just stay inside, reading,
writing, sketching ideas for films I want to
make about our experience, but mostly trying
to understand my place. I began to feel envious,
jealous, lustful, confused and angry about my
male friends' lives, love affairs, jobs, etc. I want
to be friends with more women I meet but that's
complicated by the fact that every woman has
dated every other woman plus her ex... Instead
of dealing with this head-on, I just keep busy,
busier all the time . . .*

I write her back, confessing to my own bouts with loneliness and
apologizing for failing to see how amplified this must be for her in our
male-dominated circle. My aloneness, I tell her, has something to do with
still learning who I am, still seeking my own voice. She writes back again:
*It's confusing to be so deeply identified with a community when you want to say
something or make something that's uniquely yours.*

Visits to the hospital are grimly routine now: my mother, hooked to the
machine, hair thin, body melting into the bed, mind adrift, unmoored, as
my father, Lisa, Michelle, and I circle around in chairs, talking to each
other. We talk about our jobs, my sisters' classes, about hometown gossip
and distant relatives. They ask about ACT UP. It's no longer hard for them
to understand why sick people make demands upon the powers that be. I
remember Rochelle's words, that ACT UP could spark a broader healthcare
movement. In my own family, illness has transformed awareness.

At the hospital payphone, I call Zack. He asks about my mother. Same,
maybe worse, I tell him. He says I should come to his place tonight, when I'm
done, or another night when I'm not at the hospital. "I don't know if I can,"
I say. "Do you want to play hooky one afternoon? I could leave work early."

"Can't manage that, Kiddo."

"I miss you," I say.

"We had a good week together," he says calmly, with finality. It's old
stoic Zack again, inscrutable.

On the bus back to the city, I decide I will tell Derek. I have to, we have too much history, he's too much a part of my life, and I'm driving myself crazy. But when I step into our apartment, I hear the TV, and laughter from the bedroom. Derek is in there with Michael. I thought we'd scared him away forever after the kicked-in restaurant window, but here he is, cuddled up in front of the TV.

Derek pauses the VCR, freezing an image of Woody Allen and Diane Keaton mid-argument. "Michael's never seen *Annie Hall*. Come watch with us."

Michael pats the bed. "Laughter is good medicine."

"I'll let you guys finish," I say. "I'm gonna splash water on my face."

In the bathroom, Michael appears over my shoulder in the mirror. "Derek told me about your mama. I'm so sorry. I want to help, if I can." He steps closer and wraps his arms around me from behind. I try to accept his hug, but I feel stiff, unyielding. He lets go and says, "Do you want to do a line?"

"Um, I'll just start with a drink."

I find a beer in the fridge, gulp most of it down, let the buzz come on while I settle into the couch with my journal. I want to write about the villainy of illness, the body rejecting the life that sustains it, the paradox of that, but what I'm really thinking about is a lot less grand. I put down one sentence: *What will happen to us?* Us is me and Derek, but also Derek and Michael, and me and Zack, and Zack and Raymond, our own gay panty exchange. I stare at the question I've written and the expanse of the page beneath it. Words fail.

Michael's kiss, light on my forehead, wakes me up. "Morning, handsome. Thanks for the bed," he says, silhouetted by sunshine. Then he slips out the door.

Derek emerges in his underwear, wiping sleep from his eyes. "It got late, so I figured it was okay for him to crash."

"Were you guys high?"

"A little. He wanted to squeeze you in with us, but you were out cold." He pauses and then asks, "Are you interested in pursuing something with him?"

I shake my head no. "Are you?"

"Yeah, but only if you feel okay about it."

"Yeah, it's fine. I've got pursuits of my own." *Tell him.* "While you were in Montreal I slept with Zack."

He raises an eyebrow. "Really? Wow—you'll have to tell me about that. But later. A quick shower, then I have to get to work. Will you make coffee?"

"Sure."

He heads to the bedroom, calling out, "I love you."

"I love you, too," I say, and that's that.

Howl

Larry Kramer comes and goes. You don't see him for weeks, even months, and then he's back with urgent, sometimes questionable news—like the time he demands we stop the agenda to discuss a wonder drug they're using in San Francisco, developed from a "Chinese cucumber" and reportedly stopping HIV in the bodies of gay men. The older guys like Nicholas treat "Uncle Larry" with irreverence, referring to his hyperbolic claims as "Larry facts," but I still hold him in awe. He's the visionary who understood from the start what was coming, he's the general who called for the original battle plan. If he says that a Chinese cucumber is the cure, my inclination is to stop everything else to listen, to plan. But Larry is also the apocalyptic prophet who sees only doom—"the truth no one wants to hear"—often incapable of hearing anyone else, as I learned in real time.

Facilitation often means cutting people off who speak too long, interrupting the interrupters, and trying not to take it personally when they bark back. That's the hardest part for me. I don't easily shake off conflict, which is probably why I avoid it in relationships. But there's nowhere to run at the front of the room.

In truth I had no business facilitating anymore, given the state of my life. I'd be at the hospital Sunday, facilitating Monday night, back at the hospital on Tuesday. And on this night I am implicated in one of the agenda items, our arrest at the church on Christopher's Street, and zaps in general. Are we ceding too many decisions to affinity groups, who are not accountable to the membership as a whole? Complaints resurface about past actions, like the broken glass at the FDA, or the way one small group has spent months hounding the city's health commissioner everywhere he goes. Is this harassment? Extreme actions are called for, goes one side of the argument;

on the other side, scaling the fence at that church meant additional work for our lawyers, all volunteers of course. Our resources are not unlimited.

In the midst of this contentiousness, Larry breaks in with a shout from the back: "This is a waste of time."

"We have two more minutes for discussion," I say.

"What more needs to be said? We're just going in circles."

"Please, if you don't have the floor, raise your hand—"

He raises his hand and continues, "People are dying while you—"

"Larry!" I say, voice raised. "Wait your turn!"

He rises up on his toes, an accusatory finger pointed at me: "You're a Nazi!"

Did the room hush? Did people respond? A little of both? All I'm aware of is my heart racing and my legs going rubbery. Somehow I manage to speak: "Just because you don't like this discussion, Larry, doesn't mean you get to stop it. The group elected me to facilitate. So let me do that without insulting—"

He waves his hand dismissively. "I'll be back here if anyone wants to talk about saving lives."

Later, out at Woody's, the bar and grill where we convene after meetings, I avoid the big group seated at pushed-together tables, taking a booth off to the side with Derek, Eliot, Nicholas and Amanda. I guzzle beer, neglect to eat the fried zucchini and onion rings someone has ordered, and quickly get buzzed. It's not lost on me, I tell them, that the man whose motivational scare tactics worked so well on me two and a half years ago was now someone I had to silence in public.

"If you meet the Buddha in the road," Eliot says, "kill him."

"I have no idea what that means," Derek says.

"It's from Siddhartha," Nicholas says. "Or is it Carlos Castaneda?"

"In fact, it's a first-century Zen koan," Eliot says.

"Well, darlin', either way, the message seems to be you can't be a man 'til you kill your father."

"Oh, please," Amanda says. "No one would ever say that about mothers and daughters."

"Point taken," I say. "But there comes that moment when you realize you can't learn from your teachers." I raise my beer. "To killing the Buddha."

"Is that a zap or an approved action?" Derek asks.

"Careful what you wish for," Eliot says. "One day you'll be someone's teacher, too."

Clink.

• • •

Early the next morning, Derek and I are guzzling coffee, trying to get out the door to work, when the phone rings. It's Marilyn. I can tell right away they're going to argue. It's the strained pitch of her voice through the receiver, met by Derek's defensiveness. She's expecting us the next weekend at an engagement party for one of Fred's daughters. This is the first I've heard of it, or maybe I've forgotten. Derek tells her we're not coming. She reminds him he's already promised. He says he hasn't promised but maybe she *heard* that because she needed to. She says she never asks him for anything, so why is he trying to torment her? Derek holds the phone out and presses the "speaker" button so I can hear.

He tells her I'm spending the weekend with my family, doesn't she remember that my mother is sick?, and she says, of course I remember, it's terrible, I'm just asking about the engagement party, maybe Derek will come even if I don't, and Derek says she's always asking for something, his whole life she's been making demands and not supporting him so why should he turn around and drop everything for her? She wants to know, how could he say that after everything she's done for him? He says name it. She says, your car is in our garage again, what about that? You can have the car, he says, I never asked for it, you gave it to me. It was a gift, she says, and you use it when it's convenient but it's just taking up space. Fine, I'll park it in the city, you'll have room for another Mercedes. Leave the Benz out of this, she says. Marilyn, he says, how do you think we feel going to an engagement party when we can't get engaged ourselves? Derek, it's a party, it's not like we're asking you to do chores, what's your problem—

"I don't have any problems, Marilyn, except you. Good-bye." *Slam.*

He lifts up the phone again. *Slam.* "I *hate* her! She *controls* my *life*."

"Derek, take a breath—"

"*I wish she were dead.*"

I stare at him, his words rattling in the air.

"What?" he yells, not realizing what he's just said. "Am I crazy?"

"Just clueless." I retreat to the bedroom and bury my face in a pillow.

A moment later he's beside me. "Fuck. I'm an idiot, I didn't mean—"

"I know you didn't."

"What should I do?" he pleads. "I'm sorry. I'll make it up to you."

But I'm without speech, trapped by feelings he can't share. I know it was just an outburst, but the truth is we're on different sides of a rushing river, one I've crawled out of, exhausted, soaked to the bone, one he's never entered.

I haven't spent a full weekend with my family in a few weeks. On the Friday evening bus to New Jersey, I forgo the newspaper and instead read *Howl and Other Poems*, one of Eliot's gifts. Ecstatic images gallop at me: *the best minds of my generation destroyed by madness...smoking in the supernatural darkness of cold-water flats... fucked in the ass by saintly motorcyclists...Moloch Moloch, Moloch whose blood is running money!...* The madness and smoking and ass-fucking I get, but "Moloch," this angry demon-god demanding appeasement, takes more work. Is the idea that what we're up against also liberates us? I wish I had someone to ask about it, but I'm alone on an air-conditioned commuter bus, head full of rebellion and sexuality and the paradox of poetry.

When I enter my mother's room, I don't recognize her.

I've been warned that months on the ventilator have left her body full of air, trapped under the skin. She has literally inflated. Her face now looks like a pink balloon, enlarged and spongy.

I hold her hand, though I'm not sure she understands who I am. Her bedside writing pad is daubed with half-legible scrawls.

When my father arrives, he takes me back out to the waiting area, and tells me that she's suffering what's called ICU psychosis. The longer a person stays in this unreal environment, the harder it is for the mind to absorb reality, the way a hostage or a prisoner in solitary confinement loses all sense of time.

After dinner that night, the four of us collapse in front of the TV, barely speaking, passing time until the mercy of sleep. The sitcom that's meant to be an escape feels instead like an assault, with its insistent laugh track and intrusive commercials. I quietly excuse myself and go upstairs to my old bedroom. I used to complain how small this room was; now I've been in New York studios not much larger. I sit on the edge of the bed, elbows on my knees, chin in my hands, taking in the detritus of my teenage years: a Brooke Shields poster, my high school yearbook full of boys I had secret crushes on, a brass crucifix on the wall.

In the mirror over the dresser I catch sight of myself. I see an unwelcome guest, the adult who has come to visit the teenager who once lived here, bringing only bad news: *Your mother is going to die.*

My mother is going to die. She's going to die. That's how this ends. That's the truth, rising up from my guts. There I am in the mirror, mouth open, face contorted in a silent scream that's not actually silent, because I'm howling, a siren of despair, louder and louder, and I can't stop.

"What's wrong?" My father, in the doorway. "Say something!"

"She's going to die."

"Was there a phone call? I didn't hear the phone."

"No," I say, sobbing now. "But she's going to die."

"Don't say that!" he shouts.

My sisters appear behind him, their faces twisted in alarm.

I need them to understand, to admit this truth that has overtaken me, but my grief must be terrifying, I must look completely unhinged.

Lisa comes to the bed and puts an arm across my shoulders—her touch is so calming that at last I can catch my breath. "Come downstairs," she says.

"I can't watch TV."

"We'll turn it off."

"I'll pour us all a drink," my father says. "We'll talk."

He's pulled Michelle under his arm. She's only eighteen, and so vulnerable. She's hardly been in the world at all.

Everyone's crying now.

Sorrow is contagious.

In the kitchen, my father pours expensive Scotch he's been saving for a special occasion. The only light comes from the over the sink, casting long shadows across us at the table, where we sit in a darkened version of our six o'clock family meals. We talk about Mom, trading good memories and trying to avoid the past tense, because she's not yet gone. But we can't avoid our awareness of the ventilator, the shock of her puffy face, the terrible sound of *psychosis*. We can't ignore what I voiced. It can't be unsaid. The cancer is winning.

Before returning to the city, I spend a final hour in the hospital. Mom is more alert than she's been in days. She's trying to tell me a story that has something to do with the words she's written on the pad:

Bunny rabbit.

"I don't understand," I say.

She jerks the pen across the page, making crooked letters: *Followed it.*

"You followed a bunny rabbit?"

She looks from me to the pad, then tries again. It takes forever to write three more words: *Cross the field.*

"Are you in a field?"

She nods and writes: *Patrick and Martin.*

"Your brothers?" She smiles—what passes for a smile on her distorted face—her eyes shining like a child's. I met my uncles on a visit to Ireland years ago. One was older and prematurely gray, the other younger and very tall, both soft-spoken village cops who told funny stories. I've seen pictures of them as boys, with my mother between them, all in raggedy clothes. They had no money. She came to America with nothing. Now she is remembering, or imagining, those days when she lived in a tiny, rural house amid endless unfenced fields.

I want to understand. "Did you and your brothers see a rabbit in a field?"

Her eyes brighten again. She points: *Followed it.*

"Did you find it?"

She nods and writes: *Go back.*

"We should go back," I say, my eyes filling with tears. I take her hand, rubbery and warm. "We'll go to Ireland, all of us, together. We'll see your brothers. It'll be beautiful."

For a flash she seems to be fully alert, and through the weakness and the puffiness I see her as she's always been: a strong, kind woman, prone to worry and uncomplicated in her love for me. She looks happy with the idea that we'll return to the place where she was a girl. And then it passes, and confusion flashes in her blue eyes, and the glazed, unfocused look returns. "Mom?" I try, but she doesn't respond, and she doesn't write anything else on the pad. I stay with her until her eyes close and she falls asleep. Then I kiss her burning hand and leave.

Gone

The call wakes me from a deep sleep. My father's voice: "She's gone."

He tells me it happened in the middle of the night. He wasn't there. The doctor called. I try to find words, but all I manage is, "I'm sorry. I'm so sorry."

I walk to the kitchen for a glass of water, then stand there unable to remember what I wanted. Derek follows, pulling me in for a hug while I repeat my father's words.

Gone. Left and not coming back.

The sky is shading from violet night to pale morning blue as we walk toward 14th Street to the lot where Derek has started parking the car he used to keep at Marilyn's. A few random partiers weave past us, club kids in their bedraggled costumes, coked-out businessmen in untucked shirts and expensive shoes, women suffering in heels with boyfriends' jackets draped over their shoulders. At Tompkins Square, the homeless who've slept the night in the park shuffle around their shopping carts, ignoring the cops who lean against the fence, keeping watch, menacing. We stop at Odessa and order two coffees each, one to gulp immediately, one for the ride.

When we get to New Jersey, my father says there's a family appointment at the funeral parlor. Lisa and Michelle are already in the car. I kiss Derek good-bye and join them. My father starts to back out of the driveway, and then jerks to a stop, rolling down the window. He calls out to Derek, "Get in."

I meet my father's eyes in the rearview mirror. "Your mother would want this," he says.

Derek slides into the back seat with me and Michelle. My father turns to look at him. "You're part of the family."

In a quiet voice, Derek says, "Thanks." His face bears a mixed expression: honored to be included and unsure what to do or say.

At the home, the funeral director speaks in a flat, patient voice about "arranging things," as if we are simply moving furniture around. And, indeed, furniture is discussed: the layout of the room, the chairs, the model of casket.

"Will you be keeping the casket open?" he asks, to our stunned silence.

I'm sure they're all thinking, as I am, what she looked like in the end.

Lisa says, "I don't want to see her like that."

"Open is creepy," Michelle says. "That's how I feel."

"She cared about her appearance," I say. "Even if she was just putting on a sweater to go to the store, she made sure it was the right one."

"I can prepare the body," the director says, "and then you can determine, once you see her, if you want an open viewing."

Dad says, "That's best." We all nod, relieved to put off the decision for another day.

We have to pick out clothes—Dad mentions a dress she wore to a wedding, their last truly good time before her breathing became labored. They danced for hours that night. I mention a favorite necklace, garnets set in gold. Derek says, "I remember that one. Beautiful."

The director's eyes land on Derek, whose role here has not been explained. I take his hand again, making sure the gesture has been seen by the director, who doesn't react in any notable way, doing his job, professional, discreet.

We spend the next two days at the "viewing," amid the soft lighting, pastel carpeting and countless floral arrangements. The casket sits at the far end, lid open, a decision we reach after seeing how the funeral parlor has managed to erase the traces of illness from her face. I kneel alongside the coffin, taking surprising comfort from the physical presence of her body— more tangible, more real, than I expected. I lay my hands on hers, which are cool, not pleasant to touch, but still somehow *her*, and I speak to her, which feels like prayer.

Come back, I plead. It seems impossible that she won't.

Evenings are crowded, and I move through the room with Derek at my side, dropping the awkward "significant other" once and for all and coming out to everyone I've ever known. "This is my boyfriend," I say to friends from high school, who I haven't seen in years. "This is my lover, Derek," I say to my mother's friends, who no doubt heard her call us The Odd Couple. "This is my partner, Derek," I say to more conservative relatives. Derek rolls with it, smiling his open smile, accepting condolences and coping with the rare chilly reaction by whispering in my ear: "That one's not invited to brunch."

At the funeral mass, in the modern, blue-tiled church, he sits up front next to me, and anyone who hasn't already met him, or who misunderstood what I meant by "partner," will likely get the picture. Later he tells me that he hasn't been in a Catholic church since traipsing through cathedrals on a visit to Europe in high school. He's surprised by the carpeting, the sleek varnished pews, and the Risen Christ—not a crucifix—above the altar, not to mention the air conditioning on a muggy summer day—all the stuff I take for granted after years of guitar mass and Sunday school. He follows my lead, standing and kneeling when appropriate, exchanging handshakes or hugs for the Sign of Peace and letting others step past him when it's time for that strangest of rituals, Holy Communion. When we exit the church, we're stunned to see Marilyn and Fred there, dressed in black, her eyes glistening as she offers condolences. She and I hug. It may be our first.

Back at the house, people carry in more casseroles, platters and chafing dishes than we have table space for. Guests fill the living room, dining room and kitchen; those of us who can bear the August heat spill into the yard. Voices grow louder and laughter creeps into conversations, a welcome lift to the dreary mood but also, for me, the unwelcome sign that life is already moving on.

On the back stoop, I'm stopped by my mother's best friend, Barb, a wonderful gossip with a thick Jersey accent, who enlists me to carry a cooler of drinks from the kitchen—an excuse, I realize, to grab time alone with me.

"Your mother would'a gotten a kick outta seeing The Odd Couple in the first row of St. Andrew's," she begins.

"Between you and me," I say, "I half expected the roof to cave in. The last time I was near a Catholic church, I was taken away in handcuffs." It's a bit of a provocation, but Barb and I have always spoken frankly.

"Was that for the AIDS group? She didn't always like the tactics, but she told me, *Good for him, he's speaking up.* People like us, we were raised to listen to the Pope, but eventually you wind up thinking, *Maybe if you gave out a few condoms you wouldn't have to worry about the abortions so much.*"

"We argued about that stuff," I say. "Though she was coming around."

"She knew you had homosexual tendencies since you were two years old. Oh, listen to me—*tendencies.* I sound like Sister Mary Rose. You know, my cousin Louise's first husband went gay. We all knew it was coming. He opened a flower shop."

I smile. "I'm glad she talked to you about it. She and I weren't as close as we used to be. I guess it was my fault. I have so much going on in the city—"

"She loved everyone, no matter what," Barb says. "That was your mom." For a moment she chokes up, and I feel myself get misty, too. She waves a hand in front of her eyes to clear the air for both of us. Then she gives me a slap on the shoulder. "Though she wasn't thrilled when you shaved off your hair!"

We're interrupted by a sight that surprises everyone and thrills me beyond words: walking up the driveway, into the backyard are Amanda, Hillary, Nicholas, Timmy, Dale, and Michael. I feel the crowd make way, as you would for visiting dignitaries, which I suppose they are: emissaries from my life on the other side of the Hudson, that curious life with my boyfriend-lover-partner. Here are Amanda and Hillary in vintage dresses and heavy boots; Timmy in a HEALTHCARE IS A RIGHT t-shirt and Dale with his long hair tied in a ponytail and his camera around his neck; Nicholas in a slim-fit blazer with a bright scarf around his neck like a dandy; and Michael the Southern Gentleman with a neat haircut and a good suit. "What are you doing here?" I ask, amazed to see them.

"We took the bus," Amanda tells me, then leans closer. "How could I not be here?" We hug, and then the group converges around us. Derek hurries over from across the yard and we fold him into our group hug.

"I hope this all isn't too weird," I whisper.

"I grew up Catholic on Long Island," Timmy says. "These are my people."

Dale steps back and snaps a picture of our huddle.

I introduce everyone to my father, who embraces them one by one, touched, I can see, to meet these friends his son has kept from him. Following that moment in the car with Derek, it's a sure sign that in the aftermath of my mother's death, things I'd thought unchangeable have already begun to shift.

We regroup around the picnic table, and I wave over Lisa and Michelle, a couple of my high school friends, a cousin or two, and Barb and her husband, and we pass around cans of beer from the cooler, and just like that everyone's mixed together. Derek relaxes the tense posture he's held for days, and I think about how much easier everything has been with him at my side and how taxing he must have found it all. He's clearly relieved to have our friends here, and maybe Michael in particular, who stays close by his side, attentive, offering help as he always does. I think of Zack, too, and how if he were here I could ask him, another son who has lost his mother, what happens next.

• • •

I've been at one job most of the summer, a secretarial position in the "corporate communications" department of a magazine company that puts out glossy publications for car and motorcycle enthusiasts, professional photographers, interior decorators. The older women I work with love to comment on my appearance and tease me about my age. "What's with the crew cut? Are ya in the Army?" "Those baby blues—don't tell me you're not wearing colored contacts." "You wanna get a drink? Call me when you're twenty-one." I haven't directly come out to any of them, and no one ever asks about my life outside the office, but I assume they know I'm gay, that I *read* gay, and that this, along with being baby-faced and male, is why they treat me like their little pet.

When I return to work after a week in New Jersey, Donna, the woman in the next cubicle, calls out, "Where you been, Blue Eyes? We had no one to pick on." Most of our conversations take place like this, over truncated cubicle walls, only the top of her head visible to me— an auburn helmet she probably dyes every weekend, because she's sixty without a single gray hair.

I mutter, "Personal days."

There must be something in my tone that piques Donna's interest because she wheels into view on her desk chair. "You get a better deal somewhere else?"

"No," I say. "There was a death in the family."

"Oh, Jesus, I'm sorry. Anyone you were close to?"

A pause. "My mother."

"For the love of God." Her hands rush through the sign of the cross. "That's terrible! Are you all right?"

"I'm fine. Thanks for asking." But she's waiting for more, so I tell her Mom had been in the hospital since the spring with a rare cancer. "It wasn't sudden," I say. "I've had a little time to get used to the idea."

"A few months *is* sudden! There's never enough time." Her mouth is firmly set even as her eyes well up. "My father died ten years ago, after a very long illness, and I still can't believe he's gone. I miss him every day. You only get one father. Or mother." She lays a hand on my shoulder, fingers glinting with rings and polish. "If you need a break, you take a break. On the clock. Leave early if you want to. I'll tell the boss."

Later, I overhear her at the copy machine talking to a coworker. "He says, *a death in the family,* then he tells me it's his *mother!* He's obviously in shock."

I do take a break after that, a long cigarette break on the sidewalk, listening to taxis honking, watching midtown pedestrians file past, feeling my heart thump amidst the infinite stream of city life. Across Broadway is the theatre where *Cats* has been playing for as long as I can remember. I think about Mike Savas and his Broadway stories—Mike's still at ACT UP meetings all the time, even after Christopher's death. I think of Eliot saying he still expects Christopher to walk through the door. Were they in shock, too? People die every day, their surviving loved ones returning without fail to the workplace, to school, to the local grocery, telling their coworkers and acquaintances, "My mother just died," "My lover just died." Every day, a person in mourning must confront the well-meaning, pitying look I saw on Donna's face, a reminder that the losses we think we've assimilated are actually extraordinary events we can hardly comprehend. The finality of my mother's death—the foreverness of it, the never-againness of her presence—still does not compute. It'll be years before it does. Donna's prediction will turn out to be true: I'll never completely get used to it. I *haven't,* even now, when she's been gone more than half my life. But the question that lingers is why I treated my grief as a private matter, not to be shared, when I felt like I could have walked into the middle of Broadway and screamed until traffic stood still.

Part 6

Snap

The sun is shining, the sky is blue, the September air is balmy and sensual. A perfect day for an afternoon in the park, except that I'm wearing a wig and makeup, a pair of heels and a polyester blouse that doesn't breathe. No one warned me that a wig holds in body heat, like a ski cap in winter, or that a layer of foundation feels like a clammy rag on your face. Tendrils of blonde wig hair stick to my lips. Lipstick, I've quickly learned, tastes like crayons—or maybe that's just because we bought the cheap stuff. The three-inch slingbacks I got at Payless are scrunching my toes. Before we even walk the two blocks to Nicholas's apartment, Derek and I are a couple of messy misses. On the street, it seems like everyone is staring at us, but I feel protected behind my shades, their frames the same scarlet color as my lips.

"Hello, ladies," Nicholas greets us. "And I use the term loosely."

"We are the loosest type of ladies," I say, punctuating with a *snap* of the clasp from my heart-shaped vinyl purse.

"Snap, sugar," he replies, clicking his fingers. "I hereby christen you Sugar Snap. A queen is born. Now come to Nurse Nicky." He's wearing a white tennis dress and a fluffy blonde bob with a nursing school cap already attached. From a hip pocket he produces a thermometer. "Temperature time!"

Derek opens his mouth and says *aah*.

"No, no, no. I am an R.N. The R is for rectal."

"Please, Nurse," Derek protests. "I'm a virgin."

"Take mine, take mine," I coo, wiggling my butt and peering back over my shoulder like a centerfold.

Nicholas frowns at my boyish cutoff shorts. "Your look needs surgery."

We've arrived half in drag, our wigs purchased the week before, under Nicholas's watchful eye, at a shop on 14th Street. "You can wear anything,

Babyface," he'd said to me, eyeing the bouffants and beehives, pageboys and Summer of Love locks. He turned to Derek. "You, not quite." Derek's five-o'clock shadow, dark eyebrows and strong nose resisted femininity. We convinced him to get a short brunette flip, which Nicholas assured him was very *That Girl*.

"*What* girl?" Derek asked, looking skeptically into the wig shop's mirror. "All I see is a butch version of Marilyn."

"Every gay man in drag becomes his mother," Nicholas said.

This is true for me, too: I keep a photo of my mother as a gorgeous young woman of twenty, dressed up for a night on the town in a shiny, pale yellow party dress, legs crossed coquettishly, eyes limpid. It is her pretty chin I've inherited, and her cheekbones. In this photo her hair is platinum blonde, a loose up-do lending the illusion of a regally long neck, like Kim Novak in *Vertigo*, floating around San Francisco, glamorous and haunted. My drag debut would pay homage.

The occasion is Wigstock, an outdoor party in Tompkins Square Park, organized by Lady Bunny, the cutting queen who wrangles downtown's nightlife stars into daylight. Everyone who attends is supposed to get dressed up, too.

Twenty years after Stonewall, there is a definite portion of the gay male community who strongly believes that drag queens put "the wrong face" on the movement. That is not the dominant view in ACT UP, though our aesthetic is so hyper-masculine—all those leather jackets, shorn scalps, broken-in denim and heavy black boots—that you might wonder where all the gender deviation had gone. But aren't we just presenting another brand of drag? Every time I buzz my skull and lace up my Doc Martens, I feel like I'm putting on a *look*.

"Just don't get your picture in the paper," Lisa said to me over the phone, her tone halfway between joking and deadly serious, when I told her I'd be going out in drag for the first time.

"I doubt it's going to be a media event," I said, responding lightly but in fact kind of irked. I thought she'd find this a fun idea, not a worrisome one. She was studying fashion design; she had at least one gay friend; I figured she'd "get" drag. But for her, it was inexplicable that I was dressing up like our mother in her youth just a couple weeks after she'd died. Maybe she was right; maybe this was a questionable strategy to offset the grim reality.

Nicholas turns on the radio, finds Z100 just as "She Drives Me Crazy" is segueing into "Wild Thing," and soon we are catwalking the length of his tenement toward a full-length mirror. My drag discomfort disappears now that we're working it. Nicholas rolls a joint, which slows our decisions but speeds up our giggling. The doorbell buzzes, announcing Amanda and Michael, who've struck up a friendship since showing up in New Jersey after the funeral. She wears a white spangled cocktail dress and a wig straight from Diana Rigg's wardrobe in *The Avengers*. "Mod glamour!" I cry. *Snap*.

Michael is serving up a pert black bob and a poof skirt, like an uptown girl on a blind date. "Daytime pass!" Nicholas proclaims, and we can all see it: Michael is remarkably *real* in drag.

Eventually we get back out in the sunlight, promenading up Avenue A to the park. Nicholas has put me in fuchsia velvet leggings, too glam-rock for my look but far better than the cutoffs. Derek has been completely remade in a slutty micro-miniskirt and tube top, earning him the moniker Mary Tyler Whore. At the corner, a few older, beer-bellied men send us wolf whistles. "That's right, you know you want this," I parry, with a snap of my change purse. No longer uncomfortable and sticky-sweaty, I am larger than life, fearless. I've never fully considered the phrase "drag *queen*," but now I get it: we are royalty, the world is subject to us, and I'm not taking shit from anyone.

Entering the park, we hear dance music from the band shell. Everywhere we look are boys in wigs, skirts, tights and heels, first-timers like me with misguided makeup alongside seasoned queens in full face, and women butching it up in glued-on facial hair, or like Amanda, femmed-out to the point of camp. Some people wear original costumes—one made of balloons, another constructed from cigarette packs, someone in a George H.W. Bush mask, encouraging everyone to boo. People drink beer from paper bags, lowering them as cops saunter past.

On stage, a queen spins in circles, shedding her dress to reveal a detail-perfect Wonder Woman ensemble—but Wonder Woman as a 180-pound muscular Black man. One of our local favorites, RuPaul—not yet "Supermodel of the World"—delivers an increasingly filthy comic monologue about the appropriate occasions to celebrate with the "sparkling malt liquor" known as Champale. A band called French Twist plays early sixties cocktail-lounge music, introducing themselves one at a time: "On drums, Monique. On guitar, Monique. Lead vocals, Monique." We're most excited about the headliner, Deee-Lite, an East Village success story, just signed to a major label. Between acts, Lady Bunny hurls hilarious, trashy insults while a DJ spins records.

We congregate toward the back of the crowd, where we run into friends, reintroduce ourselves with our clever new names, preen and pose for pictures.

At some point I become aware of a group of four teenage boys, two of them carrying lacrosse sticks, lumbering through the crowd, aggressively bumping into people. I point them out to Nicholas, who frowns but says, "They're outnumbered." He's right: why should four have any power in a crowd of four hundred? Here we are, in the light of day, in all our queer glory, claiming this space for ourselves. It's not a march or a demonstration. It's performers and outfits and fun. Even the homeless are dancing to the DJ.

I see a video camera pointed my way. I'm posing before I realize that behind the expensive-looking lens is Raymond. "You got a new camera!" I call out.

He lowers the lens and smiles, his mouth covered in cherry-red lipstick, but smeared, like he's been making out. Then I see who he's with.

"Hey, Kiddo," Zack says, his mouth also a slash of red.

"Oh, hey," I stammer, unsure what to do next: Hug? Kiss? I let Sugar Snap take over, improvising a girlish curtsy.

Zack—in a long hippie-chick wig and a flowered headband—curtsies back. He's shirtless beneath the bib of his patchwork denim dress, his sexy chest straining against the straps. Last I knew, he and Raymond couldn't even be near each other. But I haven't seen Zack since my mother died; we haven't even talked, and maybe they've cleared the air. Maybe they've been kissing. Anything's possible. I'm glad for my dark glasses, masking whatever my eyes would reveal.

Michael, the prettiest in our pack, pushes himself forward, playing the coquette, one hand over his mouth, the other flipping up his skirt to flash a lovely bit of ass. Zack takes Michael's hand and disco-twirls him, the skirt flaring out like petals on a daisy. Raymond crouches and shoots.

Then Zack gets drawn away to another friend calling hello, and Raymond follows, aiming his lens at the next fabulous posse to float by.

Michael, post-twirl, camps up his dizziness, staggering between me and Derek. And then I hear someone say, "Watch it, faggot, don't gimme your AIDS," and we're face to face with the aggressive boys I saw earlier.

"Excuse me—*what?*" Michael says, dropping the dizzy ballerina pose.

"Get the fuck out of our park," one of them says.

They're outnumbered, I repeat to myself, though at this moment we're three and they're four.

"Be gone," I say, "This isn't your day." I look at the stockiest one, a Puerto Rican with slickly combed hair and a sheen of perspiration on his brow. I stick my change purse in his face. *Snap.*

I see in his eyes what he's going to do, right before he does it: his lacrosse stick comes at me like a missile and strikes me in the face.

An explosion of pain. I topple off my heels. I hit the ground. My jaw, my busted jaw, that's where he hit me. Then he's on me, fists swinging, joined by a second guy, both of them landing blows, so many, so fast.

I see Michael face down, a few feet away, while a big dude raises a lacrosse stick over his head and brings it down across his shoulders. Derek's trying to pull him free. I scramble across the concrete, get to my feet, shake off my attackers. Michael stands, transformed by pure fury, screeching, "You motherfuckers. You fucking motherfuckers!"

For a flash it's just the three of us in our busted drag facing off against the four of them with their fists and sticks looking hungry for more. I feel the heat of blood on my face. "Bashers!" I shout. "Right here!"

Derek is yelling, "These guys just attacked us."

Faces in the crowd turn.

I see Raymond rushing toward us now, camera raised, shooting footage. Zack has gone off in the other direction, toward two policemen leaning against a fence—he gets close to them, and they go rigid at his sudden presence. One of them steps back, and Zack steps with him, and that's all it takes. The cop seizes Zack, spins him around, pins him to the fence. The cuffs come out.

"No, no, no," I'm shouting, trying to get their attention. "*These* are the guys you want, these guys!"

The second cop is coming at us now, pulling his nightstick from his belt. He steps up to our attackers, leans in and speaks to them in a low voice. They start to move away, to disperse. What the fuck? Has he *told* them to leave? But there are enough people in wigs and costumes who've figured out what's going on, and they form a circle around the lacrosse boys, preventing their escape.

Cop number one is walking Zack away, toward a brick building farther back in the park. Zack is pleading with him to no effect. He looks back over his shoulder and calls to me, "Get help!"

But that guy is the help, I think incredulously.

So I turn and run through the crowd, toward the band shell, where the emcee is on the mic, telling jokes.

"Stop!" I yell from the foot of the stage.

Startled, she glances down at me.

"We just got bashed. The cops arrested our friend."

She steps away. Either she hasn't heard me, or I look too crazy to take seriously. I try again, straining to be heard. "There are gay-bashers in the crowd. Tell the police to arrest them."

She looks at me again. "What's this?" she says into the mic, widening her eyes in campy amazement. "You say you got attacked? Honey, when you girls get dressed up, you drive the boys crazy. Anything can happen."

"Stop the show!" I demand.

"Oh, honey, the show must go on, everyone knows that." She walks as far across the stage as she can. "Y'all want a show, right?"

The audience cheers. Did no one else hear me? I tear the wig off my head and hurl it at her. It bounces at the base of the mic stand and then slides from the stage, a blonde puddle at the feet of the dancing crowd.

On the other side of the park, a crowd chants, *"Let him go, let him go,"* outside the brick building where Zack is being held. The idea of Zack—biracial, queer, in drag—handcuffed and surrounded by bashers and cops terrifies me. Maybe they've discovered pending charges from his last arrest. We've called our lawyer friends, but no one's here yet.

Derek, still in drag, has been hoisted onto Nicholas's shoulders and is speaking into a bullhorn. (I don't question where the bullhorn came from. Word has gotten out, and here it is.) "We demand," Derek says to the crowd, as Raymond videotapes him, "that the police release our friend and put these criminals under arrest."

"Arrest the real criminals," the crowd chants, *"arrest the real criminals—"*

I need a moment alone. I step out of the crowd. From my change purse— that fucking purse with its fucking snap—I retrieve a cigarette. An old lady with a grocery cart moves past me, and I observe her take it all in. She turns to an old man sitting on a park bench and asks, "What's the hubbub?"

He answers, "They beat up the drag queens."

In the crowd I recognize a friend, Anton, who's a reporter for the weekly gay magazine, *Outweek*. I wave him over. He says he's already talked to Michael, who is in pain and trying to figure out what to do next.

"No one offered us medical treatment," I tell Anton. "No one's taken a statement."

"Would you call this police insensitivity?"

I pause. I read *Outweek* regularly; I don't want to be a story in its pages.

But I guess that's inevitable now. I ask him, "Do you think if four men walked into the St. Patrick's Day parade and assaulted three Irish ladies, that things would have played out this way?"

He nods, writing on a notepad.

Rationally, I understand that the police were caught off guard when Zack charged at them, that once they'd grabbed him they probably felt they couldn't let him go. It was a cop thing. I didn't like it but I *got* it. What I didn't get was why the entertainment on the stage continued without pause, why a drag queen bashed at a drag festival wasn't enough of a reason to stop the festival cold. Amanda and Nicholas have spoken to the organizers but were rebuffed: "People are here to have fun. This isn't an ACT UP meeting." I tell Anton that, too.

In time, the police leave in a van with the perps inside. My stomach plummets, knowing Zack is in there too. The crowd swarms onto Avenue A, failing to prevent the van from driving away but sitting down in the street in protest anyway.

That impromptu protest, thinned out but vocal, is still there when Zack and I return hours later from the precinct, long after Wigstock has finished. He's been charged with "obstructing government administration," which he'll have to fight, but at least they're not holding him. The bashers were still in custody when we left, facing more serious charges. Michael went to St. Vincent's, accompanied by Derek, to get his shoulder looked at. On Avenue A, we tell the protesters that our demands have been met, and they disperse. Traffic flows again. It's a holiday weekend in the East Village. The regular nightlife takes over.

At Houston Street, where Zack and I would normally part company, he surprises me, saying, "Brooklyn seems really far away." He looks exhausted.

"My place is right there," I point, and we continue on together.

At the apartment, we shower, and I find clothes for him. He holds ice to my lip, which is cut open, and kisses the painful bruise on my face where I was hit. I break out the blender and make us a smoothie, telling him how my mother brought it here after my last injury. He tells me that he heard about her death, he even made me a card but didn't send it, he's not sure why, he's really sorry. I tell him I understand. It's not clear what we are to each other. I think we both know that to close the distance between us is to open ourselves to emotional risk.

167

Derek and Michael return with a final terrible twist to this terrible day: emergency room personnel mocked Michael's appearance; he overheard them refer to him as "the faggot." After he left the treatment room to get Derek, they didn't want to let him back in. "One more fight," Derek says wearily. "My hero," Michael replies. His shoulder blade is fractured, and he's been fitted with a soft brace, but he's doped up and ready to crash. Derek sets him up in our bed, on ice, then comes back out to fill a glass with water.

I meet Derek in between the bedroom and living room, facing him under the amber light of the hallway fixture. He says, "When Michael told me they called him a faggot, I thought he was delirious and was talking about the guys in the park again. But no, at St. Vincent's, this actually happened."

"Imagine if he were alone?"

"He kept *me* calm. I wanted to kick in a window." As he heads back into the bedroom, he pauses. "Is Zack staying?"

"Is that cool?"

He raises the water glass, an affirmation.

I return to Zack, sitting at the edge of the couch, questioning me with his eyes. "Let's get this bed open," I say.

It's another marker. A day meant to be a celebration became a battle: with bashers, with the police, with hospital workers, with our own community. There is so little reprieve in wartime. But at the end of the day, when Derek and I needed comfort, we didn't look to each other. We turned to different lovers.

I Will Survive

Does the virus take a vacation? No, but Derek's therapist says he, or actually *we* should. Together. I don't actually know what happens in therapy. Derek doesn't tell me much. He said he started off talking about me, but since everything's good between us (really?), he's been focusing on his mother. He knows she loves him, but why, *why* does she criticize, second-guess, insist he's wrong all the time?

"Maybe she's changing," I suggest. "She came to Mom's funeral."

"It's not about what she does, it's about how I respond to her."

This sounds like a line he's memorized, but it also sounds like the truth.

It's early September. His car isn't working; it's last-minute to make a reservation; my Visa is full. But Dr. Essen, Derek's therapist, says these are minor obstacles and tells him, you can solve this.

"What do you want to do?" he asks.

"Surprise me," I tell him.

And he does, with a note *(Pack for the beach. Don't forget sunblock.)*, a train ticket to Sayville, and my Adventurers Camp for Boys t-shirt, folded neatly.

Before I go out to Fire Island, I meet with my family to say good-bye to Michelle, who's leaving for college. They drive into the city and meet me at Kiev, on Second Avenue, a restaurant crammed with wobbly tables and chairs whose vinyl seat cushions are all cracked, more down and out than they likely expected when I suggested brunch.

"What happened to you?" Lisa asks, looking at the split in my lip, the bruised side of my face.

"Nothing to worry about," I say.

169

"Was this a police thing again?"

I shake my head and point to the menu. "You should try the pierogi."

My sisters share a concerned look, but they go ahead and order—cheese blintzes—while Dad chooses the pierogi, which he says he hasn't eaten since he and Mom had one of their first dates at a Ukrainian street fair. We joke about her unadventurous eating habits—all those buttery egg noodles and iceberg lettuce salads—and her nervous driving, and her penchant for nicknames like The Odd Couple. I share with them the story of Mom and the bunny rabbit in Ireland; Lisa and Michelle had the same exchange with her during that last week. Whatever it was, that image was the final fixation of her life.

Dad clears his throat. Says there's something else. "She had a life insurance policy through her job, and you're each getting fifteen thousand dollars."

I manage a *whoa* or a *wow* or some similar stupefied reaction; this is an extraordinary amount of money. I barely earned more than that last year.

"I don't want it," Lisa says. "It's blood money." Her face is pained but firm. Next to her, Michelle has cast her eyes downward.

"I guess I don't see it that way," I say carefully.

"If she wasn't dead, we wouldn't be getting it."

Dad says, "Your mother worked that job, in part, for the benefits. She named you on her policy because she wanted to take care of you. It's a gift."

"Maybe I'll give it to the American Cancer Society," Lisa says.

I tell her what I learned about that group from Rochelle, how it's been criticized by community organizers as a bloated bureaucracy tied too tightly to the pharmaceutical industry. I say, "I could get the names of organizations attacking the factors that contribute to cancer, like corporate polluters dumping toxins into the environment."

"And the tobacco companies?" she says.

"Sure—"

"I saw you smoking with your friends at the funeral. I don't know how you could, after Mom."

"You're smoking?" Dad asks.

"Mom hadn't smoked in twenty-three years," I say. "Smoking didn't kill her."

"Smoking causes cancer," Lisa says.

"So does living in New Jersey. Do you know how much radon is produced by chemical companies in the state?"

"That just proves my point. Mom worked for a drug company. This is their money."

"I can live off that money for months and do healthcare activism."

"Would you two *stop it?*" Michelle shouts, so forcefully that we all go mute. "Who cares what you do with the money? You do one thing, you do another. Why do you have to be *right?*" Her eyes are shining with tears, but they don't fall, as if she's willing herself not to come completely undone.

Dad puts his arm over her shoulder. "That's what Mom would want, right?"

"I feel like I'm leaving her behind," Michelle says, quieter now, "like I'm going to forget about her."

"You'll never forget her," Lisa says. "No matter how much you like college or make new friends—"

Michelle is shaking her head. "You didn't even take your finals. How am I supposed to start from scratch? I don't want to go." I reach over to lay a hand on her arm, but she pulls back. "And *you* won't share anything about your life."

"My life would just upset you."

"If Mom was here you'd tell her what happened to your face."

Now they're all looking at me. "I got gay bashed."

Lisa says, "Why didn't you say so?"

"Because I was in drag, and the last thing you said to me was don't wind up in the newspaper. And, guess what? I did." Lisa draws back into her chair. "Michelle's right," I say. "It was easier to talk to Mom."

"Well, that's not possible anymore, so why don't you try letting us know when stuff happens?" Dad says. Out of words, out of energy, I simply nod.

Our good-byes are intense: long hugs on the sidewalk, tears, then we go our separate ways. Dad is driving Michelle to school. Lisa is meeting friends in Soho. And I have to catch a train, which I'm probably late for. I feel nearly frantic with excess energy, a nervous buzzing in the aftermath of our emotional meal. Even with an overstuffed bag, I break into a run, dodging people, pigeons and garbage. My breath feels heavy, my legs are strained, the meal I've eaten is tight in my stomach. I'm trying to separate from my family's sadness, which is mine, too. I want to burn it off or puke it up or just run so fast that the only pain I feel is in my body, physical, identifiable, not this invisible, incurable loss.

• • •

Fire Island is more beautiful than I remember. Arriving under a blue sky, I take in the glinting light on the bay, the deep green of the trees, the soft sand beneath the boardwalk, and the men on the dock, half-dressed and sun-kissed, though some of them, of course, don't look physically well, even here in paradise.

I see Derek waving as my ferry pulls in. He took a day off from work to come here early with Mike Savas—who, I realize with a shock, is one of the men I'd judged from the boat as looking unwell. Mike seems less bulky, more attenuated, his KS lesions multiplying, though none of that has stopped him from going shirtless, a *fuck you* to anyone who'd prefer not to witness illness in the midst of vacation. Mike strides toward me, still a warrior, and I— still trying to absorb his glory—more or less throw myself at him for a hug. "Easy," he says. "I'm tender."

Then another voice calls my name, with a particular Southern lilt that can only mean Michael—Derek's Michael is how I think of him now. There he is, fit, lithe and pink from the sun, in a speedo and shoulder brace. "No big hugs for me, handsome," he says. "You might re-break my bones."

"I didn't know you'd be here."

"Sure you did," Derek says. "I told you."

Did he? "Maybe when you said Michael I thought you meant *Mike*."

"I hope it's a good surprise," Michael says, flirty as ever.

"The more the merrier," I say.

"Good, because I'm filling up Adventurers Camp with boys," Mike says.

I catch Derek's eye and send a silent question, but either he doesn't catch on or elects to bank it for later. He takes my bag and starts down the boardwalk alongside Michael, a study in physical contrast: one hairless and precise, the other all ottery fur and agitated angles, but still somehow in sync.

Mike's flag now flies over a different house, enormous and bright, with white furniture, chrome fixtures and glass walls framing the Atlantic on one side and a swimming pool on the other.

"Who'd you have to fuck to get this?" I ask, taking it in.

"Just myself," Mike says. "I cashed out my life insurance policy."

"You can do that?"

"A viatical settlement. People do it to cover medical costs and other needs you can't afford because you're *dying*, but I figured—" he throws his arms wide, sweeping across the bright, shiny, seaside room, and bellows, "—I want to *live*."

"It's divine," Michael says, voice carrying down from a landing overlooking the main room. "I'm gonna get me one of them viaticals, too."

Mike gazes up at his younger guest, with some small adjustment of perception on his face. Maybe he didn't know Michael was positive. I forget it too, sometimes. It's stupid to say Michael doesn't look like he has HIV, since looks have nothing to do with it. Zack doesn't "look" positive. Neither does Dale, neither do a lot of people. But there's something about Michael's unblemished presence that seems to defy not just illness but aging, trouble, worry. Maybe all those affirmations are working for him.

"You found the Evita balcony," Mike calls up. "You're required to give the royal wave when you're standing there." Michael complies, using his good arm.

The room Derek has claimed for us looks out on the ocean. A path cuts through the dune grass to the sand, where bodies sprawl on blankets. "Mike gave us the one with the best view," he says. "I told him this was our weekend."

"Is it still?" I ask. "Sounds like a party."

"It's a big house, you won't even notice everyone."

The room has two beds, one slept in, one not. "Are we sharing the room?"

"Hopefully not. And Michael's going to sleep on the couch tonight."

"Tonight?"

"Well, you weren't here—" He stops, trying to read me. "You're mad?"

"Just getting the lay of the land," I say, but I wonder, *am I mad?*

Voices from downstairs announce new arrivals: Timmy, Dale, and—surprisingly—Raymond, who once told me he thought Fire Island was the epitome of A-list gay elitism. Raymond seems to carry the city in with him, wearing black jeans and a black sleeveless t-shirt, lugging an overpacked bag. He keeps his sunglasses on as he scrutinizes the real estate, getting his bearings. Dale wears a Hawaiian shirt, a concession to the beach, though otherwise he's got all his usual accouterments: camera around his neck, bandana over his long hair, unfiltered cigarette balanced on his lip. ("Smoking on the patio only!" Mike barks.) Timmy, however, is transformed: espadrilles, Jackie O. sunglasses, flower-patterned parasol. He proclaims at full volume, "I am *thrilled* to be making my firthst voyage to the Island of Fire." They've brought along a bag of beach toys and Tupperware containers.

Timmy announces his intention to build "a big motherfuckin' thand castle."

On the beach we drink from a thermos of cocktails, add obscene details to Timmy's castle, and let ourselves get tossed around in the rough Atlantic. Saltwater tingles my lower lip where the basher's blow has not yet healed. When I swallow a mouthful, a long-ago memory ignites: my mother rubbing sunscreen on her skin, my sisters, so tiny, rushing at the breaking waves and then back again, my father in a terrycloth beach jacket chasing seagulls away from our lunch. And me, thrust beneath the surface, helpless for a long moment, water up my nose, down my throat, then standing, sputtering, recovering, alive. Where were we? Cape Cod, I think, an early family vacation, enveloped in feelings of freedom and wonder. The little me in this memory is amazed that the sun is so strong, the water so powerful, my own existence so small and contained—

"Heads up!" Derek yells. I'm spacing out, not noticing the curl of the next big wave. I dive in and propel through the tumult, rising out the other side.

Back at the house, Mike puts on a Gloria Gaynor album and we all shriek. Beach towels are transformed into couture and the poolside becomes our runway. Timmy dons a coconut-shell bikini top, and Michael, in a thin sarong, flashes his cock and balls, cooing, "My privates won't stay private." But Raymond wins the moment when he wanders out from the house in a jock strap and high-heeled pumps, announcing, "Serving butch *and* femme." Everyone takes a turn in the heels. One after another we prance to the diving board lip-synching to "I Will Survive," concluding each catwalk with an increasingly melodramatic signature plunge into the deep end.

"Old friends, meet the new friends," Mike announces, introducing his housemates, Neil and Trey, blond, tanned hunks in their thirties wearing tank tops and snug designer shorts. Neil is friendly, making a point to get everyone's name, checking to see if we eat shellfish because he's brought along a stocked cooler for his seafood stew. "If it hasn't all rotted by now," adds Trey, launching into complaints about the interminable traffic and the unseasonable heat and the woman on the ferry with a yappy dog, "a bitch with a bitch," and how is it already the last weekend of their share and he really just wants to enjoy the house to the fullest. As the grievances pile up, I spy Timmy and Dale sharing an enormous eye-roll.

Mike throws a consoling arm over Trey's shoulder. "Trina, you need a cocktail," he says, then turns to me: "You're on martini duty."

"I will do my best to serve Adventurers Camp for Boys," I say with a salute. Then I stage-whisper, "What's in a martini?"

Neil says, "Follow me," and leads me to the kitchen, where he delivers step by step instructions as if passing on esoteric tribal knowledge: "Chill the glass, but don't freeze it. Use only the best vermouth, but use almost none." He places his hand over mine to demonstrate how to wave the bottle over the shaker so that only the tiniest drop slips out. We down the first batch together—just testing—and after he gulps most of his second, he coos, "You're a fast learner," and lays his hand on my crotch. For a hot moment I'm engulfed by a fully formed fantasy of life as a kept boy to a Pines power couple, but the idea fades as fast as it comes on.

"Let's not," I say, moving his hand away. "I've got enough drama."

"Which one is yours?"

"Derek—furry, thinning hair, big smile."

"Oh, he's not with the little cute one?"

"He sort of is, but he's my partner."

"That's tricky," Neil says, giving my crotch a second, lingering squeeze. "Do me a favor? Don't mention this to Trey."

"Mention what?"

He lifts his hand to trace the cut on my lip. "What happened here?"

"Homophobia," I say.

At the dinner table, Mike encourages Trey, who is an entertainment lawyer, to give us celebrity gossip, and Trey launches into a rant against Madonna—how she is "manipulated" by David Geffen, how "her body odor is notorious," how she'll never last because "her videos are too provocative"—statements that get the rest of us in an uproar.

"We love Madonna," Timmy protests.

"She's one of the only celebrities who talks about AIDS," Derek says.

"That's true," Trey says, "but she alienates a lot of people."

"She's pushing the boundaries of sexuality," I say.

"She's dancing in leather at the foot of a crucifix!" Trey exclaims.

"Oh, Trina," Mike says, "that's you at the Eagle on a Saturday night."

"Could we drop 'Trina'? We're not in drama club anymore," Trey says.

Neil leans in to explain. "We were the Three Sisters: Trina, Nina and Mina."

"And now we're three grown men," Trey says.

"What's *her* problem?" Timmy says, and the rest of us explode into a chorus of "her" and "she" and "girl." We rechristen ourselves Tina, Dina, Pina, Dana, Rayna, and Marlena. Trey doesn't stand a chance, but doubles down, all lawyerly argumentation: "Our community is in trouble, and playing into stereotypes of gay men as women is not helping. You don't change people's minds by provoking them. We have enough trouble fighting off the idea that we're all out there spreading disease."

This silences the table. All our eyes go to Mike, who says, "Really, Trina?"

"No offence, Mike, you know what I mean."

"What *do* you mean?" Raymond asks.

Trey crosses his arms. "When AIDS started, we didn't know what was causing it. Mike didn't know, it's not his fault, none of us knew. But now we know how it's spread, so we should stop spreading it."

"We are, through condom use," Raymond says. "Gay men invented and have promoted safer sex against enormous cultural resistance."

"But we aren't promoting monogamy."

Groans all around. "What about people who say they're monogamous," I ask, glancing at Neil, who casts his eyes away, "but actually aren't?"

Trey says, "Yes, of course, use condoms. But I'm trying to make an argument about our values."

"I have HIV," Michael says, "and I don't have a permanent lover, and I'd like to continue to have sex, so I've packed my condoms. Those are my values."

Mike fixes his eyes on him. "My bedroom's upstairs at the end of the hall."

Dale pushes back from the table, chair scraping noisily. "I'm taking my AIDS out to the patio for a smoke."

Trey waves his hand, surrendering. "Food for thought, fellas. We're all friends here."

Exiting, Dale asks, "Are we?"

At the end of the night, a drunk Neil and a crabby Trey already in bed, the rest of us shed our clothes under the stars and jump into the pool to play Marco Polo—or a version of it we call "Julie Andrews." Raymond asks Mike, wrapped in a towel to stay warm, how he can put up with someone like Trey. Mike says, "When you get a little older, you'll understand why you hang on to friends, even when you change and grow apart. Trey likes to stir shit up, and Neil suffers through it, but they're loyal. They bought me the plane ticket to Christopher's funeral. I didn't even ask, they just did it."

Mike's earlier invitation to Michael, which sounded jokey, turns out to be real: off they go to Mike's bedroom. I watch Derek watch Michael be led away, and I can see how crushed out he is, how *crushed*. Timmy and Dale say good-night, too, so then it's just me, Derek and Raymond.

I've kept one eye on Raymond all day long, as if looking for clues. I don't understand his on-again, off-again with Zack; I don't know if Zack has confided to him about *our* affair. When Raymond casually mentions that he's organizing a birthday gathering for Zack the following Sunday, I feel stung. "His birthday?"

"He's very lady-doesn't-reveal-her-age, but yes, it's his Big Three-Oh."

"His *thirtieth?*" I feel myself deflate. How did I not know this?

The booze is still flowing, and we're all naked, and Derek keeps complimenting Raymond's body, and I can see Raymond likes the attention, though he's too naturally unaffected to really let on. His fitness, on full display, is super-hot and superficial at the same time. Derek's coming on to Raymond gets more and more overt. We've done this before; *they've* done this before without me; maybe it's in the cards tonight. I consider it, but not seriously, not with Zack on my mind. When they start making out, I get up and announce, "Gonna walk to the beach."

Derek says, "I'm too drunk for a walk. Stay."

Raymond slides away from Derek. "I can leave you guys to yourselves."

"I need some space," I say.

Later, in the bathroom, as I rummage through my Dopp kit (better stocked now than on my previous trip to the Pines), Derek steps up behind me and clears this throat. "Nothing much happened with Raymond."

I find his eyes in the mirror. "This isn't really what we planned on, is it?"

"Don't be mad, I'm just trying to enjoy the weekend."

"I'm not mad. I'm sad. The beach stirred up memories of Mom."

I turn around, and suddenly our faces are inches apart, like when actors on screen stand closer than anyone ever does in real life unless they're about to kiss. We aren't about to kiss. We've barely kissed since I arrived. I want us to be that magical couple who can be there for each other no matter what, who can be sexually open without losing their emotional bond. But I'm not fully in it, not the way I used to be, and I'm not sure he is either. Still, this is supposed to be our therapy weekend, so without any more processing, we crawl into bed and hold onto each other for a little while before rolling apart and falling into separate dreams.

Sad and Free

Two of the four Wigstock bashers, the two with the sticks, have been charged with bias assault. The assistant district attorney assigned to the case is named Miller. He has a thin neck, a soft chin and a smile that indicates he wants to please. "We're all on the same side here," he says, as if that needs to be established. "This is assault, plain and simple. We have witnesses, we have medical records, and we have photos. Open, shut."

"Is the fact that we were in drag going to be a problem?" I ask.

"You won't be in drag in the courtroom, right?"

"No. I'd never been in drag before that day."

"Good, good," he says, writing that down.

"But don't you want to establish their motive?" Derek asks.

Miller nods in a deliberate way that doesn't necessarily convey agreement. "It was a festival, this Woodstock event?"

"Wigstock."

"So everyone's in wigs? Is that the idea?"

"Pretty much everyone is dressed up," I reply. "The guys who attacked us were *not*. It was a gay party. They knew that."

More thoughtful nodding, more jottings on the pad.

We go over our witness list. The two of us and Michael will definitely take the stand. Miller says, "I've been in touch with Zachary Jones, but it sounds like he might not be around for the trial. Says he's moving to San Francisco."

"Zack said that?" I ask sharply.

Miller assures us we'll get a deposition from Zack if he isn't around. I can hear Miller continue, can hear Derek asking follow-up questions, but little of it sinks in. Zack is *leaving?* When we spoke a week earlier, Zack told me his charges from Wigstock had been dropped. He'd gone to court but the cops didn't show up to testify, so the judge dismissed the case. He didn't mention anything about leaving New York.

Later, I call him from a payphone. "You're moving to San Francisco?"

"Change of pace," he says vaguely.

"*Zack*—"

"I know this woman who needs a subletter, and I'm thinking of trying it out, if I can get work there."

"And if you do?"

"Maybe it's the next place for me."

What about me, what about us? I think, but I have no ground to stand on. "I just wish I didn't hear it from the stupid DA," I say.

"Kiddo, you got a lotta living to do. Most of it ain't going to involve me."

"I should go," I say, crushed.

"Let's get together after work," he says.

I meet him at Veselka, where over plastic cups of hot tea and bowls of mushroom barley soup, he says, "Look, nothing's set in stone, but I've been in New York ten years and I've never seen it so bad. Bashings at Wigstock?"

"But your life is here."

"There are things I want to do, just for me," he says. "I want to drive cross-country. I've never done that. I want to hike in the mountains, real mountains. I want to feel an earthquake—that kind of power."

"You want to be overwhelmed." He looks away, perhaps embarrassed. "And what happens if you get sick?"

"It's San Francisco, they know what to do there."

"Great, no problem then."

He falls silent. It's the one thing we never speak about.

I try again. "If you stay here, you'll have people to take care of you."

"People?"

"*Me.*"

"I would never ask that of you. Plus, you're someone else's boyfriend."

"You don't think I'd take care of you if you needed it?"

I watch his face soften, a hint of surrender revealing a reservoir of need. "Let's just do what we do well, you and me, for as long as we can."

I leave Derek a message saying that I'll be home late, not to worry.

It's autumn. The temperature is dropping. On the F, Zack throws his arm over my shoulder, and we sit like that all the way to his stop, while other passengers do that New York thing of looking without staring, noticing without reacting, imprinting and then turning away.

Strangely, after everything I've been through, I don't worry about being harassed or bothered. Next to him, I tell myself, I'm safe.

Some guys smile after an orgasm, breaking out of the intensity with a grin that seems to say, wasn't it silly how worked up I got? Derek was like that, diffusing the panting aftermath with a joke. The threeways we had with friends usually ended in dopey grins and a quick return to conversation.

There's another type of guy who goes blank after coming, reverting—willfully or unconsciously, I've never been sure—to the unknowable person he was before he let down his guard. Throughout my life, I've tricked with guys like this and always left unfulfilled, no matter how good the sex.

And then there are the guys whose faces stay enraptured, bodies quivering long after the last spurt. That was Zack. He never cut an orgasm short. He would let it buoy him like the weight-bearing surface of a salt lake as he floated in the sun. I remember him holding my hand on his cock after he came, making me make him endure every last wave of painful pleasure; he would gasp for breath, and I'd cover his mouth with mine, ready to suffocate together. I was ecstatic to have finally met someone with the same physical hunger as mine.

Back at his apartment for the first time since June, I feel unexpectedly but deeply at home among the clippings and clutter, the art in progress, all the pieces of his unguarded self on display. As if catching up on lost time, we fuck all night, making each other come with our hands, our mouths, with me inside of him. A hallucinogenic drug trip, I think, might be like this: no sense of the clock, the outside world, or anything beyond the heightened, feverish present.

Is he like this with other guys? In my mind I manufacture jealous whispers: I'm not special, I'm just the latest conquest, he didn't tell me his birthday is coming up or that he wants to move cross-country. I ask, "Is sex always this intense for you?"

He rolls toward me and runs his fingers across my cheek, still discolored from that basher's bruise. He says, "You sound concerned."

"Because you're older—"

"Watch it!"

"OK, more experienced. And I don't usually top. So I don't know if I'm doing it right, and—" *Oh hell, just say every stupid thing you're thinking.* "I don't know if I'm big enough down there."

He laughs so merrily that I have no choice but to join him. In that moment I feel myself releasing what feels like a lifetime of insecurity.

I float out of Zack's on a high, but on the cold journey back to the East Village, rehearsing the story I'm going to tell Derek about where I was from five o'clock until midnight, my mood quickly tanks. It's not just that I'm torn between my feelings for Zack and my relationship with Derek, it's some other nugget of sadness at my core, easily incited by almost anything. It's the old woman in a torn, filthy coat, her life in the bags she carries, dry-heaving over a garbage can, who scurries away from me shamefully when I ask if she needs help. It's "Like a Prayer" on my Walkman, Madonna singing *Just like a dream, you are not what you seem,* and the way I can't help but cry while the gospel chorus soars.

With thirty years' distance, I can name what was happening: I was grieving. Back then I thought grief was limited to the immediate aftermath of death, not something that stretched on without an expiration date. If you'd asked me at the time, I might have said I was frustrated with temp work, confused about my relationship, angry about AIDS, and I would have pointed to all the ways life went on like always—busy, active, even fun at times. I'd be *fine.* I believed that *time would heal all wounds* and that I was already healing. I didn't know it would take years, even decades. I was twenty-three. What did I know about time?

We all go to specific clubs on specific nights—Rock and Roll Fag Bar on Tuesdays, Boy Bar on Thursdays. On Sundays, it's Mars Needs Men, in an industrial building at the edge of the West Side Highway, three stories plus a roof deck overlooking the dilapidated piers rotting in the Hudson. There's a big dancefloor downstairs, ruled by go-go boys in white briefs, and a smaller one upstairs, where a few times a night a drag performance erupts, fierce queens with names like Glamamore and Perfidia lip-synching with expressive mouths, giving ironic twists to standards and pop songs. Sometimes we dance until Monday's sunrise, then walk home through the meatpacking district: spent, drunk gay boys wearing ACT UP t-shirts with bloody handprints—One AIDS Death Every 10 Minutes—fluttering past butchers in white smocks smeared with actual animal blood.

This Sunday night at Mars, we're celebrating Zack's birthday. By the time Derek and I arrive, Zack is on the dancefloor, feet planted and hands fisted, arms pumping from the elbow. Friends surround him, celebrating his thirtieth. He's a clunky dancer, but beneath the disco ball's sparkle, he's luminous. He spots me through the crowd and smiles, meeting my wave with a nod and then closing his eyes, as if giving me permission to watch. Dancing just for me.

Derek and I check our coats, then head to the bar, where Raymond is lining up tequila shots, passing lime wedges and a saltshaker from hand to hand. When he sees us, he calls to the bartender for two more, then says, "Make it four!"

"I've hardly done tequila shots since college," I say, voice raised above the dance beat. "Remember, Derek? That lousy Mexican place?"

"I remember you got so drunk on margaritas you puked on my car."

"As a rule," Raymond says, "*on* is better than *in*."

Down go the shots, first one then the next. The buzz hits me right away.

The dancefloor is bumping to "Everybody Everybody," the Euro-disco hit from Black Box that's quickly becoming the song of the season. I sway in place, wailing along, diva-style, "Set me free-ee-ee-ee, set me free-ee—"

"S*ad and free*," Raymond interrupts. "Not set me free."

"Are you sure?"

"It's clearer on the twelve-inch."

"Don't argue with a DJ," Derek says.

"I like my version better."

"She's *been* set free," Raymond explains. "She's just not happy yet."

I love this song, so I slip out to the dancefloor, weaving through the crowd to Zack. He throws an arm over my shoulder. "You've been shining those big blue eyes on me. Where's my 'Happy Birthday'?"

"Oh, it's your birthday? How would I know?" He pulls me in tighter, refusing to take my bait, and his scent, instantly familiar, fans across me. I drop the sarcasm. "I wish I had a present for you."

Zack steps in closer, leaning into my ear, his breath hot against me. "I have a present for you."

"You do?"

"I started a new painting, inspired by you."

"That's incredible. I don't know what to say."

"Say you'll come over and see it."

"Yeah, of course I will." But I don't say when. I don't *know* when.

I move my lips to his. He's ready for it. The kiss knocks everything else out of focus, sends time out of whack. For an infinite moment, it's just us.

Then reality returns, the sound of Derek's voice: "Aw, look at that." He's going for a light tone, but his eyes seem less certain. He and Raymond are leaning into each other, with Derek looking back over to me and Zack between whispers. Is he jealous? That doesn't make sense, after everything we've been through.

Zack pulls me back toward him, and I step in closer, and I stay there for what seems like hours.

In the men's room, two guys are saying that Elizabeth Taylor is dead.

"Wait, what? What have you heard?"

One of them says that she had a stroke, or maybe a heart attack; the other heard it was a severe allergic reaction. I'm horrified. She's one of the only celebrities who speaks out about AIDS, calling for more research, better policy, less stigma, using her Hollywood fame as leverage to shift public opinion.

Back before the Internet, a rumor like this could float through the club all night and cast a pall for hours.

I find Derek and ask if he's heard anything. He hasn't, but he snaps to alertness. "They'll know at my job," he says, and he goes in search of a payphone.

At the bar, ordering a drink, I catch sight of Zack with a boy named Brian who I recognize from treatment and data. Brian leans in for a kiss. Zack receives it and gives back. Their lips hold, Brian's hand resting on Zack's upper arm, Zack's hand gripping Brian's waist. Brian has a flop of brunette bangs that drape across their locked lips. He's younger than me, a twink, and he's HIV-positive, which he's been open about. I'm struck by the sudden, strong thought that Zack should be with someone like Brian who also lives with the monumental knowledge of the virus in his body. What good was I to him when I could hardly raise the subject? Positive guys getting together made sense. The idea of sero-sorting wasn't yet a given, as it later became, in part because we still operated under the idea that everyone had the virus, so you used condoms with everyone. People talked about different "strains" of HIV, so even if you were positive you might use condoms with another positive guy because the HIV he had might not be the HIV you had. We knew so little, so many years into the epidemic, and we clung to half understanding all the time.

Then Brian is gone, and for a moment Zack is all alone in the midst of the pumping, crowded club. He lights a cigarette with a series of gestures I already know so well: cigarette dangling from the right side of his mouth, right hand giving the lighter a reflexive shake, left hand cupping the flame, lips drawing in, ember flaring, eyes narrowing to a squint as the smoke releases. He does old-school cool like it's second nature.

"Take a picture," he calls out. "Lasts longer."

I step toward him. "You think he's sexy?"

"Brian? Come on, Kiddo. Don't pout about one kiss."

"I'm not pouting."

"You're about to." He touches my chin. "Don't be jealous. It doesn't make sense for us."

"Sorry." Am I allowed to say, I only want to kiss you, I only want you to kiss me? Am I like Trey on Fire Island, promoting monogamy in my own mind (but with someone who's not my boyfriend)? What's happened to the liberated sexuality I've been cultivating since I got to New York? Why do I feel less and less like having sex with anyone other than Zack?

Derek is suddenly here again. "It's not true."

"What?"

"Elizabeth Taylor is not dead."

"Was she sick?" Zack asks.

"She's in the hospital. The media reported it. But I talked to my boss, and he talked to someone in her circle who says she's fine. My heart is really beating fast. I think I'm not in the mood to be here."

Zack points to a cocktail table lined with four full glasses. "Have one of these. Everyone's buying for me, I can't drink them all."

Derek throws back the amber liquid, drops the glass heavily and says, "Enjoy your birthday." Then he walks away.

I scurry behind, following him toward the coat check. When I reach his side, he says, "You can have him all to yourself."

"Come on, Derek."

"You like him. Don't pretend you don't. You slept with him."

"I'm too drunk to process this right now."

"Big fucking surprise," he says.

"You've had more to drink than me!"

His shoulders slump. His eyes flicker wetly. He says, "I need to go."

Maybe something else is wrong, maybe I should try harder to convince him to stay, enjoy the night with our friends, push out of this mood. Or maybe the right response is, *I'll go with you,* so we can talk at home about what's going on, where we're at, how we're going to move forward with all this swirling emotion. Maybe if I'd done that, things wouldn't have played out the way they did later, the next day, in the days and weeks and months to come. Maybe maybe maybe.

But I say good-bye and remain at Mars Needs Men without him. I return to Zack's side and we drain a couple more drinks and we dance and kiss as much as we want. I try my hardest not to fret about Derek, and when it's time to go, I go with Zack. We walk the dark streets, through blasts of cold air from refrigerated meatpacking plants, past trucks filled with carcasses, across gutters running red.

The next morning, Derek is sitting motionless on the couch, his face striped by shadows from the window blinds. As he watches me enter the apartment in last night's clothes, only his eyes move, like an animal on alert.

"Did you get my message?" I ask. I'd placed a call in the early morning hours.

"Your non-message."

"I said I wasn't coming home."

"Don't you think I deserve a little more information?"

"I guess." We've stretched the limits of our relationship; am I breaking a rule if the rules have become unclear?

"Were you with Zack?" I nod. "Why didn't you tell me about him?"

"Tell you what?"

He points a finger at the coffee table, at a stack of my journals, speckled black and white composition books. I hadn't noticed them there, though now the pile pulses luridly in a slanting beam of light.

"Did you read them?" I ask.

"Did you *want* me to? You're always scribbling away at the table, and then leaving it right there, like you're daring me to look. His name is all over it. *Zack—*"

"This is fucked up, Derek."

"You wrote that you're in *love* with him."

"I wrote that for myself."

"I tell you everything," he says, voice cracking.

I scan the notebooks as if checking for muddy fingerprints. *He read my journal?* I cross the room to the kitchen, open the freezer, reach for the coffee, see a bottle of vodka, grab that instead.

"Oh, now you're going to get drunk?" Derek says. "Because I read about that, too. '*Should I be worried about my drinking?*'"

"Don't fucking quote my journal to me."

"How many times have you been with him? It started before Montreal, didn't it? Because that was the first I knew of it."

"I just wanted something for myself." I gulp the vodka. It carves a cool channel to my stomach. Derek hasn't moved from the couch, his stillness a measure of the righteous indignation he feels. Or perhaps he's hurt so deeply that he's simply trying not to melt down.

Amidst my anger I feel a pang of empathy. I need to speak the truth. I say, "Zack's positive."

"Yeah, I read that, too."

"We use condoms—"

"What about your fantasies? Mike Savas? Have you seen Mike lately? Have you seen what he looks like?"

"That was a *fantasy*. I wrote that years ago. Wait—how far back did you read?"

"I had all night," he says.

"This is so incredibly fucked up."

"Your lying is what's fucked up."

"When this thing with Zack started, I wanted it to be mine, not something I shared. Everything else in my life has been *ours*. And then it got deeper."

"That's not our agreement! Are you even in love with me anymore?"

"Not after you've read my journals."

"I knew you had a secret. I tell you everything. God, you suck." His voice has never been so raw. He stands up and walks to the bedroom, returning in a winter coat. "I'm going to work. I don't want to see you when I get back."

"Where am I supposed to go?"

"Figure it out," he says, and is gone.

I reach again for the vodka.

I leave the apartment intending to walk until I find some clarity, but I'm not dressed warmly enough for the weather. Winter in New York means every street corner is a wide slushy lake, every curb a pile of rot-colored mush. Cold wind blows through your clothes, gripping your skin, freezing your bones. People disappear beneath thick, shapeless coats and face-concealing scarves. Everyone—pedestrians, drivers, store owners, the homeless—seems tense.

I think about calling Zack, but something makes me hold back. I go to Amanda's building on 10th Street instead. I press the grimy little doorbell. "I'm on a deadline," she says through the intercom.

"Relationship crisis," I say.

She buzzes me up, and I tell her what's happened. "This is good," she says. "You guys needed to put everything on the table."

"But if it's over with Derek, where will I go?"

"Raymond just told me he wants to move out, so there's space here."

This is the best thing I've heard in forever.

She returns to what she's working on—an application to NYU film school—while I slip into her bed and under the covers. I stare up at the Christmas lights strung around the apartment, never unplugged. I count each individual bulb, beads on a glowing chain, like days in the year, and when counting doesn't bring on sleep, I try to calculate the number of days I've been with Derek. It's two years and many months—I can't do math in my head—something like nine hundred or one thousand days since that student conference when Larry Kramer first demanded we do something about AIDS. Since then, every day has felt crammed to the limit, my heart always pulsing at full strength, Derek at my side, partner in crime, significant other. Looked at one way, it seems as though we've just moved in together, signed a lease, installed cabinets. So much still ahead. But looked at another way, enough time has passed to prove that we're not getting closer, not going deeper. We've gotten emotionally attached to other people. We don't trust each other. Is there a way back from that?

It's Monday, so there's an ACT UP meeting that night, and we both have to be there. But we arrive separately and keep apart.

During a break, I find Derek on the sidewalk, ranting to Nicholas about me and Zack, loud enough for anyone to hear. Nicholas catches my eye and waves his cigarette, a signal: *Go back in, I'll handle this.*

That night, at home, we argue, bargain, blame. Am I still planning on seeing Zack? Derek asks incredulously. Can we work something out? I wonder. You're deluded, he accuses. Zack might be moving to San Francisco, I tell him. So you just expect me to wait around until he leaves? he asks.

What if we adjust our relationship? I try. Are we still in a relationship? he asks. Back and forth until we exhaust ourselves and fall into bed. After so much tension, this physical proximity is completely charged, and when I look at him, I see hunger in his eyes. We kiss furiously, ready to chew each other up and spit out blood. Combative, clawing, rough. I know what I want: I want to *feel* something with him. To be affected by him. To get fucked by him. He must feel it too, because we get there quickly, my legs up and him spitting on my hole and going in roughly without a condom. I urge him on, *harder, don't be nice*, and he complies, a cold look in his eyes. It's never before happened like this, all the way to the end, him letting loose inside, both of us climaxing at the same time, moaning like demons. Done, we roll apart and lie there panting, eyes to the ceiling. When at last we look at each other again, I see an unmistakable finality in his expression. It's there in mine too, I'm sure. We both seem to understand: Nothing is left. We've spent it all. It's over.

Zack's response to the news that Derek and I are breaking up: "It's about time."

"I'm all yours," I say.

"No, Kiddo, you're all *yours.*"

This conversation happens on the phone; he's leaving that night on a red-eye, for San Francisco, where he'll be working for a couple of weeks at an agency, a freelance gig that might turn into something longer. He uses the word "exploratory," and my stomach drops to my feet. I won't get to see him before he flies away. It feels like I'll never see him again.

"You're going to forget about me," I say.

"Never," he says.

Part 7

The Devils

Stop the Church. That's what we're calling the next big demonstration, at Saint Patrick's Cathedral.

ACT UP has been everywhere lately, from the floor of the stock exchange, calling out price-gouging of AIDS drugs, to the Centers for Disease Control in Atlanta, raising hell about the lack of data about women with AIDS. On nights when I facilitate, I move through the agenda marveling at our capacity to always do more. Now we're taking on the Catholic Church, alongside WHAM, a women-led reproductive rights group, by protesting at St. Patrick's.

But here's the problem: Unlike the government, which operates at least nominally according to democratic principles, the church answers to none but the God of its own definition. I'd been to Mass every weekend of my childhood, and I felt pretty sure that our demands would be ignored, rendering our actions symbolic, which had never been ACT UP's way. We did not operate out of symbols or theory. We succeeded by making concrete demands. Even the name of this action spoke to the impossibility of success. Stop the Church? Stop what, exactly? Stop it *how?*

Listening to me rant, Amanda advises, "Take a break."

"From facilitating?" She nods, like this is obvious, though it hasn't yet occurred to me. No one takes a break. You get involved and you stay involved.

And so on a cold Sunday in December, I stand outside St. Patrick's Cathedral among many thousands of protesters at our largest demonstration ever. Counter-protesters across Fifth Avenue shout *"Burn in Hell,"* while police stand arm to arm in greater number than we've ever seen. Our affinity groups deliver campy theatrics: someone dresses as "Cardinal O'Condom"; others carry signs that say KNOW YOUR SCUMBAGS, with the cardinal pictured in profile, his pointed miter like the tip of an unfurled rubber. A caravan of taxicabs rolls up, unloading circus clowns who dash along the sidewalk handing out leaflets proclaiming AIDS IS NO JOKE. On the picket line, among our steady chanting, I see faces so enraged that I guess this is what I looked like the night I hopped the fence in the Village. Inside the cathedral, an unknown number of activists plan to stand during the cardinal's homily and turn their backs, or lie down in the aisles, a silent die-in that will surely lead to arrests.

But as the demonstration becomes the top story of every news outlet in New York (and many more around the world), the media focuses only on the handful inside who stood on pews and shouted at the cardinal until he gave up trying to deliver his homily, and the single protester who takes communion—*The Body of Christ, Amen*—then drops the consecrated wafer on the floor. The tabloids declare the entire thing a desecration.

The next morning, I'm reading the *Daily News*—GAYS NABBED AT ST. PATS—when the phone rings. It's Javier, from the media committee, who needs a Catholic to talk to a reporter on camera. I pin a STOP THE CHURCH button to my red shirt, the newest, cleanest garment I own, and within an hour a guy from ABC News with an Irish surname shows up with a cameraman. I try to talk about the issues, like the Church's political influence. He keeps asking about that crumpled wafer.

"I know it probably seems that ACT UP likes to cause trouble for its own sake," I say, "but the truth is, we give a lot of time and thought to our tactics."

That night, before heading to our general meeting, I watch the broadcast:

> Reporter: *Those of you who saw the*
> *shocking images of protestors shouting*
> *in the aisles of St. Patrick's yesterday*
> *might be surprised by these words*
> *from one of the organizers:*
> Me: —*we give a lot of time and*
> *thought to our tactics*—
> Reporter: *Though this might seem*
> *closer to the truth:*
> Me:—*ACT UP likes to cause trouble*
> *for its own sake*—

Every time they cut to my face, I'm scowling, my busted lip still swollen; my buzzed head makes me look like an inmate; my red shirt is like a taunt to a charging bull. The caption reads: FRANK MURPHY, ACT UP. *Frank Murphy?*

At the Center, an unhappy Javier finds me. I explain how my words were edited out of order. "That reporter's on our shit list," he says. "He'll be sorry."

Larry Kramer catches sight of me and says he saw the report, too. "Why did you give them an alias?" he asks.

"I gave him my name. Maybe he didn't write it down."

"I figured you didn't want your parents to know."

"Larry, I'm out to my parents."

I've stood in front of our five-hundred-person meetings every other week for more than a year. My name and phone number are on the contact sheet. I faced down Larry himself not so long ago. But it seems I might still be seen as a coward, a boy in the closet. I feel my face flush, red as the shirt I'd stupidly worn on camera.

Most of that night's meeting is about the fallout from St. Patrick's. Many people voice concerns that we've set back our cause. Tempers run hotter than ever. I feel nearly dizzy at times trying to manage it, and I can tell that Timmy, facilitating with me, also feels the frenzy. So it's with some relief that we come to an agenda item that has nothing to do with the church.

Two men from the actions committee announce a new model of protest: the actionette. "It's smaller than a full-scale action, but not as spontaneous as a zap," says one of them.

"We need actions that don't require thousands of people to show up, or even hundreds," says the other.

"But at the same time, they're not totally reactive, like a zap."

"An actionette is an action-lite."

"Less filling. But tastes great."

They've targeted a cocktail fundraiser for the New York Republican Party. An affinity group will infiltrate; a larger number will protest outside.

"OK," I say to the room. "There you have it. The actionette. Let's discuss."

People ask questions about demands and logistics, and after the allotted time, I say we're ready to vote. Then I see one more hand. I call on Essence, a teenager involved with Treatment and Data who has proven to be an indispensable researcher, though she's only eighteen. She's super smart and has great style: Buddy Holly glasses and a Louise Brooks bob, homemade t-shirts and shit-kicker boots. She makes me feel over the hill.

I ask if she has a question before we vote on the actionette.

"A comment: the use of the feminine suffix *ette* to describe something that is considered *less than* is sexist." Her face is set, her stance firm.

I look to Timmy. He gives me nothing. Stumped, I say, "We'll definitely put that comment in the minutes." I see other hands go up.

"Language matters," Essence says. "I move to withdraw the term *actionette*."

The guys from the actions committee also look completely caught off guard. One says, "It's just a name."

The boy sitting next to Essence, a punk kid with green hair, jumps to his feet. "Why can't we just call it an action? Even though it's smaller? Why not just call it an action regardless of the size?"

"Can we have a point of order about it?" Essence says.

"Yeah, or we can just laugh about it and move on," I say.

From several directions I hear an extended hiss, the universal sound of gay disapproval. Hands fly into the air. I've fucked up. I've been patronizing. And somehow, I've still got to manage the discussion.

I know then—clear as anything I've ever known—my time as facilitator is over.

The person I want to talk to about this is Eliot, who has stepped down as administrator. I miss him at the front table, his hand steadily recording, his face retaining its Buster Keaton calm. He was an anchor amid the fluctuating dynamics, needing only to lift an eyebrow and pause his pen mid-stroke to register his opinion. How I wish he'd been up there with me on my last night.

I leave several messages before he returns my call and invites me over.

"You've been avoiding me," I say as he greets me at his apartment door.

"It's not personal. Burnout is a bitch, and recovery is her cruel sister."

"Why do people say *burned out* and not just *tired?*"

"My dear, burnout is not simple exhaustion. It's the nastiness that comes when you *ignore* the exhaustion, when you're out of steam but keep pushing the machine to do more."

"I have no idea what that's like," I say dryly.

"I thought the ship would sink without me," he says, "and then I realized it wouldn't, which was worse! *ACT UP is not going to collapse? Why the hell not?*"

I tell him about "Frank Murphy" and Larry Kramer, about Essence and her friend and their objection to actionette. "I liked *actionette*," I say. "It's the exact silliness ACT UP used to be good at."

"*ACT UP, Fight Back, Fry Eggs!*" he says, raising a martini glass.

When I tell him that Derek and I are ending things, he protests, "But you're our Paul Newman and Joanne Woodward!" When I tell him about Zack, he recasts me as Liz Taylor, dumping Eddie Fisher for Richard Burton—which I suggest doesn't bode well for our future.

"What went wrong?" he asks.

"I don't know. We've changed? Maybe we're both burned out."

"Different types of crazy, you two."

"Derek's neurotic and I'm psychotic?"

"There are medications for that," he says.

Tonight's installment of my Queen's Cinematic Education is *The Devils*, a terrifying, psychedelic story of hysteria among medieval French nuns, who are accused by an evil cardinal of being possessed by Satan. "How timely," I say.

"ACT UP has nothing on these sisters," Eliot notes.

We drink too much and forget to eat. When it's time for me to go, he grips me tightly, and I feel what I've often sensed in his good-byes, that he treats each one as if it were the last. "Get home safely," he urges, and though we are at his apartment, I drunkenly reply, "You too."

Love Is a Stranger

I've never been through a breakup and am unprepared for its acid taste. Dividing our belongings doesn't take long because we don't own much— some furniture, basic cookware, an embryonic CD collection—though it feels like an epic tug of war as we try to be "fair," a word we throw around a lot. *If you take the sauté pan it's not really fair to also get the pasta pot...* Monetary value substitutes for emotional hurt. I'm bitterly aware of the things I don't like about Derek, and when he looks back at me through pained eyes, I see that he's doing the same calculation. At night, pulling out the sofabed's heavy steel frame, it's like lugging our one thousand days from the shadows. There I am, at the tail end of this long run, alone on an uncomfortable mattress.

Zack calls from San Francisco. They're working him hard, he hasn't seen as much as he wants to see, the city is pretty but small. "Every other gay man seems sick," he says. "In New York, AIDS feels hidden. Here, it's out in the open. It's kind of scary for me, but also more real." This is possibly the most I've heard him say about living with HIV. Maybe San Francisco makes sense for him, I think, and then squelch the thought. When he asks about me, I complain that I'm still waiting for Raymond to move out of Amanda's. Zack says I should stay at his place. The super has a key. "Do it," he says. "I like knowing you'll be there." He's calling from a payphone, and the sun, he says, is shining through a rainstorm. "Oh wow," he exclaims, "there's a rainbow right above me!" In his excitement he shouts at someone passing by, "Look up!," as buoyant as I've ever heard him.

Being in Zack's apartment without him eases the longing. I can see, smell and *feel* him everywhere, reliving the nights I've spent here, imagining more to come. I can block out the fear that he might actually move across the country for good.

On the weekend, without quite planning it, I have an entire Saturday and Sunday clear. I stay in his apartment all day except to get food, which I carry back and eat on the mattress where we fuck. I throw open the windows, despite the winter cold, because the smell of paint is intense—have I somehow ignored it before? It can't be good for his health to be smothered in fumes like this. There's a second room at the back of the apartment that I've never been in before. I always assumed it was a closet, but it's bigger than that, a small bedroom he uses for storage: cardboard boxes gape open, full of art supplies, fabric, tools. Stacks of magazines and books rest everywhere, some of them—textbooks, store catalogues, illustrated encyclopedias—cut up, plundered for collages. There are novels I've heard of but never read, like *Last Exit to Brooklyn*, the Frantz Fanon tome *Black Skin, White Masks* that I saw on Raymond's nightstand a year ago, and James Baldwin's *The Fire Next Time*, which Floyd told me to read. Outside the window is a fire escape above an unkempt yard: busted concrete, a rusty fence, spindly bushes waiting for spring. For a couple hours in the afternoon the fire escape is awash in sunshine. Even in the winter air I'm able to stay out there, on a cushion, wrapped in blankets, reading. From somewhere hip-hop plays loudly, Public Enemy, "Fight the Power."

You were born into a society which spelled out with brutal clarity, and in as many ways as possible, that you were a worthless human being. You were not expected to aspire to excellence: you were expected to make peace with mediocrity. Zack has underlined these words, addressed by Baldwin to his young nephew. *And when he realizes that the treatment accorded him has nothing to do with anything he has done, that the attempt of white people to destroy him—for that is what it is—is utterly gratuitous, it is not hard for him to think of white people as devils.* Floyd's words come back to me: You don't know the truth about yourself. And maybe it's the book, or the music, or just being here on Zack's fire escape at this moment in my life, but I finally hear what Floyd was trying to tell me, that racism is a problem for white people, who don't know who they are without their, *our*, categories, bigotries, hatred, othering. I wonder, too, what Zack does with this knowledge. He doesn't define himself as Black or white. I've heard him say *mixed* and *biracial*; I've heard him say *passing*. His own story is a variation of the one being breathed in fire on these pages, in the music blaring across the yard. His own story—I get it now—is the one he makes into pictures, mixed media, a hybrid of paint and varnish and paper and glue.

Moving day finally comes.

"What about these?" I ask Derek, pointing at the violet curtains in the bedroom. We stare at them together.

"I guess they're yours," he says quietly.

"They were made for this apartment. I should leave them."

He looks away from the curtains, looks at me, looks away again, like there's nowhere safe for his gaze, and says, "They'll just remind me of you."

"They remind me of *her*," I say. "I'll take them." I pull a chair to the window and start easing the fabric off the curtain rod. I hear him exit the room behind me. It's a quiet moment that gongs loudly in my brain: *This Is Really Happening*. I'm leaving him, leaving this apartment, leaving the "us" I fought so hard for my family to accept, and my mother is gone, too, a real person now a memory, a collection of mementos. She made these curtains with her hands. I touched her cold hand in her coffin, pleading with her to return. There is no return, there is only forward.

Amanda and Hillary help me haul out my stuff: three boxes of books, a lamp and end table I bought at a flea market, the VCR, a boombox that plays cassettes, which I've owned since college, a big armchair, a futon I found through the classifieds, which will be my new bed, files of articles I've clipped, and the notebooks I've filled with my scrawl. There's a box of photos and letters, a few bags of clothes, the coffee maker, my mother's blender, my Farrah Fawcett drinking cup. Nicholas waits at the curb in a double-parked station wagon, a heap, borrowed from one of his artist friends. At Amanda's, we quickly unload everyone on the sidewalk. "Is your apartment locked?" I ask her.

She hands me a key. "It's yours now, too."

We pile everything into the center of the flat, where I'll sleep. Then Nicholas leaves to return the car. Hillary, who has said very little throughout all of this, announces she's leaving too and slinks away with an understated good-bye.

Amanda scurries around the apartment as if determined to get me settled as soon as possible. There are drawers cleared for my clothes and shelves emptied for my books. We unfurl the futon on the floor between the half-wall to the kitchen and the doorway-without-a-door that marks Amanda's space. The big chair I brought doesn't really fit. She wedges it between the two windows that face the street, right up against her bed. Standing back and looking at it, she shakes her head and covers her face with her hands. Is she crying?

"We can get rid of that chair," I say. "It's too big."

"It's not the chair," she says. "It's me and Hillary. We can't work it out."

"What's wrong?"

"She refuses to get rid of that straight girl, Shanna."

"Shanna's straight?" Last I saw her, she'd shaved her head, pierced her nose and wore a button that said "Don't Assume I'm Hetero."

"She was until Hillary. But what the fuck do I know about sexuality?"

I give her a hug but she can't relax into it. She wants to take a bath. In the kitchen, she lifts off the slab of wood that covers the tub and props it against the front door, covering the multiple locks and the sliding peephole.

We strip down and climb in as the water rushes forth with an airy screech, filling in warmly around us, bubbles rising to the surface. We scrub each other with a sliver of soap and scoop up water in a plastic take-out container, dumping it across our bodies. I brush out her tangled hair.

"There is some good news," she says. "My name is on the lease now."

"How'd you manage that?"

"I just walked into the landlord's office downstairs, and I gave them the name of Raymond's ex, who held the lease, but I said he was *my* ex and that I had kicked him out because he beat me."

"You convinced him to turn over the lease?"

"First he wanted $100 more a month but I bargained him down to $50. I told him, 'I have nowhere to go,' which was not a lie. If he kicked me out it would be hard to find another place I could afford."

"Good for you."

"Yeah, it's mine. And yours, for as long as you want it."

We stay in the bath for more than an hour, adding hot water and analyzing our exes, thrilled with our resentments but also castigating ourselves for our monstrous shortcomings: my dishonesty, her mood swings, her confusion about what she expected from Hillary, my cowardice in not telling Derek about Zack. A shared cigarette sits perched in an ashtray on the lip of the tub, and in between puffs she wipes away tears. I don't cry. I'm not even sad. I'm in a state of measured anticipation. What happens next is unknown, but right here, in this room filled with steam and smoke, we're preparing ourselves. Out the open window I hear dance music from a passing boom box, fading up and then away. I hear car horns, a bouncing basketball, an ambulance siren. I hear a voice calling across an invisible distance, and I hear a reply.

When Zack returns, we spend nearly every night together, so much so that I start fantasizing about living with him in Brooklyn. I tell him how much I liked being in his apartment while he was away, reading his books and thinking about what *he* thinks when he's here, and maybe understanding a little more what his art is about, or for. He clamps me into his arms while we sleep, but he doesn't ask me to move in, doesn't ask me to move to San Francisco.

"Do you think he's trying to get away from me?" I ask Amanda.

"Drama queen."

"What?"

"You just left a long relationship. He's doing you a favor."

On a weekend morning at Zack's, I wake to the squishy sound of paint squeezed from a tube. He stands in front of his easel, wearing loose jeans and a long-sleeved shirt, all smeared with color. There's a paintbrush in his mouth, two more in his left hand and another in his right. He steps close, makes a mark, steps back and studies it, then moves forward again. From the mattress, I watch this dance, as stroke by stroke he transforms negative space with light blue, darker blue, some deep green, then a slash of rusty red, stirring some flat form to life. It looks like—I think it *is*—a map of New Jersey. When I ask him about this, he acknowledges me for the first time since I woke, and nods.

"Put some music on," he says, brush still in his mouth. "Too quiet in here."

His boombox—splattered with paint like so much of his stuff—has a mixtape in it. I press play, and the Eurythmics sing, *"Love is a stranger in an open car to tempt you in and drive you far away."*

"You know I'm from New Jersey, right?"

He nods. "My father lives there now. Near the shore."

"Do you see him much?"

He shakes his head. "No reason to." After a moment he removes the brush from his mouth and wipes it on his sleeve, smearing red. "New Jersey is this in-between place," he says. "I grew up outside of Philly, and I've been in New York for years, and there's this densely packed state in between that feels like, I don't know, the mental distance between one and the other."

"Between who you used to be—"

"Yeah, and what I became." He shakes out a cigarette and then throws the crushed pack and the lighter to me. "My dad married one of her friends—this white woman, she was in a book group with my mom. They used to meet at our house, and I'd hang all the ladies' coats in the hall closet and fill their wine glasses and empty their ashtrays. I was raised on secondhand smoke."

"My mother was a big reader, too," I say.

"Yeah?"

"She'd order these historical novels from the Book of the Month Club, these big sweeping sagas, and leave them on the coffee table, and I'd pick them up and start reading along. There'd be one bookmark for her and one for me."

"Aw, that's sweet," he says.

"She used to tell me I would write a book of my own one day."

"So when are you gonna start?"

"When there's a cure for AIDS? Does the virus stop to write a novel?"

"The virus doesn't stop at all, Kiddo."

"Enough with 'Kiddo.' I'm not a kid."

He looks back at the canvas. "I'm trying to tell you—I put off my art for a long time."

"I don't know what I'd write about."

"Just look around."

He stubs out the cigarette and picks up his brushes. Conversation over.

I get up and find my overnight bag, pulling out the new notebook I started when I moved out from Derek. This one is blank. I told myself no more diaries. Just start writing creative stuff. Stories. Poetry. Anything that feels like imagination instead of regurgitation. I prop myself up against the wall under the window, morning light falling onto the blank page. I look around, like Zack told me to do. I write:

> Zack wipes paint on his shirt,
> working beneath a picture of Billie Holiday
> listening to Annie Lennox
> talking about his dead mom.
> Painting is messy, paint gets all over.
> Turns out that Zack, so cool and controlled

is disorderly and not easily contained.

I keep writing, listening to the sound of his brushes imprinting the canvas, until it's time to leave. He comes downstairs with me, buys me a coffee at the bagel store. We share a cigarette as he walks me to the subway. He kisses me good-bye and turns away, and I luxuriate for a moment watching him head back home in his paint-stained clothes.

Out With the Old

When I call Dad, he speaks only of Mom. Her kindness and gentleness, her shy smile and bright eyes. The love my parents felt for each other isn't news to me. They held hands in public, giggled over inside jokes, expressed romantic appreciation for anyone to hear. "Hot stuff," my father would call as she came down the stairs in a new dress, ready for a night out. I once caught her looking with bald lust at him; he'd been working in the yard and came into the house pulling off a sweaty t-shirt, torso gleaming. All of this is lost to him, the gifts of a lover, stolen by the shock of death. He's like a castaway, stunned in his isolation.

Amanda suggests we have him over for dinner.

"I don't know if he'll come into the city."

"What if I invite him?" And she's right, that clinches it. They've met only once before, after Mom's funeral, but she made an impression by looking at family photos with him and listening to his stories of courting Mom in the '60s, taking her to see folk singers in the Village and stand-up comics doing "risqué material."

When he arrives, he pokes around the apartment, intrigued by the tub in the kitchen, the mismatched furniture, my futon on the floor, the bookshelves everywhere. After he uses the toilet, he comes out chuckling at the message Amanda has written in Sharpie on the underside of the toilet seat: Boys Must Return Seat to Girls' Position. "Place has got a lot of character," he says.

I'm not at all practiced in the art of the dinner party, but together we pull it off. First, a hunk of brie from a gourmet store on Third Avenue and a round of martinis concocted according to my Fire Island lesson. Next, lasagna—a one-pan entrée I've successfully made before, though the boiled noodles confound me, breaking apart or sticking together, wriggly as freshly caught fish. We open a bottle of Tuscan red, recommended by the guy at the "wine club," a cramped store with a better than average selection where Amanda is a "member." (Buy ten bottles, get the eleventh for free.) We finish with salad—salad *after* dinner is how they do it in Europe, Amanda insists. She whips up a perfect vinaigrette by hand and laughs when I treat this like some culinary marvel.

I've been vague with Dad about the breakup, saying only, "We grew apart." When he asks how Derek's doing, and I tell him I don't know, he says, "That's a shame. Your mother always liked him." Amanda talks about her application to film school, and I tell Dad I'm trying to write stories, but he has little to say beyond, "Don't put off what you want to do with your life," which lingers heavily in all its implication. I raise the subject of the protest at St. Patrick's, hoping for a little debate, something to catch fire, but all he says is, "You can't change the church the way you can change government," which I don't disagree with. His castaway gaze roams aimlessly, his eyes staring out into the void, scanning the horizon with no hope for rescue.

After he leaves to drive back home, we stand at the window, looking out at a fresh coating of snow. Tompkins Square is outlined in white, pretty instead of forbidding, and the streetlights glow with wet halos, disguising the grit of 10th Street. At the curb, people scrape snow off windshields and pack snowballs.

Ninety minutes later, the phone rings. It's Dad. "I'm in the emergency room," he says. "I had an accident."

Driving up the FDR, he came around a bend to find a car stalled in the left lane, no lights on. On the wet surface his brakes were useless. The impact came fast and hard. His head hit the windshield, his chest slammed the steering wheel, his knees banged into the dash. He was brought to Bellevue in an ambulance, and he's been lying on a gurney for an hour. "Everything hurts," he says.

You never really get used to hospitals—I haven't, all these years later—but a public emergency room on a December night in a snowstorm is a world of pain. Every chair has someone in it, and some of them seem like they have nowhere else to go. People are skeletally underfed or ungainly and obese, in clothes thin as dishrags but layered thick as mummies. Mothers ignore children, then shout when they stray. An old man moans for a nurse over and over. Someone wails, and someone else yells "shut the fuck up." A synthetic Christmas tree stands in the corner, colored bulbs blinking rapidly on and off until a man complains it's going to give him a seizure. A nurse silently yanks the plug from the socket.

Dad is having trouble finding a way to sit or stand that doesn't hurt. He's doing his best not to complain, helped by the Tylenol they dosed him with before they forgot him altogether. His forehead has been hastily bandaged, like a stock photo of a soldier in a battlefield hospital. A gash on his hand is spotting blood. Amanda and I bother the nurses until one of them attends to the wound. It's midnight, then one a.m., then two. A doctor finally emerges, tells us he'll be back soon, and then scurries off before anybody else can claim his attention.

"Barring someone with a gunshot wound to the head," I tell my father, "I think you're next."

Moments later sirens roar up to the sliding doors. Two ambulances. Two stretchers carrying bleeding bodies surrounded by medics. Controlled chaos takes over. From the nurses' station I hear the word "gunshot."

Dad raises an eyebrow to me and says, "Did you have to jinx it?"

We bring him back to our little apartment, where he sleeps uncomfortably for a few hours on Amanda's bed, while she and I curl up on the futon. At dawn, I call a car service that takes us out to New Jersey, to the hospital where Mom died. Lisa and Michelle meet us in the emergency room, which is quiet, orderly and empty. A doctor sees him right away, determines that nothing is broken or internally damaged, and reprimands me for letting Dad sleep: "You're lucky he doesn't have a concussion."

Dad releases a blast of dark laughter. "Yeah, I feel really friggin' lucky."

Back at the house, he closes himself into his bedroom—so recently *their* bedroom. Lisa looks at me and Michelle and says, "This is getting ridiculous."

"Totally ridiculous. Like, the goddess is angry," Michelle adds.

"The goddess?" I ask.

"She's taking a women's studies class," Lisa says. "Now there's two of you to gang up on me."

"Would a non-patriarchal goddess be this mean?" I ask Michelle.

"You're right," she says. "It's probably the Judeo-Christian God."

"Whoever it is," Lisa says, "they're totally fucking with our family."

"The house will probably catch on fire tonight," I say.

"First we'll all get food poisoning," Lisa says, "and we'll be too weak to crawl out of the flames."

"Trapped in a burning house with explosive diarrhea dying slow painful deaths."

"We probably already all have cancer," Michelle says.

"Or AIDS," I say. "Or both, cancer *and* AIDS."

"And untreated concussions," Lisa says.

"Hi, I'm a person with AIDS, cancer, food poisoning and a concussion."

"And my house is on fire."

We keep going, working ourselves up until it's not even complete sentences, just horrible words: food poisoning…explosive diarrhea…house on fire. We laugh so loudly we wake our father, who stumbles out and looks at us like we're nuts. We are, no doubt. We've earned it.

Nicholas throws a New Year's Eve party, just a handful of us there: me and Zack, Amanda and Ginger (her latest galpal, very WASPy and femme, not her usual butch, which makes me think it won't last), Dale and Timmy, still going strong, and Raymond, who's brought along Tony, a new guy he met at Stop the Church, who can't be more than twenty-one. Tony has a hot pink, needle-spiked Mohawk, wears a black t-shirt with the name of a band I don't know, and pegs his jeans over sixteen-hole Doc Martens. His fingers shine with silver rings: skulls, goat heads, other creepy stuff. He looks like an underage punk grubbing for change on St. Mark's, but his long-lashed eyes are flirty, and when he opens his mouth his voice has the same gay timbre as the rest of the guys in the room. He doesn't drink alcohol, so at midnight, when everyone raises glasses of champagne, Tony's contains seltzer.

"Out with the old," I say, toasting the end of an awful year.

"Here's to 1990," Tony says, voice bright with hope, "the year of the cure."

We all repeat it: "The Year of the Cure!"

Art Is Not Enough

Note to Self #9: Life as Amanda's roommate

She always had the radio on. It was either NPR or classical music, which I felt entirely ill-equipped to appreciate. Amanda's favorite was Mahler, so she got us tickets to hear the Philharmonic playing Mahler's Fourth, which starts with sleigh bells and ends with a soprano singing a child's vision of heaven. I was amazed at how much more of the music I heard in the live performance than on the recording. Seeing musicians lifting and lowering their instruments—bows sawing then stopping, percussionists striking things, arms raised then resting—distinguished the parts from the whole.

She had little patience for the inane lyrics of all the pop I loved, but it turned out she liked house and techno, the stuff we heard in clubs and, more and more, listened to at home, rehearsing moves we'd try out on the dancefloor.

She was always watching something on VCR. Her favorite film was Times Square, a teen-girl buddy pic that we watched over and over. She loved screwball comedy and worshipped Preston Sturges, Billy Wilder, and the Thin Man films. I made her watch experimental shorts that she puzzled over, wondering aloud if the fact that I'd get stoned beforehand was part of the reason I liked them so much.

She was unafraid to talk to strangers and had gotten to know everyone in the building. She bought food at the bodega for homeless people if they asked.

She hated washing silverware so it piled up in the sink.

She really didn't like when I left the toilet seat up.

She worked on her scripts with seriousness at the kitchen table, every night.

She did the NY Times crossword puzzle. She had a membership to MoMA. She subscribed to The New York Review of Books. I didn't know anyone else like her in 1990. She was a twenty-four-year-old feminist living on a temp salary without healthcare or a credit card to her name. She had a radical lesbian critique of power and had helped write ACT UP's "Women and AIDS" handbook, but could fall into a fugue state listening to Callas's recording of Tosca's "Vissi D'Arte," translating the lyrics for me with tears in her eyes: I lived for my art, I lived for love, I never did harm to a living soul . . .

Hillary leaves an invitation on Amanda's answering machine for a new affinity group using art for activism. There's a meeting at Timmy and Dale's. She says to invite me and Zack, too. The message is brief, her voice steady, no-nonsense.

"You'd think she'd at least acknowledge your breakup," I comment.

"That's Hillary," Amanda sighs. "Never any drama. Which is its own kind of drama—the thing everyone's thinking but no one's mentioning."

"Are you gonna go? What if Shanna's there?"

"Maybe that's best. Get us all in a room together and just deal with reality."

I haven't been able to talk to Derek, much less be in a room with him, for months. Our friends have been forced to navigate it: hanging with one or the other, never both of us at once. Nicholas told me, at New Year's, that Michael moved in with Derek, which I can't quite compute. Michael, downtown? Did he leave his fancy apartment? Did he quit his bank job? But I didn't ask for details. Didn't want to know.

At Dale and Timmy's, Hillary tells us that she's "not creative" but wants to be part of art-based activism. I watch Amanda watch her (and ignore Shanna, who sits across the room).

First up, Floyd unveils a new poster, white letters on a black background:

ART IS NOT ENOUGH.
TAKE COLLECTIVE DIRECT ACTION
TO END THE AIDS CRISIS.

There's a buzz of approval and immediately people start talking about where to wheatpaste and distribute it to reach its intended audience.

Then to my surprise Zack speaks up. "So you're not just saying, come to a demonstration, you're saying, make something explicitly political?"

"The art world has been decimated, but privileged artists hide in their studios, schmoozing wealthy buyers, instead of using their talent for social change," Floyd says.

"But artists make the art they need to make," Zack says. "I mean, I do."

"Yeah, otherwise it's Official Art," I say. "It's the Cultural Revolution."

"Mao and Stalin were dictators," Floyd says. "We're dissidents." I hear a patient indulgence in his voice. It's been a while since I've had that tone directed at me.

"We could do a whole series," Zack says, irony under his uninflected delivery. "Your Desk Job Is Not Enough. Driving a Truck Is Not Enough."

"This is a meeting about art and activism," Floyd says, pointing emphatically at the poster. "I suggest we target the art world."

"Everything's on the table, right Hillary?" Amanda asks.

Shanna answers, "Yeah, we're brainstorming." Amanda shoots her an uncertain look, trying to figure out if she's just been backed up or challenged.

Hillary says, "Did anyone else bring something?"

"Pick me, pick me," Dale says, waving a lit cigarette.

Hillary smiles. "The facilitator recognizes the queen in the bandana."

"The art world is all about slow art," Dale says. "I don't have time for that. I want fast art." He's been wheatpasting copies of his photos around the city, black and white images of himself, Timmy and our friends, together in parks, in apartments, having fun—anywhere but at demonstrations. At the bottom, he writes captions in his own hand. He calls it his "Extended Family" series. In one, Timmy is shot against a graffitied wall, making a silly face, above the words I LOVE TIMMY. In another, taken at Derek's pool party, a group of us are lined up on the diving board, over the words BOYS LIKE BOYS. DIVE IN. There's one from Mike's house in Fire Island in which Derek and I, in tank tops, sit on a couch in a brightly lit room with our eyes closed, the kind of candid shot you might typically discard. The caption reads, IT'S OK, YOU CAN OPEN YOUR EYES. The coaxing tone makes me smile, as if we're newborns entering the world, but seeing us together like this, unguarded, is like being confronted by ghosts.

We discuss, argue, take a break, eat quiche and salad that Timmy serves, and eventually reach a consensus: we'll go out in teams wheatpasting Floyd's poster alongside Dale's photos. Side by side they fuse together powerfully—political manifesto plus personal testimony—a model of living through this crisis.

"What Dale said about fast art, I really clicked with that," Zack says. We're walking back to my apartment with Amanda, arms linked in the chilly night air. "Makes me want to get back to my canvas right away."

"I admire Dale for just pushing ahead, not thinking about it too much," I say. "I started writing ideas down about my mother's time in the hospital, but it's like, I don't know what to do with it."

"I'll give you a deadline," Amanda says. "Then you'll have to finish."

Zack nods in agreement, and right away I feel like I can do it. "Deal," I say.

"I have a draft of my short film script," Amanda says. "For my grad school application. It's about Hillary. Sort of." She asks if she can read it to us, to hear it out loud, which is how we wind up back at 10th Street, spread out on her bed.

Amanda sits cross-legged in front of us, script clenched in her hands. She scans the page, gaze focused, striking me for a moment as uncharacteristically vulnerable. Then she begins to read.

It starts with a voiceover: "Max was a grown-up tomboy on her way to the bodega to buy groceries for dinner." We follow Max through one encounter after another with strangers she meets along the way—a homeless woman, a man who wolf-whistles at her, a guy very sick with AIDS. Each one leaves her more and more unsettled, until, at the market, she's unable to remember what she came to buy. She gets disoriented. The guy behind the register tells her, "Everyone in New York is upset these days," and she shouts at him, saying, "I'm not upset." Back home, she realizes she forgot what she needed to make the dinner she'd planned, and she breaks down in tears, saying out loud, "I can't go back there." She makes a phone call, cancelling the dinner she was going to cook—which is when the narrator, in voiceover, reveals herself to be a woman in love with Max. "I'm telling her story to figure out why she cancelled our dinner. Why she won't love me in return." The end.

Amanda's eyes rise slowly from the page. "That's it," she says.

"I like how compressed it is," I say. "Every moment counts."

"I like how mysterious the emotions are," Zack says.

"You think so?" she asks, eyes uncertain. We both nod.

"But it definitely feels emotional," I add. "Like it's all about figuring out how to live in this city and still have your feelings."

"And the way you pull back the curtain at the end is cool," Zack says.

She plans to give it to Hillary as a gift, a way to make up for some of the harsher things that were said at their breakup, and we talk about what it means to make art for an audience of one. "I couldn't have written it unless I knew who was going to read it," Amanda says. "It's like writing a letter."

In that moment I realize I can write about Mom in the hospital if I think of it as a gift for my family. I'll write it to let them know what is in my heart—all the feelings I've been unable to articulate.

I write, longhand, while Zack paints, or while I'm at my kitchen table, Amanda's classical station playing. I bring my notebook to work and type it into the computer, hovering over the printer while it slowly spits out pages.

I work to find the words to summon back that brutal time in the hospital, which seems like just yesterday and also like a time long ago, receding into dimness. I call up details and try to find meaning in them, like the way the sedatives that dripped from the IV bag through a tendril into her arm seemed like a slow numbing for me, too, an erosion of clarity and certainty. I try to invoke emotions without naming them. Just describe the room, the nurses, her body.

I read a draft to Amanda. She says I should insert more of myself as a character. How do you do that? The challenges are all new. I cross out words and replace them with better words, more *precise* words. I make so many changes I lose track of where I started. One day, out of ideas, I decide it's done. I give it a title—"The Rabbit," after her hallucinatory vision—and bind the pages at a print shop. I hand one to Amanda and another to Zack. I save one for Derek, unsure if I'll ever give it to him. I mail copies to my sister. I mail one to my father. Two days later he phones, saying, "You got it right, but it was tough to read." Michelle says, "That was hard to read." It was hard to write, I say. Lisa says, "That bunny is going to haunt me forever." Me too, I agree.

The next time I see Zack is when we meet up with the art affinity group on a street corner in Soho, carrying buckets of wheatpaste and brushes. We split into teams, each on a different block near a major gallery, slathering paste onto billboards or the wooden barriers around construction sites, fixing a grid of Floyd's poster and Dale's photos.

ART IS NOT ENOUGH.
I LOVE TIMMY.
TAKE COLLECTIVE DIRECT ACTION
TO END THE AIDS CRISIS.
IT'S OK, YOU CAN OPEN YOUR EYES.

One of us wields the brush, one holds the bucket, one keeps watch. I feel an adrenaline rush, the trespasser's high, as we make fast work of it.

When we're done, walking back home, I prompt Zack about my story. Yes, he's read it, he says it was intense and felt like it came from the heart. But he's holding back, I can tell. I push for more. Is it good writing? Does it feel true? He throws a question back at me: "Kiddo, what do *you* think of it?"

I admit that I suspect I've treaded too carefully. I was writing not just about my family but *for* my family. There's not enough tension between the narrator and his family; there are no arguments between the boyfriends in the story, no dynamic of dissatisfaction, no affairs or confessions. I wanted my readers—my loved ones—to like the story.

Zack says, "Art isn't about pleasing other people."

Burden of Proof

Derek and I don't speak all winter. Now it's spring and the Wigstock trial is here, and we meet outside the courthouse. He's with Michael, who gives me a hug and whispers in my ear, "Miss you," and Nicholas, who says, "Hello, darlin'," and plants a kiss on my cheek. Derek lifts his chin without a smile, the kind of stiff greeting coworkers send each other at my workplace. An acknowledgment, neither hostile nor polite.

In this courtroom, my eyes go right to the defendants, brown-skinned boys with newly close-cropped hair and stiff suits, already at the table when we enter. I recognize the boy who struck me with the stick and the one who joined him in beating me on the ground. I force myself to make eye contact with each of them right away, wanting to overcome my own intimidation before the testimony begins. They each look away, perhaps under instruction not to engage. One of them whispers to the other, a simple gesture that for some reason fills me with dread.

D.A. Miller—hair gelled, shoes shined, face pasty—begins his opening remarks. He pauses frequently to consult his notes, hands rifling through papers. His presentation strikes me as designed not to offend anyone. Our attack, he says, took place at a "festival" while we were "in costume." The defendants approached us and taunted us with "biased comments." They struck us without provocation. They were arrested on the spot. "You'll see images to prove this," he says, which is the moment I remember that the burden of proof is ours. Until we get through this, these boys are innocent.

The defense lawyer, Cohen, immediately establishes himself as a seasoned veteran who's seen it all and relishes a good scrap. He's not a public defender, which means someone is paying for his services. The defendants are Puerto Rican guys from the neighborhood, but I recall reading in the *Times* that at least one of them attends a private high school. They got those lacrosse sticks from somewhere. I'm confused by the mix of race, class and sexuality here, of how power will play out in this legal arena. The judge is a stern-looking white man with a conservative haircut and a look on his face like he's above all of this.

Cohen's wild hair is more salt than pepper, and he slumps, but strangely this all makes him seem vibrant, as if he's too full of purpose to bother with a comb or to stand up straight. He speaks with the accent of a lifelong New Yorker. I can tell he'll get loud if he needs to.

"The prosecution," he begins, "will have you believe that these teenagers came to this park to start a fight. In fact, these neighborhood boys, who use this park for recreation, found themselves surrounded by a large homosexual gathering, where they were provoked with inappropriate sexual comments and gestures. They weren't taunting the plaintiffs, they were being taunted! What the prosecution calls a bias crime is actually bias in the other direction—because as you will see, the accusers belong to a radical homosexual organization called ACT UP, which most recently went into Saint Patrick's Cathedral to disrupt a Roman Catholic Mass. Their aggressive behavior toward my clients led to an act of self-defense, one that you will find to be completely justified once you hear the facts."

Derek, Michael, Nicholas and I exchange wide-eyed, open-mouthed, head-shaking stares. Has Miller known this was coming? Why didn't he warn us? At the first break, we converge on him, and he hurries us to the hallway, out of earshot of the other team. "This isn't surprising," he says. "They don't have a case, so they're trying to drum one up. We have the facts on our side. That's what I'm going to present, the facts."

The first person Miller calls to the stand is the arresting officer—not the one who nabbed Zack, but the second cop, who went toward the bashers and tried to get them to scatter. He doesn't mention that, of course, but he does say in a neutral voice that the kids stood around with their sticks while we were on the ground, injured. We pointed them out, and they were apprehended on the spot. Miller introduces still images, freeze frames from Raymond's videotape, of the boys in the park in the aftermath of our beating. When it's Cohen's turn, he asks a series of questions: Did this officer see the attack take place? Did he see what precipitated it? How was he alerted to it? This is the first time Zack's name comes up. It's established that he was the person who pointed out the attackers to the police and that he too was arrested because, the cop says, "He was acting erratic."

Cross-examined by Miller, the cop admits that charges against Zack were dropped. There was a lot of confusion in the moment. So no, he wasn't found guilty of anything, but his behavior was "aggressive."

I'm up next.

Miller asks me to describe my actions that day. I describe having seen the defendants in the crowd bothering people. It's clear to me they were looking for a fight when they came over and started bothering us.

"What did they say to you?"

"They called me a faggot."

"That's an insulting term, is it not?"

"For a gay man, it's a very offensive term, yeah."

"Did you say something back?"

"I said something like, 'Get lost.'"

"Did you touch, hit or otherwise move toward him?"

"No."

I don't mention the change purse—that fateful snap. My first untruth.

I describe being hit while on the ground. I describe Zack's arrest, and the arrest of the defendants. Miller introduces into evidence a photograph showing the bruises on my face.

Then Cohen begins. "Please describe what you were wearing that day."

Miller objects. Cohen responds that since "costume" was already mentioned in the opening arguments, it's relevant. Objection overruled.

"I was in drag. Wigstock is a drag event. It's like Woodstock, with wigs."

"So you were wearing a woman's wig?"

"Yes. It was blonde. I was going for Kim Novak."

"And you had women's makeup on your face?"

"Not enough," I say, drawing out laughter from somewhere in the room.

"What else?"

I describe the blouse, the scarf, the leggings.

"These are women's garments?"

"The leggings were unisex. I borrowed them from a hippie."

Chuckles from the courtroom again. I want the jury to warm to me. I know what Cohen is doing, trying to make me into a freak.

"Did you solicit sex from the defendants?"

"Objection!"

"Overruled. Please answer the question."

"No."

"Did you put your hand on the genitalia of the defendants?"

"Objection!"

"Mr. Miller, I'm allowing this line."

"No, I did not put my hand anywhere on the defendants. Why would I?"

"So you did not in any way, verbally or physically, suggest to the defendants that you wanted sexual relations?"

"Absolutely not."

"Do you know what 'rough trade' is?"

I look to Miller. He frowns, makes his objection, is overruled.

"'Rough Trade' is a record label," I say, trying again for humor but maybe coming off too glib.

"Sir, please, do you know its common meaning?"

"I guess it's a butch guy who—" I've never stopped to define this before. "I don't know."

"Objection," Miller calls again.

"Your honor, he can't object to the witness," Cohen says, perfectly dry.

"Ask your question."

"Have you heard of the definition of rough trade which is: a heterosexual man whom a homosexual man solicits for sex, usually for money?"

"Objection."

"Sustained. You're leading, counsel."

"Withdrawn."

Even withdrawn, the question lingers. I glance at the jury, looking back at me, some of them likely wondering, *Did this guy dress up like a woman so he could pay a straight boy to have sex with him?* I suddenly feel queasy.

Cohen shuffles through his notes. "You say you were hit with a lacrosse stick. Can you describe that?"

"It came right at my face."

"Were you moving toward the defendant at that time?"

"No."

"Were you snapping your fingers in his face?"

"No."

"I'll remind you, you are under oath."

I press my lips together and wait. Cohen stares directly into my eyes, as if assessing this pause. I hold his stare until he speaks again: "Did you pull the defendant to the ground?"

"Pull him? No. I fell. After he hit me."

"You say you fell to the ground. Were you in high heels?"

"Not very high."

"Were you drinking alcohol that day?"

"No." I don't mention the pot I'd smoked.

"Were you under the influence of anything besides alcohol?"

"No," I lie.

"So how is it you fell to the ground?"

"Objection."

"Sustained. Mr. Cohen, the defendant answered the question."

"Yes, Your Honor. You were with a group of people, is that correct?"

"I was with my boyfriend, Derek, and two friends, Michael and Nicholas. Actually, Nicholas wasn't with us at that moment. Just the three of us."

"So there were three of you, and two of them?"

"There were four of them. I don't know why the other two aren't here."

"But you had friends in the crowd?"

"Yes."

"How many?"

"I don't know."

"Would you say you had ten friends in the crowd? Twenty?"

"It was a festival. A lot of my friends live in the East Village."

"Are these people part of a group called ACT UP?"

"Objection."

"Sustained."

"Are you yourself part of a group called ACT UP?"

"Objection."

I look at the judge, waiting. He waves Cohen and Miller to the bench. There is some back and forth consulting sotto voce. When it's through, I am dismissed from the stand.

Derek is next. Same line of questioning—drag, rough trade. He wasn't attacked in the same way, so there are no injuries to discuss, and Cohen makes a big deal of this: Derek was unharmed.

Then a new piece of Raymond's videotape is called into evidence, from the protest that followed the attack. Cohen plays it for the jury—there's Derek up on Nicholas's shoulders, in his That Girl wig, bullhorn at his mouth, fist raised.

"What was going on here?"

Derek says, "A crowd formed to protest, and I was addressing them. The police had arrested our friend Zack, and we wanted him released."

"Why was that?"

"He tried to tell the police about the bashers, and they arrested him."

"But they also arrested my clients, correct?"

"Yeah, after they arrested Zack."

"Did you pressure the police to arrest my clients?"

"We told the police that these were the guys who hit us."

"But in this tape, you're telling the crowd that Zachary Jones should be released, and that my clients should not be. Correct?"

"Yes."

"Looks like a big crowd. How many people would you guess?"

"I don't know. Fifty?"

"Were you telling them to do anything?"

"I was trying to let them know what had happened."

"Did you tell them to march into the street?"

"No."

"You told them to chant, right? That's what it sounds like."

"We probably did some chanting."

"Probably? Aren't you saying, 'Arrest the real criminals?'"

"We wanted them to release Zack, and to charge these guys with assault."

"And that's what happened?"

"Eventually."

Miller takes over. "The bullhorn. Where did that come from?"

"Someone went and got it."

"Why?"

"So we could communicate with everyone."

"The crowd was already there, at Wigstock, right? You didn't summon this crowd from some other location, right?"

"Right. These guys had walked into the middle of our festival and attacked us. Everyone thought that was a big deal."

"The police have not always been responsive to anti-gay violence, have they?"

"Objection."

"Sustained. Rephrase."

Miller releases a gust of frustration. "Was there a reason you thought that pressure needed to be brought to the situation?"

"Yeah, these guys could have walked away scot-free. And Zack, who was only helping us, was going to be charged, even though he didn't do anything wrong."

"So you were unhappy with the fact that Mr. Jones was taken to the police station?"

"Of course. It was unjust."

"To be clear: You did not go to the park that day with a bullhorn to organize a political protest?"

"No, we did that after we were attacked."

The next day, the trial continues with Michael's testimony. His hospital X-rays are entered as evidence, and he's subjected to the same line of questioning. Cohen makes a big deal of Michael's skirt, calling it "provocatively short." Miller rests his case, and the defense does not call witnesses. I take this as a good sign—proof that the defendants are lying, that their story won't hold up under oath—but that night, at Zack's, he tells me he has a bad feeling about it. Without testimony from the defendants, the case will be decided on whether or not we are to be believed. I lie on his mattress thinking back on the faces of the jurors—men and women, Black, white, Asian and Puerto Rican, none of them as young as us, none who in any way look like they live lives like ours. Justice is in their hands.

A day later, I'm at home when D.A. Miller calls. "I'm sorry," he begins.

The defendant who hit Michael has been found guilty of second degree assault. The guy who slammed his stick in my face and punched me has been declared not guilty on all charges.

"I don't understand," I say. At the kitchen table, Amanda looks up. I mouth to her, "They got off."

"You're fucking kidding me," she says.

Miller says, "His closing argument painted you all as activists who pressured the police to arrest these innocent guys."

"But what about our injuries?"

"Michael's injuries were serious enough. They couldn't deny that. With you, we only had that one photo—"

"And my testimony?"

From what seems like a long way away, Miller lets out a sigh.

As soon as I hang up, the phone rings again. It's Derek, his voice raging in my ear. "He didn't prove the case. He didn't do his job. Their lawyer appealed to the jury's homophobia. They only needed half a day to reach a verdict! I told Miller that would fucking happen! *The facts were on our side.* The facts don't fucking matter if they think faggots in drag deserve what they get!"

I mutter my agreement, but his voice is slowly dissolving, sucked down a tunnel into an abyss, the place where unresolved, unjust events churn and fester. My ears hum, my feet carry me to the white door of the refrigerator, my hand pulls out a bottle of vodka, I watch clear liquid fill the glass, feel it drain into my mouth, down my throat. The light around me is intensifying, the room is growing pale, it's the merciless light of the courtroom, the shameful light of interrogation—

"What are you doing?" Amanda is asking.

I see that I have raised my arm, that I'm ready to throw the empty glass across the room, I'm already imagining the impact, hearing the satisfying smash—but she's stepped in front of me, her face tight with alarm, to gingerly take the glass from my hand.

In my ear, Derek is asking "Are you listening?"

"Sorry, what?"

"We have to do something."

Self-Defense

Fourteen of us stand in a circle, in a mirrored dance studio in an old mercantile building on a grubby block in Soho. All eyes are on Lily, who doesn't look much like a Lily to me. She could be a Jan or a Pat, a gym teacher, barrel-bodied and solid through the shoulders, with parted hair pulled into a ponytail. Her t-shirt, tucked into charcoal cotton sweatpants, reads BROOKLYN WOMEN'S MARTIAL ARTS. She's here to help us learn to defend ourselves, for the next six weeks. Derek is here, Raymond is here, as are Michael, Timmy, Dale, Nicholas, Rochelle, Floyd, Gilberto, Javier, Hillary, Shanna, and Amanda. The person who I really miss is Zack, but he's already packing for San Francisco.

"We start with your stories," Lily says in a voice that has a musical, coaxing quality, like a clarinet. She asks us to talk about the violence we've experienced. Derek and I are not the only ones with a story. Dale and Timmy were spit on while they were out wheatpasting. This guy shouted, "I'll stab you in the head for spreading AIDS," to which Dale replied, "Please, stab me so I can spread it to you."

Timmy picks up on Dale's story. "It was scary, but it was also like every obnoxious straight guy ever, going back to kindergarten, when I skipped across the playground like a little nelly queen and someone called me a girl."

Javier tells of being chased through the West Village by guys with bats who called him a "diseased spic." He escaped into a gay bar, where he called the police, who took hours to show up and had to be badgered to take a statement. Javi heads ACT UP's media committee but he couldn't get any of his contacts to write about the incident. "Happens all the time," one editor told him. Gilberto was with Hillary and Shanna on the Upper West Side handing out safe sex literature at a private high school when a couple of boys charged at them, punched Gilberto in the head and then ran away. Around the circle, my closest friends tell stories I've never heard.

"I was injured twice in the last year," I say, "once by the cops at a demonstration and once because I was in drag. The first time was worse physically, but the second one *felt* worse."

"It felt personal," Lily says, and I nod.

"It all feels personal to me," Floyd says. "Harassment from the cops, racism from white gay men, homophobia from the straight Black boys on the block."

Raymond speaks up suddenly. "I'm glad to be here and *share* and all that, but part of me is, like, why don't I just carry a knife?"

"We're going to talk about knives," Lily says calmly. "But if you carry a knife, you will get cut. You will have to be mentally prepared for a knife wound."

We're all very quiet after that.

"This starts with our stories, with our voices," Lily says, and asks us to go around the circle again, this time stating, "My name is," followed by a first, middle and last name. Hillary goes first. After she's spoken, Lily says, "Good. Now say it again, but look me in the eye, and hold the eye contact."

Hillary speaks again: first, middle, last.

"Did you feel how you looked away from me in the middle?"

"I hate my middle name," Hillary jokes.

"There's nothing wrong with your middle name."

"It's too girly."

"Go ahead and say it again, the whole thing, and keep your eyes on me."

Hillary exhales, closes her eyes, opens them again, and then nearly shouts: "My Name Is Hillary Dawn Costello."

"Good. You feel the difference?"

Hillary nods intently.

Lily pivots to face Amanda, who seems to have absorbed Hillary's lesson. Her own voice doesn't waver. Next is Derek. Lily tells him, "Now do it again without smiling. Don't try to make me like you. Just make me hear it."

We go around the room, one at a time . *My name is—. My name is—. My name is—.* Then it's my turn.

"My name is—" But I choke before I finish, and I can't catch my breath. I'm shaking. I start to cry.

"It's okay," Lily says, "stay in it."

The moment elongates, and quickly someone else starts sniffling, and then someone else, and I fear that my emotions are derailing the class, which only makes me cry harder. I remember that night in New Jersey when I upset my father and sisters with my hysteria. I remember being cross-examined in court. *Did you snap your fingers in his face?* I hear Derek saying *God, you suck,* and I hear Zack saying, *You've got a lot of living to do without me.* I see my mother's swollen face behind the ventilator mask. I hear my father saying, "It's cancer."

Raymond, at my side, drapes an arm across my shoulders. I feel stiff at first, until I hear Lily say, "It's all right to take comfort," and then I let myself sink into his meaty chest. He wraps his other arm around me and pulls me closer. I feel someone else embrace me from behind, I'm not even sure who it is, but the extra touch unleashes everything I'm still holding back. Now I'm sobbing. I feel another body step close and join the huddle, then another, then another. We hold each other in that cocoon, and we grieve together.

When I finally catch my breath, and my heart rate begins to slow, I signal that it's okay to let go. As we pull apart, I turn to meet Derek's gaze—it was he who held me from behind, and I whisper *thanks*. Everywhere in the room, faces are damp.

Even Lily's eyes glisten, though her voice stays firm: "The emotion that you feel is the main reason people avoid self-defense. The moves aren't hard. They can be learned by anyone. What's hard is everything that brought you here, everything you've talked about today and all those things you can't put into words yet. Over the next six weeks you'll feel sad, enraged, elated and embarrassed. At times you'll want to cry, and at other times you'll want to make jokes. To be in this room is to make space for all that. All right? Good." She looks at me. "Ready?"

I nod. I lift my chin. I say my name.

Zack presents me a canvas, a gift. It's about three feet by three feet, and it shows the main room of his apartment: our mattress beneath the window, surrounded by beer bottles and our overflowing ashtray, the wall behind it collaged with shrunken photocopies of the actual images on the actual walls. He's painted his easel displaying a painting, a miniature of one he's been working on. It isn't like anything he's done before. His brushwork is looser than usual, blurring the edges of objects. He watches me look it over and take it in, and I can feel the stress this causes him. "I love it," I say. "It's like a memory of us, here, together, right?" He nods. "And you don't want to take it with you?"

"I want you to remember it. This is our place."

Our love nest, though we've never called it that. "Are you worried I won't?"

"You'll make your own memories. But I want you to have mine."

He's been purging his stuff, anticipating the date when he'll begin his cross-country drive. He's removed his paintings from their frames and rolled them into tubes, leaving them with Dale and Timmy, who have the space to store them. He places an ad in the *Voice* to sell his furniture, and I help him haul an armchair, a chest of drawers, a microwave and more down his stairs to the vehicles of strangers, who show up with cash and try to bargain him lower than the price he's set over the phone. Each solid item that goes out the door takes a memory with it: I sat in that chair while writing a short story, I used that microwave to heat up leftovers, I pulled a t-shirt from those drawers, borrowing Zack's clothes when I forgot my own. Piece by piece, our time together is dissolving. As the belongings thin out, as the floor appears from under the clutter, as images are peeled from the walls, I feel nearly dizzy with awe. This purge is so unmistakably adult. I've never watched anyone pack up the contents of his life. Zack approaches everything with clarity. He's always been like this, I realize: he quietly chooses, and that's that. When he decides something, he does it.

One strangely windy night, as the glass shakes in the windowpanes, I sit on the empty floor watching him attack a shoebox filled with photos. He flips through them quickly, then slowly, then quickly again, returning just a handful to the box.

I watch as a photo of him taken outside of City Hall flutters from his hand to the trash. In it, Zack smokes a cigarette, as a protest sign he designed—HEALTH SCARE, with a picture of Mayor Koch—leans against his thigh. His stance in the photo reminds me of our mornings before work, when we'd stop for a cup of coffee at the bagel shop, sharing a cigarette before getting on the subway.

"You're not keeping this one?"

"This is better," he says, offering another from the same demonstration. Here, he's holding aloft the poster, mouth open in mid-chant, t-shirt wet at the pits. It's a more vibrant image, calling up the anger of that demonstration.

"Maybe you want one of these," he says, handing me a 10x12 envelope containing a series of black and white portraits of Zack posing in his activist gear: black jeans, ACT UP t-shirt, Yankees cap. In one photo, he sits on a park bench like a model positioned to look casual: leg bent, elbow on knee, face turned to the light. In another, he leans against a tree, jacket fanned out over his shoulder so that the sticker on it can be read: THE AIDS CRISIS IS NOT OVER.

"These are sexy," I say.

"They're contrived." He holds the bench picture up to his face and tilts his head to the side with a forced smile, mocking himself. In that gesture, I see an admission that he knows the effect he has on others, that he posed for these photos to capitalize on his visual appeal. But now they're headed for the trash.

At the bottom of the stack, I find a shot not part of this series: taken indoors with studio lighting against a gray wall. He's shirtless, and his chest has been shaved and oiled, gleaming with the hard, shiny relief of a new coin.

"I'm not sure how that got in there," he says, frowning.

"When was this?"

"Five or six years ago."

"Was the photographer a professional?"

"A professional asshole. Actually he was, I don't know, a fuckbuddy, I guess. A drug buddy, really."

"What kind of drugs?"

"You name it. Pot, pills—after a while, heroin."

"Really?" I've never done heroin and can't picture Zack doing it, either.

"We'd chase the dragon and have this halfhearted sex after we smoked. One night I went to his place and these people were there. I'd never seen them before. They had words, and I watched him stick the needle in his arm, and so I tried it, too. Did it a couple times before I got scared and stopped seeing him. Shit got way too heavy." He stares into the space between us, silently debating if he'll continue. Then: "I think I got it from him."

"Got what?"

"The virus."

"Oh—" No one ever talks about that—when they got infected, who passed it to them. It's impossible to know, really. Plus, it's too close to how right-wingers talk about AIDS, in the language of blame. "How do you know?"

"Just the way it all timed out." He looks again at the picture. "Fuck, I've gotten so..." He doesn't finish, but I know what he's seeing, or rather isn't seeing: the bulk he's lost, the thinness in his face.

"I like how you look now," I say.

"A bit of infection does wonders?"

I'm not in the mood for gallows humor. "Zack, I don't walk around thinking of you as *infected.*" He exhales heavily—I'm on shaky footing. "All I meant is, you look more like a man now. You're a boy in this picture."

"Just take whatever you like," he says, gesturing to all the discarded photos. I keep the one of him smoking, plus one of the park photos. I return the studio shot of shaved-chest Zack to the envelope. I don't need to preserve him the way this other guy saw him, this guy whose name I wish I knew so I could track him down and murder him.

A week later, in a station wagon found through the classifieds—the owner needing a driver to take it one-way to San Francisco—Zack leaves New York. I hold onto him tightly, shocked, angry, stunned. Even after all this preparation, I can't believe it: he's choosing a path that takes him far away from me.

"Come to San Francisco," he says, his parting words. "Don't wait."

Part 8

Spin the Bottle

We'd broken the seal, Derek and I, and it seemed we were going to try to make room for each other again, just a little. My gut told me that even a little was too much, too soon; we hadn't worked through what happened between us, but our lives were so intertwined, something had to give. In our world, your ex didn't have to be your enemy, not when you had real enemies.

Violence was escalating against queer people, alone or in pairs, harassed on the street by groups of young men, all over the city. It was always men, and they were always in groups, which told you that individually they were cowards. The mainstream press wasn't covering this, though the queer press knew this was *the* number one issue, after AIDS, in our community. Leo, our former media whiz, is now the editor of *Outweek,* and he wants to interview me and Derek about the self-defense class. We set up a meeting at the apartment on Norfolk Street. It's the first time I'll be back since I moved out.

There's the monument store with its gravestones in the ground floor windows; I passed them so regularly when I lived here, I've forgotten how spooky they look. There's the stoop, with Wilson, the drunk super, smoking a cigarette. As I climb the familiar stairs, Michael is on his way down. We share an energetic burst of small talk: How am I doing, have I heard from Zack, was I practicing my self-defense moves? He says he's thinking of leaving New York, he wants to return to playing piano, he's quit his job and is sharing rent with Derek. A quick kiss on the lips, and off he flies, on his way to volunteer at the Anti-Violence Project. When I first learned he was living here, I assumed he and Derek were sharing a bed. But inside I see that Michael has put up a tall folding screen in the main room, blocking off half of the living room for himself. The couch and coffee table are pushed to the opposite wall.

Leo is here with Tony, the Mohawked, many-ringed punk Raymond brought to New Year's, who now works as his assistant. Leo's questions about our self-defense class are answered quickly, and conversation turns to what's really on their minds: the need for a new activist group to confront problems like bashing. "It should be separate and different from ACT UP," Leo says. "We don't need another group bogged down in procedure."

"Agreed," Derek says.

"A new group should be fun," I say. "Make it so that people *want* to join."

"An affinity group," Tony says. "Something that, like, moves fast." He tells us he was part of the gang of clowns that tumbled out of taxis in front of St. Patrick's. He also went with the group that crashed a Republican fundraiser wearing buttons reading, "LESBIANS FOR BUSH"; he removed his rings and tucked his Mohawk under a cap to get past security. He says he wants to do protest in drag, and he mentions Rollerena, who rollerskates through ACT UP demonstrations dressed like Glinda the Good Witch, waving her magic wand over cops and protesters both. "I saw her picture in *Outweek* when I was living in Pittsburgh and I was like, I'm going to New York to meet my fairy godmother."

"And now he's working for *Outweek*," Leo says, clearly charmed.

"The group doesn't need to meet regularly," Derek says. "We can get together whenever we're inspired, and do something different every time."

"We can keep changing the name," Tony says. "A moving target."

"This is perfect," Leo says, beaming. "But I can't be the one to organize it. I'm too associated with the magazine. It needs to come from you guys."

Tony says, "I'm in!" Derek says he's in too, and looks at me. I nod my head yes. Their excitement is contagious.

On my way out, Derek stops me to ask, "You sure you're up for this? After everything?"

"Yeah. I've had a little break from ACT UP. I can take this on."

Later, I'd realize he was trying to give me an out, and if I'd been smart enough to foresee how much energy the group would demand, I might have taken it. But instead, I got on the phone, reserved a room at the community center, and began telling our friends to show up and bring their best ideas.

We get about fifty people, more than expected, not just the usual friends but folks like Eliot, who emerges from seclusion accompanied by his boyfriend

Lenny, blinking behind his scholarly glasses. Word has spread. Chairs are gathered from other rooms in the center and arranged in a large, lopsided oval.

Derek begins by recounting our original conversation, and I see heads nodding in agreement—but he's soon interrupted by a man I recognize from the actions committee who very sternly says, "People are concerned about what you're doing here. It seems like an attack on ACT UP—a competition for bodies."

Someone else chimes in, "Is this *Outweek's* way of co-opting ACT UP?" Leo jumps in, explaining that he's not here as an editor but as an activist. He seems unruffled by the accusation, but I'm thrown. I hadn't expected pushback.

Derek says, "We can take the pressure off ACT UP by being the place for queer issues that aren't about AIDS."

"The AIDS crisis is not over!" someone shouts.

"Who said that?" Tony calls out defiantly. "We know it's not over."

I wave my hands to get everyone's attention. "The four of us are not in charge. We just thought this was an idea that would bring people together."

"This meeting has probably been infiltrated by the NYPD." The speaker was someone I'd never seen before. With his tinted glasses, shapeless jeans and heavy-soled shoes, he looks as likely as anyone to be an undercover cop. This prompts me to recite the familiar litany that opens every ACT UP meeting: "If there are any members of the New York City Police Department..." But no one self-identifies. *They never do.*

I can't believe I'm facilitating again. Didn't I just step down?

Gilberto, who used to facilitate with me, is here, and he asks to speak next. His concern is how few people of color are in the room. Derek tries to respond, but Gilberto isn't having it, and why should he? It doesn't do any good to remark that we contacted people without a plan, spreading the word among those we'd done actions with, because that only reinforces the point that our movement has been majority white and majority male, and here we are again. "I'm not here to accommodate your lack of outreach," Gilberto says, and then he gets up and walks out, just like that. Derek chases after him, and their muffled voices are audible as they go back and forth in the hallway while I try to center the room, regain focus, acknowledge Gilberto's concerns without sounding like another clueless white boy. Javier raises his hand to speak. "I may be the only other Latino in the room, and I feel torn. I don't want to leave, but I want to say Gilberto's right. This could have been done better."

"I'll own that," I say. Where I got this phrase I'm not sure. It's in the air: politics, therapy, consciousness-raising. Around the edges of our action-oriented activism, there's a lot of talk about personal responsibility. We can't fix the world until we fix our own community, clean our own house, *own our shit*. I keep having to relearn this, which is to say there's a lot to *un*learn: attitudes and assumptions and negligence so deeply lodged it had to be mined, surfaced, crushed. But at the same time: I know that self-correction becomes its own intoxicating end. Utopia looks inward, fixated on perfection.

Hillary stands and speaks. "I'll bring more women with me next time, but let's talk about what's possible now, while we're here." A few people clap, which isn't a comfort, either. It's not a game show or a popularity contest.

Discussion moves around the circle, and slowly ideas start to pile up—doing zaps, activating the phone tree, using the ACT UP info table to spread the word. Targets are suggested. There are more ideas than anyone can deal with, too many.

Dale stands and says he wants to do something fun. "Let's have a kiss-in," he says, and I sense a surge of approval. Kiss-ins are the most fun, and when onlookers react badly, their bigotry is so easy to tear down.

Debate starts to swirl around this idea:

We should go to straight bars to do this.

That could get people bashed.

They already bash us for no reason at all.

But if you start kissing your boyfriend in a straight bar, where people are drunk and looking for a fight, you're just going to get more queer people hurt.

That's your internalized homophobia talking.

ACT UP always has clear demands. What's the demand here?

Do we need demands? Can we just show up and be?

"Does anyone want to address that last question, about goals?" I ask, trying to steer this toward closure.

I see Amanda's arm arc upwards. She's been quieter than usual, in listening mode, sitting in the chair next to Hillary. At one point I saw them whispering privately back and forth. But now she has the floor. "My goal," she says, "is to terrify, mystify and enchant."

We go to McSorley's, the East Village pub that's been around since before the Civil War and didn't allow women inside until forced by law to do so in the '70s. During the day the place is a den for old-timers who've been drinking here since World War II; at night the place fills up with NYU jocks and bridge-and-tunnel types who get really wasted and wind up puking in the gutter in the wee hours of the morning.

On our chosen day, about two dozen of us enter and file to the back room. The regulars observe us with suspicious sidelong glances over the rims of their pints. The bearded bartender's ruddy face stays blank as he takes our orders.

At one large table, there's a big, noisy group of guys and girls, some of them in NYU sweatshirts, throwing a bachelor party. We fill a couple of tables, pulling up chairs, our conversations fueled by nervous energy. We're all acting *big*: men sissy it up, women butch it up. Raymond drains a bottle of Rolling Rock and then announces, "Let's play Spin the Bottle." He spins the glass on the tabletop, and we watch it slowly stop in front of Derek, who dives across the table and plants a lip-lock. Everyone whoops and hollers.

The NYU kids take notice, and one of them enthusiastically shouts, "We should play Spin the Bottle, too!"

Dale calls out, "Queer kissing only!" which elicits both cheers and groans from their table.

I take a drink order, an excuse to slip away from the game; even at a kiss-in, it seems best to avoid the possibility of kissing Derek. Amanda has the same idea, kissing Hillary would be too fraught. When the bartender tells me the total, Amanda makes a big show of pulling out her wallet and counting out bills. I guess this is part of our demo—women paying for men—because I know she doesn't have extra cash while she's saving up for school. Behind us the empty bottle spins circles, until it creaks to a standstill and everyone cheers again. I watch Nicholas make out with Timmy, who is wearing false eyelashes and lipstick, while Dale snaps pictures. "Adorable," Amanda says.

"What's this business about?" an older man on a barstool asks us. His fluffy white eyebrows furrow above a nose red with burst capillaries. His voice is pure New York—*dis bizness*.

"It's happy hour," I say.

"There are bars in this neighborhood for your crowd, you know," he says.

Amanda says, "But this place is perfect."

"We always go to gay bars," I say. "We wanted somewhere new."

"Why cause trouble?" he mutters.

He returns his gaze to his pint. But Tony is behind us, and he's heard the whole thing. "This man thinks we should go away," he announces loudly.

From our group, there's a chorus of boos. Timmy slides onto the table, sprawling pinup style, head resting on hand, leg crossed coyly over leg. "But there's so much *room* here," he purrs.

Someone else calls out, "Why don't *you* go away, man?"

The fight some of us are itching for seems likely to erupt.

The bartender has until now been on alert but silent. Now he speaks: "If you're going to climb on the table you're going to have to leave. All of you."

Nicholas says, "We're going to buy *a lot* of beer."

"I'm not putting up with this kind of shit," the bartender says.

From the bachelor party, a young guy in a baseball cap stands and says, "They're ordering beer. We're ordering beer. Everyone's having fun, right?"

"Right on, sister," Timmy lisps, as he slides off the table.

A woman from the bachelor party calls out, "More beer!"

From our table, someone answers, "More beer!"

Then everyone at both tables is chanting those words. The bartender scans the scene and with a shake of his head, he lines up a row of plastic pitchers and starts filling them from the tap, as if to say, *I'll give you more beer. A lot more.* We keep drinking, spinning the bottle, and bantering loudly with our new friends at the next table. Later, Derek dubs them our first straight allies.

We leave after a couple of hours—tipsy, energy dissipating, all kissed out—offering hugs to the bachelor and bachelorette and waving to the bartender, who nods, inscrutable.

Terrifying, maybe. Mystifying, definitely. Enchanting? I could only hope.

One thing is clear: people want to do it again. So the next Friday at happy hour, we gather at the South Street Seaport, swarming into a bar called Flutie's. Instead of a bartender persuaded by our cash, we're met with bouncers who want us out quickly. Instead of newfound allies, we get tourists pointing their cameras at us. Here, we're either a nuisance or we're local color, like the Three-card Monte players on the sidewalk or the guitarist strumming chords to "A Hard Day's Night," a case full of coins at his feet. Perhaps this is what it means to enchant: you kiss on film while a German backpacker or a Japanese couple clicks the shutter, capturing a souvenir to bring back home to their friends, like a t-shirt proclaiming, "I Love NY."

Before Zack left, we watched movies set in San Francisco, priming him for his trip. Our favorite was *Vertigo*, with Kim Novak playing a mystery woman who tries to kill herself by jumping into the Bay. So when I receive my first piece of mail from San Francisco, a homemade postcard with a sketch of the Golden Gate Bridge, I smile at the tiny cartoon self-portrait Zack has drawn, with a speech bubble commanding: "Kim Novak, get out of the water." He's pasted a cutout of Kim's blonde updo among the waves, plus a lone seagull in the sky and a Tom of Finland leatherman on the shore. On the back, he's written:

> *Roommate is moody, but there's enough space to make art. I've found the activists, but it's hard to be angry in a city so pretty. Write me at this address. I'm a man of few words but I miss yours. Wet kisses, Zack*

I read his note once with a thrill, then a second time trying to determine if I detect a strain of doubt in all those *buts*. Is he lonely? Regretting the move?

I've been writing letters to him every week, stories of our friends, our kiss-ins, my writing and the books I'm reading. I transcribe an Adrienne Rich love poem for him. It's about sex between women as a form of dissent in a patriarchal world, but it makes me think about sex between men of different sero-statuses, and how condoms are an insistence on intimacy in the face of illness. But I also fantasize about sex between us without condoms. This isn't the old Eros-and-Thanatos appeal of Mike Savas. In this fantasy, there is no virus. Am I allowed to unshackle my imagination this way, revealing to Zack by inference a wish that he wasn't positive? It's not something I've ever said to him. After I've mailed this letter, I wonder if I've made a mistake, and this nervous energy keeps me walking from the mailbox all the way to the West Village, where the piers jut out into the Hudson and all the young Black and Puerto Rican kids hang out, snapping and vogueing.

Across the wide, dark river is New Jersey, my family. They know almost nothing about Zack. I've told them I was seeing someone, a painter, who moved away. I mention that he left me a painting, hanging on my wall now, but I do not mention HIV. They are too scarred by loss. They'd think of him differently if they knew, and they'd worry too much about me. I have my reasons to be secretive, but it gnaws at me: I've put myself in another closet.

Zack is out there, far, far beyond what my eye can see, all the way west. My letter will make its way to him, while I remain here, stuck on this island.

Take Back the Night

There's a line of police cars outside of Uncle Charlie's. The bar's entrance is cordoned off with yellow police tape. An onlooker tells us there was a "bomb scare." *At Uncle Charlie's?* Derek and I used to frequent this bar on weekend getaways from college—I ordered some of my first legal cocktails there—but I haven't been inside for years. The clientele is too squeaky clean, the cruising too uptight. Derek has jokingly dubbed it an S&M bar, for "stand and model."

On this spring afternoon, I'm with Derek, Tony and Leo. We're here in the West Village scouting locations for a kiss-in. This neighborhood was once the center of the gay universe, but now the bars feel ghostly, casualties of the epidemic. On weekends young people from the 'burbs and the boroughs maraud like herds of drunken rhinos, trampling on the decimated community that still calls this place home. When someone in our new, unnamed activist group talked about "taking back Christopher Street," Derek and I looked at each other nostalgically. It would always be *Christopher's Street* to us.

We approach a cop outside of Uncle Charlie's to ask about the bomb scare. "More than a scare," he says. "Pipe bomb went off in a trashcan."

We exchange alarmed glances and pepper him with questions. Was anyone hurt? (No, it was after hours.) Are there suspects? (Could be Mafia-related.) Are they treating this as a bias crime? (These things are usually about money.) Then the cop decides he's said too much and shoos us away. The four of us agree: people should know about this. Leo says he'll get an *Outweek* reporter to follow up with the police about the investigation. Tony, Derek and I head back to the East Village to activate the phone tree. Everyone we talk to reacts the way we did: a bomb exploding in a gay bar is about homophobia. We need to respond.

That night at nine o'clock, more than a hundred people are on the street in front of Uncle Charlie's. Within twenty minutes, the crowd has doubled. The police are there, too. Bryn, who trained me in civil disobedience years before, is acting as head marshal, talking to the commanding officer, who's unhappy that we're impeding traffic. He wants to know our plan. We don't have a plan. We hadn't expected a crowd this size. Derek is talking to a reporter from *The New York Times* who is wondering what the story is. We don't yet know the story. This is not ACT UP; we don't have our sound bites rehearsed.

A group of us huddle together. There's a quick consensus that we should march somewhere, release all this energy. To the police precinct? To City Hall? Someone mentions Washington Square, where a lesbian couple was assaulted just a week ago. This triggers an idea: a march across the Village, west to east, stopping at sites of recent bashings. A Take Back the Night March.

A route is mapped. Marshals are enlisted. We comb through the crowd to find people willing to speak along the way.

Derek gets on Nicholas's shoulders with the bullhorn, and I feel a rush of anger, like a dog straining against a chain, like it's Wigstock again: Derek rallying the masses, the police on alert, all of us feeling threatened. It's not just this pipe bomb, it's this whole wave of beatings and harassment. People have been saying the uptick in violence was payback for Stop the Church, that we went too far and our enemies were pushing back. *What did you expect?* But I was bashed months *before* protesters stepped into St. Patrick's. The more out we are, the more they come after us. Plain and simple: we're in the midst of a violent backlash

"We want the police to treat this as a bias crime," Derek booms, neck taut, face as serious as I've ever seen it. "We want the media to investigate. That's why we're here. We will not be silent." The crowd is with him, defiant, urging him on. In this electric moment, he's the voice of the uprising. "We are the queer nation," he roars. "They better get used to it."

Hillary starts a chant: *We're Here, We're Queer, Get Used to It.* I haven't heard this one before, though it immediately catches on, and soon it will be ubiquitous, so familiar it becomes ripe for parody, like *Harmony Moore Has to Die.* But in this moment it takes hold and thunders. Even now, I can feel the rising reverberation in my bones, our collective fury unleashed.

"Well done," I say to Derek as he dismounts.

Nicholas looks dubious. "The queer nation?"

"They seemed to like it," Derek says.

At Washington Square, under the grand stone arch, one of the women who was attacked takes the bullhorn and tells us her story. Unexpectedly, another guy steps up to share a similar harrowing episode: strangers, unprovoked, hurling names and swinging fists. I've never seen these people before, and I don't think they're on our phone tree, but they've found us. They need this.

We spill onto Fifth Avenue and move north. At Eighth Street, we encounter new hostility, a handful of young men on the sidewalk taunting *faggots, homos, stop spreading AIDS, ugly dykes, die queers die*. An egg flies from above and drops into our midst. Another egg splatters on the concrete near my feet. A group of five marchers breaks away and charges at the tormentors. The egg-hurlers take off, followed by the five, followed by cops, and then I lose sight of them all. I find Bryn, who tells me to keep the march moving. She'll take a few marshals with her and chase down whatever is happening.

Our numbers swell at our next stop, Astor Place, and then at the next, Tompkins Square, where, at the corner of Avenue A, I'm handed the bullhorn. I speak in my most militant voice, recounting Wigstock, linking it to what just happened on Eighth Street: *We show ourselves, they want us to go away. We live freely and they attack. We fight for dignity and they grow murderous.* Afterwards Derek tells me I was on fire, but I was only half aware of my words, transported out of my body even as I felt flooded with adrenaline.

In the next day's *Times*, there's a report on our march: "A peaceful protest turned violent when onlookers attacked the homosexual rights group Queer Nation…"

Three men, the ones who threw eggs, were arrested after cops confiscated a golf club, a baseball bat and a hunting knife from their car. The situation was more precarious than we'd known. But our number-one demand was met: the office of the new mayor, David Dinkins, issued a statement that the explosion at Uncle Charlie's would be treated as a bias-related crime. We count it as a victory.

The next time our group meets, after extensive debate a vote is taken and it's decided that we need a name for future organizing. We're no longer an amorphous gang of friends kissing each other in straight bars. We are Queer Nation.

Leave a Message

A gay man named Julio Rivera is brutally stabbed to death in Queens, in a cruising area called Vaseline Alley. A small group of us from Queer Nation go there to hoist our signs and make demands, coordinating with neighborhood activists who are shaken by this murder and outraged at the tepid police response. Not long after, we travel to Staten Island, where a gay man named James Zappalorti was stabbed to death at a gay beach. As in Queens, our numbers are modest, nothing remotely near our Take Back the Night march. Maybe the outer boroughs are too far from downtown Manhattan. Maybe deaths in cruising zones are harder for people to rally around. Maybe we are still lousy at standing up for ourselves, too burned-out to do it over and over again, too scared, or deep down, too ashamed. Still, even poorly attended demonstrations draw attention to Queer Nation and our anti-violence agenda. Energy is surging.

Derek's phone number—formerly mine—is the contact number for the group. When you call you hear, "Leave a message for Queer Nation," and you also hear, "If you're looking for Paul, call—" and then Amanda's number, which is why she and I now get messages from the media needing a quote, or the police looking for information, or the paranoid guy instructing us how to root out police informants: "Begin each meeting asking everyone to cross their legs. Then look at their ankles, which is where the cops strap their guns. Plus if they're doing surveillance on you, you'll see the wire…"

I apologize to Amanda. "Yeah, it's getting kind of intense," she says.

"It's making me paranoid," I say.

A weekday night. I'm home alone, writing. The phone rings, and before the machine picks up, I grab it. I'm thinking it's Eliot, who I've been trying to reach, who once again seems to be dodging calls.

"Is this the Queer Nation?" A male voice, Southern accent.

"Well, it's my home, but—"

"I just got bashed."

"Oh. Fuck. Tell me what happened." I grab a pen and paper, pin the phone against my neck, mute the classical radio station.

The words come out in a rush. "I was with this guy, we met at a bar and were walking to my place and, I don't know, we weren't *doing* anything, just talking, maybe we were touching a little, nothing *blatant*—"

"Sure, sure, go on—"

"And these goddamn breeders, like maybe ten of them, total straight motherfuckers, went after us—"

"Went after how?"

"I started running and I asked these other people for help, but when they saw what was happening, they just said *sorry*—"

Think, think. "When did this happen?"

"Just now. I'm at a payphone."

"Are you hurt?"

"One guy punched me in the stomach—"

I want to ask if he hit back, want to ask about self-defense; I'm wondering if I would have been able to use what I learned in the moment. *Think.* "What about the other guy, from the bar?"

"He ran. He just left me."

Help him. "Can you get home or anywhere safe?"

"I was two blocks from my apartment but I ran the other way."

"What about the police?"

"The police?"

"No, scratch that." *Jesus, Paul, you know better.* "Is there somewhere you can go, a bar or a restaurant? Just to get off the street?"

"I can't find my wallet." He might be crying. "I've only been in New York a little while. I don't know people."

He says he's near Sheridan Square. I tell him to go to the diner there and order. I'll come meet him, I'll pay, and we can talk. "We'll figure it out."

He says his name is Dennis. *Din-niss.* I tell him my name. "Yeah, I know who you are," he says, "from Queer Nation."

On my way out the door, thinking, *You are in way over your head,* I grab an issue of *Outweek*, which always lists the hotline for the Anti-Violence

Project. I wait for the bus, which takes forever. I watch cabs go by, then I decide this is stupid, I should get there now, and then of course there are no more cabs. The bus eventually pulls up then lumbers like an elephant across town.

At the diner I spot him right away: skinny, floppy platinum hair, hoops through both earlobes, a shearling-lined jacket and a SILENCE=DEATH pin. He could be any guy who shows up at meetings, hovering in the back. He has the look.

"There you are," he says with clear relief. An empty porcelain mug sits next to a squashed teabag. The handwritten bill lies face up.

"Are you ordering?" This is the waiter, a brusque queen clearly impatient with the pace of things at this table. I tell him I want coffee, and he snatches up the bill with a sigh.

I slide into the booth. "That took longer than I thought."

"I'm going a little crazy," he says. He repeats the outline of the attack, which is hard to follow. How was it that he lost his wallet? What happened to the other guy? And why was his first thought to call Queer Nation? I'm fighting back the nagging notion that he isn't telling the truth, that this is a setup and he is one of those fabled informants, ready to entrap me. (But entrap for what?) He's new to the city from Georgia, he wants to sing on Broadway. He went to an ACT UP meeting in Atlanta once, so in New York he tracked us down and put his name on the phone tree. The protest outside Uncle Charlie's was his first. "I ran away from the rednecks back home just to get queer-bashed in the Big Apple."

"New York is hard," I say earnestly.

"You got bashed at that festival, right? I heard you speak at the march."

"Yeah, that was me."

He clenches his fists. "They'd wipe us all out if they could."

"Seems that way sometimes."

"I'd like to kill every last one of them, and their rotten children too, and you know who else, the faggots who don't speak out, who run away at the first sign of danger—" and then he says the name of the guy he'd been with, the one who fled the scene, and says he'd add him to the list, too.

I pay the bill and we walk out to the street. Across the whooshing traffic of Seventh Avenue is Sheridan Square, where the Stonewall Riots exploded twenty-one years ago. I'm thinking about Dennis's wish to kill, the rage of the victim who is supposed to slump into hiding after an attack, licking his wounds, but instead emerges with a vengeance. I've barely tapped into such blazing emotion since Wigstock. At my self-defense class it came out in sobs. At the march I channeled it through a bullhorn. Tears, words, but not anger, not payback. What would it take?

"Can I buy you a beer?" I ask.

"I just want to go home." He lives on the other side of NYU.

"Why don't we walk past where it happened, so you can show me?" I have this desire to retrace his steps and map out his story, which still somehow seems abstract, full of gaps, marred by (my) doubt. But his face flashes in alarm. He wants to avoid Washington Square, the scene of the attack. Of course, of course he does. We go down Seventh to Bleecker, then across toward Broadway, fumbling through conversation. When we get to his doorstep, I move in for a hug and feel him freeze. He looks behind us, alert, on guard.

"Here, I almost forgot." I hand him the magazine I brought along and show him the hotline number. "Call them, they're trained for this."

"Okay. Sorry I bothered you." He goes inside, pulling the door shut. I feel awful. And I feel a little scared, on my own, not far from where he was jumped.

At the first payphone, I call Nicholas, who says, "Perfect timing. Derek's here, hanging out. Come over."

Not so perfect, but I don't have anywhere else to be.

At the door, Nicholas hands me a joint and points me to the chair next to Derek. As I feel the high, I recount Dennis's story, and what seems so clear is how I fell short: I waited for a bus instead of rushing over in a cab, I was suspicious of him, I asked to revisit the site of his assault. Just showing up was a pose—playing the hero—when he needed real support. Derek asks if I got his number, to follow up. I forgot to do that, too. "I'm not cut out for this," I say.

"Don't be hard on yourself," Derek insists. "You did a good thing."

"I'm just not ready to be the voice of Queer Nation."

Derek reaches over and rubs my leg. "But we need you," he says.

On the wall behind him, amid Nicholas's array of flea market paintings, is one that I recognize immediately as Zack's. It depicts the façade of an apartment building. Framed in a window are two women, one Black, one white, each with half a face. The Black woman's face is completed by the arc of a Ferris wheel, the white woman's by a clamshell. In front of them is a pile of cigarettes, stacked as if for a bonfire, smoke starting to rise. Mother, identity, race, danger—I sense the swirl of his ideas in the tight brushstrokes

245

and the cool, surreal tone. Surrounded by more decorative canvases, Zack's stands out, a confrontation.

Nicholas is sizing me up. "Zack gave that to me before he left."

Derek looks at the wall, then back at me. "Even when he's gone, he's here."

"I didn't mention him," I say, defenses rising.

"Are you still in touch with him?"

"Should I *not* be?"

"You boys never really worked this out, did you?" Nicholas asks, looking from one of us to the other.

At the same instant Derek says, "No," and I say, "We've moved on," and then we stare at each other, simmering with awkwardness.

"You could still go to couples' counseling," Nicholas offers.

"We're not a couple," I say.

"People do that? With their exes?" Derek asks. Nicholas nods.

"Counseling costs money," I say.

"But there's low-cost therapy, interns getting their hours," Derek says.

"Remember that intern dentist I went to? That disaster?"

"Oh, so this is like a root canal—"

"Well, a root canal is when they dig out the rot."

"*Rot.* Nice."

I bite my lip. I don't want to hurt him. But I don't want to go to therapy with him, either.

Nicholas pops to his feet and moves to the fridge for a beer. "All righty," he says, changing the subject, "Who's got plans for Pride?"

I turn to Derek. "I'm not trying to—"

He can't look at me now. "Don't bother, okay?"

"I should go."

"Yeah, just fucking go."

As I stand and move to the door, Nicholas waves his hands, "Hey, hey, darlin's, maybe it's not my place, but why not keep talking this out—"

"Thanks for trying," I say to him. I look to Derek one last time.

"What?" he demands.

"Can you take my name off your answering machine?"

"Gladly."

Don't Hold Back

Oh, Eliot. Oh, no.

The call comes from Lenny on a weekday afternoon, while I'm at my desk at my more or less permanent temp job, filing faxes. It takes a sec to register Lenny as Eliot's boyfriend. He's never called me before. "Eliot's in the hospital," he says.

"Last time I saw him he was on pentamidine. Isn't it working—?"

"It's not AIDS-related. It's, well, you see—" He needs a moment to collect himself. "Eliot attempted suicide."

"Fuck—"

"He cut his wrists—"

"No. Fuck fuck fuck fuck."

"—but I was on my way over so I found him, and he's going to make it. I thought you should know. He cares about you, and if you can handle a visit—"

"Yes, absolutely."

Amanda and I go together to New York–Presbyterian Hospital, on the Upper East Side. His windows look back downtown, from where we've traveled. I find myself remembering the time Eliot visited me when my jaw was busted, and he showed up with a VCR. We don't have anything nearly as impressive, but we've come bearing gifts: the *New York Times* crossword puzzle, the latest issue of *Outweek*, a frosted layer cake from a bakery near the hospital.

Eliot takes in our display with little cooing noises. His expression is drugged, drained. His wrists are swaddled with gauze, and IV fluids feed his veins through long, clear tubes. A chart on a clipboard hangs at the foot of his bed, etched with a doctor's scrawl.

"Birthday cake! Your favorite!" I announce grandly. "I couldn't sneak the cocktail shaker past the nursing desk, or else we'd be making martinis."

"But you're not allowed to throw it out the window," Amanda says.

Lenny signals to us with his eyes: *bring it down a notch.*

I park myself on his bed and take hold of Eliot's hand, which is cool and papery to the touch. "Do you want to talk about it?"

His lips seem to quiver. "I was just so tired."

"You've been burned out, I know."

"Christopher managed to get it done." He's rubbing his eyes beneath his wire-rimmed glasses, looking very tired himself.

"Please, Eliot, don't talk that way."

"We love you, Eliot," Amanda says. "We don't want you to go away."

"I suppose my heart wasn't fully in it," Eliot says. "I'm like Susan Hayward, *I want to live.*" He pushes himself upright. "Is that one on your cinema list?"

"We can make a date for it," I say.

"Turns out I'll be around," he says.

On the subway downtown, standing in the midst of a crowded car, I ask Amanda, "Why did we do that thing with the crossword puzzle and the birthday cake? It was embarrassing."

"What should we have done?"

"I don't know. Let him rant?"

"He was too doped up to rant."

"He mentioned Christopher."

She shakes her head, perplexed. "Why is he chasing Christopher's ghost? It's selfish. Think of Lenny."

"But if he wanted to get it over with—not suffer through some horrible death in the future—who are we to say?"

"He's alive. We showered him with love. That's what friends do."

I have a sudden image of him—dark hair, pale skin, bandaged wrists—throwing open his hospital window and screaming like that guy in the movie, *I'm mad as hell and I'm not going to take it anymore!* This vision is like fuel, and I speak with fire on my tongue. "We should have thrown away his sedatives and sprung him from the ward and let him run through the streets, just let him *exhaust* himself, just get it all out. Why don't we *all* do that—howl out the truth, make the world stop for a second and *listen* to us?" My voice has gotten louder, my gestures bigger, and I can feel the passengers around us taking note, shuffling away. "Look at all these people just going on about their business while this war is being fought in our bodies. Like people aren't dying by the tens of thousands in this city. That's why Eliot opened a vein! He wanted people to *see!*"

"We see you. We hear you too," a man nearby mutters.

"What the fuck did you say?" I yell.

"You startin' something?" The guy is bigger than me, with a confident stance. But I've taken self-defense and suddenly feel itchy to use it.

"Mind your own business," I snarl.

The train pulls to a stop. Amanda grabs hold of my arm and yanks me out of the car. "This isn't our station," I protest.

"Take a breath," she commands.

"Why are you silencing me?"

"Do you have more to say? Then say it. But don't pick a fight."

I watch the train pull away. Furious, I shake her off me and retreat to a bench until the next one pulls in.

"Look," she says, "Eliot is where he needs to be. Maybe tomorrow he'll be happy to eat a slice of cake."

We take the next train, but we don't talk. I'm in turmoil, and I want to empty my heart of this pain, but not like Eliot, not with a razor, not by sacrificing myself. And not by stirring up shit on the subway, either. But how?

Don't hold back was a mantra Lily hammered home during our self-defense class. Learn the moves, absorb them into your body, and if you have to use them, go for it. For weeks in that studio we shouted *No* and *Stop*. We bellowed our names with voices that didn't waver. We aimed the heels of our fists toward the noses of imagined assailants. We learned to be ready for the unexpected.

So when Hillary asks me to contribute a five-hundred-word piece of writing about gay bashing to an affinity group publication, and she says, "Don't hold back," I don't. I write about Wigstock, about the murder of James Zappalorti on Staten Island and our single timid demonstration in response, about how self-defense taught me to break an attacker's nose and gouge his eyes. I end like this:

The straight world has us so convinced that

we are helpless and deserving victims of the violence against us, that we queers become immobilized when faced with a threat. BE OUTRAGED! These attacks must not be tolerated. DO SOMETHING. Recognize that any act of aggression against any member of our community is an attack on every member of the community. The more we allow homophobes to inflict violence, terror and fear on our lives, the more frequently and ferociously we will be the object of their hatred. Your life is immeasurably valuable, and unless you start believing that, it will be easily taken from you. Defend your community. Defend yourself.

I wasn't signing my name. None of the contributors were. The only author identified would be "Anonymous Queers."

On Pride Sunday, we meet along Central Park West, where ACT UP's contingent is gathered, waiting for the kickoff. I've arrived with Raymond and Tony, who shows up in glorious fright drag: pancaked flesh, black-rimmed eyes, lace-up boots. His Mohawk is flattened under a platinum wig as big and sculptural as Divine's. Over a black minidress he's draped a white satin sash with the words Ms. BASH BACK, and he's carrying a baseball bat. "My own personal bodyguard," Raymond says, voice dripping with admiration, as Tony twirls in the street, brandishing the bat.

Our art affinity group is all together when Hillary and Floyd arrive, pushing a dolly stacked with a tabloid-sized newspaper. Floyd holds one up for us, displaying its huge, unambiguous front-page headline, bold black type set off against a geometric red and white design: *QUEERS READ THIS*.

"Very Bolshevik," Nicholas says.

"I was going for *Ebony* circa '65."

"Ebony Bolshevik," Nicholas said. "Your new drag name."

He points to the second largest headline: *I HATE STRAIGHTS*. "That's subtle."

Floyd smiles, but says nothing more. Spirits are high. We're all seeing this for the first time, grabbing copies and flipping through it. The pages are dense with unfiltered rage, manifestos of what we've been living through:

I'm sick of waiting for straight people to help...
I'd like to kill a straight man for every gay man
who has died because of indifference... Fuck you,
Women's Movement, for ignoring lesbians...
I hate the cops—state sanctioned sadists who
brutalize street transvestites, prostitutes and
queer prisoners... Teenage boys spotting my
Silence=Death button begin chanting "Faggot's
gonna die," and I wonder, who taught them
this?... Tell your straight friends not to dismiss
you by saying "You have rights," "You have
privileges," "You're overreacting," or "You have
a victim's mentality." Tell them "GO AWAY
FROM ME, until YOU can change." Go away
until they have spent a month walking hand in
hand in public with someone of the same sex.

Seeing my own words typeset and laid out amid these pieces from my friends is a thrilling but also alien experience, like hearing myself on tape and not immediately recognizing my voice. That's what I sound like? But it's more than that, because my voice is part of a chorus, and I have no doubt it will reverberate.

"Grab what you can carry and pass them out along the route," Hillary tells us. We spend the next few hours moving down Fifth Avenue, thrusting our words into outstretched hands.

Tony, our drag mascot for the day, leads the way, drawing attention, calling out "Queers Read This!"

People are excited for a handout. Then they scan the headlines, and I watch their faces change.

At the next ACT UP meeting, Javier, giving the media committee report, stands during the "new business" portion of the agenda. He holds aloft our broadside, points to *I Hate Straights*, and asks, "Are we going to talk about this?"

A dozen hands go up. Timmy is facilitating, and since he was part of our collective, he knows what's coming. He calls on Floyd first.

"Brothers and sisters, this was an art piece," Floyd proclaims. "We wrote it out of our pain, our rage, our passion. You know these feelings, you share this with us, don't you? We happened to be moving alongside ACT UP at the parade because this has always been our activist home, but none of us ever stated or implied that these were official ACT UP statements. I will happily answer your queries, but the rest of our group is anonymous, and I will honor that." I think about how he's always been there, from my first ACT UP meeting, to the Outreach committee, to Fire Island and self-defense and now this, the face of this action that so many in the room take issue with. Commenters center on the backlash this publication will create, alienating straight allies at the very moment we were getting beyond St. Patrick's. No one is talking about the content of the essays, just the one headline, with its capital-letter HATE. ACT UP had allowed for anger, civil disobedience, even militancy, but was hatred somehow too far?

Amanda and I walk home together, talking all the way, as stimulated as we've ever been by a meeting. Neither of us had known we were participating in a manifesto. We were told to write from the heart, from the gut, *don't hold back*. The result was as raw a display of emotion as any I'd seen in years of political organizing. But the irony is that we wrote less out of hatred than out of love, out of the urgent need to care for and defend each other.

Words, I think. Words did this. Print, on paper, passed hand to hand.

I mail a copy to Zack. I write, *We are using art to shake things up.*

I get a postcard in return, with just two sentences:

Time to visit, Kiddo. Bed too big without you.
—Quaking for you, Z.

Part 9

The Right Person

From the air, San Francisco looks like a city only half tamed: high verdant hills, white fingers of fog, dark, jagged coastline. This is the farthest from home I've traveled since I did a college semester in London, a time that seems so far in the past I hardly remember it.

As I emerge from the jetway, I spot his Yankees cap first, then his handsome face, those soft lips and big brown eyes, which brighten when he sees me. His skin is sun-browned, and he has on a new, safety-orange jacket, like a utility worker might wear, instead of the black leather he wore in New York.

"Kiddo," he says, pulling me in for a kiss. I'm aware of my bag slipping off my shoulder and the passengers exiting past me on either side, the two of us like a rock in the middle of a rushing stream.

"Excuse us," a voice says. "Please." We make room for an old woman pushing an even older woman in a wheelchair. They pass by us as if they see two men kissing every day. I'm definitely not in New York anymore.

"Come on," he says. "I'm gonna pop your San Francisco cherry."

He takes my hand as we walk to the parking garage, while I steal glances at him. His hair is longer, more natural. His ears are pierced, silver hoops through both lobes. Around his neck, on a thick silver chain, is a shiny hunk of metal. His body seems not quite as bulky, and of course I wonder about his health, though the effect is more like he's taken off a layer of armor, unburdening himself of weight he is tired of carrying around.

He drives me into the city in a junky little car that makes so much noise I can't help but laugh. "It was free," he says. "My roommate's friend died, and there was no one to take it."

"He didn't want it?"

"She. Raven."

"I'm guessing that's not her birth name."

"Birds are apparently big among the queers here. I bought a pot brownie off a faerie boy named Blue Jay. And I met a person at ACT UP named Sparrow, whose gender was unknown. At least to me."

"You told her I'm staying with you, right?"

He grins at the worry in my voice. "It's not like at Amanda's. Our place actually has walls. I don't really need a car here, but I like getting in it and just—" He sticks a hand out of the window and lets it fly in the breeze.

"Where do you go?"

"North to the Marin and Sonoma coasts. It's so rugged there, cold and wet, with redwoods. And down to Santa Cruz, which is still torn up from the earthquake. Yosemite's next, before the snow. Or maybe after, so I can ski."

"You're getting crunchy, aren't you?"

He laughs. "Honestly, I've never felt so much like a New Yorker. I had to learn how to make small talk with cashiers and cab drivers. At every corner, I have to remember to stand on the curb instead of stepping into the street. If you do that here, you'll get hit by a bike."

San Francisco stretches wide under dramatic clouds, with sunlight and blue sky breaking through unexpectedly. Houses climb up hilltops. It seems like a city you could fall in love with fast.

Zack lives on Baker, just off Haight. ("You don't say 'street,'" he tells me.) He points toward Buena Vista Park, a rise of gnarled trees, feral shrubs and cracked staircases hinting at faded elegance. ("Super cruisey," he says with a shrug. "Gets old fast.") His building is three stories, Edwardian, a "flat" on each level, with scrollwork around the windows and doors. Inside his front door, a long hallway extends, with rooms down the length of it. There's a big living room with scratched wooden floors, secondhand couches and a lopsided rubber tree filling a Bay window. "This would have been a double-parlor once. Raven's room," he points, "is behind the pocket doors."

At that moment, I get a glimpse of Raven, an older butch in a man's blazer, with a shorn head and a vivid tattoo on her ropy neck. She gives me a visual once-over, salutes and then vanishes.

Zack's bedroom, on the far end of the apartment, has a queen-sized bed, not just a mattress on the floor, and two closets, a small one for clothes and a big one with enough room for his easel and paint supplies, set up beneath a small, high transom window. When I ask how he works with so little light, he points to the realistic landscape on his easel: gray-green ocean, rocky shore, the orange towers of the Golden Gate Bridge. "You're painting outside?" I ask.

He nods. "It's corny, but it makes me so happy."

That night he takes me to a Thai restaurant. I've eaten a gummy rendition of Pad Thai at a sushi restaurant in the East Village, but this is full of fresh mint and crisp vegetables. We walk from there along a hilly street to the Castro, passing calla lilies popping up from patches of dirt and trees flowering with yellow trumpets. "Where's the filth?" I ask.

"In New York."

It's Friday night, but the Castro is quiet. Inside a leather bar with a window and counter open to the street, men overlook the sidewalk, clutching pint glasses. Most of them are older than us, with bushy mustaches and jeans sanded at the crotch to show off the goods. When I comment that it's like the West Village twenty years ago, he replies, "They call San Francisco a retirement home for the young."

We pass a woman in a shabby wig sitting in a doorway holding a hand-lettered sign: TRANSSEXUAL AND HOMELESS. I LIKE SPAGHETTI AND MEATBALLS. Zack digs a couple of quarters from his pocket. Sensing my surprise—I've never seen him hand out change in New York—he says, "How could you resist her?" She bats her eyelashes and offers a raspy thank you.

At the corner donut shop, crowded with a cross-section of what I immediately dub San Francisco characters, Zack nods toward a quartet of two gay guys and two lesbians, all wearing leather jackets plastered with Day-Glo stickers that say POSITIVELY QUEER, LESBIAN MENACE, PROMOTE HOMOSEXUALITY. I knew there was a Queer Nation in San Francisco—in just a few short months, Queer Nations have popped up all over the world—but it's hard to connect the dots between our early exploratory kiss-ins and these proudly stickered strangers. Zack says he'll take me to a meeting and introduce me as the founder, an idea that makes me want to run for cover. "I'd rather be a fly on the wall," I say.

He drives us up a twisting road to Twin Peaks, in the center of the city, where we stand in the whipping wind, his arms wrapped around me, his chin on my shoulder, his voice in my ear. All of San Francisco is revealed below like an illuminated map, with the slant of Market Street running from the base of this mountain to a faraway bridge, a rope of jewels against black water and sky.

"Is that the Golden Gate?"

"That's the Bay Bridge, which goes to Oakland." He pivots me to the left. "*That's* the Golden Gate. I call it the Bridge of Souls. It's mystical out there."

"Souls?"

"When you're on it, so high up, you feel the harshness of the wind, you taste the salt from the ocean. It's a new perspective—how violent nature is."

Back at his flat, we crawl into bed—the one he deemed too big without me—and we're kissing and stripping off our clothes when I see the rash along his underarm. "Let me look at that," I insist.

He twists his arm toward me. "I'm getting it checked at the clinic."

"Are you doing any treatment yet?"

He shakes his head. "No, but at ACT UP they were talking about a drug trial for an anti-retroviral, ddI or d4T—one of the nucleosides."

"Is it easy to get into those?"

"I'm making connections. I went to the wrong ACT UP meeting at first—"

"What do you mean?"

"ACT UP split into two groups here. One is focused on drug treatment. The other, the wrong one, is obsessed with HIV not being the cause of AIDS."

"That's so upsetting." I've heard rumors of this split and want to know more, but what I'm really concerned about right now is Zack's health.

He says the scaly patch on his arm has been there a while, but he has no idea if it's a symptom of HIV or just something else he's picked up. He alludes to other minor complaints without going into detail. "Let's just spoon," he says, voice as sweet as I've ever heard it. "I want to feel close." We fall asleep without having sex, which is another first.

We spend the next day driving around the city, Zack playing tour guide. "Different neighborhoods have different weather," he says, though everywhere we go is a version of wet: rain, fog, mist, dampness that seeps into my bones. At Community Thrift on Valencia I buy a knit cap and gloves. We eat deliciously stuffed burritos and go to the Castro Theatre, a beautiful, battered movie palace still damaged from the '89 quake. The movie is *Breakfast at Tiffany's*, but half the show is the audience: hissing at Mickey Rooney's racist caricature of the Japanese landlord—buckteeth, Coke-bottle spectacles, impenetrable accent—sniffling when Audrey sings "Moon River."

"Did that make you miss New York?" I ask Zack as we exit.

"New York was never like that for me. I always lived like a slob in dangerous neighborhoods."

"I used to have that uptown fantasy when I was a kid," I say. "My mother had a friend on the Upper West Side, she was sort of my Auntie Mame—stylish, ageless, with great stories about New York in the '50s and '60s. I still see glimpses of that era under the soot."

"You're an incurable romantic."

"Me? You're the one."

"I'm just incurable." He means this to be funny, but I feel my stomach clench.

We have quick sex that night, hands and mouths and easy orgasms, then back to cuddling. He sleeps with an arm draped over me, keeping me close. The feel of his pulse through his warm skin is divine comfort, but questions about the rash on his arm keep me hellishly awake. When people die from AIDS, there's always a best friend or lover who takes charge of caretaking and a wider circle of friends who share the burden. Who will fill those roles for Zack, so far away from home? What happens to people in his situation, without support? I know the statistics—there aren't enough hospital beds for long-term patients, and the neediest are often warehoused in overcrowded rooms. ACT UP's housing committee does good work for homeless people with AIDS in New York, but I don't know what San Francisco can offer. I can't picture what the future will bring if—*when*, I correct myself—Zack gets ill.

The first item on Queer Nation–San Francisco's agenda is a suggestion to send a thank-you note to openly gay Congressman Barney Frank, who recently made a statement praising "a new generation of lesbian and gay activists." Ten minutes later it's still being discussed. Is Frank too mainstream and not queer enough? Is thanking politicians what Queer Nation should be doing? "Let's send him a t-shirt and ask him to wear it on TV," someone suggests, and then another voice calls out, "They don't come in XXL." Hissing follows, then a request for "an agenda break to talk about sizeism." An agenda break, I discover, is part of the procedure here. It can be called by anyone at any time to address offensive remarks.

We're standing in the back of a big meeting room in the Women's Building. The setup is familiar—facilitators up front, folding chairs in rows, an info table near the door—but the energy is different. I feel caught up in process, not spurred to action. There's a long discussion about money to purchase a bullhorn, which seems like a no-brainer, but it turns out everyone present has to agree, or abstain, in order for the request to pass. The group runs on consensus, not majority vote. The measure fails after one man announces, "I'm going to block consensus because a bullhorn gives one person a greater voice than everyone else."

I turn to Zack, my mouth agape. Ripping a piece of paper from my notebook, I write: "Should I get up there and facilitate?"

Zack scrawls his reply: "You should take me home and fuck me."

It's taken us three nights to fuck. So much about Zack has changed—what he wears, what he paints, how he spends his time—but not this. In bed, I take charge, putting him on his back, rolling on a condom, squeezing out lube. I lift one of his legs, put my other hand on his chest, press my cock into him, entering the familiar warmth, our bodies locking together. He keeps his eyes open as I pick up rhythm and we rock together, deeply connected. I could stay here forever.

It's when he gets on his hands and knees, with me behind him, that I see it: another rough patch on his left shoulder blade. I don't want to believe it's that same rash, so I keep going, moving in and out with increasing force, telling myself that I can save him, can fuck away this opportunistic illness, if that's what it is, before it takes root. It's the inverse of that long-ago wish for Mike Savas to infect me. What I want now is to pull off the condom and flood Zack with uninfected seed, as if I could transfuse strength and crush death.

But after I come and pull out, the condom hanging like a limp, gooey rope, I feel the opposite of savior. I'm just a guy behind a barrier with a hero complex.

"You have that same rash forming on your back," I tell him.

I follow him down the hall to the bathroom, where he looks over his shoulder into the mirror. "Maybe," he says.

"You need to get treatment," I say. "Let me help you."

"How? You're leaving in two days."

"Come back to New York, where you have a community."

"Why don't you stay here?"

"My apartment, my job—"

"Amanda's apartment? Your temp job?"

"Zack, whether or not I move here—and this is the first time you've even *mentioned* that—you have to deal with your health *now*."

He starts coughing at that moment, pushing out of the bathroom to the kitchen, where he fills a glass and guzzles water. For half a minute, the coughing persists. I rub my hand on his back, until at last he calms.

"I want to ask you—" I pause, unsure.

"Just say it."

"Did you move here because you decided it's where you're going to die?"

His face falls. "I'm here because this is where I want to *live*. I want to be in a beautiful place where I have room to breathe and just *be.*"

"You shed all your possessions, you move to a place where you don't know anyone, you're not monitoring your health—"

I'm bracing for a backlash, but he says nothing. His eyes seem to plead for silence. Which is when I realize that his reticence about living with HIV is not just a matter of privacy, not just his "cool" personality. He's in denial—emotionally unequipped for what illness will bring.

Is this common? Does Eliot talk with Lenny about his fear of death? Does Dale talk with Timmy? When the guys on the treatment and data committee meet to compare notes on drug research, are they also opening up their emotional lives to each other? Those conversations must be happening among the activists I know, but as a negative guy who had a negative lover for years, I've never been part of them.

"I'm operating on instinct," he says, finally. "When I think about the end, all I come up with is, I won't be able to make my own choices. It's going to happen *to* me." He reaches out to take my hands in his. "I know it's too much to ask, but will you? Move here?"

He's terrified. I haven't actually known this. But of course he is. Anyone would be, and Zack—though he's so special to me—is also like anyone else.

"I'll think about it," I say, "if you think about moving back to New York."

On my last night, we go for beers at the Detour, a place that reminds me of The Bar, but darker, more sexual. A chain-link fence runs down the length, creating a corridor on one side. Shafts of light passing through the fence cast back-alley shadows on us as we sit on a bench, his arm over my shoulder. We watch men drift by, some of them circling in loops, cruising to the throb of techno music.

I get up to buy another round, and when I return, Zack's in conversation with a guy who has a Fu Manchu beard and a long leather coat. "This is Mel," Zack says. Mel extends a hand. His fingers, like Tony's, are covered in rings, though Tony doesn't crush you with his grip like this guy does. He strikes me as slightly menacing, or maybe just a little sleazy.

"Where'd you come from?" Mel asks.

"New York. I'm staying with him."

Mel sends Zack a knowing look. "So that's why I haven't heard from you."

"This one's keeping me busy."

"You need any help with that?" Mel asks flirtatiously.

"No one needs any *help*," I say.

"This one's feisty," Mel says. He has a confidence that unnerves me, a competitiveness I'm not used to. Have they had sex? Except for a single mention of a cruisey park up the hill, Zack hasn't spoken of his sex life here.

Mel leans in and says quietly to Zack, "You let me know about that other thing, if it gets bad again." He smiles at me, and then he's gone.

Zack explains that he met Mel through Raven, his roommate. Mel makes jewelry. The chunky piece hanging on a chain around Zack's neck is one of his. "He's not what you think," Zack says. "He's in nursing school."

"So what did that mean—if it gets bad?"

"There was this night, about three weeks ago . . ." He describes being doubled over with cramps, diarrhea that lasted two days, a trip to the emergency room. Raven stayed with him at the hospital, held his hand, monitored his care, which surprises me. My glimpse of her hadn't suggested a nurturing side. "It turned out to be a parasite. Nothing too bad. It could have been MAI, what they call the 'diarrhea of death.' But luckily it wasn't. I got better pretty quickly."

"So Mel gave you something for the pain?"

He lowers his voice. "Morphine."

"Morphine's the same as heroin, isn't it?"

"I only took a little. It got me through a bad night."

I look at him. The face I love. The troubled eyes that draw me in. We've been living our lives without each other, which seems unbearable now. I don't understand any of the choices I've made in the past few months. "You were suffering," I say, "And I wasn't there. That seems wrong."

He pulls my head against his chest. "How did I get so lucky to find you?"

"I put myself in your path."

"Like a kid playing in traffic."

For a moment the bar goes away—no more chain-link fence, cruisey lights, driving music. It's just me up against him, absorbing the thump of his blood and the rhythm of his lungs, as if a spell has been magically cast upon us and only us. But that same magic casts shadows, too: secrecy, isolation, the limitations of what the two of us, absent anyone else, can actually take on.

"This guy gave you morphine?" I ask. "That's so hardcore."

"Shh," he says. "Don't worry."

The doorbell wakes me. The airport shuttle is outside, but we've overslept, so I send the driver away with a few bucks, checking that there's enough cash in my wallet for a taxi instead. Zack scrambles into his work clothes—buttoned shirt and pleated trousers—looking like an earlier version of himself, only with more jewelry. We both need to rush, so there's no time for more than a kiss on his front stoop, an unromantic good-bye. I watch him dash to catch the bus downtown.

I have no idea when I'll see him again.

"I'll give you a ride to SFO." This is Raven, the roommate, standing in the hall. I politely say thanks, no, you don't have to. But she insists.

As she drives, she gnaws on a toothpick, the tape player blaring a riot grrl band. She keeps her foot on the gas, like she's in a race. She's as stone-cold a butch as I've ever met. I'm making small talk when she interrupts. "We gonna talk about your buddy Zack?"

"Yeah, let's," I say, catching the serious look in her eye, suddenly bold myself. "You took him to the ER."

"It should have been a wake-up call. He's not doing enough for himself."

"I want him to come back to New York, but he gave up his apartment—"

"Can he live with you?"

"I've got a futon on the floor of a friend's railroad. How much do you know about New York real estate?"

"Not much. But I know a lot about AIDS."

"He told me he's getting info from ACT UP about drug trials."

"Does he know his CD4 count? When's the last time he did blood work?"

This silences me. I can't answer her questions.

She eases up, just a bit. "Look, I've been through this before with my boys. I can do it again if I have to. But Zack's not really *mine*, see?"

"What if I'm not the right person?" I ask her.

"Anyone can be the right person. But you have to rise to the occasion."

At the airport, she gives me her card. Just her one-word name, and beneath it, a list of odd jobs, everything from carpentry to Tarot readings. "One more thing," she says. "You know he's been up to the Golden Gate Bridge, right?"

"With his sketchpad—"

"He's been up there more than once. Think about it."

What I think is: Kim Novak in *Vertigo* jumping into the Bay. And my breath catches in my throat.

At the airport, I find a payphone. I call Zack at work.

"What's this about you going up to the bridge?"

"Whoa—what?"

"Raven told me."

"I don't know what she said, but I'm at work, I can't talk."

"I'm getting on a plane. *Talk.*"

I hear the rolling of chair casters, the closing of a door. Then he's back, voice lowered. "I went up there, and yeah, I thought about it. People jump every day. But I couldn't do it, and I won't. I'm in a different state of mind now."

"Oh, Zack." I swallow to hold back tears. All around me is the airport, hard surfaces, echoing announcements, travelers on the move, lives in flux. I'm standing near the spot where we kissed just a few days ago. Since then the world has tilted on its axis.

I make myself say the words. "You can't kill yourself."

"I don't want to. I wanted to kill *it*. The virus. Do you believe me?"

I try to make sense of this. "I think so."

"I'm not depressed. I'm painting. I'm living."

"So fight the virus. Get treatment." And then, as if I too am throwing myself out into the unknown, I add, "I'll help you, Zack. I promise."

I hear him release his breath. He's been holding it in, uncertain of what I might say. "I believe you, too," he replies, and then we just breathe together, across this distance.

We've Only Just Begun

The night I return to New York, Timmy and Dale are throwing an anniversary party. They've been together three years, as long as any couple in our extended family. The theme is Junior Prom. When Dale invited me, he said, "In high school, after three years, you get to go to Junior Prom. But since none of us went—"

"Or if we did, it was awful," Timmy interjected.

"—we're having our own."

As I walk back into our apartment, Amanda is getting in costume, and Hillary is with her. Their costumes are role-reversed: Amanda is in a man's suit, cuffed at wrist and ankle, too wide all around for her petite frame, like Judy Garland's tramp in *A Star Is Born*. Hillary is nearly unrecognizable in a blonde wig and a poofy, shiny pink gown. She's excited to hear what I thought of San Francisco. "It's such a historic city," she says. "I bet you'd do great there."

"I'm not even entertaining that idea," Amanda says. "You are not allowed to move three thousand miles away."

"You're just saying that to disagree with me," Hillary says.

Amanda leans toward me. "We're totally in a fight tonight."

"So I guess that means you're back together?" I ask.

They exchange glances, neither wanting to answer. I decide not to push it.

I'm worn out from traveling, but when I suggest that I'm not up for getting into drag for the party, they won't hear it. Amanda dresses me in a vintage kaftan she pilfered from her mother's closet—"She worked the '70s like Mrs. Roper"—and in a fit of inspiration, I run down to the corner Korean market and buy some daisies to braid into a crown.

Stepping into the party, I announce, "I have returned from San Francisco with flowers in my hair."

The welcome I get is so enthusiastic it's like I was gone a year. Everyone wants to know if I'm planning to move there. "That's what happens when New York queens visit San Francisco for the first time," Nicholas says. "They forget where they're from!"

The biggest surprise is Eliot, in his Harmony Moore cocktail dress and scar-concealing opera gloves, featuring newly bleached hair cut into spiky tips by Tony. "Harmony," I gush. "You've been reborn."

"More lives than an alley cat," he says. "Don't count me out yet."

Lenny is at his side, in a powder blue vintage tux he claims was the one he wore to his actual prom. "I never get rid of anything," he says, sending me a wordless, *weathered the storm* glance when Eliot turns momentarily away.

Dale says he'll never speak to me again if I move to San Francisco, and Timmy says, "Oh, good, maybe I'll move, too"—a bickery-sounding statement that nevertheless leaves the two of them giggling, as if this is a running joke, the kind that has kept them together.

Nicholas hands me a tall cocktail. "Nurse's orders. Now tell us about Zack."

"He loves it there, but he's isolated. He wants me to be with him."

"It's wildly romantic to move cross-country for love," Eliot says.

"Never mind that Zack doesn't have any friends in San Francisco," Amanda says, "what about the fact that *you* don't?"

"I know," I say. "I think he should come back here."

Tony lowers his voice and says to me, "Your ex-husband is in the kitchen." At that moment, Derek appears, not in costume, crossing the room toward the front door. With him is a hunky boy in a Queer Nation t-shirt, holding out Derek's coat and opening the door for him. Derek's eyes find mine and linger for a moment before he exits, his face a tense mask.

"Did he just leave because I showed up?" I ask Tony, who reports that Michael moved out of Derek's this weekend—he left with little warning, announcing he was relocating to Miami with a rich Cuban he'd recently met. "This guy has a big apartment in South Beach with a grand piano, and Michael's going to play music and, like, be kept by him, I guess. I hung out with Derek, and it was so messy. He played 'Nothing Compares 2 U' on repeat all night. I mean, I love Sinead, but girl, really?"

"Michael means a lot to Derek," I say.

"Yeah, but the drunker he got, the more he talked about *you*."

I drop my head into my hands, muttering, "Catholic guilt."

"Drama," Raymond says, not very nicely, and then slips away. I hadn't even known he was here.

Raymond's DJing the party, in drag—a bobbed Dynel wig and a beaded dress that won't zip shut across his broad back. We all dance for hours, full of celebratory vibes for Dale and Timmy, though for me, Derek's dramatic exit lingers, punctuating all the longing and confusion I've carried home from my visit with Zack. I drink too much, too fast. At the end of the night, when Raymond changes up the mood with a scratchy vinyl recording of "We've Only Just Begun," it hits me like a queer broken-hearts ballad. I slow-dance with Amanda, tears in my eyes as Karen Carpenter croons *So much of life ahead* . . . then the tempo quickens and the tambourine shimmers and we find our swing again, harmonizing, *Sharing horizons that are new to us, watching the signs along the way,* and I disco-twirl Amanda from my extended arm right to Hillary, who grabs hold of her without missing a beat. I watch them grapple for lead until Amanda gives in with a laugh as Hillary takes command, a butch prom queen.

At the end of the song, the whole room forms a circle around Timmy and Dale. I pluck the wilting flowers from my hair and pass them out, and we shower the boys with anniversary petals.

When the party is over, Raymond offers to give me a ride home. He's recently bought a dented pickup truck that he's dubbed "Maude." I squeeze into the passenger seat with Tony, as Maude gurgles unsettlingly down the West Side Highway, around the Battery toward the East Village. From this vantage point downtown Manhattan strikes me as dense and towering. "This is a lot to visually absorb after the open sky of San Francisco," I say.

Tony says, "Girl, you've only been gone for a long weekend."

"But it's the farthest from home I've been in years," I say. "We live in an extreme place, but we act like it's the most normal way to live."

"That's why I adopted Maude," Raymond says. "To carry me away from the craziness every now and then."

"I'll be happy if she gets to the East Side without a breakdown."

"Shh. She can hear you," he says, running a hand across the dashboard.

Raymond drops Tony at home first, then drives me back to 10th Street. He parks and turns off the ignition, but he doesn't make a move to get out. "I have to get this off my chest," he says. "I'm just *not happy* about you and Zack."

"What are you talking about?"

"First of all, I thought it was crazy, you and Derek breaking up. I mean, you'd figured out the whole non-monogamy thing, you had that great apartment, you were fun together—"

"Not every couple is meant to last. We were running on empty."

"Plus—Zack is such a problem child. I've known him since before ACT UP. His whole strong-silent thing just covers up a giant stewpot of neediness. He told me once that he wanted what you and Derek have—*had*—and I just feel like, he shouldn't be looking to you for that. I thought it was good that he got away, and now you're talking about moving there? Really?"

"You sound jealous," I blurt out. "I mean, I know your whole history."

He grips the steering wheel so tightly I can see his knuckles whiten in the light coming through the windshield. "I'm having fun with Tony. I like him a lot. Okay, sure, I'm probably a little jealous, but it's more than that! Zack is so important to me, and I think you're just toying with him." He stares at me with serious eyes, a bit glazed from a night of drinking. "I think Zack should stay in San Francisco, without you. Without me, too, for that matter. I'm sorry, but I do. Let him spread his wings and figure out who he is."

"Raymond, listen to me," I say, taking a deep breath. "He's developing symptoms—diarrhea, heavy coughing, a rash that won't go away."

His mouth falls open, like he's going to speak, but I continue.

"Maybe you're right," I say. "Maybe in an ideal world he'd have this beautiful life in California and find an HIV-positive lover who was perfect for him. But I think we should find him a job *here*, and bring him back."

"Fuck," he yells. "Just fuck the fucking world." And then he bangs his hands on the steering wheel, over and over and over and over.

A few days later, Zack calls me at work with the news that he's been fired.

"Insubordination, once again," he says. He clashed with his boss over a proposed campaign. Didn't give her what she wanted. Didn't do what she ordered. "Then I showed up to the pitch meeting with a Day-Glo sticker on my jacket that said 'Fuck Your Heterosexual Privilege.'"

I'm at my desk, at the same magazine company where I've worked for well over a year now, handling administrative tasks so mindless I sometimes can't remember what I've spent the day doing. At some point after my mother died, I switched from temp to "perm," as they call it, and went on the payroll, freaked out that I didn't have health insurance. Now I dial the extension for Human Resources and ask about any open design or production positions in the company. It turns out there's one, at our interior decor publication. I take the elevator up three floors to that office, where I know a gay editor named Jared who has been to ACT UP meetings. "I need a favor," I tell him.

A month later, Zack is back in New York.

In those days, it was still pretty easy to find a rental in the East Village. Wealthy go-getters hadn't yet taken over. Rich kids came downtown to *slum*, as they called it, their taxis and limos idling while they scored heroin and crack at fortified storefronts on 2nd and C, but they weren't yet renting apartments in the neighborhood. The elite playground of today's downtown Manhattan had not yet taken root, though change was absolutely on its way.

Mayor Dinkins had ordered the police to close Tompkins Square Park, first kicking out the three hundred people living there and bulldozing their tent city, then installing a ring of uniformed cops around the perimeter, standing guard day and night. The homeless relocated to the doorways of abandoned buildings, many of which were being squatted by anarchists, who pulled power from streetlights, coming and going through busted fences. The Eastern Europeans, Koreans and Puerto Ricans who ran the restaurants and bodegas all lived nearby. It was still possible, if you were waiting for a paycheck and the guy behind the counter of the hardware store or the lady running the dry cleaner's knew you, to pay what you owed "next time." The only fast food was a McDonald's on First Ave., and why would anyone get a Big Mac when for the same price, a block away, you could eat homemade Ukrainian meatballs? When a Gap opened up on St. Mark's Place, its glass was smashed by vandals, and smashed again every time it was repaired, until they just pulled up stakes. It was still a neighborhood, and the locals resisted gentrification fiercely.

Zack finds a studio on Ave. C and 13th Street, just four blocks from me. It's like we're living in two wings of a manor, joined by a long, filthy hallway. Most nights we're at his place, which is smaller than his old Brooklyn apartment, with fewer windows. On some nights we stay at mine, where we watch movies with Amanda and talk long into the night, drinking wine out of juice glasses and flicking our cigarettes into a big ashtray on the bed. Yes, he's smoking again.

As he assimilates back into New York, the open, San Francisco side of him goes AWOL. At the office where we both now work, I visit him at his desk, three floors up from mine, and he grumbles about everything and anything: the lines at the post office, the pushiness of people on the subway, the supermarket's crappy produce. He's incensed every time he comes to my apartment and has to pass the cops stationed around the park across the street. "Fucking police state," he'll mutter. But he's also incensed about the intimidating drug dealers who have the run of his block and lend an air of menace to the dark streets.

He plods through the paperwork for health insurance, which means concealing his HIV status; he needs three months on the job before benefits kick in. Meanwhile we visit a doctor at the clinic where Nicholas is getting his nursing intern hours, where Zack's records will be kept confidential. His T-cells are just below four hundred, not good but not yet dire. Raymond shows up one night with a clipboard and pen and tells Zack, "Write down the names of anyone you're comfortable with to be part of your support team. I'll contact them and set it up." I can see how hard this is for Zack, who never asks anything of anyone.

I worry to my friends that Zack will never be happy again. It will pass, Nicholas insists. Give him space, Amanda advises. This is what you wanted, Raymond reminds me.

Spending more time with Zack makes him more real to me, but also more complicated. Every morning before work, he wordlessly toils at a new canvas. We eat our meals together, mostly takeout from places in the neighborhood, though I'm cooking more, too. I get good at stir-frying chicken and fresh veggies, the savory steam filling his apartment and masking the odors of paint, solvents and tobacco. My mind fills with doubts—*he's getting tired of me, all my babbling is annoying him*—while my grievances accumulate— *why is he so laconic, why are so many subjects still off limits?* His masculine inexpressiveness, once seductive, now irritates. The flip side of this is that his silence means I can write in peace. Inspired by Amanda's acceptance at NYU, I want to go back to school for writing, though I haven't said anything about it to anyone, not even Zack.

"I'm going to ACT UP tonight," he says one Monday.

"It's been ages since I've been to a meeting," I say, surprised.

"So come with me."

My recent involvement with ACT UP has been limited to a few key actions, like when we protested Governor Cuomo's slashing of the AIDS budget right before election day. I'm like a lapsed Catholic who goes to Mass on high holy days out of obligation. It's become harder and harder to drag myself back into the fold. So I hesitate. But he pushes, and after a while I agree.

The group now meets in the East Village, in a slick assembly hall at Cooper Union, bigger than ever but also more contentious, as people I don't know argue about issues I haven't kept up with. Zack is riveted. He joins the treatment and data committee which is focused now on a detailed plan to combat five major opportunistic infections associated with the virus, and they've become intricately bound up with the National Institutes of Health. The outsiders are advising the establishment, people like Dr. Anthony Fauci, who we once protested.

On the walk back home that night, somewhere on Avenue A, I say, "I'm proud of you."

"No pity, please."

"I'm not pitying, I'm admiring."

"I don't need your admiration. I'm not doing anything special."

A cold silence descends. After weeks of this, I've had enough. "Just tell me what's on your mind," I demand.

"You don't want to hear it," he says, but then lets loose: "You gave up AIDS activism for Queer Nation. You gave that up, too. For what? Writing? What are you actually writing? I'm painting in that tiny fucking apartment, filled to the walls with fumes, it's fucking killing my lungs. I had to push you to come to this meeting. Do me a favor, don't patronize me if I want to get involved."

I return his accusations with my own: after my mother's death, the bashing, the trial, things falling apart with Derek, him leaving—I almost say "abandoning me"—how can he yell at me, how dare he? As I try to defend myself, I hear Amanda telling me it was too soon to get involved, I hear Raymond warning of Zack's *stewpot of neediness*. "Fuck off, Zack, I'm going home, and not with you."

"Sure. Punish me because I called you out."

"Deal with it," I say, and rush away.

I hear his bootsteps advancing from behind. He grabs me and yanks my arm. The look I see in his eyes is furious—I've seen it only once before, years ago at my birthday party, when he came to blows with Raymond.

"Get off me," I shout, but I'm thinking, *Go ahead, slap me, push me, give me a reason to be free of you.* Better a big explosion than another relationship fizzling away with everything unspoken. Our anger overlaps like the growling of animals.

"What if I can't do this?" he yells. "Can't be with you?"

"You don't have to!"

"I'm fucking trapped. Why did you bring me back here?"

"I was *helping* you."

"I wanted you in San Francisco."

"It's not only about what *you* want!"

"Yeah but I'm the one who's fucking dying."

In San Francisco, I made a promise to take care of him—now, the memory of those words catches my breath in my throat. I fall silent, hold his eyes with mine, try to impart steadiness to both of us.

He looks at me, unsure.

"We're having a fight," I say.

"Yeah, I can see that."

"Have we ever actually had a fight before?"

He lowers his head. "I swore to myself I wouldn't be a rough asshole, like I was with Raymond. I'm sorry I grabbed you like that. I'm so sorry."

"No, I was defensive. I shouldn't have said all that—"

"I was calm in San Francisco. I knew if I came back here I'd get mean again."

"You're here. You made the choice. I didn't make it for you."

"I'm glad we're together, Kiddo. I am. But I feel so lost."

He steps closer, and this time I enfold him, while strangers rush past, all heavy footsteps and emphatic conversation and whistles for taxis. The air smells of pizza and cigarettes and piss. In his arms, I wait for the world to slip away, but it doesn't. The world wants to be heard, smelled, sensed, known. There is no escaping it.

"I love you," Zack says. It's just a whisper, hoarse and tense in his throat and muffled by our embrace, but I heard it, I know I did—even now, so long after the fact, I can still hear it. I whisper the same thing back to him, and I think he hears me, too.

Note to Self #10: What about Zack's health?

. . . I'm getting there. I am.

Emergency Contact

There's a war on, not the metaphorical one we fight every day, ignored by the public except for the media attention we draw to it, but an actual, bombs-and-troops war in the Persian Gulf, an invasion with an announced start date. The drumbeat to war spotlights what the federal government can do when it marshals its resources and power, a reminder that there's never been anything like this for AIDS. Congress finally passed legislation favoring research and treatment, then failed to allot enough money in the budget to make it happen. We're now ten years and 110,000 deaths since the first recorded cases. More than a thousand people die *every week*.

ACT UP's response will be known as the Day of Desperation. At the Monday meeting, the many components of the action are announced, including the shutting down of Grand Central Terminal during rush hour. After the meeting, I join a group of old friends and new faces at Woody's. There's a lot of gossip to catch up on. I'm stunned to hear whispers of embezzlement within the ranks of ACT UP; it's believed that someone has been siphoning off money after a big art world auction filled the treasury.

Talk of infighting predominates. The treatment people, mostly men, are clashing with a group, mostly women, that wants to declare a six-month moratorium on meetings with government officials. Shanna apparently authored an open letter to the treatment and data committee, addressing one treatment activist as a "co-opted piece of shit." In response, someone fired back a furious manifesto under the headline HIV NEGATIVES, GET OUT OF OUR WAY. In just a year, our rhetoric has been shifting from hating straights to hating each other. Would ACT UP New York split like in San Francisco? Would the dividing line be sero-status?

For Zack, this is all background noise. He's joined a group planning to block traffic on 42nd Street. His involvement has invigorated him, lifted his mood. He finds my eyes across the restaurant table and beams at me, and he takes my hand when we walk home. We've weathered the worst of his transition back to New York, and I feel giddily grateful to have him near.

In bed that night, he says, "For once, I won't be playing it safe."

"What are you talking about? The first time I met you was in a jail cell."

"That wasn't intentional." He grapples for words. "Courage doesn't come natural to me."

I ask if he'd feel more at ease if I got arrested too, but he insists he needs to do this without me. "Besides," he says, squeezing my hand, "who'll be my phone call when they lock me up?"

"That's a big responsibility."

"Do you accept?"

"I do."

"Then it's official. I now pronounce you my emergency contact."

We seal it with a kiss.

I wake to sheets cold and damp. I reach over and find Zack drenched in sweat, asleep but shivering, possibly in the grip of a nightmare.

I nudge him and he bolts awake, blurting, "What happened?"

"Bad dreams." I don't say *night sweats*, that dreaded phrase.

"I'm freezing," he says.

I put him in a warm shower, strip the sheets, make him tea. He goes to work but comes home early with a fever. That night I bring him hot soup from a Chinese restaurant and find him wrapped in a blanket on the couch. "The mattress still feels damp," he says. I convince him to walk with me to Amanda's, where he can rest on dry sheets. Once there, he falls asleep quickly.

Amanda and I sit at the kitchen table, talking in low voices. This is it. This is Zack getting sick, this is what I signed up for, what I promised. I stammer out my worry that it's more than I can handle. "You're already handling it," she says. She takes a pragmatic approach: focus on the tasks at hand, ask the questions you need to ask. Don't waste time on fear, not where there are things to be done.

Evening rush hour at Grand Central is total chaos. There are thousands of us, organized into cells, each one blocking an access point to the commuter trains at exactly five p.m. We link arms, form human chains, face off with enraged commuters and provoke them further with the language on our flyers: *1,175 people died of AIDS last week and you murdered them.* A group that Tony is part of scales the ticket booths to drape the departure board in a banner: One AIDS Death Every 8 Minutes. Another banner rises on helium balloons into the station's cavernous vault: Money for AIDS, Not for War.

After a fixed amount of time, my affinity group leaves the station to join the march going down 42nd Street toward the United Nations. When the march grinds to a stop, that's my cue: I break away to find Zack.

It's one thing to throw myself into danger, to risk jail, to put my own body on the line. It's another to spot my lover yanked roughly by cops through the disarray of a demonstration, hands cuffed behind his back, face contorted. I feel a flood of protective adrenaline as Zack trips, stumbles, is yanked back to his feet. Pandemonium swallows him up, and I lose sight of him.

Arrests are happening all around, more than I've ever seen at a single protest. The police refuse to talk to those of us doing support even as we shout that they are legally bound to tell us where our friends are being taken. A few of us get in cabs, pleading with our drivers to tail the police buses, communicating on walkie-talkies that slip in and out of range. Once we locate the precinct, we're still kept in the dark. We aren't given the names of those arrested, how long they'll be held, what the charges will be. We are seasoned and good at what we do, but it's nerve-wracking to wait for hours, knowing that many of those being held overnight are immune-compromised. I eventually fall asleep on a hard plastic chair, waking herky-jerky to barking voices, the buzz of fluorescents, the slamming of doors, the cry of sirens near and far.

Finally, there's Zack, sleepy-eyed, a little wobbly, blinking in the light. The first thing he asks about is media coverage—I tell him the big news, that activists stormed PBS and CBS, disrupting the evening news. He says he slept on and off in his cell and woke up with a painfully raw, sore throat, but he's excited to tell me about the people he bonded with behind bars. "You're the one who looks wrecked," he says, holding my face in his hands.

I take him home with me and put him in the bathtub.

"Darlin' you really don't need to be sleeping on the floor of an unheated cell all night," Nicholas says. He's come over at my request.

"This one mattered to me," Zack says. "I'm trying to save my life."

"You think you can save your life without putting your health at risk?"

"Yes, Nurse Nicky."

Nicholas lights a joint and passes it to Zack. "Seal it with a puff."

Zack inhales and then erupts in a fit of smoke.

"Some nurse," I grumble.

The pot mellows Zack, but he complains that his throat is on fire.

Nicholas takes a look. "When's your insurance kick in?"

"It just did. Why? What do you see?"

I pass Zack a hand-held mirror.

"That white stuff on your tongue?" Nicholas says. "It's thrush."

They do all kinds of tests, and while we wait for lab results, which are oh-so-slow in coming, Zack gets a high dosage of antifungal medication. It helps. After a couple of days of rest, he's back at work. I take on domestic duties, including altering our diet to eliminate yeast, sugar, and fermentation, all of which feed the thrush. No more soy sauce in my stir-fries, and no more cigarettes, either. I'm also lugging dirty sheets and clothes four blocks to the laundromat, and keeping his place passably clean.

His apartment is just one room plus a bathroom. There's a kitchen area to the right when you walk in, with a tiny table where we eat and where I write the stories I'm now working on with some dedication. The bed takes up most of the space. Against the far wall is an old mulberry-colored sofa and a coffee table cluttered with art supplies and magazines. He's stopped painting, the fumes too much on his lungs. Instead, he's making collages. He sketches with ink and charcoal, glues images on top, draws on top of that, and keeps layering. If he decides it's worth preserving, he'll throw open the windows and cover it all in varnish. His energy can feel manic, head down and hands fluttering—so different from those quiet mornings a year ago.

He's begun using text snipped from publications or written in his own hand: medical lingo, political speech, curses, slurs. He does a series with "New York City" and a random word: New York City Germs. New York City Make-Believe. New York City Disappearance. He says, "I think of them as poems. Not that I know anything about poetry." I scour Amanda's bookshelves for poetry collections; I go to St. Mark's Bookstore and ask for recommendations. I read out loud to him from poets who wrote about New York—Dorothy Parker, W.H. Auden, Frank O'Hara—and poets who wrote about illness, like Blake and Ginsberg. He finds an Emily Dickinson poem that he likes and reads it to me:

"My loss, by sickness—was it Loss?
Or that Ethereal Gain
One earns by measuring the Grave—
Then—measuring the Sun—"

"'Measuring the grave' freaks me out," I say. "It's too final."
"Yeah, but it goes with 'measuring the Sun.' You have to do both."

I'm at his apartment one night when he returns from a meeting with Mike Savas. Mike's become a shrunken version of himself, hair thin as an old man's, walking with a limp. The many flights of stairs up to the apartment must have been hell for him. We hug, and he says, "You've gotten buff," sweetly impressed. I've taken to doing multiple sets of push-ups and sit-ups on the floor, expending the stress I feel all the time, and it seems I've gotten stronger, becoming more like the man Mike once was. It's a cruel exchange.

I ask if I should leave, but Zack says, "No, stay, it would help me if you heard all this."

"You're not planning another arrest, are you? You promised..."

"It's not civil disobedience," he says.

"Then what?"

"Political funerals."

Mike says his affinity group is studying dissidents in other countries who parade their dead in open coffins as a form of protest, holding the powerful accountable for casualties, bringing activists together to mourn. "A solemn, dignified, public display of a corpse demands attention," Mike says. "It's a way to humanize AIDS statistics."

Zack says, "So we've been having a conversation about doing something with the bodies of people after they die—"

"The bodies of people?"

Mike raises a hand to quell my agitation. "Some of us are changing our wills to indicate our wishes for political funerals. There's a whole protocol to get family members to make the arrangements."

"So this is a thing that's happening."

"You don't seem convinced."

I've always idolized Mike, and I guess I foolishly expected the numbers on his handmade sign to go up and up indefinitely. How can I tell him this sounds to me like defeat?

"At my first ACT UP meeting," I try, "we were planning for the Pride parade, and someone wanted to send a pile of coffins down Fifth Avenue. Back then you were arguing against that. You said coffins were the wrong image, the opposite of our fight for survival."

"But people aren't surviving, and the world should know it."

"I'm sorry, it just sounds like we've run out of ideas."

At this, he stiffens. "It's a new tactic for the movement."

Zack jumps in, fervor in his voice. "What I'd really love would be if they marched my coffin to the Brooklyn Bridge, set it on fire and dumped it into the East River."

"That's gruesome," I say, and Mike quickly intervenes, telling Zack there are rules if this is to work. No burning, no dumping, just a display, a procession, a rally with a permit.

For all his depletion, Mike is as passionate as ever, the moral barometer he's always been. His imminent death, he says, feels like an assassination, a willful murder on the part of the powers that be. He wants to put his corpse in the faces of those who've killed him. He wants to take a stand, even beyond his last breath. I don't argue further. It's not my place.

After he leaves, Zack turns to me. "I know, it's a lot all at once."

"I was freaked out by the word *grave* in a poem, and now we're planning your funeral—"

"Not *planning*. I'm interested in what Mike has to say, and I wanted you to hear it. I didn't trust myself to explain it right. You don't have to take this on—"

But I wonder, is this what it means to be his emergency contact—carrying out his final wishes, no matter what?

I catch sight of myself in the mirror. I've changed. My every surface looks *hard*. My cheekbones have lost their gloss, my neck has thickened, my jaw is more prominent. My shaved head reveals the shape of my skull: wide above the ears, round on top, forehead high and shiny. I look like a bomb ready to go off.

In the dark hours of the early morning, I wake to find Zack sitting naked at the table, aglow in lamplight. Before he brought Mike over, I'd been writing, and I left my notebook on the table, open to a new story, which he's now reading. It's about the first time a young boy is called "faggot" at school, based on a memory of mine from second grade. At home, the boy locks himself in his bedroom and refuses to open the door, sending his family into an uproar. Eventually he asks his father what a faggot is, and his father takes him outside to teach him how to fight.

"What do you think?" I ask.

"I think it's about how the parents don't get it," he says. "When their son's called a fag, it's an insult, but it's the truth, too."

"Yeah," I say, joining him at the table, "an inadvertent epiphany." He pushes a glass of water toward me, and I drink.

"I blame them," he says.

"Who?"

"My parents—my father and my stepmother."

"For?"

"For what's fucked up about me, my emotional constipation, the poses I put on, the straight-acting shit. What am I trying to do—pass? As straight? As white? And why didn't I take care of myself? Why did I get infected?" He points to the story. "It starts when they try to beat the faggot out of us."

I see that I've written something truthful enough to draw this reaction from him. My words did this. That's powerful—but the pain it's pulled out of him is so open and raw, it's hard to feel good.

"Listen, my father will want to make it Catholic," he says. "But don't let him. No Mass, no scripture, no last rites."

"What if I find a hot gay priest to rub oil on you?"

"Well, if he's *hot*," he says, allowing a smile. "I'm serious though."

"I know. But Zack, I don't even have their phone numbers."

He goes to a drawer and digs out an address book, well-thumbed, filled in with pen and pencil entries, most from long before I knew him. He flips to "J" and points to the name *Stacia Jones.* "Start with her, if it comes to that," he says.

"Who is she?"

"My sister."

It's only later, much later, after he gets sick, that I think to ask, does she know you're positive? The answer is no.

Army of Lovers

It's Gay Pride again, my activist anniversary, the date from which "Paul from New Jersey" marks his life as a New Yorker.

On the Saturday night before the Pride parade, we all go to the West Village for a "funeral" for Judy Garland on the anniversary of her death. I'm with Zack, Raymond and Tony, all of us wearing white t-shirts, silk-screened by hand with a graphic Zack designed: a purple fist raised above the words QUEERS BASH BACK. It's been a long spring helping Zack cope with symptoms and side effects, but the t-shirt is a signal that he's still engaged, not giving up.

At the microphone, a feathery drag queen talks about the importance of divas, citing the oft-told tale that Stonewall happened because the queens were so wrecked by Judy's untimely death that when the cops raided the bar, they snapped. A cabaret star follows with "Over the Rainbow," and then we're led in that well-worn chant, *Out of the Closets and into the Streets.*

What happens next is unplanned: the crowd, too big to be contained, flows from Sheridan Square onto Sixth Avenue, stopping traffic. It's less a protest than a street fair, with music playing and people exchanging kisses and hugs and plans for Pride. I have one arm around Zack, Raymond is holding my other hand, and Tony is on the other side of him. Zack, looking happier than he has in ages, proclaims us an "army of lovers."

The gathering starts moving without any apparent goal, an organic display of people power on our High Holy Day. We turn off Sixth onto a side street, further messing with motorists who've gotten stuck with nowhere to go. The chant shifts, *Out of Your Cars and into the Streets,* and people do get out of their cars, giving over to the vibe, turning up the volume on radios, joining the party. Other drivers are less excited, attempting to squeeze through openings in the crowd, pleading their cases through open windows. One woman stands on her hood and announces that she has kids in the car and food she's trying to deliver to her elderly mother, and can people please make room? A group steps aside to clear a passage for her, guiding her car out of the throng. But mostly the swamp of bodies is too dense, and cars trying to maneuver out just make it worse, the way struggling in quicksand gets you sucked under faster.

As the sky falls into darkness, drivers grow impatient, laying on horns, yelling insults. We amble past, meeting threats with blown kisses. There's one driver in particular who sets off an alarm for me, the way those guys with the lacrosse sticks at Wigstock did the moment I saw them. He's just ahead of us, standing next to his open door, dressed in a polo shirt and backwards baseball cap, arms gesturing furiously, voice bellowing, "You people better get the fuck out of my way." His car, a smallish red four-door, is trapped on Charles near the corner of Seventh. His girlfriend, dressed for a night out, sits stonily in the passenger seat. Finally the guy yells, "That's it! Fuck this shit!"

I watch him get back in his car and slam the door. I hear him gun the engine and blast the horn. The car starts to move. I hear shouts and see bodies lurch away. The driver takes advantage of this gap and floors it, knocking people off balance. I see one marcher get swiped by the front bumper, spin on his feet and topple to the ground. I hear shrieks as others leap out of the way.

The car careens to the left, clomping over the concrete curb onto Seventh. Tony starts to chase him, then Zack takes off, too, waving for me to follow. Raymond says, "Let's go," and then we're all running.

I hear someone yell, "He drove into us." There's a whole group of us running now. Up ahead, the car approaches a traffic light. The driver doesn't wait for the green but swings right onto Christopher Street—*Christopher's Street!*—where it's too crowded to pick up speed. We're closing the distance. People on the sidewalk are turning to watch. Someone throws a can of beer toward the car. I watch it hit the back window and spurt out foam.

Halfway down Christopher, the car stops moving. Traffic is at a standstill. There's nowhere for him to go. He swerves onto the curb at the Lucille Lortel Theater. The marquee is lit up: *The Destiny of Me,* Larry Kramer's new play, hovering there in a gorgeous display of cosmic irony.

We surround the car and bang on the hood, the trunk, the windows. Tony climbs up onto the roof and slams down his boot. I hear the metal give in. I step to the front of the car, lift my foot and kick hard into a headlight, feeling the impact rumble up my leg, and I see a vision of Derek kicking in that restaurant window all those months ago—it seemed so pointless, an act of pique, but now I get it, that need to strike out, the desire of the punished to punish in return. I kick harder. Zack steps up to the other headlight and kicks that one in. He's feeling it too. Destroy this. All of this. Rain down destruction.

Through the windshield, the girl in the passenger seat starts to scream. It stops me cold. I back away, just as she flings herself out of the car, onto the sidewalk, clutching her purse, hobbling on heels. The driver tumbles out too and pushes her toward the theater, shouting, "Leave us the fuck alone!"

People who've given chase start to close in on them, shouting back, calling him a maniac, *you drove into the crowd, you hit someone, you could have killed people.* I wonder if he's the one who'll be killed. I can see it, the mob tearing him to pieces, a scapegoat, a sacrifice.

The car is swarmed. Fists hammer the hood, the trunk, the doors. Legs are raised and aimed at windows. Glass shatters into spider webs. I watch Tony, on the roof, swing his boot heel into the windshield—the impact frozen for a split second by a camera's white flash.

Streetlight ripples across the glowing red metal, dented and puckered under the nonstop barrage. A wall of bodies leans against the length of the vehicle, rocking it, lifting it off the ground. Zack is with them, his neck tense as he joins the chant: *Queers Bash Back! Queers Bash Back!*

The next morning, Amanda is cooking a frittata and pouring mimosas. The smell of coffee fills our apartment. Flowers have been arranged on the kitchen table, pinks and purples in a beam of sun.

We're all hovering over the cover of the *New York Post*, with its headline GAY MARCH TURNS SOUR. There's Tony in the photo, on the roof of the ravaged car, mid-kick. "Should I be worried?" he asks.

"You can't really see your face," I say. "But the Mohawk…"

"Zack's t-shirt looks fabulous on you," Raymond says.

Queers Bash Back. Zack's words had seemed like a slogan, but slogan became fact. Last night's retribution is today's image of what pride looks like in 1991. We recount the night to Amanda, Hillary and Nicholas, who weren't there. We debate what it means. We've seen so much death, maybe we have to create suffering to balance the scales. But we're not anarchists, we're people with day jobs and apartments. We're *brunching* for fuck's sake. Raymond says that smashing up the car unfurled like a dream. Time stopped.

The normal rules were suspended. "But then I woke up, and it scared me a little," he finishes.

"New York is a gunpowder factory," Zack says. "You work your shift, go home at the end of the day, but sometimes something blows the fuck up."

"What I see is a lot of testosterone," Amanda says.

"There were dykes there, too," Tony says.

"I wasn't even going to chase that car," I say, turning to Zack. "You took off running—"

"You didn't need any convincing," Raymond says. "That's what I mean: dream state."

"I want to put all of this into the movies I'm going to make," Amanda says. "I want to create, not destroy."

"What we destroyed was his weapon," Zack says. "That's self-defense."

"I wonder if it counts as self-defense if you're chasing them," Hillary says, sounding genuinely curious.

"I'd like to not get arrested for this, okay?" Tony says. From his bag, he pulls out his electric clippers. "I came prepared."

Raymond pushes a chair to the center of the room. Tony takes a seat with a towel over his bare shoulders. We pass around the clippers, each of us taking a turn slicing off a section of his blue Mohawk. Another sacrifice. When he's been completely shorn, we all lay our hands on his head, rubbing his scalp, like fortune-tellers trying to see the future in a cloudy crystal ball.

Part 10

Monsters

Raymond calls me at work: Zack's been admitted to St. Vincent's. Raymond drove him to the emergency room this morning with a high fever and intense cramping. I knew Zack hadn't felt strong enough to go to work, but I didn't realize he was this bad. I catch a cab downtown, counting out the change in my pocket to make the fare. "I can't give you a tip, I'm sorry," I tell the impassive driver, and it seems so apt: I'm running through life with just enough to get by, nothing more.

At the sight of Zack in a hospital bed—an oxygen mask over his mouth and an IV in his arm—I feel myself recoil. Visions of my mother in the ICU, my father in the emergency room after his accident, Eliot with bandages on his wrists. Zack lifts his head and looks my way. "I'm better already," he says. "I was dehydrated, but they're giving me fluids."

"Why didn't you call me?"

"I needed to get here, and Raymond has Maude."

"That bucket of bolts."

"Don't be mad."

"I'm not." I'm scared. It's all so far beyond my control.

They've put him on Septra, a prophylaxis against pneumonia. They're going to start him on AZT, but he's pushing for a low dosage because the toxicity can be ruinous. Zack doesn't complain, but when I ask, he describes his symptoms bluntly: "My throat is shooting pain into my skull… My skin feels like it's been burnt… Everything I eat turns my stomach sour."

It's past the time that I can deny, even in the smallest measure, what's happening. "What's happening" is just like every story from everyone who's been through this, but of course this feels different, because it's here, it's him.

The stay lasts for days, and it sends me mentally back to Mom's bedside, remembering the texture, the details, the dueling impulses: you want to stay close at hand, keep a watchful eye, be on guard for whatever is needed. Attend. But you also want to run screaming from the smells, the glare, the anxiety. I think of my father, and I call him from a payphone, telling him I'm back at the hospital with someone I care about.

"How are you doing with it?" he asks.

"I want to flee. I want to be out in the sunshine."

"One thing I've learned, you can't run from reality." He asks when we'll see each other. We're overdue, I agree, and I promise to call again soon.

Every now and then, there's a good day.

I hear footsteps outside Zack's apartment door, then Nicholas's Southern drawl announcing, "Decorating committee, darlin'!" He enters with Raymond and Tony carrying shopping bags filled with fabric, which they immediately start draping across the walls, covering the dingy white in bright colors. Zack sits up and smiles at them: Raymond in his tank top, pectorals bulging; Tony's silver rings clacking; Nurse Nicky pushing pins into the wall like she's casting spells. Nicholas has baked pot cookies, which Zack nibbles, then eats in bigger bites, falling into a goofy-smiled haze. I skip the cookies but drink vodka with Raymond. Amanda brings over a tape of her first film school project, about a woman on a park bench who keeps running into every gal she's ever dated. She flirts, she argues, she makes out, all to an opera soundtrack. It's so shot through with humor and hope it seems nearly magical, and when it's over we break into applause. "It's just a rough cut," she says, but I can tell she's pleased.

Hours later, tipsy and tired, I get into bed with Zack, and for the first night in forever, we both sleep soundly.

After his hospital stay, I beg Zack to call his sister, Stacia. He puts it off, and when at last he gives in he reports back that it didn't go well. "She asked me how I got it," he says. "She asked me how long I have to live. She asked me why I didn't tell her sooner, and I said, 'Because I knew you'd react like this.'"

Two weeks later, Stacia drives up from Maryland with her husband, Doug. They're staying in New Jersey with Zack's father, who isn't coming into the city with them. I make a reservation at a white-tablecloth restaurant. Zack isn't happy about it. His sister's a phony, her husband's a Republican, they're not part of his life, why even bother? "I get to decide who my family is," he says.

But we both know: when the time comes, the hospital will decide.

"You're doing this for me," I tell him. "For your emergency contact."

"Fine, I'll meet them," he says. "But I don't trust her."

Her physical resemblance to Zack puts me at ease: same light brown eyes, ochre skin, and dark hair, though hers is smoothed into a helmet, with soft bangs, while his keeps getting longer and more natural. She asks me about my job and the writing workshop I'm taking, and she expresses sympathy when I mention Mom's death. "We never stopped missing our mother," she says, at which Zack crosses his arms. There is no *we* for him. He eats little, says less.

Doug is a buttoned-up type, deferential to his wife until halfway through the meal, when he takes over, asking what procedures and medications Zack will need "as this develops" and how they'll be covered. It turns out he works for an insurance company, which seems like good news; we might need his expertise. But Doug's prying, all-business tone sets Zack on edge.

Doug says he can arrange for a home care nurse through a family plan, which they can put Zack on if he agrees to move back in with his father.

"Why would I do that?"

"Because as I understand it," Stacia says, "you're in a tiny apartment in a building without an elevator, and your situation is getting worse."

"Better than a house with a father who can't admit his son is gay."

She stares at her hands. I notice that her nail polish is chipped and she bites the skin around her fingernails. I clear my throat. "Why don't you pay a nurse to come to Zack's apartment, if he needs it?"

"The plan doesn't work that way," Doug says.

"We're not wealthy," Stacia says.

Zack slides back, throws bills on the table and says, "I'm done here."

"This is on us," Doug says, pushing the money away, but Zack is already walking out. Stacia and Doug stare at each other, silently communicating. Then she gets up and follows Zack. I watch them through the restaurant window, arguing on the sidewalk. Doug looks at me sheepishly. "I hardly recognized him," he says. "But that attitude hasn't changed." This infuriates me, and at the same time, I'm unsurprised: Zack and his infamous *attitude*. I pocket the money Zack has left on the table and excuse myself.

On the street, I find Stacia. "I don't know what went wrong," she says.

"You guys came on pretty strong," I say.

"No, I mean, we used to be close. I can't tell you how many hours we spent listening to records, dancing in my bedroom. He used to draw me. I was his first model."

"He's still making art."

"I don't doubt that. It's what drives him. He'll be making art 'til he drops." Then she gasps and covers her mouth.

"I think you should try again, and just hear him out. He doesn't react well to being told what do."

She urges me to stay in touch, and I write down my phone number for her.

Back home, I find Zack bent over the table, paintbrush in hand. "She's diabolical," he says. "She had my father call while we were out and make the same offer. *Come back to the house, we'll get you a nurse.* No contact in years and suddenly he wants me to die under his roof?"

"Maybe he's trying to make up for everything," I say.

"She put him up to it."

"I think she genuinely cares, and this is her way—"

"No, no, no, my family does not get to take over, not now, not later, not ever." He stares at me hard. "Do you understand?"

"Yes. I hear you. No family."

"Thank you."

I step in closer to look at his painting—it's a watercolor, a medium I've never seen him use. Pages lie scattered across the table, buckling as they dry. Some suggest fogged images of San Francisco, its *bridge of souls* looming ghostlike, but most seem purely abstract, color for color's sake.

"They're pretty," I say, unsure.

He scrunches his nose: wrong word. "I'm trying to find a new way to be expressive. The collages aren't working for me."

After that, an idea fixes in my head: he needs a Polaroid camera. Snap the picture, get the photo. *Fast art.* I comb several photo stores until I find a camera I like, a flat rectangle that pops into shape, its accordion sides giving it a whimsical look. I present it to Zack with great fanfare.

He looks at the camera curiously, then aims it at me, taking a moment to frame before pressing the button. The sound as the mechanism pushes out the photo is so satisfying, but Zack just puts it down, no further interest. He goes back to the table and his vague watercolors.

I look at the image after it develops. My face and posture seem tense, but he's captured something in the lighting of the room and the framing of the colored fabric on the wall behind me. "You have a good eye," I say.

He studies it and shrugs. "I'm just not into the documentary aspect."

"Oh, for fuck's sake," I say.

"Don't make this a fight, I'm just asking for some space."

"Fine, take all the fucking space you want." I gather up my belongings and I'm out the door, rushing down flights of stairs, ignoring his calls from above. I walk back to Amanda's—still officially *home* though I spend so little time there.

I find her cross-legged on the bed, hair tied up and pages of a script spread out in front of her. She's in the middle of editing—the pages are slashed in pencil, with sections crossed out and arrows drawn in different directions—but I can't stop myself from launching into a harangue about Zack's ungratefulness. "He barely looked at the camera. The world doesn't need more abstract watercolors! Zack's work has always had a subject. This feels like he's giving up."

"You know you can't tell Zack what to make."

"He needs me when he's feeling like shit, but as soon as he can cope on his own, he needs *space.*"

"That seems normal," she says carefully.

"But he's such an asshole about it."

"Just because he's getting sicker doesn't mean he'll miraculously become a better person."

I know this is true. I've observed it in ACT UP. When people get sick, their personalities intensify. Like dying stars, they flare into brighter versions of who they already are. The loudmouths get louder, the sweethearts get sweeter. My mother, falling ill, became gentler; Eliot has slipped deeper into irony. But I can't simply sit back and let Zack's worst qualities take over, because I've seen the best of him, too, in San Francisco. Maybe it really was a mistake bringing him back here.

Amanda pats the bed, calling me close. I sit and smoke with her. I look around: the Christmas lights, the overflowing bookshelves, the radio playing Mahler. Amanda's sympathetic ears. Everything here welcomes me, everything says stay. But I feel like I should be with him.

I call to apologize. He's sorry, too, he says. He suggests we take a few days apart. We've been on top of each other. I tell him I don't feel comfortable leaving him alone. Just in case. "I'm covered," he says. "Raymond's here."

"Already? I just left."

"You're relieved for the night," he says.

● ● ●

Another night with Zack: he wakes up coughing and can't stop. I lead him to the shower and hold him tightly under the water, but he nudges me away, saying that my grip makes it harder to breathe. He sucks up steam, and eventually he calms. When I dry him off with a towel, he flinches under my touch, which is too rough I guess. "I thought I'd never stop," he says.

"But you did," I say. "You got through it."

"For now."

He doesn't go to work the next day, and when I stop by to talk to Jared, his boss, I'm told that someone from the benefits department was sniffing around, asking leading questions. Was Zack sick before he started? Had he failed to disclose a *pre-existing condition?* "I told them to fuck off unless they wanted a lawsuit on their hands," Jared says. "I'm guessing it'll all blow over, but you should know, things are iffy around here."

I spend the day seething at my desk, hating the corporate structure that defines how we get our healthcare. I call Nicholas and ask if I can come over after work. I need someone to talk to.

Nicholas greets me at the door saying, "You look like hell."

"The stress has to show up somewhere," I say.

I'm surprised to discover Raymond standing in the kitchen—and also not surprised, because Raymond is always just *there.* Empty beer bottles are lined up on the counter. He and Nicholas have been hanging out a while.

Raymond greets me with a strong, tight hug. It's stupid that I still feel jealous of him, eternally jealous even though we're on the same team. He hands me a beer, and I tell them about last night's coughing fit, the questions from personnel at work, and the blowup when Stacia visited. "Is it really worse to wind up at his father's than at some city hospital?" I ask.

"He wants to die at home," Raymond says.

"Yeah, but you can't plan for that."

"No," he says, then adds cautiously, "I mean, you *can*, if—"

I wait for more, but it's Nicholas who finishes the thought: "You'd have to get hold of enough morphine to give Zack control over the end."

"Oh," I say, looking from one to the other, then back again. "That's pretty fucking heavy." Somehow, I can tell that *this* is what they've been talking about: *assisted suicide.* In theory, I'm not opposed to it, but when I try to imagine it, my hands start shaking. I picture Zack's arms, lately so thin, veins raised to the surface. I picture a syringe full of morphine, a thick sludge plunging into the needle piercing his skin, Zack's body shuddering at the lethal dose. "That can't happen," I hear myself saying. "He could get better. People do get better."

"In some places, like in Europe—" Raymond begins, but I wave him quiet.

Nicholas reaches out and gently rubs my arm. "Don't mind us, darlin'. Just thinking out loud."

Monsters. Both of them. Gathered here like conspirators.

"Don't you dare talk to Zack about this," I say. "He needs us to believe."

"Of course," Nicholas says.

Raymond nods, but his gaze, locked on me, is inscrutable.

I nearly run the eleven blocks back to Zack, completely spooked. Just hearing about this concept leaves me heavy with guilt, as if I've wished for his death, as if their idea has poisoned me. I worry Zack will see it in my eyes.

I find him passed out on the bed. The apartment stinks of shit. In the bathroom I see that he's missed the bowl, soiled the seat, the tank, the floor. I'm on my knees spraying disinfectant everywhere when Zack staggers in, apologizing, blaming it on sushi he ate, insisting that he'll clean it up. I shush him, send him back to bed, and call Dr. Leone, who asks, "Can he last the night?" a chilling phrase that stops me cold, though all the doctor means is, could he stay hydrated and comfortable until morning? "I need you to drink a lot of water," I tell Zack. He sips from a cup. "Chug," I command. "All of it."

"Please don't be mad," he says weakly.

"I'm not mad, baby. Please, drink it all."

The next day, Dr. Leone calls with results from the lab. There's a diagnosis—a scary opportunistic infection called histoplasmosis—and a treatment, amphotericin B. ("Amphoterrible," Eliot calls it.) Leone recommends a PICC line—a catheter under Zack's skin to deliver the larger doses of medication he'll need. When Zack objects, Leone says, "Do you want to look for a vein every time?" The procedure sends him back to the hospital; the catheter goes into his arm and up to a vein near his heart. We get instructions about keeping it sterile and avoiding secondary infections. He gets new prescriptions to deal with the nausea and diarrhea, plus stronger painkillers. I take notes, go over them again when we get home. Zack apologizes for resisting the catheter. "It seemed too final," he says. "Why is it so hard for me to accept help?"

"We're way beyond that, Zack." But I see that this is true for me, too. I'm not reaching out enough to friends—as if my promise to take care of him means that I have to go it alone. I've been slow to see that caretakers can burn out, just like activists. I find Raymond's clipboard with its names and numbers, and I pull out a day-planner. I pick up the phone and start signing people up for shifts.

Deliverance

Stacia shows up unannounced at the apartment. She stands just inside the door, coat on, hands clutching her purse. Seeing him through her eyes, I realize how Zack's appearance has deteriorated, even from a few weeks ago. "I wish you would come with me to Dad's," she says.

He shakes his head. "You'll go back to Maryland, and me and Dad will kill each other. You know it won't work."

I jump in, trying to avert the argument that seems sure to erupt. "You're here after a bad spell, Stacia, but Zack got new medicine and he'll be better soon."

They send me identical, piteous looks, brother and sister silently commenting on my wishful thinking. I feel my face redden.

Zack clears space on the couch. "Let's sit while we talk," he says.

She joins him there, loosening her coat and accepting a glass of water from me. I'm not sure how, but Zack is able to stay calm. Maybe he's burned through his anger, maybe this is a new strategy. He shows her the catheter and explains why it's important for him to be near his doctor. He gives her Dr. Leone's number.

"I want you to be comfortable," she says, wiping her eyes before tears can fall.

"I'm comfortable here, with my lover," he says.

Stacia glances in dismay at our dirty dishes, the clothes on the floor, the damp towel on the bathroom doorknob. Even the bright fabric on the walls seems to sag. I have to stop myself from manically tidying up.

She says, "Zack, I don't know what to do."

"You can start by asking me what I need, instead of telling me."

Her shoulders slump and heave.

After a moment, he sends me a look, and I know what to do. I get up, grab my jacket, and move toward the door. Right before I step out, I glance back and see him reach out his hand and intertwine it with hers.

Stacia's visit felt like a small breakthrough, but later, as we go through our routine, and I watch him in his dozen daily struggles, I worry that she might still intervene, take over, take him away. I make him write out his wishes, signing and dating the paper with me and Nicholas witnessing it. Zack writes that he does not want his family to oversee his care, that his friends should be consulted about medical decisions. I insist that he spell out the names of the friends he has in mind. He puts my name down, and Raymond's and Nicholas's. When I ask him about his funeral, he writes: *No Catholic Mass. No funeral of any kind. Just cremate me.* He hands the paper to Nicholas, who signs it with a flourish. It won't carry legal weight, but it might convince Stacia and Doug of his wishes. Still, I'm not family. I'm not a spouse. I'm a twenty-five-year-old trying to take charge of his dying boyfriend's life. I am literally holding onto a scrap.

One night, I enter to find him banging a nail into the wall. "Turn around, close your eyes," he says. When it's okay to look again, I see that he's stretched a large piece of fabric, navy blue in color, across the apartment's longest wall. It hangs like a taut curtain from nails. "Is there something underneath?" I ask, moving toward it.

"Don't," he sings out, mischief in his eyes. He says he's begun a large new art piece, which he's keeping behind the fabric, "until I'm ready to show you."

I remember an early visit to his apartment in Brooklyn, when he flipped over an unfinished painting, shielding it from my curiosity. It's been a long time since he kept his art from me. I don't want a secret between us. But now, instead of letting myself in with a key, I'm supposed to knock, announce myself, and wait in the hall while he shuffles around. This becomes the new routine: I smoke in the hallway, waiting for him to unbolt the door. Inside, I smell paint and glue, see paper cuttings on the floor, note an empty box of Polaroid film on top of the trash. He's using the camera. He's using everything at hand, it seems. He's been newly energized by whatever it is he's doing. It matters to him. I know I have no right to feel locked out from it.

It's so hard not to peek behind that blue sheet. But I can't. That would be like reading his journal.

Right around then, the call comes that shifts everything. The bedside phone rings, and I pick it up. "This is Mel, from San Francisco." Mel of the Fu Manchu mustache, the metal jewelry and the opiate stash. When I met him at the Detour, I distrusted him intensely. I had no idea Zack has stayed in touch with him.

I pass the phone to Zack, who curls away from me and lowers his voice. I hear him say, "like we talked about." I leave the room, give him privacy, sit with my writing and my cigarettes in the hall, dropping butts into a coffee can. Back inside, Zack doesn't want to talk about it.

A few days later, there's another call from Mel. Something's going on. I look at Zack and say, "Just tell me."

He asks, "Have you ever heard of self-deliverance?"

He's talking about the same idea that Nicholas and Raymond brought up: deciding the moment when he will end his life. Mel is part of an underground buyer's group with access to morphine. If Zack sends him money, Mel will ship a package to an anonymous mailbox in one of those storefront mailbox businesses. There's one just down Tenth Street from Amanda's. In the package he'll find enough of the drug for a lethal dose. As he tells me this, my hands start shaking to the point where I can't keep a match lit. Is he actually planning to do this? He doesn't know. Who else has he told? Nicholas and Raymond. Nicholas because of his experience, Raymond because "he's the only other person I know who's shot drugs." If I hadn't heard him talking to Mel on the phone would he have told me? Yes, eventually. Why did he wait? He says, "To protect you."

"Is this something you're *absolutely* planning to do? Is it up for discussion? *Can we talk about it?*" With each question, my voice cracks. My throat constricts, like I've swallowed something sharp.

"Kiddo, *breathe.*"

I breathe, deeply. Then again, and again until my heart stops racing.

Calmly, he says, "One day this might get so bad that I'll wish I could end it. I'm exploring options, that's all."

I feel so immature in the face of his steadiness, and angry that I'm not the first to know. Maybe he's right. Maybe I do need to be protected from this. I'm ashamed that I can't meet him where he's at. This is a way to take control of a catastrophic situation. I understand that. It's also illegal, unpredictable, and scary.

All week, the knowledge of Zack's flirtation with assisted suicide is like a radioactive pellet implanted under my skin, emitting a dull, regular pulse. It's like I'm being monitored, like someone is keeping track of my every move. When Nicholas first raised the subject, I cast him and Raymond as nearly mythical betrayers. But it was Zack's scheme all along. Now I'm in on it, too.

Breaking the law is nothing new. It's the lifeblood of justice that runs through our lives. But this doesn't feel like civil disobedience. It feels like anarchy.

I ask Nicholas to come over to Amanda's, to talk me through this. We pick a night where she'll be at school, editing her project. We're just settling in at the kitchen table, drinking cheap Italian wine, when she shows up, early, exhausted, heading straight for the tub to start a bath. "Darlin', we're about to have a private conversation here," Nicholas says.

"Really? Can you talk in my room so I can unwind?"

But there are no walls in this apartment, no "rooms," no place where we won't be heard. "Maybe you should hear this," I say. Nicholas shoots me a warning look, but I suddenly feel like I must have Amanda's perspective.

She slips into the tub, while I begin. "Zack told me he's been talking with his friend in San Francisco about self-deliverance."

"Is that what he called it?" Nicholas says. "Leave it to San Franciscans to come up with an empowering euphemism." I smile despite my serious mood. It's true, the phrases on my mind—like mercy killing—are cold and judgmental. *Self-deliverance* sounds spiritual.

It didn't occur to me that it could be.

Amanda takes it all in without pause. "I'm not surprised. The subject is all over the news. There's that book, I read about it in the *Times.*"

"*Final Exit,*" Nicholas says. "The doctor who helped his wife end her life. I read it. Lots of legalese, medical info, all very carefully presented. But people do it, you know, without all of that in place." With a flash of some emotion in his eyes that I can't quite read, he adds, "I've been through this before."

I look at Amanda, who no longer seems tired. She has me pour her a glass of wine, light her a cigarette. The mist from the tub seems to soften the room.

"I rarely talk about this," Nicholas says, "but I told Zack, and I'll tell you. There was this boy I loved named Harper; you've heard me mention him no doubt. Pretty as a sunrise, and just as rosy. He was a drifter, a runaway really, crashing at the commune. For a little while, we were lovers Years later, he showed up in my cab, pure serendipity." He pulls a photo from his wallet of a dreamy-eyed, feather-haired fellow of about twenty posing on the mall in Washington, D.C., the Lincoln Memorial gleaming in the distance behind him. The photo is creased, the colors muted, a relic from the '70s. "I couldn't keep Harper as mine. He flirted with everyone, he loved sex, and there was so much sex back then. He could make me squirm with jealousy. But he was a delight to be with, even when we reunited and he got sick. He was always rubbing essential oils on his skin and making special teas. He'd feed pigeons, which I thought was disgusting, but he made it seem like God's work. He wasn't the first person I knew with the so-called *gay cancer*, but he was the first one I took close care of. When it got bad, he made me promise I'd help him end it. Which we eventually did, though not with needles. We crushed a bunch of pills and stirred it into his tea."

"Did that work?"

"It knocked him out. Then he laid for two hours in a coma before dying."

"That's a hellish two hours," Amanda says.

"Interminable. But it was not as horrible as the previous two months, when he went blind and his bones started breaking."

It's going to get worse. Much, much worse.

I reach out to squeeze his arm. "Did he choose the day, or did you?"

"He did. The day and the hour. It has to be him, you see?"

He tells us what he told Zack, that he should talk to three people before proceeding: a person with legal knowledge, a member of his family, and a spiritual counselor.

"He'll never tell this to his family," I say.

"That's why he talked to you," Nicholas says.

"I guess I reacted like family would: I didn't get it."

"The legal part won't be hard," Amanda says. "We know lawyers."

"I don't know anything about religious counsel," I say.

"I advised him to think of what gives him *meaning*," Nicholas says. "He can't make this choice in a void. For lack of a better word, he has to think about his soul."

● ● ●

Some days later, I overhear Zack on the phone with Raven, his San Francisco housemate, who is giving him a long-distance Tarot reading, turning cards on her end of the line and interpreting their meaning. Does this count as spiritual guidance? I suppose it's no less superstitious than Catholicism. After the call, Zack bobs around the apartment buoyantly. "I had the Fool at the center of the reading. It's the beginning of a journey."

"It doesn't mean you're making a foolish decision?"

"Well, foolish not like stupid, but like, brave and determined."

"Is that how you feel?"

"It's an image, that's all. A way to focus my mind. When I've thought about death, all I've been able to see is a pile of ash. It's felt like a prison, like annihilation. But maybe—I don't know—maybe I'm *going* somewhere."

Whatever he envisions this new journey to be, wherever he imagines it might lead, Zack's mood evens out after this. Our bickering around the apartment tapers off and then ceases. He doesn't mention anything further about self-deliverance or secret packages sent to mailboxes, and there are no more calls, that I know of, from Mel. Zack stays focused on his art, which he continues to shield behind that blue fabric, and I let him be.

Forever

We're in a taxi, on our way back from Dr. Leone's office in Chelsea, when Zack tells the cabbie to pull over. He says he wants to walk the rest of the way. His legs have been suffering flashes of numbness and pain, a symptom of neuropathy. The doctor gave Zack a cane to ease walking, and I guess this is the moment he's going to try it out.

I pay for the ride and help him to the curb. We're at St. Mark's and Second. I tell him to wait at the corner while I run into the newsstand for a paper. I'm only in there for a few seconds, but when I come back out, I don't see him. I turn this way and that, growing panicked, until I realize I've looked right past him. He doesn't look like the Zack I know—his bulky coat emphasizes how frail he is beneath, his dark glasses are like goggles over his sunken cheeks. He's leaning his weight on the cane, a black stick shaking in his grip.

"Take a picture, it lasts longer," he says. At least his voice is the same. Same attitude. I smile. We walk.

At first he doesn't seem to know what to do with the cane, but his mental acuity takes over. He's resolved to walk even if, or maybe *because*, it's difficult and public. People glance at him then glance away, looking without staring. It doesn't matter to Zack if anyone pities him or is spooked by him or projects bravery or nobility onto him. He wants to be out in the sun for these few blocks. That's what matters.

Back at the apartment, I ask how he is, and he says, "Horny."

This surprises me. "What are you up for?" I ask.

"Show off for me," he says.

I start up a slow, corny striptease that makes him laugh. He calls me a goofball, compliments my body, says I'm becoming a man. He lies back on

301

the bed, and I straddle him, feel his hands roam over me. I touch his skin and watch him shudder. His cock stirs but doesn't get fully hard. Mine is like a rocket. I still feel everything I've ever felt for him, and I want him to know. The attraction, the infatuation, the love hasn't gone away, it's just buried under other, harder emotions: confusion, sadness, fear. I have to fight them back every minute. Have to show him I am still *in* this, am still here for him. He's telling me I'm sexy. I tell him to keep touching me, keep touching me until I cum. It builds and builds until I'm splattering across his skin. I lie down next to him, and we find a way to embrace that's comfortable for him. Then, exhausted, I feel myself going under.

I am writing in a strange notebook that might be a Tarot deck, but my pen doesn't work. There are deep indentations on the page, but no ink, no story. Loud voices outside draw my attention—it sounds like the police, or maybe soldiers. I run out of the apartment, into the hallway with its sleek walls and modern fixtures—*I'll have to ask Zack when we moved into this new building*—and I climb the stairs, adrenaline pumping. I hear men in pursuit, their boots pounding behind me. With all my weight I push against the door to the roof.

I'm on top of the World Trade Center in the dark of night. In every direction, the city is lit up: there's the Empire State, there's the Chrysler, it's all so vivid, bright, magical. But the noise! Helicopters swarm above me, military snipers leaning out, aiming their weapons, pinning me in their sights. I'm on top of the world, but I'm cornered. I'm going to have to jump. *Where's Zack?* At the very edge, I peer down—*fuck, I'm up so high*—but there, way down below, I see my friends, faces I recognize, Nicholas, Amanda, arms outstretched, a bolt of navy-blue fabric pulled tightly between them. It's so far down, but it's somewhere to land. From every direction I hear the sound of triggers being pulled, weapons exploding. I leap—out into the black night, out and up, up, up—

I wake to the click and whir of the Polaroid camera.

Zack sits up in bed holding a fresh photo, fanning a little breeze with it.

"I had to jump," I say.

"Go back to sleep." Warm sunlight is edging the windows. "It's early."

"You took a picture of my nightmare." It's still so vivid. The snipers, the roof, the leap—

He shows it to me. Inside the square frame, I'm naked, with the white bedsheet snaked around my body. The look on my face is not of a man on the run for his life. I look like I'm in ecstasy.

In my dream, I wasn't falling. I was flying.

My father is coming into the city. It's a Saturday in August. Two years since Mom's death. Time has flown by. The night before, I stay at Amanda's, so Dad can pick me up there. It doesn't make sense for him to come to Zack's. The place is a clutter of art supplies and medical supplies and the general disarray in which we live, and besides, they've never met before, and I think we're past the point that it makes sense. I wake and bathe and sip coffee with Amanda over the Sunday crossword puzzle. We talk about missing out on a meeting of our affinity group, which is participating in a big action in Kennebunkport, Maine, where President Bush vacations. ACT UP is going to invade this small coastal town with the message "The AIDS Crisis Can End." Not long ago it would have been inconceivable for us to miss a demonstration this big. "Do you feel guilt?" I ask her. "I mostly just feel removed."

"You're a caretaker now," she says.

"But that's not activism."

"Honey, activism isn't *better* than everything else."

"It's not? Isn't that what we've believed for the last four years?"

"I made a decision at some point," she says. "I didn't even know I made it. I still want to change the structure of things, but I want to do it culturally. I want to make a movie that affects people, a lot of people. I don't want to write another fact sheet. I don't want to get arrested."

I tell her about Zack's artistic burst, his secret project hidden behind the sheet, and how we've found a new, calm rhythm together.

"People bounce back," she says. "It happens."

"With my mother, it all just went in one direction. Bad to worse."

"There will be a lot of ups and downs. You have to be prepared."

The buzzer intrudes—my father, on the street. We ring him up, and he once again pokes around. "Looks different in the light of day," he says.

"You can see how badly it needs a paint job," Amanda says.

"Pick a Sunday," Dad says. "I'll lend the elbow grease."

"You will?" She looks delighted.

"Be careful what you offer, Dad. We'll take you up on it."

"I've got a lot of time on my hands," he says. "Put me to work."

I'm thrilled to see him in such a good mood. It's been a long time.

He drives us to Battery Park. We stroll the waterfront, listen to a guitar player singing "Imagine," buy roasted chestnuts and a hot pretzel. New Yorky stuff. We look out onto the harbor, the Statue of Liberty, the shell of Ellis Island, soon to be rebuilt as a tourist attraction. Dad's parents were immigrants from Germany who came through the port of New York. Their names are on an official registry of those whose citizenship started here. Dad was raised in New York City, then fled to raise a family in the suburbs—and I've come back. Full circle.

He says he's starting to try new things, like scuba diving, something he's always wanted to do but put off because Mom wasn't a swimmer and didn't like going underwater, even to dunk her head. He says he's thinking of placing a personal ad. "I'm ready for human contact," he says. I tell him I approve. "I can't help feeling like I'm dishonoring her," he continues. "People say, time to move on. But what do they know?" He confesses that after the night of his car accident, he became overwhelmed by thoughts of death. What if he'd been killed on the FDR Drive? Would that have been better than going on living, so lonely all the time? Would he have found Mom in the afterlife? He couldn't shake these questions. Then came a night, driving on the George Washington Bridge, when he was struck by the idea of driving over the edge. He even dared himself: *Do it*. He gripped the wheel and sped up the car, believing for a few seconds if he swerved hard enough into the guard rail, he could flip the car over and drop into the Hudson.

"What stopped you?"

"Another car came speeding by, honking its horn, this complete nut-job, and I thought, *That guy better slow down, he could'a killed me*—and that made me laugh. The instinct to live is so strong." I laugh too, hearing it. He continues, "I put my foot on the brake, got control of myself and drove home. Just like that, it had passed."

"I'm glad you're still here," I say.

"We need each other." He looks me in the eyes. "Let's try harder to be close."

At lunch, over glasses of wine, I loosen up enough to mention "the painter" I'm seeing, who's back in New York. He says he'd like to meet him. I speak vaguely: *we'll see how things go, the future's uncertain*. I'm so close to telling him.

He drives me back to the East Village. I ask him to pull over so we can talk about one more thing. He finds a spot on Tenth Street, across from Tompkins Square, still ringed in cops, and he turns off the engine. I ask him to tell me about Mom's final days, which I wasn't there for.

"You see the person you love in such pain, nothing prepares you for that," he says. "I thought at the time that we'd been robbed, because she was leaving us so fast. But now, knowing where it was headed, I wish, for her sake, it went even faster. Hooked up to that machine, that was torture for her. We might have taken her off sooner."

"Did you ever think about assisted suicide?"

He hesitates. "I was raised with certain beliefs. We can't play God."

"But taking her off the ventilator, that would have been similar, right?"

"Letting it happen," he says, nodding his head. "I can't say I have the answer. Maybe what God wants is for us to evolve until we know how to do the right thing, and maybe the right thing is to help people in terminal cases, in great pain, to suffer less."

"We do it with animals," I say.

"They don't know any better."

"So you go back and forth on it?" He nods. His eyes are wet, and as he takes off his glasses to wipe them, my own eyes fill up, too.

He says, "My biggest regret is that I wasn't there on the last night. I wasn't at the hospital. I went home. I assumed we had more time. And so she was alone. That wasn't right—we did everything together. How could we be apart for the end? It wipes me out, every time I think about it. That's the thing with assisted suicide—you could plan to be together."

My gaze travels out the car window. In the park, behind the cops and the fence, are a bulldozer and a backhoe—machines turning over the earth, making room for the new. Plans are proceeding. Things move in the direction they're supposed to. Zack will die sooner rather than later. I don't want to believe it, but it's true, isn't it? I can be there at the end, with Nicholas, Raymond, whomever Zack chooses. If he wants to plan his *final exit* how can I object? I'm almost resolved to this. Almost.

I call Zack from the corner, tell him I'm on my way up. I dutifully wait in the hall as he scurries around on the other side of the door. When he finally opens it, he looks eager to see me. Then he picks up on the emotional state I'm in after leaving my father. "How'd it go?" he asks, clearing room for us on his bed. It hits me in that moment that if he decides to go through with a plan for self-deliverance, this is where it will happen. He'll be right there, under the sheets, and I'll be sitting on the edge of the mattress, syringe in hand. I try to picture the fatal dose being administered, and how it will look for Zack's life to end right there in front of me—but I come up short. My inner vision goes dark, blank, cold. I shudder.

"Are you okay?" he asks.

"I don't understand death," I say emphatically. "Even after my mother, even after so many memorial services and hospital rooms, I just don't get it. I want death to stop happening to everybody I love."

"You want the impossible."

"I keep thinking somehow I can stop it, *I* can keep you alive. I want to believe that. I want *forever.*"

"I know, Kiddo. I know that about you." His voice sounds wise and elevated, as opposed to my own, which sounds lowly and beaten down. When he tries to soothe me, drawing his bony hand across my thick forearm, I feel ashamed.

I clear my throat and say, "Enough about me. What's going on here?"

He stands up and says, "Close your eyes."

New York City Do Over

I open my eyes and there it is, the art he's been working on these past weeks: a big collage, densely layered in places, spare in others, on a canvas painted a bruised, inky shade of violet. Thin lines in yellow or white connect clusters of overlapping or adjacent images, some cut from catalogues or magazines, others originally photographs, now torn or painted around the edges. My gaze falls first on a photo of Zack in his Yankees cap over which he's painted a curly cartoon Afro and pasted atop that a dingy embroidered "NY," which I realize he's cut from the blue cloth of the original cap. He's been wearing that cap since the moment we met. I turn to him in surprise, but he nudges me back to the canvas, wanting me to keep looking.

In the upper right corner is a photo taken at night of Zack and me in action, wheatpasting an ART IS NOT ENOUGH poster onto a boarded-up building. "Did Dale take that?" I ask.

"I've been holding onto it."

"I've never actually seen a photo of us together."

He smiles, and I can see it's been worth it for him, to create this in secret.

"This whole thing was behind that blue sheet? How big is it?"

"Four by six."

"It seems bigger."

I see fragments of fact sheets: WE DEMAND THE CATHOLIC CHUR–, SEIZE CONTROL OF–. I see a prescription scrawled in Dr. Leone's terrible handwriting. I see the Polaroid of me in bed, with sunburst lines radiating from my naked torso. I see Zack's torso from that old photo he'd shown me, when his chest was shaved. He's ripped off his head, and a syringe, a light bulb and a pill bottle float out from his jagged, exposed neck.

The longer I look, the more I detect an underlying order. The yellow and white lines direct the eye into a story that winds through the painting. Lower left of center, a baby is drawn in a pale brown outline on a calendar from the year 1960. Spiraling around it are trees and suburban ranch houses and then an exploding church and a dismantled crucifix, cross and savior floating separately, and then a porn image of a beautiful brown-skinned boy gripping his erect cock with a look on his face as if he's amazed at his own pleasure. A white line points toward a Tom of Finland couple kissing amid a cityscape at night, lit up in neon and surrounded by painted flames. Some pieces are quite literal: a photo of the Wigstock bashers brandishing their lacrosse sticks—a still taken from Raymond's camcorder footage, used as evidence in court, trimmed to the outline of the bashers—overlapping an *Outweek* cover about anti-gay violence. But scattered throughout are the enigmatic icons from Zack's earlier works—light bulbs, exploding buildings, a trio of beautiful Black women with sculpted hair—their meaning elusive, evocative, unfixed.

Above and to the right of dead center is a Bridge of Souls watercolor. Above that, on a square of white, in an austere typeface—created from meticulously applied black paint—are the words NEW YORK CITY DO OVER.

"Is that the title?" I ask.

"I think so," he says. "It took a long time to get those letters right."

I had assumed whatever he'd been making in secret was therapy, a visual diary, an experiment, but this is so much more.

"When you said you wanted 'forever,'" he says, "that's what this is for me."

"It's your whole life."

"And my afterlife. Will you take care of it for me?"

"Of course," I nod. "I'm your emergency contact."

We spend that night and all of the next day together in the apartment. He wants to tell me everything about the collage, all the ideas that drove him through it, the influence of Rauschenberg that got him started; the nods to Haring, Barbara Kruger, Romare Bearden; the moment when he realized he needed the lines to map it out, like David Wojnarowicz used in his paintings. Zack didn't have a ruler long enough to make the longer lines. So he leaned the table against the wall and traced its edge. (I see that the table's edge is now marked in yellow.) He describes how he moved images from one part of the canvas to another, and tells me about things he decided to leave out, how he'd wanted more and more negative space. He talks excitedly and without interruption for long stretches. He hasn't seemed this vigorous in weeks.

In the morning, he says he's not going in to work.

I tell him I'm worried about his future at the job, but he says it'll be okay.

He keeps delaying my departure with kisses, with lingering embraces, more expressive than he's been in a long time, the residue, I assume, of having shown me his work. Sharing it must have been such a high for him. Later, I would see there'd been much more on his mind.

That afternoon, he doesn't pick up the phone when I call.

I keep trying. No answer. As the day goes on, I grow concerned.

When I get back to the apartment that evening, he isn't there.

He's made the bed. In the middle of it is a note to me:

> *P —I'm sorry to do it this way, but I had to leave before it was too late. I can't ask you to be part of what's coming next. I know that what's right for me isn't right for you. Please don't be mad and don't come after me and don't be afraid. I'll be taken care of, it's all planned out, it's what I have to do. Just remember us the way we were. You know I love you. I will love you until my last breath. — Z*

I'm frantic. I call everyone, but no one has heard from him. The only person I can't get hold of is Raymond, and then Nicholas tells me that he's loaned Raymond a few hundred dollars, which seems to add up to something. On a hunch, I call Raven in San Francisco and leave a message. As the night grinds on and she doesn't call back, I become sure that this is where they've gone. I call a guy I know from ACT UP who moved to San Francisco, Kyle, and ask him to go to Raven's flat and question her. He calls a day later and confirms yes, Zack is in San Francisco, he's with a friend, that's all Raven would say. I don't understand. Hadn't he written down instructions that I was to be consulted on his decisions? How could he just leave? How long have he and Raymond been planning this?

I fall into a state of anger and dread. I understand what his note implies, what's going to happen, and I think I should fly out there, to be part of it— but he wanted me to stay here, with his art and his good-bye note and my rage and my tears. I go to work, I have to, I've taken too many days off caring for him, and anyway he has my number at work if he decides to call. At night I stay at his apartment, staring at the artwork on the wall, tempted to tear it down and set it on fire. I think about calling his sister, but I hold onto some hope that he'll come walking through the door.

On the third night, Amanda and Tony drag me back to her place and put me in the bath. Nicholas shows up with Valium, which I wash down in vodka. After that I lie down and sleep for twenty hours.

I wake to Amanda sitting on my futon. From the look on her face I can tell something's changed. "Raymond called," she says. "From San Francisco."

I sit up. "What did he say?"

"He said that Zack died last night."

"No. No, no no—"

"Raymond was with him. He said there were a few others there too."

I feel the air leave my lungs. I feel my blood freeze in my veins.

"He was calling from a funeral parlor, arranging the cremation."

"*No.*"

"I told him to talk to you, but he wouldn't stay on the phone."

"It can't be."

She tells me to breathe. It takes such effort. Finally I find the words to ask her what we should do. "I think you should call his sister and tell her that Zack took a trip to San Francisco and that he died at a friend's house."

I am absolutely not ready for that.

I make myself get dressed. I step out to the street, anticipating the cops surrounding the park, imagining myself charging at them, brazenly, crazily, a threat they'd have to meet with drawn guns and a shower of bullets. End it for me, please. But they're not there. The cops are gone, the construction fence is being pulled down, the siege is over.

A city bus rolls up and spits out passengers, and as it moves away again it replaces my suicidal vision with the most ordinary glimpses of daily life: a man hurrying out of the Korean market carrying flowers, a lady pulling a grocery cart and whistling a tune, two winos stumbling along sharing a bottle from a paper bag. I turn left toward C and walk all the way to D, into the projects, tall brick buildings I usually avoid but which now seem like cardboard cutouts I could blow down with the force of everything churning inside of me. An old man loaded down with grocery bags lurches out of my way. I'm a zombie, a lumbering half-alive thing, frightening to others.

I take a pedestrian walkway over the FDR toward the East River. I walk out onto a wooden pier where men are fishing in pairs, and I look across to

Brooklyn—Brooklyn will always be Zack's borough. That first night, when he told me he was positive, I was already in love. I was ready to upend my life for him. I *did*. How had it led to this, me here, alone? I grip the splintering wooden railing with my hands and lean into the brisk wind that skims the river. I think I should scream, or cry, but to do so would be giving in to facts I don't fully believe. Zack is dead? A seagull squawks above my head, as if taunting me, and behind me the fishermen converse in Spanish. I hear gleeful laughter from somewhere. I hear a boat on the river blasting its horn. And then for a moment everything falls absolutely silent, as if the whole world has paused, and even the wind is still.

In Memory Of

Word spreads. At Amanda's the phone rings all the time. I let the machine pick up, listen to condolences: Hillary, Rochelle, Floyd, Dale and Timmy together, Eliot terse and awkward, Tony saying, "This is fucked." I talk to some, put others off.

A day later there's this message, the speaker either a femme boy or a butch girl: "Hi, it's Lee from ACT UP letting you know about an upcoming action—a political funeral for Mike Savas—"

Mike. I pick up the phone. Lee tells me that the funeral will start at Tompkins Square and move through the East Village. I say I'll come. "Can you call other people?" I say I will. I'm given three names and numbers, people I don't know—the phone tree, evergreen. I'm so overwhelmed I don't even think twice, I just do my part. Bit by bit, I learn more details. Mike died in the hospital. The body was transported to a funeral home that has helped arrange the march. His affinity group, with help from his brother, is making this happen.

On the appointed day, hundreds are gathered in the newly opened park, on the rebuilt plaza where the bandshell once stood. A wrought iron fence marks off a garden. A banner hangs from it, adapting Mike's famous sign:

HE LIVED WITH AIDS 6 YEARS, 6 MONTHS, NO THANKS TO YOU, AMERICA.

In front of that is a coffin holding Mike's body, placed more or less on the spot where I threw my wig in helpless rage. The lid of the coffin is open, and a line of observers moves past, paying respects. I wait to the side, not ready to look into it.

The microphone is flicked on and people begin to speak. One of them is Floyd, who knew Mike as a performer on stage before they met in ACT UP. When he says, "I'm not the only one here who fell in love with him from a distance," I hear an acknowledgment ripple through the crowd. He talks about Adventurers Camp for Boys and the stolen flag, about Mike's humor and fury. Mike's brother speaks, saying he's here to represent the family. I can see a resemblance, the big eyes, the prominent nose. He tells stories of childhood, saying, "Mikey was always the ringleader." After him, a woman named Judith I recognize from ACT UP steps to the mic. "Mike wanted this," she says. "He wanted accountability. He wanted the so-called general population to look AIDS in the face, the way *we* do every day. He wanted blame laid at the feet of our enemies. We know who they are. We've branded them guilty in public over and over. And they're still not listening to us."

I feel an old fire alight inside, an unmistakable flickering.

Pallbearers, their faces familiar, lift the coffin and proceed out of the park. I hang back, waiting for the crowd to thin before I join, wary of standing at the hot center of so much sorrow.

Then I see someone moving toward me from across the plaza.

It's Raymond.

The afternoon light hits him at a slant and plunges everything else into shadow. He becomes a glowing shape—bulky physique wrapped in a t-shirt, the wide black straps of a backpack binding his shoulders, his jeans cut off at the knee, his shiny boots laced tight around his thick calves. I feel the impulse surge through me to charge and knock him to the ground, pummel him for taking Zack from me. But in fact I take a step backwards and bump into the railing, pinned in place. My heart pounds. I'm damp with sweat. The crown of Raymond's head is circled in sunlight that lands brightly on his white shirt. He waves his arms, which blur into enormous wings, a supernatural messenger come to snatch me away. I'm overcome—the afternoon heat, the muggy, sooty air—and then I'm teetering, I'm *swooning*, and I feel myself going down.

He catches me before I crumple, before I pass out completely, and steadies me with his strong hands. I'm aware of the shape of his skull, the thickness of his neck, the gap between his teeth. "I got you," he says.

At the sound of his voice, I think, *It's Raymond, not some angel of death,* and I'm able to catch my breath and bring him back to scale. "I can stand," I say.

"Do you want to go with them?" he asks, pointing toward the funeral procession turning down Avenue A. "I was going to tape it."

"I want to say good-bye to Mike, but no. I don't think I can right now."

"We should talk," he says.

I nod. "You have a lot to tell me."

We go to Zack's. The place smells of garbage and ash. I open a window, throw a bag of trash into the hall, run water over the dishes in the sink—a bowl crusted with rice pudding, a spoon that had been in his mouth. It's so stuffy in here, and I haven't been back for days, and everything seems to sag and droop. His art piece looks like it might melt off the wall. "Have you seen that?" I ask, pointing to it.

He nods. "I bought him art supplies and did the stuff he couldn't do— like stretching the canvas and spreading the gesso."

"So you guys made it together. He didn't tell me that." Angry again.

"I just helped."

"Why didn't he give it to you?"

Raymond cocks his head, like the answer is obvious. "You don't see *my* picture up there."

"There are pictures you took, though."

"He made it for you."

We both stare at the collage for a while, seeing different things, remembering differently. I'm trying to imagine them here, working in secret and planning their trip to San Francisco. It's like discovering an affair going on behind my back, though maybe the opposite is true: I was the interlude. Raymond was the one with the history.

"What happened in San Francisco?" I ask.

We take seats at the table, each of us with a glass of water. He gulps before he speaks. "I know this is absolutely fucked up and terrible for you, and I get it if you never want to speak to me again." Then he tells the story: Zack died in the apartment of someone who was a friend of Mel's. Mel set it up. He arranged for a doctor and a nurse to be there. They provided the morphine and another medicine as part of the injection. The doctor gave the final dose. Raymond was at Zack's side. He'd been at his side from the moment they left New York. Once Zack got to San Francisco his health plummeted: diarrhea, difficulty swallowing or keeping anything down, pain, labored breathing.

"He didn't seem that bad before he left," I say.

"I know, when we got on the plane at Kennedy, he was okay, and we talked about not going through with this because he only wanted to end it if he was truly in bad shape. But by the time we landed at SFO, he was feeling worse, and over the next two days his fever went up and everything just sort of collapsed." Raymond takes a cigarette from the pack I put on the table.

"I don't remember you smoking."

"Stress." I can see it on his face. He doesn't look like old carefree Raymond strutting around with a camcorder or DJing with his hands in the air. He says, "I had this idea that being in San Francisco would revive him. I hoped for it, really. You have to understand, I did not want to do this."

"Right."

"You don't believe me?" His expression conveys defiance and pain—the two sides of what he's been through.

I need him to be a monster I can vilify, to carry the burden of this horror. But of course that's not the truth, and I make myself keep asking questions. "Did he know what was happening? Did he know where he was?"

"Yeah, but it got a little psychedelic. He was talking about climbing a mountain with no food or water, taking off his clothes, lying on a rock overlooking the world and staying there until it was all over. He kept saying, 'The mountain lions and the eagles can have me.' I don't know where that came from."

"Sounds like a vision out of Blake," I say. "He'd been reading poetry. Or maybe it was dementia. My mom got like that at the end, living in another reality."

Raymond stares at the cigarette. "I was mostly aware of the smells and raspy breaths and how freaked I was that I was the one he picked to be there. I really don't know why it wasn't you. He said you couldn't handle it—"

"He didn't give me the chance—"

"And it's not like I was so fucking eager to be there. I mean, it was the right thing to do, but Jesus fucking Christ, it was intense." He tightens up his mouth. "Afterwards, they left me alone with him. Just for a few minutes before they had to take him away. He wasn't breathing, it was really quiet. And I sort of felt him passing away, or passing on, or *through*, you know? I can't explain it. I just knew something was shifting." With an intake of breath, he says, "I'm a materialist atheist but I was experiencing this spiritual, I don't know, *presence*." Then he wipes his eyes and asks, "Is there anything else you're wondering about?"

"What did Stacia say?"

He looks at me, dumbfounded. "When I talked to Amanda, I asked if you'd call—"

"I wasn't there!" I shout, absolutely furious, all of it ready to come out—but then Raymond lets loose a torrent of tears, sobs from his throat, his shoulders slumped and heaving, and my rage is gone. I circle the table and tighten my arms around him. We stay like that, both of us wrecked, him sobbing and me holding on.

I'd always treated Raymond as a rival, I'd been intimidated by him, and jealous of him, but he was just a year older than me, and only a little more experienced at life—and now, from all these years past, looking back on that moment, I see how young, how ridiculously unprepared we both were for everything that happened. We were all unprepared—every one of us, even the people who seemed old to me at the time. We rose to each terrible challenge as best we could. We often failed. We failed to understand ourselves and our actions and each other. But we just kept going. That was part of being young, too. Taking the next step. Always going forward. Doing what we had to.

He tells me he has something for me, and reaches into his backpack to pull out a box. "I brought back Zack's ashes, and this is for you."

Inside, in a thick plastic bag, is a substance like ground gravel. I jostle it, and the top powdery layer drifts aside to reveal larger chips beneath. With a terrible awareness I realize these are bits of Zack's bones.

Raymond says, "They call them *cremains*."

"They do?"

"Zack would've used that, right? 'New York City Cremains.'"

"What do we do with them?" I ask.

"Girl, I have no clue. I'm not putting them on the mantle in a Faberge urn."

There's a lot to handle: emptying out the apartment, donating Zack's stuff to a thrift store, distributing his sketches and drawings and unfinished pieces among friends (or else throwing them away, which is really hard to do), transporting the couch across town to Dale and Timmy, and finally, removing "New York City Do Over" from the wall and carrying it through the neighborhood to my apartment, where we hang it over my bed.

I call Stacia, breaking the news and then handing the phone to Raymond. He doesn't tell her the full story, just that Zack died at a friend's house in San Francisco. Zack has at this point been dead nearly a week, and she is stunned to have been kept in the dark, letting loose on Raymond and then on me, with a hurt I can barely absorb. She asks for some of the ashes.

Later, I will carry them to a church in New Jersey, where she has arranged for a memorial Mass. Raymond will wait in his truck while I get out, hand over the box to Stacia, and exchange some words with her and Doug. I will consider staying for the service, but what stops me is the sight of an older white man in a crisp suit and tie, with ramrod straight posture and a cold inscrutable look on his face. He turns toward me briefly, and I recognize him as Zack's father. I can't do it, can't talk to him, have to leave. But his green eyes, so like Zack's, stay with me, and later that night I find myself calling my own father and telling him what's happened. All of it, no more secrets.

The evenings, after work, are the hardest. The hours of open, unplanned time are suffocating, but conversely I can't bring myself to go to meetings, do activism, hang with friends. I start roving downtown with my notebook and pen, parking myself at the counter at Veselka, drinking a lot of coffee. I tell myself I'm starting new stories, though mostly I'm venting, ranting, unloading my unvarnished emotions in barely legible scrawl.

I go to Times Square, to "buddy booths" where for a few tokens I can push a button and raise a partition revealing a guy in the next stall. It doesn't matter who he is, what matters is that I can see the need and desperation in his eyes, which I know is also in mine. As we jerk off on either side of the plexiglass, everything else vanishes, and of all the people in the world, only this stranger matters—until the climax, and then he's just one more thing to flee. Or I go to a bar where I can be anonymous, and I drink until I'm buzzed enough to get picked up by someone who shows interest, anyone really; the less I'm into him, the better. We burn through sex, sucking and jerking to quick orgasms.

In my apartment, I lie on my futon and stare up at Zack's collage. I focus on a particular image or piece of text and then reverse-engineer it through whatever gestures he might have used, his hands, his stance, his face in concentration, letting the art conjure him back into physical form. Some nights it's so vivid I can sense him in bed with me, a phantom lover, curled around my body. Other times, craving flesh and breath, I'm aware only of paper and paint and glue.

My neck feels stiff. My joints ache. I catch myself chewing on pen caps and biting my nails and barking at strangers over tiny offenses that New

Yorkers are supposed to shake off, like someone cutting in line at a checkout or grazing my shoulder on a subway staircase. I cough a lot, a smoker's hack that I convince myself is a sign of immunosuppression.

I go for another HIV test. I live like it's just a matter of time before I get sick, too. I look at every pimple and blemish on my skin as if it were the beginnings of KS. But when the results come in, I'm still negative.

Washington, D.C.

We enter the Metro separately, in groups of two and three, and take our positions.

Some of us are on one platform, and some are on the other, with the tracks in between. We're waiting for trains to arrive from both directions, carrying other members of our affinity group, who will disembark with banners and balloons.

The balloons are filled with helium and tied with strings that have clamps on the ends; the clamps attach to the banners. The banners will rise, which is when the rest of us, waiting on the platforms, will open our canisters—stink bombs—before we exit. That's the action.

We've coordinated our plan with the Metro schedule. We've picked this station because it's in the heart of Washington, and we picked Washington because ACT UP is at this very moment demonstrating in front of the White House—the Ashes Action, at which protestors will reach through the fence to pour the ashes of their loved ones onto the White House lawn. Raymond is there, with his portion of Zack's cremains. He asked me to come, but I declined. It's too much like a political funeral to me, a spectacle of death I can't quite reconcile, though I'm largely alone in this feeling. ACT UP has embraced this tactic. Eleven years of death, no relief in sight, this is our civil disobedience now.

In the lead-up to the Ashes Action, our affinity group decided to do something in tandem. Our plan began at Timmy and Dale's loft. That day, we gave ourselves a name: "The Joneses."

Dale and Timmy are here now, in the Metro, on the opposite platform from where I stand with Tony and Rochelle.

I'm the lookout. I'm supposed to signal at any sign of trouble: the signal is the word "Jones" and a wave of the hand. Rochelle holds a copy of *The Washington Post*. Tony stands near a garbage can, clutching the canister with the smelly stuff inside. We wait among the commuting throng beneath the Metro's brutalist vault. We're wearing brimmed caps and nondescript clothing. I attempt to stay cool and calm, but my heart is thumping and my fingers twitch.

A train rolls in. People on the platform inch forward, ready to board: a sea of suits, dark skirts with blazers, briefcases. People in D.C. are clean-cut, with a governmental sheen, which is part of our theater: to stink up their orderly, unblemished world.

Passengers spill out. But our people are not here. Did not disembark. No balloons, no banners.

I look at Tony, at Rochelle. When the trains pull away, I look across the platform, where Timmy and Dale are also wondering what's happened. The plan has gone awry, and we now seem quite conspicuous.

Tony shrugs. Rochelle looks around, squinting, as if for cops. We don't have a contingency plan. Everyone holds their place until headlights appear again in the tunnel.

The next trains pull up. On our platform, Hillary and Nicholas step out. *Finally.* She holds two bunches of balloons. He holds the rod from which he starts to unfurl the banner. She goes to work clamping the balloon bouquets to the rod. I hope that on the other side, as the other train empties, Amanda and Floyd are there, as planned, doing the same. I keep watch as passengers stream past.

Rochelle is in front of the trashcan, with the *Post* opened up like a shield. Behind her, Tony is uncapping the stink bomb. Then he's done, walking to the escalator, while Rochelle folds the newspaper under her arm and takes the stairs.

The trains zoom away, first this one and then the other. Over there, I can see Amanda and Floyd letting go of their balloons. Their banner rises up, light-colored cloth with dark lettering. The message proclaims:

WASHINGTON: YOUR AIDS POLICIES STINK

I'm supposed to walk away, too. But I don't, I stand there, not ready to go. The stench is not yet apparent. I need to smell it. How else will I know it's worked?

On this platform, Hillary is struggling with the balloons. Only one side of her banner is starting to rise.

Nicholas has already let go. He's walking away. Everyone is supposed to walk away, not get caught, that's the plan.

I say, "Hillary!" but I should have said "Jones!" She looks at me, her eyes warning, *Don't help, you did your job, keep walking.*

I can smell the stink bombs now. Rotten eggs filling the station. Garbage. Sewage.

Everything is working except for this second banner, which is the one that matters most to me.

I run to Hillary. Our fingers fumble together with the balloon strings, the clamps, the rod, the banner, all these tricky things. I'm aware of my breathing, my heartbeat.

And then she says, "That's it."

"What?"

"Let go."

I release my grip, and the balloons begin to lift the rod and unfurl the banner. Up it goes, toward the roof of the cavernous station. I can read it clearly.

IN MEMORY OF ZACK JONES
KILLED BY GOVERNMENT INACTION

I've witnessed the message, I've smelled the foul stench. We've been here longer than we've planned. I turn to the exit, remembering to keep my head down.

Then I hear the next train arriving.

I have to turn around one last time, like Lot's wife, on the upchugging escalator. Disembarking passengers immediately begin waving hands in front of faces, assaulted by the smell, looking for the source. People point to the banners overhead, scanning our words. That's what I needed—that's the whole point. Without thinking, I raise my arms in triumph.

Then I see some kind of station cop, rushing across the platform, looking up at me, following me with his eyes as I get to the top of the escalator and find Dale, snapping photos. I grab him and we take off running. We cover our mouths, the odor now overwhelming. I hear a commanding shout from behind. We don't look back, just keep running, out and up, hitting the street where we shed our coats and stuff them in trashcans, which is also part of the plan.

I listen for sirens, sure we'll be caught. But as we run, I hear only the sounds of the city at rush hour. We're soon out of breath—two smokers after a sprint—so we tuck into an alcove between buildings, nearly doubled over with exertion, and we wait until it feels safe.

Later, we rendezvous with the group over beer and burritos, trading stories, what it was like on one side of the platform versus the other, the cause of the initial delay, all of it. There's a sense of elation at having gotten away with a brazen action, one that put us at risk for federal charges. Everyone's anticipating Dale's photos, with much faux-lamenting that they won't be scratch-and-sniff. We did it, whatever it was: a prank, a zap, an actionette. A memorial. Later, we'll meet up with Raymond and others who've been at the Ashes Action, and they'll convey entirely different emotions, telling how the names of the dead were called out as their remains were scattered on the White House lawn.

Even before the stink bomb action, I considered leaving New York for good. Now, during this conversation, something unexpected occurs: *a click* like the one I had when I knew I was finished with facilitating.

This is it for me, one last big risk, a final *getting away with it*.

I no longer want to terrify, mystify and enchant. I want to rest.

Be the Witness

I begin applying to writing programs, submitting my application with the story about the boy who locks himself in his bedroom, locking out his parents. I name the boy in the story Zack, another memorial. I apply to several schools and am turned down by all but one, in San Francisco.

It seems I will not outrun him, not yet. If anything, I'll be going there as part of an unspoken pact: to live an artistic life, as he wanted for himself.

Before I leave New York, Derek calls. He's heard about Zack's death and the action in the Metro, and is it true that I'm moving away? Over dinner at a little Italian place on Second Avenue, just a few doors down from The Bar, I lay out the details of our action in the Metro, the planning that went into it, our hope that the banners stayed up in the rafters long after the smell had dissipated. He smiles in delight—that winning smile, which hooked me at the start. For a moment, I can see a glimmer of the boy I first fell for. He tells me he's been hired to manage a new, glossy gay magazine with national reach. "I'm joining the Gay Establishment," he says. "More shaking of hands, less shaking of fists."

"Less kicking in windows?" My joke makes him cringe.

He says he's in therapy again, analysis this time, which means lying on the couch, free-associating, three days a week, every week for months. He says it's the best thing to come out of our breakup.

I ask, "Would it have been better or been worse if I left you for a guy who was more like you? Because Zack was so different, and I needed something different." He says there's no way it wouldn't have hurt.

"There's something I need to say," I continue. It's time for my apology, which I've planned in advance but which still feels hard to do, and I need a moment to get the words out. "You were my first love, the first person who let me be myself. And I betrayed your trust. I cultivated something in secret. I waited for you to find out and then I tried to shift the blame back to you. And for all of that, I'm sorry."

Derek, being Derek, the guy who can smile in every situation, and will always make a new friend, or open himself up to a new adventure, tells me he understands, or thinks he does. "I was jealous that he gave you something that I couldn't," he says, "but jealousy seems irrelevant now." Then he surprises me with a question: "How did he die, in the end?"

I tell him what I know, unsure if I'm breaking a confidence, aware only that this is a moment to be truthful. When I'm done, we sit in silence as a waiter clears away food we haven't finished.

I ask about Michael, and Derek's face clouds over. "I visited him in Miami, and we spent the first night running from one club to another, and it took me a while to realize he was chasing his dealer around." Coke dealer? He shakes his head. "Crystal. And oh my God, we didn't sleep for forty-eight hours, having all this sex and inviting other guys over. It was hot at first, and then, like, not hot at all. Just messy and wired, and we ran out of condoms so . . ." He clears his throat. "When I got back to New York, I was plunged into depression, this brutal coming down from the high."

I cautiously offer some words about taking care of himself. It's not really my place to advise Derek anymore, but I feel a pang of protectiveness, for him, for all of us. We're so wounded, our brotherhood, always grasping for escape, for meaning, for new ways to compensate for the self-hatred lodged deep under our skin, the poison the world made us drink in childhood, always bubbling up as new damage. The fact that we as a community have been able in any way to survive one crisis after another is astonishing.

"You and me, we were a good team," Derek says.

We seem mature in our post-breakup dinner by the light of a restaurant candle. I can see our profiles in a mirror on the wall, two people with a long history, their gestures reflecting both deep familiarity and unresolved tension. The meal itself looks like a placeholder, a rehearsal for the easier, freer conversations that a long friendship will someday allow.

Life moves quickly when I get to San Francisco. I get busy with school, grow my hair out, join a gym. I find a studio apartment with a wall big enough to fit Zack's collage. Visitors inevitably ask about it, and my answer depends on who they are and what emotional state I'm in. "Is that you?" they'll ask, pointing to the Polaroid of me sleeping. "You look younger." I *was*, I think, though it was just months ago.

One night, I go out to the Detour, the bar with the chain link fence where Zack took me. There, a guy with a nice face and a decent body flirts and buys me drinks. When he asks me home, I say yes, because it's been so long. I haven't been laid in a while, and he lives nearby. I'm drunk, and he's aggressive, and before I know it, he's fucking me, and he's not using a condom. "Wait," I say.

"Right. We shouldn't do it this way," he says. But he stays in. "I'm negative."

"Me too."

"Feels so good."

"It does," I agree. "Maybe just a little more and then stop."

The warnings rattle in my skull—*How do you know he's negative? How does he know for sure?*—as he keeps pumping into me.

I think of Derek and Michael in Miami, of sex with strangers without condoms—condom fatigue, we'll come to call it, as if it's something we can just sleep off, as if we're not traumatized.

"You want my load? You want to feel it?" this guy asks, looking now like any other white boy with mousy brown hair and dull brown eyes. He's nothing to me. Why him, why now? But I do want to feel it, so I tell him yes.

Through a friend of a friend in ACT UP, I find a job working in a bed and breakfast, a Victorian mansion in the Mission District, with a backyard garden in the shade of a cypress and a fig tree. My job is to greet guests and answer their questions, which means pretending to know the city better than I do. One Sunday afternoon, a lesbian couple from out of state approaches me at the front desk. They'll be receiving a visitor, they say, handing me a business card for a minister from the Metropolitan Community Church, the queer house of worship in the Castro. This man is going to marry them, here, today.

They are two women in their forties, one a bit stockier, with a graying mullet, wearing a man's suit that fits her loosely; the other more athletic, with auburn hair pulled neatly into a long ponytail, wearing a blouse, dress pants and sensible heels. The minister turns out to be a fiftyish guy with a shiny bald head, muscular chest and pierced ears, like Mr. Clean. I walk him to the back garden, where the women sit waiting, holding hands.

The day is clear, and the garden is in full bloom, dappled with light. The minister ushers the women beneath the bent boughs of the fig tree. I'm curious about what will happen, never having seen two people of the same sex wed. The butch is holding a small camera, so I ask if she wants me to take pictures. "Would you?" she responds gratefully.

I listen as "Jackie" and "Paula," voices quavering with emotion, read their simple, heartfelt words to each other off index cards. *Jackie, I'll love you forever. Ever since we met I've been the luckiest woman in the world... Paula, you're the only one for me. I'm so excited to spend my life with you. For better or worse, in sickness and in health, until the end of our days.* When they finish, the minister tells them their union is sacred, and he offers the blessing of "whatever universal force you understand to be God." They exchange rings and kiss, and I snap pictures, trying to steady my own trembling hands so I can document this private testament of love. So I can be their witness.

Letters come and go. It's the twilight of letter writing, the last moment before email takes over and everything gets faster, more fleeting. I learn that my father is seeing someone, a woman who answered his personal ad. He hasn't yet told my sisters; he's worried they're not ready for him to date. Lisa has met someone, too, a guy who wants to take her on an around the world trip, the plans for which have already begun, but which she isn't quite ready to tell Dad about, for fear he'll grow anxious with her so far away. Michelle confides that she has a girlfriend she met in a women's studies class. They're planning to move into an off-campus apartment together, one where the landlord will allow cats. She's worried how Dad and Lisa will react. Somehow, I've become the person who collects everyone else's secrets, a natural extension, I suppose, of having kept so many of my own.

My friends, it seems, are all doing something new. Amanda is writing a feature screenplay that she plans to direct. Tony cuts hair in a salon and has gone back to school for social work. Nicholas has a nursing job at a clinic working with HIV clients. Raymond is editing years of documentary footage into an experimental film, though he hasn't yet settled on a unifying form. Late one night, he calls me and tells me he's tested positive, but new research is pointing to promising treatments, and he swears he's going to survive. Hillary is taking a break, burned out by the split in ACT UP that led a group of treatment activists to leave and form a new organization called TAG. The divisions got too personal, she writes, the dogma too absolute. She's not sure what she wants to do next. Something meaningful, she says, the way AIDS activism was meaningful, but without the burnout.

Javier is working as an editor at the magazine that Derek manages, and he asks if I'm interested in writing an article for him called "What Happened to AIDS Activism?" I tell him I'm not that person, that I'll need twenty years before I can figure out what we've been through.

It turns out I've needed thirty, and I'm still not sure I got it right.

And then there's Eliot.

The AIDS Crisis Is Not Over

Eliot writes me nearly every week, full of musings on politics, often in the voice of Harmony Moore, whom he has fashioned into an advice columnist. Sometimes he includes "letters" Harmony has received from "readers":

> *Dear Harmony: I'm uncomfortable calling myself queer. Is there an alternative to this alternative?*
>
> *Sincerely, Label-less*

> *Dear Label Lass: You'll be interested to note the increased use of the "acronym" LGBT, especially among the executive directors of nonprofit agencies and academics expanding their Sexuality Studies programs, though I must caution that this is not a proper acronym—just try to pronounce it—and so surely will not catch fire. I myself prefer to use the word "Clever." Doesn't it have a nice ring? The Clever People. And it's so inclusive! We're here, we're clever, get used to it!*
>
> *Yours in the struggle, Harmony Moore*

I return to New York at the end of my spring semester and make a plan to have cocktails with Eliot, but as the evening approaches, I can't get him on the phone. I track down Lenny, who tells me Eliot is back in the hospital with some kind of intestinal pain. When I call him there, Eliot says, "My insides are on fire. And this time it's not the greasy spoon on Ninth Avenue."

I can hear he's putting up a brave front, but Lenny warns me that the doctors are worried. Eliot has not been taking his AZT regularly. When I ask him about this, he says, "I've got the blues. It makes me forget."

Lenny asks me to round up friends to visit, to help lift Eliot's mood. "He's been isolating himself," Lenny says grimly. So I make the calls, give out the bedside extension, tell people to check with him before visiting.

When I phone before making my way uptown, Eliot asks me to bring him clean underwear. "Pick something festive," he says.

I go to a store on Fourteenth Street, not far from the shop where I bought my first wig with Nicholas. As I try to figure out what size underwear I should buy, imagining Eliot wasting from L to S, I begin to cry, right there in the aisle. One of the store's Puerto Rican sales ladies comes up to me as I'm wiping my cheeks. "Cheer up, Papi," she says. "It's a beautiful day."

Indeed it is. From the window of Eliot's hospital room, the sky is clear between tall buildings, reflecting the late-day sun, and the city gleams below us, a metropolitan utopia. But Eliot's skin is so white it appears green, and he looks, as I expected, like a depleted version of himself. When I give him the underwear, he thanks me and says, "Put them over there."

I follow the line of his long arm, skeletal but sturdy, like that of an old dowager pointing to her bounty. There on a side table are other packs of underwear, the ones Eliot has asked each of his visitors to bring. His smile is triumphant, and I burst out laughing, thrilled that I can still be caught off guard, that my understanding of life, marked by so much loss, still has room for joy. Over the next few days, I'll watch the wrapped packs of underwear pile up—briefs, boxers, bikinis, some bearing fancy designer labels, others garish and patterned, more than he'll ever need. When the stack gets high enough, I ask, "Would you like to make a sacrifice, Harmony? We can throw them out the window."

"No, the gods are never appeased, no matter how much we sacrifice." Then he adds, "I'll make sure they get distributed on the AIDS ward. There are some very down and out people here."

Without quite making a firm decision, I put off returning to San Francisco for the summer, so that I can be part of Eliot's care team. Back in his studio apartment, his sofabed, piled high with pillows, remains open all the time. There's an IV pole in his room, a sharps box for discarding syringes, and a couple of bedpans. Visitors stream in, telling stories, providing gossip, reminiscing. People bring organic home remedies, holistic tinctures, Ayurvedic recipes, chicken soup, green tea, bottles of liquor, Valium, pills. There are bouquets of flowers, stuffed animals, love beads and wigs. Eliot either has fun and lets his guests stay for hours, or else grows quickly exhausted. I have time to spare, so I visit every day, and sometimes sleep overnight, too, lining up the couch cushions on the floor beneath his overloaded bookshelves, not unlike sleeping on my futon at Amanda's. It doesn't hurt to be there, the way it sometimes did at Zack's, when I felt alone and frightened all the time. Here I feel useful.

I grow attached to Lenny, who has a sweet, grave maturity, with his wireframe glasses, ever-present beard stubble and high forehead. When I tell him he looks like a character from a Russian novel, Eliot starts calling him Lenin. The joke expands and soon I'm Pavel and Eliot is Eliotsky. When we bring in a home care nurse named Doreen, she gets a Russian handle, too: Dorinova. She's butch, thirty-something and Irish, all business until she breaks into song at the end of her shift, coaxing Eliot to sleep with lullabies. She tells us that she's part of the Irish lesbian and gay group protesting the St. Patrick's Day parade, demanding queer inclusion. She's exactly what we need, not least because, for me, she's an echo of my mother, an Irish nurse with a sweet sense of humor.

The visitors trickle off after a week, and the days become quiet and monotonous. The deteriorating functions of Eliot's body predominate all activity. He sleeps, he's in pain, he's sedated. We all understand the end is close.

One morning, after a night on his floor, I wake to a commotion. Doreen is hovering over Eliot, who is thrashing in his bed. His eyes are rolling back in his head, his mouth is agape and wet with foam. "It's a seizure," Doreen calls out to me and Lenny. "Hold him down, keep him from choking." She gives me a plastic tongue depressor which his mouth clamps upon so forcefully I can almost feel the force of his teeth on my own skin. Doreen jabs him with a syringe full of sedative, and at last he calms, his breathing shallow.

"Should I call an ambulance?" Lenny asks.

Doreen looks at him very pointedly and suggests that we all just wait with Eliot for a little longer.

I see that she knows what's coming.

I hold one of his hands, and Lenny holds the other, and we stay at his side. At first, Eliot seems to grip me back, but soon there's no strength at all.

Time passes, it could be fifteen minutes or fifty. Lenny speaks softly to Eliot, telling him he loves him, saying the words over and over until they become a chant, a meditation. "I love you, Eliot. I love you. I love you, my man." I imagine this is a way to calm Eliot and make him well again, to keep him alive, but I soon understand that Lenny is fashioning a vessel of words to float Eliot out of this life. The chant flattens to a hum, all breath and rhythm, sustained by Lenny until he no longer has a voice, and then Doreen steps in and fills the silence with a tender melody I've heard her sing to him before. I know it well enough to hum along, and when she gets to the end, we repeat it. Lenny's wet eyes are locked onto Eliot, an unbroken gaze. Our song goes on, and Lenny's tears keep falling, until at last there's a change in the soft breaths coming from Eliot's throat. To my ears it's a gust forced up from under his ribs, wet and dense and then finally, absolutely over. He's gone. I look at Eliot's face, the pale, pale skin, the dark, wispy hair, and the dark eyes, now unmoving yet still somehow telling a story of mischief and rebellion and intelligence. There's some remnant of him, of Harmony Moore, imprinted there, or so I want to believe. Eventually I let go of his hand. Lenny keeps holding on.

Three days later, accompanied by Amanda, I return to Eliot's apartment. We meet Lenny in the lobby and take the old, narrow elevator one last time. When we get to Eliot's floor, we find his door crisscrossed in yellow caution tape, which Lenny explains is because he died at home. The medical examiner's office treats it like a crime scene until the cause of death is confirmed and the death certificate issued, case closed. Tearing off the tape is like ripping a bandage from a fresh wound.

We're here to clear things out. Amanda finds a bottle of whiskey in the tiny kitchen, which we finish while we go through his things. Lenny tells us that he spoke with Ralph, Eliot's long-ago boyfriend, the lawyer from Calgary, who told the story of meeting Eliot—at the time failing his freshman year of college and trying to make rent money by hustling at the only gay bar in that corner of Canada. "Apparently Eliot made a lousy hooker, because he scared all the cowboy johns away with his brainy, crazy commentary," Lenny tells us. "Ralph said, 'He had no family to speak of, and until all of you came along, I was it.'"

In the drawer of a file cabinet, Amanda finds photos from Eliot's legendary birthday party. "Oh, my God, remember this?" she exclaims.

"Didn't he throw a cake out the window?"

"He threw all the cakes," I say.

"Are you sure? Not just one or two?"

"I remember eating birthday cake that night," Lenny says, "So he must have saved at least one."

Looking back and forth between them, I wonder: are their memories faulty, or is mine? That party took place five years ago. In that time, have I begun replacing facts with an amplified version of the truth? Have I already started rewriting what happened to us? There in the photos is Eliot as Harmony Moore, in that beaded dress and uncombed wig, mouth open in half-crazed joy, wailing "Stairway to Heaven." It's startling to see him so vibrant and strong, and I stare at the picture long enough to overpower the image of his face at the moment of death, which has dominated my thoughts in the days since, and which I now need to clear away.

Before I return to San Francisco, to my studies and my job, I have one more thing to do—one more thing I'll relate before bringing all of this to an end, though this story of friends in the midst of crisis doesn't end here. Others will die, like Dale, quite suddenly, after a reaction to new medication in the hospital, and his death will send Timmy on a month's-long journey through Central America, where he'll sit atop a pre-Columbian pyramid in the jungle, tripping on acid, waiting for the universe to reveal to him the truth of death; like Floyd, who'll be surrounded by family members who come out of the woodwork to sing Christian hymns while he passes away in hospice care; like Michael, whose end will reach us via gossip from Miami, talk of rehab and homelessness and an overdose, none of which I can reconcile with my memory of the cheerful volunteer and his commitment to the healing power of affirmations.

The one last thing I do before I leave New York is this: I take the box containing the portion of Zack's remains that Raymond gave to me, and place it in a shoulder bag, and I get on the F train heading toward Brooklyn.

I wait until the train leaves its last stop in Manhattan and begins its descent, and then I open the door and step between the cars. In the darkness, I remember the last time I did this, with Zack, and I remember how even in the low, intermittent light and dank air, deep in the earth beneath the river, his face had been alive with the thrill and the risk of the ride.

I speak out loud—my voice fighting the screech of the train—saying a few simple phrases like *I love you, I miss you, I forgive you. Please forgive me.* I don't fret about precise language. There is no perfect memorial. I simply reach into my bag, pull out the box, scoop out a handful and let the rushing air begin the work of scattering the last of him.

Some of the ashes hover and swirl. The heavier pieces stay in my hand, rough at the edges until I shake them free.

I am, at this moment, the age Zack was when we met; I'm more like the man I always wanted to become, less like the boy I was so eager to shed. Soon I will be older than he ever got to be, not because he did anything wrong or I did anything right. Life is not a heroic achievement, not a victory built on correct choices but something more mysterious: a bit of ash caught in a current of air, glittering in a flash of passing light, then swept away. On that noisy moving train in the dark, my body shaking from the vibrations, I feel some of him blow back to me. He is in my hair, on my lips. I wish that I had Eliot's ashes, too, and Mike's and Christopher's, and most of all my mother's—everybody I have loved and lost, every body.

I breathe in the dust of all of them, and then I open my mouth and howl.

—San Francisco, 2022

Acknowledgments

This is a work of fiction, years in the making. It exists today because I've been uplifted, cared for, and challenged by many people along the way. I'm sure I've lost track of some who have influenced the telling of this story. I humbly offer these acknowledgements knowing that they are bound to be incomplete.

Top of the gratitude list: Michael Nava at Amble Press for rescuing this project when I'd all but let go of it. To Salem West and Ann McMan at Bywater Books, thank you for welcoming me into the fold. To photographer Eurivaldo Bezerra, thank you for permission to put your stunning *Hands* on the cover.

To the beloved friends who read drafts, pushed me toward better writing, and helped me persevere when the light at the end of the literary tunnel was neither visible nor guaranteed—Maria Maggenti, Dave Hickey, Christine Murray, John Vlahides, Sonia Stamm, Aron Kantor, Lewis Buzbee, Christine Troy, and Alia Volz—you were my lifelines. To the writers' group that embraced my earliest attempts to tell this story, I thank Elizabeth Costello, Catherine Brady, and David Booth. To David Groff, your keen storytelling eye when the manuscript needed a fresh look made a great difference. Thank you.

To Monique Jenkinson and Marc Kate, thank you for artist dates and mind-sharpening conversations. To John Rossell, thank you for your bottomless support and your caring friendship. To Paul Festa, James Harker, Linda Plack, and Les Plack, in California, and Tami White, in New York, thank you for sharing your space for retreat, contemplation, and work. To Seth Eisen, thanks for your collaborative energy and endless affirmation, plus a room in which to edit at a key moment of revision.

Conversations with comrades from ACT UP New York helped clarify and sometimes complicate memories of the days recounted in these pages. They include Jay Blotcher, Heidi Dorow, Joe Ferrari, Michael Goff, Ron Goldberg, Jim Hubbard, Paul Isaacs, Andrew Miller, Emily Nahmanson, Michael Nesline, Steve Nesselroth, Michael Paller, Jim Provenzano, David Robinson, Sarah Schulman, Peter Staley, and Charlie Welch. I'm in awe of our community of survivors, and I thank each of you for keeping the fire burning. A special thanks also to Terry Schy for opening up the archives and sharing Lee's beautiful photos.

Alan Klein, consider this the tiniest drop in the deep ocean of gratitude I owe you for the adventures we've shared and the support and love you still provide.

To the creative community spread along the San Francisco–LA axis, I am lucky to be among you. I offer sweet shout-outs to Liam Passmore, Trebor Healey, Marcus Ewert, Graham Smith, Matthew Clark Davison, Dare Williams, Kirk Read, Ed Wolf, Chloe Hennen, Robbie Sweeny, Alvin Orloff, Michelle Tea, Daniel Handler, the University of San Francisco MFA in Writing Program, the Djerassi Resident Artists Program, Shotgun Players, RADAR Reading Series, Literary Death Match, Litquake, Babylon Salon, Quiet Lightning, Why There Are Words, Inside Out, Lambda Literary, the De Young Museum, the San Francisco Public Library, and anyone anywhere who let me read from this work in progress over the past decade.

To the Moss Boys, the Crabby Queens, the Oscar Watchers, the Pigmalions, the Driftwood crew, the Cubby, the Biggest Quake-ers, and the Gratitude Exchangers, thank you for the energy expended forging our circles, clubs, camps, and tribes. Writing is the calling; friendship is the reward.

For the people who've known me the longest—my father, Karl Soehnlein, and my sisters Karen Woodhull and Kimberly Soehnlein—we lived the toughest part of this together, and we've helped each other remember, heal, and move on. I love you with all my heart.

Last, first, and everywhere in between: Kevin Clarke. You know what this took out of me, but I hope you also know how deeply these pages are filled with your spark, smarts, hand-holding, yes-saying, daisy-watering, check-marking, big-adventuring, birthday-countdowning, affirmation-camping, never-going-to-bed-angry Taurusaurity. I believe in miracles since you came along, you sexy thing.

About the Author

K. M. Soehnlein is the author of the novels *The World of Normal Boys, You Can Say You Knew Me When*, and *Robin and Ruby*, along with essays and journalism in numerous publications. He is the recipient of the Lambda Literary Award, Henfield Prize, and SFFILM Rainin Grant in Screenwriting. He received an MFA from San Francisco State University and teaches at the University of San Francisco MFA in Writing Program.

Raised in New Jersey, he lived in New York City during the AIDS crisis, participating in direct action with ACT UP and cofounding Queer Nation. He currently lives in San Francisco.

Amble Press, an imprint of Bywater Books, publishes fiction and narrative nonfiction by LGBTQ writers, with a primary, though not exclusive, focus on LGBTQ writers of color. For more information on our titles, authors, and mission, please visit our website.

www.amblepressbooks.com

CPSIA information can be obtained
at www.ICGtesting.com
Printed in the USA
JSHW031154171122
33142JS00007B/7

9 781612 942476